T

Tales

stone

Published by Kashallan Press, 2021

The Hunted Kashallan

Tales of the Kashallans, Volume 2

Celu Amberstone

Published by Kashallan Press, 2022.

This is a work of fiction. Similarities to real people, places, or events are entirely coincidental.

THE HUNTED KASHALLAN

First edition. March 22, 2022.

ISBN: 978-1777537944

Written by Celu Amberstone.

Prologue

Within the confines of his covered litter, Combaron Dingay raised himself up on one elbow, groaned and pulled back the curtain. "Watch where you're going, you putrescent pieces of Begta filth!" he snarled. "Are you trying to kill me?"

The Warlinga lizardman nearest the open side of the litter flattened his head crest and mumbled a reluctant apology. Combaron glared at the man a moment longer, then jerked the curtain closed and flopped back on his pillows, clutching his head.

With another dramatic groan, he closed his eyes and waited for the pain to subside. "Clumsy brutes, they will pay for this."

Lying on his side, he gingerly reached up with a furred, four-fingered hand and touched the back of his head where someone had struck him. "Damn the Caltia witch and her blue-eyed accomplice! It hurts," he whined.

"Damn them to the black pit—and double damn them for stealing all the Loti, forcing me to use these clumsy Warlinga to carry my litter. Ow, not again! There doing it on purpose—just to torment me—the brutes."

How much longer must he endure this? Pulling back the curtain a crack, he opened one eye and peered out into the fading afternoon sunlight. Broad rusty fields of lamra stretched out along the dusty road. Here and there groups of Loti peasants with baskets and digging sticks worked among the tall leafy stalks of grain. The air was pungent with an acrid coppery scent. The sounds of chanting drifted across the water through the amber mists shrouding the lake.

Good, they were almost to the capital; soon this infernal torture would be over. They would be at Riath before dark, and he could relax in a warm bath and get proper medical care for his aching head. Combaron lifted the flask of brandy to his lips. He took a long drink, then lay back once more.

This journey over the Jeban Pass had been a nightmare of poor food, pain, and discomfort. Would his grandmother Enaju appreciate the suffering he had endured to bring her his news?

Enaju hadn't been pleased with him when she packed him off to Sulas to keep an eye on Sagas Caltia. She had warned him not to return to Riath until she sent for him.

But after what had happened she would have to listen—have to understand—there was nowhere else for him to go. Sulas Keep was dead.

When he had Sagas once more in his custody—and that misbegotten lay-about, Gormach Tragar had better find her—the witch would pay. Sagas and the blue-eyed Umwira mutant had tricked him with their foul magic. But they wouldn't get away with their crimes—even if he couldn't remember all of it. Damn his head hurt—his grandmother would make them suffer, oh yes, they would suffer!

On the night the outlaws escaped, Combaron could only remember cornering the blue-eyed mutant in the tiny chapel by the kashallan birthing pool, but after that he recalled nothing until he awoke later in his bed, with a splitting headache. To his disgust, he also found his senior apprentice, Dar and Gormach Tragar bending over him.

The tall gray-scaled K'San raised his head crest when he saw Combaron glaring at him. "Ah, Ata, we are blessed," the Warlinga said. "Your apprentice here was afraid we might be permanently denied your guidance." Gormach bowed over the bulge of his distended belly and displayed his yellowing fangs.

"What, are you verminous spawn of a swamp monster doing in my bedchamber? I haven't given you permission to attend me!"

Combaron tried to sit up, but any further commands degenerated into a theatrical groan the moment his head left the pillow. He flopped back and closed his eyes. When the pain subsided, he stared up at them in bewilderment.

"Please, Ata," Dar begged, "Don't try to sit up yet. Your injury—it's quite serious." Dar tucked his hands into the folds of his kilt and ran a tongue around his dark lips. "I-I've done the best I could for you, Ata, but—"

"My head hurts," Combaron whined, cutting him off. Dar's eyes were round with that panicked look he got when he knew Combaron would be angry. "Don't give me any of your sniveling excuses, Dar, get me some of the orange kavay, and be quick about it."

"Ata, I'm sorry—I've done the best I could—but there isn't—"

"What!" Combaron sat up, ignoring the pain in his rage. "If there's none in here go to my workroom and get some. Lazy slimeworm, go!"

"Ata, I have already given you all that I could find in the keep. There isn't any more."

"Stupid Begta slave, then go down to the pools," Combaron snarled.

Trembling Dar glanced beseechingly at the big Warlinga. Gormach raised his head crest a fraction, but remained silent. Clutching his head in one hand, Combaron reached out with his other and grabbed the hapless apprentice by his braids pulling him closer, then he slapped him hard. "Stupid filth, go get it!" he screeched.

As Combaron thrust him away Dar stumbled then stepped out of reach, rubbing his cheek. "Oh, Ata, I can't," he wailed, his voice quivering. "Ata Combaron, it's so awful. Ima Sagas and her Umwira demons have killed the Khutani. There aren't any more medicines."

Combaron blinked then stared at his apprentice as if Dar was babbling in an Umwira dialect. Dead? Mother, his head was killing him—why were they making him think? Cruel fiends, he couldn't puzzle this out when his head hurt so terribly.

Through narrowed eyes he glanced at Gormach. But, to his surprise, he saw a trace of fear in even that degenerate's red eye. "What are you two imbeciles talking about? The Khutani dead, Bah!"

"If the sacred Khutani aren't dead, Ata," Gormach said, "then what other explanation would you give for the fact that the pools at Sulas are now devoid of all life?"

"Impossible. You drunken, lazy Warlinga how would you know? You aren't even allowed down there."

For just a moment murderous rage glowed in Gormach's eyes, then he bowed, and when he rose his face had once more assumed its habitual mask of bored insolence.

"Ata, it's the truth," Dar blurted. "The pools are blackened and foul smelling. The Khutani must be dead. What will become of us without them?" the young man cried, his voice rising on a note of hysteria. "Oh, Ata, I did the best I could for you when we found you unconscious in that tiny chapel. Oh, Ata—"

"Shut up!" Combaron snarled. "You're making my head worse with your yammering. Shut up!" Flopping back on his pillows, Combaron closed his eyes and tried to ignore the throbbing in his head. "Stop sniveling, Dar. If there's no orange kavay, I'm sure there's at least lamra brandy around here somewhere—bring me that."

When the young man was out of the room, Combaron slitted his eyes and studied the Warlinga. The man shifted uneasily, his long whip-like tail curling and uncurling itself on the floor behind him. Hmm, he was definitely worried, and that wasn't like the toadying lout to display his anxiety so openly. Something was wrong, but the Khutani dead?

"Now that that fool Dar is out of here, tell me what's going on?"

Gormach stilled the motion of his tail and raised his head crest in inquiry. "We were hoping you could tell us the answer to that riddle, Ata. I know only what the Avairei who remain here have told me. I was hunting for Umwira—as you ordered me to do, remember? I arrived here but a short time ago—to pick up my, uh, prisoners.

"I found the priests remaining in the keep quite hysterical. They kept babbling some gibberish about evil magic and dead Khutani. When I insisted, they showed me and my cousin Tobrach the pools. They are indeed fouled." Gormach held out his empty gray-scaled hands, to emphasize his innocence.

"No one knows anything more than I've told you, and my, uh, prisoners are gone."

"Gone? Make some sense—how could Sagas be gone?"

"Your priests say that Ima Sagas and her accomplices have vanished—into thin air, or so your people claim. The Ima, the mutant slaves, all of the Loti servants, and many more of Sulas's inhabitants are gone. Your slave pens are emptied, and the pools are fouled, and the Holy Ones—" Gormach dipped his head crest. "It is a most puzzling mystery."

Combaron snorted. He hated mysteries. "What nonsense. There's no mystery, at least about Sagas. She and the mutants have fled. And that lazy good-for-nothing Hanno will pay for his negligence—"

Gormach let out a bark of malicious laughter. "Oh, he has, Ata, he already has. Your Warlinga Hunt Leader is dead. And his kinsmen don't know how it happened."

His eyes gleamed with amusement, his voice taking on a mocking tone as he added, "It seems they all got drunk and slept through the whole thing. You see, they'd been drinking a lot of mushroom beer you sent them to celebrate your—uh—victory."

Combaron gaped. "What? I never sent them beer to celebrate anything, those lying Begta."

"Mm, you didn't?" Gormach raised his head crest a little higher. "Well, if you didn't, Ata, I guess their drunken slumber is just another example of the sorcerer's magic, hmm?"

Combaron narrowed his eyes, was the big brute toying with him? "I never sent them any beer, the stupid fools," he repeated. "So—yes, it must have been magic. Magic—Umwira magic!

"This is all your fault," he accused. "You brought those evil creatures here in the first place, and now look what's happened! If those demons have killed the Khutani, I'll see that you pay—"

"I think not, Ata," Gormach growled. He stepped a little closer to the bed, his head crest flat, his clawed hands flexing. "If you think to put the blame for what has happened on to me, I suggest you reconsider."

Gormach gave him a toothy smile, his red eyes alight with menace. Combaron pressed himself back into his pillows, and Gormach's smile widened. "I am but a simple Warlinga. What do I know about such priestly matters as sorcery, hmm?" He shook his head.

"While doing my duty, I happened to discover and capture a new strain of mutants. To me they seemed harmless enough, and I will tell the High Council that—and other things."

Combaron leaned even further away from that grinning face, his eyes flicking to Gormach's lethal claws. He swallowed, his mouth suddenly dry

Twisting the blade a little deeper, Gormach added, "Yes, I'm just a poor, simple Warlinga—I couldn't possibly be expected to know how dangerous the creatures would turn out to be. Why, Ata, you examined all of them yourself.

"You even brought one of the mutant females to your rooms—just to make sure she was—harmless. Ata, you assured me that she was most satisfactory that very next morning, don't you remember?"

Gormach rumbled a most unpleasant laugh. "So, dear Ata, if there is blame to be laid here, I suggest we put it where it truly belongs, hmm? The pools are destroyed, and Ima Sagas is gone. It would seem to me that our missing priestess has a lot of explaining to do. Wouldn't you agree?"

"Yes," Combaron said, not taking his eyes from the taunting Warlinga's face. He understood the implied threat behind his words. But the fat brute was probably right about Sagas. "You must find her," Combaron hissed. "She must be brought before the High Council to pay for her crimes! It is your duty—I order you to find her."

Gormach bowed. "Your will, Ata."

Combaron would have liked to have the Warlinga kill her, but he dared not—not without his grandmother's approval anyway. But if the pools were indeed fouled, as was claimed, hmm. This could be the excuse that the Dingay clan needed to rid themselves not only of a troublesome priestess, but of her entire clan as well.

"You will find her and bring the blaspheming witch to Riath, where her crime will earn her the reward she deserves."

Gormach dipped his head crest in agreement. "And the other mutants—her demon tempters?"

Combaron waved a dismissive hand. "Kill and eat them, for all I care. Sagas Caltia and the blue-eyed one are the two that are most important to me. When I get to Riath I will have the papers drawn up to make it legal. But, as of this moment, you are officially appointed to seek out these renegades. Bring me Sagas and her blue-eyed tempter."

"Your will, Ata. Never fear, I will bring her to Riath before the Sorin Storms close off the pass."

OUTSIDE IN THE CORRIDOR Gormach smiled and congratulated himself. Yes, this was much more to his liking. The perverted priest would fix things for both of them. He would have to, or risk exposure of what Gormach could disclose about his unconventional appetites.

Gormach would find the old hag and bring her to Riath, if the Dingay needed her to further their own plans. But he would take care of the rest of that bunch of mutant renegades in his own way.

It wasn't over between him and Blue Eyes, no, not at all. Thinking of the sweet taste of the mutant's exotic flesh made him hungry. Mm, yes, very hungry.

Part One: The Dark Hunt

Chapter One

After their escape from Sulas through the forgotten passages below the keep, it had taken the fugitive humans and their native allies longer to find a refuge in which to rest than the Kashallan had expected.

Unable to see much in the gloom with the few lanterns they'd managed to scavenge from the keep, they'd missed the site and were making their weary way along the underground river path, when one of the Begta hunters in their rear spotted their error and rushed forward to tell them of their mistake.

Retracing their steps, Dunnagh saw the pitted stone walls of an ancient compound, looming out of the blackness, just as the Elder Gladdris had promised. To his professional eye the outer walls seemed defendable—in case they'd been followed. The facade looked relatively sound, save for an occasional rockslide.

Peering through the gap where a gate once stood, he could see there was little left inside but piles of rubble. Though it appeared deserted, his battle-companion Nathan, and new, "Hunt Leader," made the civilians wait while he had his squad of Caldoni mercenaries and the Begta check the place thoroughly.

A hasty camp was well underway by the time the natives surrounding Dunnagh, known to them as the Kashallan, opened their protective circle and allowed him to enter. The Loti he'd been riding stopped and he slid trembling off her broad muscular back.

Dunnagh mouthed a curse and leaned against her, trying to find the strength to walk. Still so damned weak from the Transformation. It had been easier riding than walking, but now his leg muscles quivered from the unaccustomed strain.

Sensing his debility, his centaur-like mount took his elbow and guided him towards one of the newly ignited green fires. Dunnagh eased his aching bones onto a flat rock and smiled. "Thank you, Berren, you are always so good to me."

The Loti displayed large yellow teeth in a broad grin and patted the tangle of long red braids cascading down his bare back. "It is always a pleasure to serve you, Kashallan, in whatever way I can."

Reaching out his own hand Dunnagh curled his fingers in her soft shaggy coat. Berren always smelled to him like a mixture of lemon and wet sheep dog. All in all, a comforting scent on this alien world—something that reminded him of home. "Go now and rest while you can, my dear. I fear I will have need of you all too soon."

"I will do that, Holy One, and you rest as well." Picking her dainty way through the rubble, the Loti disappeared into the gloom.

Dunnagh took in a deep breath and closed his eyes. He was so tired. Hungry and frightened the young symbiont coiled in his middle fretted. Absently stroking his belly he hummed a wordless lullaby under his breath, hoping to sooth it.

Sagas, the former matriarch of Sulas put a furred hand on his arm, drawing him out of his inner communion. "Are you well, Holy One?"

"I'm tired and stiff from the riding, but I'm all right, Ima." He gave her a lopsided grin. "Except, of course, for being very hungry, and a little afraid." Then he said a bit wistfully, "But I shall have to learn to ration myself, I suppose, since I don't know how long the formula I brought from Sulas must last."

"It is not necessary to deny yourself, Kashallan. Too much abstinence in fact, might even be dangerous," she warned. "It is unfortunate that we were forced to leave at this time, but you must have proper nourishment. Kashallan, there is always the Blood Gift should you—"

"NO!"

Her aging cat-like face registered both surprise and annoyance at the vehemence of his refusal. Dunnagh sighed and repeated more gently, "No. We will all need our strength. If I start drinking my followers' blood—" He shuddered, then shook his head. "No, that won't be necessary."

"But, Holy One, it isn't natural for you to reject such an offer. We Avairei have been bred with supplementing Khutani needs in mind. All the priests who came with us are used to adding a measure of their blood to the young Khutani's feedings at the pools. It doesn't hurt—and there is little difference between you and the others—"

As he continued to shake his head in denial, Sagas lost patience with him. Guessing the true source of the problem, she snapped, "Ignorant alien, why are you being so stubborn? You may endanger both your own and your bondmate's life if you persist in this foolishness."

"I said no, Ima, and I meant it."

A thin upright creature with graying brindle fur she tossed the dangling braidlets of her long mane over a shoulder, crossed her arms across her chest and folded her dark lips into a smirk. "We shall see about that. You are young. And your Khutani Elders gave you into my care. And, by the Mother, I will take care of you—whether you want it or not—"

"Everything's secured, and I've got the sentries posted," Nathan announced as he drew near. "Anything else, uh, *unusual* I need to know about, or do?" He glanced from a frowning Dunnagh to the scowling Sagas.

Sagas ignored him. Grateful for the distraction Dunnagh said, "Trust your instincts on this one, Nathan. It was safe in the past, but the Gods alone know what's down here now. I hope there's nothing more exciting than the cave rats the Begta were chasing, but I don't know for sure."

It was hard for his tall beefy friend to combine bewilderment and resignation in his expression, but Nathan was doing a good job. Dunnagh would like to have pity on him, tell him what the Avairei priests and the Khutani Makers had really done to him—how they'd changed him. But that was a luxury he couldn't afford. Not yet anyway.

Soon, Dunnagh silently promised his friend.

His eyes flicking from one glaring adversary to the other, Nathan settled his steel-gray stare on Sagas for conformation of Dunnagh's unexpected pronouncement. Still looking angry, she pointed at Dunnagh.

"You heard the Kashallan, Hunt Leader."

Nathan sighed and cleared his throat. "Yeah, right." Then glancing around he changed the subject, and asked, "What is this place anyway?"

Waving a four-fingered hand to encompass the crumbling walls Sagas condescended to answer, "This is probably one of the strongholds that the ancients fled to, during the great wars."

"Great wars?"

"That was the time in this planet's history when everyone left alive, came underground to protect themselves from the Sorin Winds that burned the world above," Dunnagh added.

"Sorin winds?" Nathan asked, giving Dunnagh a puzzled look.

Damn. He'd forgotten and used a native term that Nathan would have no way of knowing. Nor should he, under normal circumstances.

Damn, keeping his secret from all his human comrades—especially his battle-bonded friend was making him crazy.

<<Then tell him, Kasha,>> the symbiont whispered in his mind.

<<I will...But not right now.>> To Nathan, he said, "Radioactive fall-out storms. I saw them when I went into the Cumarsaid trance aboard Bennett's ship."

"Oh." Nathan looked around again, this time with more interest. "What happened to those people? Were they your ancestors, Ima?"

Outraged, Sagas glared. "No! They were not. And, thank the Holy Ones in the pools for that. Those evil creatures were the ancestors of the Umwira. It was they who caused the destruction of the ancient world."

NATHAN SCRATCHED HIS growing beard, thinking. For a furred woman only about two thirds his height and maybe only half his bulk, the priestess was a power to be reckoned with, to be sure.

"Mm, I see." Nathan wasn't sure he did see, not at all, but he didn't want to take the discussion any further. Groping for an excuse to retreat he received more evidence of the unsettling changes in his friend when a young Avairei priestess showed up to tell Dunnagh that she had made up his bed and had his food ready. Dunnagh saw the carved stone flask she wore at her hip, smiled eagerly and without another word rose and followed her into the gloom.

Bemused, Nathan glanced at Sagas. She had turned, watching the retreating couple with a satisfied expression on her cat-like face. Nathan shook his head; the knot of unease in his gut tightened another notch. Was Dunnagh sexually interested in the furry little woman? Aliens had never interested him in that way before. Yuck, it was sort of kinky.

Chapter Two

By the time Nathan got the sentry assignments arranged to his satisfaction, most of the camp had settled into an uneasy slumber. The adrenaline rush that had been keeping him going for hours, suddenly dissipated, leaving him chilled and exhausted. He wanted to find Tessa, relax into her warm arms and sleep.

But when he found her, she wasn't alone. Ima Nansa was sitting beside her. Nathan set down his weapons and scowled. What was the woman up to now? The last thing he wanted at the moment was *another* problem. He sighed. "Tessa, can I speak to you for a minute? *Alone*."

Her pretty heart-shaped face wore a confused expression, but without a word, she rose and came to him. Putting an arm around her shoulder, he drew her into the shadows by the stone wall. "Tessa, what's going on here?"

"Nothing." Her innocent brown eyes stared up at him. "I was just talking to Ima Nansa. She's a fascinating old lady and—"

"Tessa," he cut in impatiently. "I'm tired. I want to go to bed."

"I know, Nathan, we were just talking while we waited for you."

"What? Wait a minute—are you telling me she's sleeping with us?"

"Well, you did bring her without even a cloak, or anything. We can't just leave her to shiver alone in the darkness, can we?"

Nathan shook his head. "No, Tessa, she's not sleeping with us! She's got kin here. Sagas wanted her to come—let the old gran sleep with her, damn it. Or she can sleep with the Loti for all I care right now, but she's definitely *not* sleeping with *us*."

Tessa pushed herself away from him and folded her arms across her full creamy breasts. Unclothed as they all were—and had been since their capture by the natives, those luscious globes were heating his blood as he contemplated their quivering ripeness.

Tessa saw his growing interest and fixed him with an angry glare. "Maybe *you* should find a Loti to sleep with yourself. How could you be so cruel to a poor old lady."

Oh, Gods, woman, I don't need this right now, please! He begged her silently. Gritting his teeth, he said, "Cruel? I am not." At her continued silence, he sighed. "Look, Tessa, my heart, I just want to be alone with you right now, and go to bed. Please."

"You're being a selfish beast," she spat back. "The only reason you want us to be alone is because you want to do—to do *that!*"

"*That? That?* Can't you even say what it is? It's called sex, Tessa. 'Making love' will do if you can't bring your high-society self to say the *awful* word. It's called sex—or fucking." He folded his arms defiantly and glared down at her, angry now himself. "Yeah, maybe I did want us to be alone so we could do *that!*

"And why not? You haven't been exactly unwilling, you know. In fact, I'd say you've been most willing to throw your legs about a rough Caldoni 'savage' like me, eh, Tessa?"

"Nathan, stop! You're being crude—and you're not a savage—I never said so." Burying her face in her hands, she began to sob.

Nathan swore under his breath. Feeling guilty now, he reached for her, wanting to apologize, but she pushed him away. Turning her back on him, she continued to cry.

Looking round, he saw Ima Nansa still sitting by the fire. Pretending to be unaware of her role in their argument, the old priestess gave him an innocent smile. Nathan scowled. Innocent his ass! He'd seen that twinkle of amusement in her sharp, old eyes, before she'd caught him watching her.

Uttering another vile Caldoni curse, Nathan gave in. Going over to their simple bed against the wall, he flung back the cover, then bowed stiffly to the women. In his best imitation of galactic high-society manners, he said through clenched teeth, "After you, ladies."

Tessa flounced past him, lying down next to the wall and turned her back on him. That left the old priestess to lie in the middle next to him. He let out a long suffering sigh, and lay down next to Nansa, pulling the blankets over all of them.

But tired as he was, Nathan found he was unable to sleep. The argument had left him tense and wakeful. Unbidden, the events of the past few hours began to replay themselves over again in his mind.

Head and neck beneath the murky water, red hair flowing out around his submerged face, torso wound about with a tangle of gray eel-like bodies, Nathan's heart nearly stopped as he recalled once more the frightening seen he'd witnessed by the pool. Who *were* those creatures, and what had they been doing to Dunnagh?

But his cousin and battle companion had been acting strangely ever since he'd performed the Cumarsaid on the ship. Nathan hadn't wanted to see it—or admit it, but it was true.

Dunnagh had tried to share his worries with him at the time, but, like the stupid fool that he was, Nathan had refused to listen. He'd been so afraid. He'd brushed off his friend's attempts to talk to him, stupidly hoping that whatever was bothering Dunnagh would just go away, if he, Nathan, ignored it. But the problem hadn't gone away. Because of his own fears, he had left Dunnagh to face this trouble alone.

Alone!

And now, *he* was alone—or at least Nathan felt that way. *I might as well be*, he thought, feeling very sorry for himself. He tried to reach out to Tessa, time and again, but she confused and angered him more often than she comforted or understood him.

Oh, if he was honest, he supposed she wasn't trying deliberately to torment him. But a Caldoni armachd and a rich, galactic society woman...? They were so different—maybe too different to make a go of their relationship.

When they returned to the base and finally got off this nightmare world, Tessa would leave—like they all did.

"Why? Oh, Dunnagh, why? Why must you leave me, too?" He moaned, feeling his throat go tight. "How could you just go off like that, forsaking friends, kindred—and me? How can I go home without you?"

Suddenly furred hands reached over and began pressing and massaging his back and shoulder. Nathan stiffened. "Don't do that," she admonished, pressing harder. "Let go, relax."

Nathan could hear Tessa's soft, rhythmic breathing. Asleep. "What are you doing?" She snorted, continuing to knead his taught muscles. "You should be asleep."

Nansa laughed softly, her fingers continuing to work. "And just how am I to do that, with you lying here so tense, crying out your pain for all to feel?" She pressed several sore points in his shoulders even harder. "Now lie still and let me work. There are other ways to obtain relaxation than exercising that thing dangling down between your legs, you know?"

He grunted, but made no further protest, giving himself up to the soothing ministrations of her skilled hands. Later, as he felt the tension receding, Nathan blurted out the one question he desperately needed answered. "What have you Avairei done to him?"

Nansa was silent for a while, her hands still moving. At last, she said, "Nothing has been done to him that he didn't choose for himself. By the Great Mother, I swear that to you, Hunt Leader. Your kinsman heard the call—he chose of his own will to come and help us."

Nathan twisted round to look at her. "But Dunnagh wouldn't just abandon me—us, if you hadn't done something to him. He just wouldn't."

Nansa pushed him back down with an impatient clicking sound in her throat. "Don't. You'll undo all my work, and I'm too old to be rubbing your back for long. Lie still—and relax."

He lay back without further comment, meekly letting her resume her massage. Nansa kneaded and stroked his stubborn muscles for some time; finally she said, "I think you are either lying to yourself, or you don't know him as well as you believe.

"The Chosen is a very honorable man. If a people were in trouble and asked his aid, wouldn't he try to help them, even if, by doing so, it meant making a great personal sacrifice? Haven't you known him to do such things before, hmm?"

Yes, damn her, he had, many times. Dunnagh was always doing something stupid and heroic—and damn him, too. He probably had agreed to whatever they wanted.

After a long silence, he reluctantly admitted, "Yes, you're right."

She chuckled. "I thought so, but why are you so sad? This is what I don't understand. Do you think he will leave you because he has agreed to serve the Khutani and help us? It is not like that. He will need his kindred, and especially you with him, now more than ever."

A muffled "Oh," was her answer.

Nansa smiled when she heard his quiet snoring. She allowed her hands to slow, and then to stop. Curling up against his muscular back, she pulled the blanket up over them and slept.

Chapter Three

Aroused by the sentries after a few marks of exhausted sleep, the band of natives and human aliens gathered around a central fire. The green flames of the burning stones gave off a dry metallic smell and little heat, but the fire's light was a welcome haven in the gloom. As their new Ce'awn or leader Dunnagh was already awake and waiting for them.

My people. May I be worthy of their trust, he prayed silently as he looked into their eyes.

<<Don't fret, Kasha,>> Tani said. <<I have my encoded memories to guide us. All will be well.>>

Dunnagh surreptitiously brushed a hand across his middle. The symbiont was so young and meant well, but there were too many unknowns in this equation for his liking. <<You are probably right, Shalla. I will try to remember.>>

<<And stop worrying.>>

Tessa, Singey and the Avairei sat in a half circle nearest to him, the shaggy centaur-like Loti stood flicking their tails nervously behind them. The Begta and his squad of Caldoni armachda were watchful, weapons ready, either at his back or scattered elsewhere round the perimeter.

Addressing the native Timornans first, Dunnagh allowed Tani's encoded knowledge to guide his words. "Your breeding was true, and I want to thank you for your loyalty, both to me as the Kashallan, and to my kindred in the pools. It took great courage to break with tradition and disobey the High Council in Riath. I am honored."

Raising his glance to include them all, he continued, "Outlawry will not be an easy path, I fear. We are hunted, and for some here capture must surely mean death.

For me personally, there are certain priorities that I must consider or I may not survive this journey no matter what our enemies do. I need to find another living pool, where my Khutani kindred can help me.

"Combaron has tried to kill me, and his powerful clansmen, I'm sure, will bar the Keeps in the Yeyen Banai valley to me. That leaves me but one option. To get what I need, I must go to Ticca Keep."

There was an uneasy stirring among the Timornans at that revelation. Finally, Nansa said, "You're correct, child, the valley would not be safe for you at this time. But Ticca is a long way, and the paths along the Rim Wall are rough and dangerous. Can you survive it?"

He grimaced. "I have no idea. But Ticca is where my elders advise me to go, so I must try it. But I can't go to Ticca directly." Dunnagh motioned to the members of his squad. "When we arrived on this world, we had others with us. We need to find out what has happened to them. We had a camp in the Broken Lands; I will go there first."

There were murmurs of agreement from the humans around the circle, and shocked protests from the Avairei. When they quieted again, he continued. "I must know their fate before I can go on. For a long time, when no one came looking for us, I thought they were dead.

"We had enemies of our own who were pursuing us. I thought, as many of my human companions did, that those enemies must have found our people and destroyed them. Now, however, I am not so sure."

"But surely," Sagas protested, "That can wait. When you are safe, your kinsman there," she motioned to Nathan standing behind him, "Surely he can take word to the others later. It is your safety that is of most importance, so much depends on you. The Khutani have told me— "

"I know what they have told you, Ima," he interrupted. "But the Sorins won't wait, either, and you know that as well as I. Besides, I have other reasons for choosing to go west to the base.

"First of all, our enemies will not expect it. They will look for us to go east over the Jeban Pass, or perhaps they will even seek us on the direct route south along the Rim Wall to Ticca.

"Or, if they believe the Dingay's nonsense about us being mutant sorcerers, they might send out Warlinga hunting packs north into the

Ghostlands. But it will be a long time, before they think to look for us to the west."

When he fell silent, waiting; there was a murmur of agreement at his reasoning. "My second reason for choosing this way is, if the camp still exists, we can pick up better weapons and supplies for the rest of the journey to Ticca.

"Those of my human kindred who want to follow me will need better weapons than a few knives and spears. Right now we are all very vulnerable. My armachda are well-trained and seasoned fighters, but they are in need of proper equipment. For all these reasons, I see no other course for us than this one. We will go west."

Sagas shuddered, but said nothing when he gave her an inquiring look. "Part of the way we can follow the River Magre through these caverns. The Begta say there are old tunnels leading back into the Broken Lands that connect with the river. When we find one of them, we will turn west, and come out somewhere near our objective. From there—" He shrugged. "Who can say? It will depend on what we find."

Singey leaned forward to catch his attention, concern apparent on his ebony features. "Dunnagh, you didn't list it as one of your reasons for returning to the base, but you have referred to your health a few times now. If you are in need of medical assistance, then, by all means, we need to get back to the base as soon as possible. If the ship is repaired then we can get you to a proper medical facility—"

"No, Philip, that isn't an option I can consider. For reasons I don't want to go into right now, I must stay here on Timorna. Dr. Bennett's medicine would be of no use to me, I can assure you. Timorna is where I belong, and where I must stay. I can't leave now—ever."

"But, Ce'awn," Oglas protested, "We would not be wanting to leave you alone here, but we can't be staying! We have kin and obligations at home. Surely you understand that. We have to go back." The rest of his squad of armachda murmured their agreement.

"I understand. I can't force you—you must do what you think best."

"I'm staying," Nathan announced. "The rest of you mangy dogs can do as you please."

Dunnagh glanced at him, feeling a smile curve his lips. "Thank you, Mo Cri."

Stunned, Nathan blurted, "Did you think I'd abandon you, after all we've been through together? You stupid ass."

Dunnagh chuckled. "I know I am, you've told me I am often enough."

"What are you people talking about?" Sagas demanded. "You can't leave Timorna, any of you. The alignment has been completed; you would die—horribly I might add—without the kavay now. Don't you know that yet? Kashallan, why haven't you told them?"

A stunned silence followed her words. Sagas glanced from one alien face to the other, her braid ornaments clacking with her distress. Finally addressing the armachda directly, she pleaded, "You can't abandon him now, when he needs you so much. What will we do without a hunting pack to protect us? If he is determined to go to Ticca, then you must come!"

As confused as the rest of the humans, Dunnagh said, "I don't understand, Ima, why can't they leave, if they want to?"

"Think, child of the pools!" Nansa said. "You know exactly what she means. You are allowing your Chosen to have too much say in this. Stop now and balance yourself."

Balance himself.

Dunnagh closed his eyes and listened as his symbiont bondmate brought up the necessary information about the Khutani-created organisms, introduced on this world centuries ago to sustain life. At last, he opened his eyes and sighed heavily. "I'm sorry. Ima Sagas is right. I remember now what I have been told about the kavay alignment. I'm afraid you all must share my fate.

"Now that the alignment is complete, the changes that have occurred in our bodies are permanent and irreversible."

"Kavay? What is kavay, Sir?" Chang asked.

"I don't know much about the scientific explanation, Armachd," Dunnagh said. "But kavay is the cause of the blue coloring in the food and water on this world. The kavay is a virus, or something like that, introduced here to help living organisms withstand the poisons left over from the old wars.

"The kavay alignment process was what caused us to become so ill while we were in Gormach's slave pens. It was our bodies adjusting to life on this world."

"But surely, with the aid of modern medicines, we can go through a detoxification period, and then we can leave," Tessa protested.

He shook his head. "Kavay alignment is not like an addiction to alcohol or drugs. Its effects on our metabolism go deeper than that. I don't know how much time Philip had to examine the environment before we were taken.

"If he had continued his studies, I'm sure he would have found that there are still a lot of poisons present here. These substances were left over from industrial wastes and a nuclear disaster that happened thousands of years ago.

"Kavay, even now, is the only thing that makes living possible on this world. But in order to maintain life, kavay must make permanent changes in the cell structure and metabolism of the body to which it is introduced. Those changes are irreversible. On Timorna, kavay *is* life, and everything is aligned with it."

Armachd Taleish swore. "Why? Why did those devils have to do that to us? They *forced* us to take it! Damn them!"

"I don't know what happened at Tragar," the elderly priest Temog said. "But please don't judge all Warlinga by your experiences with that bunch. Giving you kavay was not an act of cruelty. Ignorance, yes, but not cruelty. You must understand that until your coming, we had never heard of anyone not aligned with the kavay—" he grimaced as if in pain. "Even the Umwira are blessed by it.

"I talked to Tobrach, Gormach's young cousin; he told me about the sickness, but he thought, as everyone else did, that it had something to do with the blowgun poison. No one considered a lack of alignment as the cause of your symptoms.

"It was only in the most ancient of our writings I found mention of such an illness, and by that time—the alignment was nearly complete—and there was nothing to be done."

Singey leaned forward so he could see Temog more clearly. "Forgive me, Ata, if I seem skeptical; I mean no offense to your beliefs. I am what my people call a scientist. What I do is study and observe things in order to find the truth. I noticed the toxic traces in the soils and atmosphere, as Dunnagh implied, but, until I have time to prove it for myself in my lab, I cannot accept what you tell me about the kavay as truth.

"My people have progressed such a long way from the primitive lifestyle you have here on Timorna. I'm sure with the aid of our advanced science; I could find a way to reverse the effects kavay has made on us. I'm sorry, but if the camp is still there, I have to study this phenomenon before I believe you."

The Kashallan laughed softly. "Go right ahead, Philip. I would not expect you to do anything less, but, in the end, you will find out we are right. And Sagas is right too—I do need you—we need you, but I can't compel you to follow me. I have told you what I honestly believe.

"That belief is based on knowledge given to me by the elder race of this world, but what you do with the information must be in accord with your own hearts."

Feeling quite vulnerable, Dunnagh waited, allowing them to take their time and think about his offer. He could see their stunned expressions in the firelight. They hadn't counted on *this*.

Ever since their capture, the only thought that had been keeping them going was the hope of returning to family and friends in that normal, mundane world out among the stars.

And now, those hopes were dashed; this nightmare would go on and on. The realization was a heavy blow, they were, in effect, dead to Caldon and their old lives. But Timorna did offer a new beginning and a life of service and purpose. He hoped they would be strong enough to seize it.

At last, Marti spoke up, shattering the silence. "Ce'awn, Marnez and me, we would rather be going home, that's the Gods' own truth. But if that is not to be, then, like Patrol Leader Nathan, we stay with you."

"I'm your man, too, sir," Oglas allowed.

Eyes glistening with unshed tears, the Kashallan accepted his human companions' oaths of fealty, and pledged his own oath to them in return. They were his sworn armachda now.

Ah, but will they be, when they find out about Tani? Will they follow a creature that isn't wholly human anymore?

Dunnagh saw Nathan looking at him with a worried expression, and dropped his eyes. *Oh, Nathan, what will you do when I tell you? Can I bear it if you are afraid of me?* In his middle, Tani shifted fretfully, becoming aware of his fear.

Dunnagh took a deep breath, fighting for control. He stood up; the rest of the group rising along with him. "We had best get moving," he said, and turned away into the darkness.

Chapter Four

Among the rocks by the underground river, several wraith-like creatures squatted in a tight circle, their large, sensitive eyes picking out every detail of their leader's fearsome visage. The domesticated slaves of the Khutani called them Umwira, but they referred to themselves as the People—the Real People.

It was *their* ancestors, after all, who once ruled this world. And it was the Real People who would rule it again, someday soon. The old wizard, Barak, had promised it.

The war leader bared his teeth, reached out a sinewy arm, and dug his claws into a stammering subordinate's shoulder. "Speak clearly," he demanded. "Who are they?" The smaller, less fiercely endowed monster whined, trying to pull away. His leader held on, tightening his grip. "S-speak-k!" he hissed, shaking it impatiently.

"I-I not know, Great Avenger." The scout gasped. "There are many—Avairei, Loti, Begta, coming along the river. And, there are also some strange creatures traveling with the Khutani's slaves that I never see before."

"What about Warlinga?"

His victim shook its head vigorously. "No Warlinga."

"Hmm." Where were the fierce lizardmen that the Khutani bred to protect the rest of their slaves? The war leader hated riddles. Was this a trap, stupidity, or something else? He let go his grip on the scout, allowing the smaller creature to sink to the ground, cradling its wounded limb and whimpering.

"Don't move," the war leader's Second warned. "We tell when we finished with you."

The wizards who bred and guided the People of the Ghostlands, like the monsters who made up this warband, hated the Khutani and all that they had created, with a ferocity passed down through the ages.

Seeking to please his wizard with more new captives, the Great Avenger had decided to take his warband south over the Jeban pass. Few of the war leaders ventured that far into the Khutani's' territory, so he reasoned that the booty would be well worth the extra risk.

Luck hadn't been with them this time, however. Nearing the Jeban Pass, the warband came upon a small caravan of Avairei priests and their Warlinga guards. The temptation was too great to resist.

They attacked, but these Warlinga weren't the drunken fools from Tragar, as they'd assumed. This pack fought with a willingness that turned an easy victory into a shattering defeat. It stung his pride like a whiplash that they'd been forced to run and hide in the tunnels where their ancestors once lived, to escape the search parties sent out to find them.

With no victories to boast of, and few captives to placate Barak's anger, they had been slowly creeping homeward, when their luck suddenly changed. They were alone down in these caverns no longer.

But Avairei hadn't used these underground paths in centuries—and never without a Warlinga guard to escort them. Their presence was a tempting lure, but the Avenger's instincts warned him that there was some kind of danger here as well.

He didn't want to ignore such a seductive prize outright, but after their fight with the Warlinga by the pass, they were weakened. If unknown magic was involved, their victory might not be as easy as it appeared.

"You say there are others," his Second asked the scout. "If not Warlinga, who are they?"

The little one shook its head. "Don't know—never see that kind before. Maybe other wizard breed new kind mutant."

The unasked-for comment earned it a swift kick, but its two superiors exchanged significant glances over its groveling form. "What look like, these strange ones?" the leader demanded. There had been rumors of rival wizards west on the banks of the Shallow Sea who wanted the Southland for their own. Could these strangers be creatures of another wizard's genetic manipulations?

The scout screwed up its face in concentration. "Some big, almost like Warlinga. Got smooth skin, no scales or claws, but got Warlinga weapons. So, maybe Warlinga?"

"No claws, easy to kill?" the Second suggested. "If we kill, we can take Avairei and Loti. Master always needs more slaves for his magics. If we bring him plenty slaves maybe Barak not be angry."

"Hmm, maybe,"

When the Warlinga drove the Ghostlander's ancestors north into the poisoned waists, the People hadn't perished as the Khutani hoped. Their wizards deliberately sought out the poisoned places, and willingly paid the price of mutation. It was worth the risk of a terrible death, to claim the powers these changes brought—power to be turned against the enemy in so many delicious ways.

But Master Barak was not the only wizard who possessed great magics. They had, if not exactly enemies among the western clans, then certainly "rivals." Could these others be from across the Shallow Sea?

"Hmm. Maybe strange mutants have magics. No needs claws, if got power."

The Second growled, flexing his claws. "Mm. What we do?"

The Great Avenger rose, looking around him at the remnants of his warband. The Second was right; they needed to take home some prisoners to avert punishment. The Master would be very angry if they didn't have anything to show for such a dangerous undertaking.

And if these newcomers were indeed a new race of mutants bread by their cousins on the shores of the Shallow Sea, the Old One would also need to know about a rival encroaching into their territory. This, too, was valuable information that could avert pain.

The strangers must have magics. Why else would such defenseless-looking creatures be sent to gather slaves, unless to fool them and the Warlinga hunting packs into underestimating them? When their enemies attacked, thinking them easy prey, then the strangers would unleash their power, and their unsuspecting enemies would die.

The Avenger felt his rage mounting—how dare these newcomers raid into Ghostlander territory? He had big magics too! They would taste his magics. No. Better to watch and follow. In a menacing hiss he gave his orders.

Chapter Five

Sending his Begta scouts ahead into the gloom, Nathan walked back along the column until he found Dunnagh. He nodded to Berren, then, matching his pace to the Loti's, he studied his friend out of the corner of one eye. Since Dunnagh's return to them from the pools below Sulas Keep, Nathan had been keeping an eye on him, trying to puzzle out the unexplained changes he sensed in his beloved friend.

It seemed like he was missing something—something important, but what? At times his friend was the same old Dunnagh, the man who was the one person in the universe he cared about most. They had grown up together, sharing everything, and taking care of each other through many a dark time.

But now—well, there were times when Dunnagh said or did something that was so alien, so un-Dunnagh, that it made Nathan's blood run cold. His gut instincts told him that his friend was keeping something important from him, and that made him both angry and afraid.

Each time Nathan questioned him, Dunnagh got a haunted look in his eye, and made some excuse to run off and hide among the Avairei. Then, when Nathan tried to follow, Sagas or another of Dunnagh's new guard-dogs would look at him sternly and tell him to get lost and don't bother the "Kashallan."

Kashallan. What exactly was a kashallan, and why did they call his friend that, and treat him like some kind of God. He'd asked Tessa, but if she knew, which he doubted, she wasn't telling either. There were so many questions, all needing answers.

What had happened after the priestess took him away from the slave pen? The Avairei did something to him, or he let them do something to him—whichever—it didn't matter, it had been done. Dunnagh had changed; he wasn't the same man any more.

Like now, for example. There he was, riding hunched over, one arm cradled protectively round his middle, totally oblivious of Nathan's presence, engrossed in some internal dialogue of his own. Nathan shuddered. He looked, so—so—weird.

Trying to drive away his uneasiness, he put a hand on Dunnagh's knee. Startled out of his reverie, Dunnagh glanced around, then saw him. "Sorry, Nathan, did you say something to me?"

"I was wondering, oh fearless leader, when you planned on stopping. You've been pushing them pretty hard. I think everyone's getting tired. Don't you think we should camp soon?"

Dunnagh made a face, then sighed. "Yeah, you're right, maybe we should stop." He glanced around uneasily. "I know I've been pushing the pace a bit, but I'm worried. I can't shake the feeling that someone is out there in the gloom watching us, and I don't like it. Gods, I'll be glad to get out of these caves," he confessed.

Nathan grunted. He'd felt it too, but had put it down to the oppressive feeling of being always in the dark. He trusted Dunnagh's keener Psy, however. Trying to sound casual, he asked, "You got any idea how much farther to this side passage of yours?"

"No I don't." Dunnagh dropped his eyes when they met Nathan's. "I guess we'd better stop. It won't do any good to push ourselves to exhaustion. Tell whoever's on point to look for a suitable spot to camp."

"Your will, Kashallan." Nathan muttered, and loped off.

DUNNAGH GLARED AT THE shadows and swore under his breath.

<<You should tell him, Kasha. You told me he loves you and you him; why are you avoiding this? He needs to know, all your kin need to know. Why do you delay?>>

<<I wish I dared tell him, Shalla. I hate this as much as he does, but for us humans—it's complicated.>>

A mental snort. <<I am learning that so much about humans is 'complicated,' but I don't understand why. If you—>> Tani broke off, tasting its bondmate's emotions. Puzzled, it stated, <<You are frightened. Why?>>

Dunnagh started to protest, then fell silent. If he denied his fear, he would be lying, and Tani would know it. He was learning that his bondmate could *taste* his moods. Tani usually knew better what he was feeling than he did himself.

Once again Dunnagh marveled at how the symbiont was such a strange mixture of youth and maturity. It had its species' encoded ancestral knowledge upon which to draw, but in actual living experience, it was only a young child. The bond was so new and confusing. They were still exploring how to interact, both with each other and with the outside world. Not only did the symbiont's responses change with each new situation, but Dunnagh himself found he vacillated between different roles, as each partner's expertise was needed.

At last, he said, <<I'm afraid because there is a deep unreasoning fear among my race of being possessed by another intelligent mind. When something like that occurs, my people tend to think of that person as a monster, someone to be hated and feared, and maybe even killed. It's hard for me, because Nathan and I have been so close since childhood. I don't want to lose him, Shalla, but if I tell him, he might think me a monster too. He might not understand.>>

<<But I've not tried to take away your free will!>>

<<I know that. The point is, Nathan doesn't know that. How can I prove to him, or any of them, that in this body that we share, there still is a Dunnagh Kai who is a separate being from Tani of the Pools?>>

<<But—>>

<<Think about how lonely you have been feeling since we left Sulas. Well, I would feel the same if my kin were afraid of me, and left me. You're right; Shalla, I'm not only frightened, I'm terrified.>>

<<Would they do that, Kasha, really? Surely they would not, especially your kinsman and battle companion Nathan.>>

Dunnagh laughed low in his throat. His inner companion had a way of cutting through excuses to nip at the truth. <<I've been too scared to find out. You're right, though; I must do it soon.>>

Chapter Six

It took them a while, but at last Nathan and the scouts found a place among the rocks where they could set up camp. As uneasy as he felt, Dunnagh had to admit he was glad for the rest. His body ached from the unaccustomed riding, as well as from the biological adaptations Tani was continuing to make in their shared flesh.

His fingers tonight seemed particularly painful. Dunnagh rubbed them absently as he sat by the fire waiting for his new Avairei bride, Pela, to bring him his ration of formula.

Passing his fire, Singey paused, then unexpectedly joined him. "I've watched you doing that before, Dunnagh. What's wrong with your hands? Can I do anything to help?"

Startled, Dunnagh glanced at his hands, laughed and slid them into the shadows under his cloak. "Oh, my fingers, yes, they are a bit sore. I must have bumped them somehow. It's nothing to worry about."

His ebony face unreadable, the scientist nodded. "I seriously doubt you bumped your hands. Will you let me see them?"

Dunnagh hesitated for a long moment, then he held out a hand. Singey took it, and traced with a slim, dark finger the growing elongation of Dunnagh's middle and ring fingers, comparing their proportions to his own. Next, he felt the raised hard cases that were growing along the whole length of those two fingers. This hard outer covering had almost replaced the flexible skin and fingernails that were a part of a normal human hand. The digits were still supple, but if the adaptation continued, Dunnagh wouldn't be able to make a fist or use them properly for gripping objects.

Turning Dunnagh's hand over, he then held it up to the wavering green light of the fire, and examined the new openings on the fingertips, trying to discover what was contained within the hardening shells.

Finished with his examination at last, Singey returned the appendage to its red-haired owner. "Thank you. I was curious, though I'm not exactly sure what I just saw. Would you mind telling me what purpose these adaptations, when they are completed, will serve?"

Dunnagh returned his stare and countered. "Before I do that, Philip, first tell me what you know—or think you know."

Singey shrugged. Picking his words carefully, he said, "I don't know anything for certain. I've merely been observing you since we fled Sulas, and trying to come up with a hypothesis that fits the data."

Dunnagh chuckled. "Come on, Philip, don't go all scientific and evasive on me. You started this, let's finish it."

Singey nodded, his dark eyes solemn. "You're right; we should finish it, because it needs to be done, and it's not going to get any easier as time goes by."

He took a deep breath. "I'll start with the most obvious things. Physically you've changed. Not only your hands are different, but there are other things too. The shape of your body is thicker through the middle, yet elsewhere your bone and muscle mass appear thinner, more defined.

"There is another adaptation I have noticed besides your hands, your new pointed teeth. You have tried to conceal that too, but at times you forget yourself and smile." Singey's own white teeth flashed in an ironic grin that soon faded. "The effect is quite striking, I assure you."

Unable to keep the note of apprehension out of his voice, Dunnagh blurted, "Do you think anyone else has noticed these—uh—changes?"

"It's hard to say; the light is dim in these caverns, and we have all been under a lot of stress. I noticed, because it's part of my training to make observations. I do it automatically, without thinking about it. Nathan should have noticed, knowing you as well as he does. Hasn't he said anything to you?"

Dunnagh grimaced, then let out a heavy sigh. "He's tried. I've been avoiding the issue. But continue."

"All right. You're probably not conscious of how odd you appear at times. And this I know Nathan has noticed, because I've seen him staring at you when you're doing it."

"I thought I was hiding the changes so well, but apparently that isn't the case. What am I doing that is so strange?"

"Well, for one thing, you've developed this habit of closing your eyes and moving your lips like you're talking to someone inside your head. People who have been institutionalized for mental illness often do that when they are hearing voices. If you were hearing voices, because of some of your, uh, 'Caldoni training,' that would explain where your new-found knowledge of this world is coming from, perhaps.

"What it doesn't explain is why you often do that while rubbing or cradling your belly—or why I have seen, on at least one occasion, that same midsection move in a most unusual manner."

Dunnagh sat stunned, his mouth hanging open. <<Gods, Tani, how could I have been so careless. No wonder Nathan has been pestering me, if it is that obvious.>>

<<I keep telling you that you need to tell him—and all of them.>>

Not considering that comment worth an answer, Dunnagh returned his attention to the scientist. Singey was saying...

"And, let's talk about the priests' behavior. A lot has changed there as well. They treat you more like a god or royalty rather than a slave. Why! I wonder. The answer seems to center around the true meaning of the word kashallan. That is what the Timornans call you now, and they use the term with the highest respect. When I've asked the Avairei what the word means, however, they are most evasive—when they reply at all."

Singey leaned forward, his eyes alight with his eagerness. "Have you told them not to answer, or are they just picking up on your reluctance to speak about what has happened to you? The best I can get out of them is that a kashallan is a very old word in their language. I gather it has something to do with an oath or a bond of some kind.

"My second mystery has to do with the Khutani. Who or what are they? Are they ancient tribal Gods, as Tessa believes, or are they something else, something more real and physical?

"I know they have something to do with you, Dunnagh, or Kashallan, if you prefer, because they are usually mentioned when talking about pools of some kind. And it was to the pools at Sulas that you were taken."

Singey sat back, holding out his hands, palms upwards. "That's about it. I feel I'm close, but not quite there." Under Dunnagh's continued stare, he laughed nervously. "I would appreciate if you'd tell me the rest so I can get some sleep, instead of spending half my rest period sorting through my facts,"

Dunnagh nodded and dropped his eyes. For a long time he sat staring into the fire. At last he said, "You seem very calm about all this, Philip. You've thought it out quite carefully and logically. I'm impressed, and overwhelmed. But don't all these changes you've observed in me, don't they bother you? Aren't you afraid of all this—of me?"

Singey considered before answering, finally he shook his head. "For some undisclosed reason this is very important to you. During our capture and slavery I've grown to respect and like you, Dunnagh. And for that reason you deserve an honest answer. Certainly I've been more terrified since coming to this world than I ever dreamed was possible, but no, I'm not frightened of you, or what's happened to you. And before you press me further, I can't explain why."

His uneasy laugh came again. "How very unscientific of me, right? Should I be afraid of you?"

Dunnagh shook his head. "No, definitely not, but, to be equally frank, that has been my fear. That is—if all of you knew the truth, you would abandon me, and right now I couldn't bear that."

"I see. I thought it might be something like that. Are you able to trust me enough to tell me what did happen after the priestess took you away?"

"I don't know if I can. I've tried that before, remember?"

At the recollection, Singey grimaced then nodded.

"And, though we both have changed a lot since our first meeting, we still have little common experience in the area of the psychic disciplines that would make the telling easy. Later perhaps we can talk about it in more detail. But what I will do for you now, is give you more information about the kashallan and the Khutani. Fair enough?"

Singey nodded. "More than fair, and, I am sorry about that time when I mocked your Psy training. That was my own pet fears surfacing; it had little to do with you."

Dunnagh acknowledged the apology, then continued. "Firstly, the Khutani are not ancient tribal Gods in the way I think Tessa means. They are very real, and, with one exception at present, they live within pools like the ones at Sulas. They are the most ancient living intelligent species on this world. Their racial memories go back to a time before the Great Wars.

"You were also right, Philip, when you said some time ago that this planet's ecosystem was unnatural. It is. Over the centuries it has been the Khutani who have carried out the genetic engineering and breeding programs that were responsible for the re-population of Timorna."

"And," the Kashallan's mouth quirked, "they are also responsible for creating and spreading the kavay to act as a buffer between life and the poisons that are still present on this world."

"Are you quite sure about this?"

The Kashallan laughed, then gave him a toothy grin to deliberately emphasize the new alien part of his nature. The timbre of his voice slightly altering as Tani answered for both of them, it said, "Oh, quite sure, Dr. Singey, quite sure indeed. Now to give you the rest. A kashallan is a type of bond. It is a bond between a symbiont and a host. In this case, the symbiont being a child of the Khutani, and the host being the human Dunnagh Kai.

"But the priests were not lying when they told you about an oath as well. A kashallan bond does involve a pledge, as well as the symbiosis. Those beings who willingly choose the partnership set aside their personal lives to become the healers and guardians of all life on this so wounded world."

Taking over the narrative again, Dunnagh asked, "Do you understand now, Philip? And, more importantly, can you accept the changes that have happened to the me that is Dunnagh since I chose this path?"

After a prolonged hesitation Singey rubbed a hand across his face and sighed. "Well, I certainly got more out of this than I expected." He gave a short bark of a laugh. "I don't know what to say—it's very hard to grasp this all at once. May I ask a couple more questions though? I'm having trouble right now understanding our current situation based on what you've told me."

"Of course. I've told you this much, I'm not going to close up now."

"All right. Why you, Dunnagh, or even why a human host? Surely there was a more suitable species already here on Timorna?"

Dunnagh shook his head, but it was Tani who took up the tale once more. “Unfortunately, there wasn’t. That was the problem. The Bebech who originally served that purpose were killed off in a plague several centuries past, and the genetic patterns were lost. Since that time, we were confined to the underground pools at places like Sulas.

“As to why humans, and why Dunnagh in particular—all of that gets into the gray area that my Kasha tells me you find so hard to accept. I’m not sure I can describe this in a way you can understand, but I’ll try. The “Makers,” the Ancients of my species, tasted a 'wrongness' to things.

“They knew there was a need for us to come out of the pools so that we could care for the land and peoples of Timorna personally. Since the plague, we have had to rely on the Avairei to do that for us, and the Khutani Elders weren’t satisfied with the priests’ stewardship.

“So for that reason, the Makers divined that there was a suitable host species, out among the stars and used their power to call you to us. Dunnagh, because of his Caldoni training, could be contacted. For that reason he was chosen, and agreed to become my bondmate and host.

“Though we are the first of the new kashallans, the Elders hope that others of your species will choose the bonding in time.” The Khutani studied him speculatively, through Dunnagh’s blue eyes. “Should you ever choose to do so, Dr. Singey, you yourself would make an excellent bondmate, I would think. The knowledge you have from your own studies, combined with the Elders’ wisdom, would be of great benefit to this world.”

Singey cleared his throat nervously. “Am I correct in assuming that at the moment I am not speaking to Dunnagh, but to one of the Khutani?”

The Kashallan nodded. “You are correct, Dr. Singey.”

“May I know your name, if you have one?”

Dunnagh’s face smiled, displaying those sharp alien teeth he had so recently acquired. Sounding as pleased as a child, the symbiont said, “Oh yes, I have a name. I’m Tani, Dunnagh’s bondmate.”

“Thank you, Tani, you and your, uh, Kasha have been very open with me, and have given me a lot to think about. I don’t know what to say.”

“There is nothing that you need to say. What we have told you is difficult to grasp; you will need time to think about it.” Tani’s amused giggle startled him, making Singey jump. "I don't think, we've improved your prospects of sleep by giving you the information you requested."

Singey's lips twitched. "True enough, but I did ask for it, didn't I?"

"That you did." Catching the subtle shift of timbre this time Singey recognized the Kashallan's next words as coming from Dunnagh. "Thank you, Philip, I appreciate your calm acceptance of my situation. Tani has been pestering me to tell Nathan. After this, maybe I can work up the courage to do it.

"I also want to tell you that, throughout this whole mess, you've been someone I could count on, and I want to thank you for that, too."

His eyes suddenly luminous with moister, Singey said, "Thank you, Ce'awn, your high regard means a lot to me."

Dunnagh felt the flush darkening his cheeks and stood to hide his embarrassment. He stretched, Tani automatically shifting its position within his middle. Dunnagh looked down at the scientist, and grinned. "I'm doing it again, aren't I?"

Singey nodded. "Yes, you are."

The Kashallan put a hand on his shoulder. "I've got to go get something to eat. One of the big problems with our hasty and premature flight from Sulas is that I am short of a constant food supply. In order to complete those adaptations you've noticed, I'm supposed to be eating more regularly than I am at the moment. And, right now I'm starving. We can talk again another time if you like. I'll answer your other question about my hand adaptations then, all right?"

"Yes, of course."

Overwhelmed by the unexpected wealth of information he'd just received, Singey stared numbly into the fire. Its green flames reminded him all too clearly of the strangeness of this alien world. And if Dunnagh was right about the kavay alignment, they would have to call Timorna home forever.

And, the Khutani was also right, the answer to his riddle was not going to let him get any more sleep. He shivered, remembering the look of that cold alien gaze when the symbiont spoke to him directly.

"Philip?"

Startled, Singey glanced up as Nathan sat down beside him, a hunk of bread and a bowl of hot-spiced kavay tea in his hands. "They've got food set out over there. Go see Tessa; she'll fix you up some."

"Thanks, I will in a minute," Singey mumbled. Symbiosis? Yes, he could understand Dunnagh's reluctance to let them know his true situation. In spite of all his scientific training, it had been almost impossible for Singey to maintain his air of calm detachment, especially when the symbiont made him that unexpected offer.

Nathan ate for a while in silence, then blurted, "I saw Dunnagh over here a minute ago, seemed like you two were having a very serious conversation."

"Hmm? Oh, yes, it was. Very interesting."

Interesting? Looking back on the whole conversation, he found that, if he were brutally honest, he was both attracted to, and horrified by, what had happened to Dunnagh. His scientific curiosity was piqued by the treasure chest of information that would be opened up for him if they should have to remain on this primitive world, and he took the Khutani up on its offer, but on the other hand....

"I guess he must have seen me coming and taken off again," Nathan grumbled. "Sorry if I interrupted something important."

Reluctantly Singey gave him his full attention. Nathan didn't sound sorry, not sorry at all. Behind the remark, he heard the pain in the other man's words.

He, personally, had never been close to anyone the way he had observed some of the Caldoni were with one another. Singey supposed this closeness was a product of their unique kinship system, and the harsh conditions under which they lived and fought.

If he were honest with himself, he would have to admit that he secretly envied Nathan and Dunnagh's friendship. Growing up the only child of wealthy aging parents, in the past he had never wanted, or thought he needed, such ties.

Since coming to Timorna, however, he was not so sure. He had grown accustomed to the rough camaraderie of his companions over the course of their ordeal together, and was proud of the place he had won for himself among them.

The armachda had been wary with him at first, and he with them. Singey blamed himself for their capture, and some like Taleish did too. But over time things had changed. Now they treated him with the same respectful reserve that they gave their own Lann Gheal officers.

And here sat Nathan, reaching out for help with a problem that he couldn't solve for himself. Well, maybe both Dunnagh and Nathan needed a little help. Maybe the explanation would come easier from another, at least the first part anyway. Then it would be up to them to work it out for themselves. The Kashallan hadn't forbidden him to repeat what he'd been told. Gathering his thoughts, Singey took a deep breath and began.

Chapter Seven

From the depths of exhausted sleep Dunnagh became aware of a vague uneasiness in the waking world. He lay still in the darkness listening to the sounds of the sleeping camp around him, trying to puzzle out what had caught his attention.

Tiny green fires dotted the rocky hollow where they'd made their camp. Beyond in the eternal gloom he could hear the lap of ebony water against the river's shoreline. A sentry's bare foot dislodged a pebble and the man cursed softly under his breath. Dunnagh remained perfectly still, feigning sleep. Was something wrong—had the unseen watchers he'd felt earlier returned?

Maybe. Slipping into the Cumarsaid trance, he allowed his awareness to soar outward into the blackness, but he sensed only Nathan's guards and small animals in the rocks. Coming back out of the trance, he took a deep breath and let it out slowly. The camp seemed quiet,

But that didn't mean they were safe, though. His gift had been tampered with before on this alien world. He suddenly wished there had been more time to spend with Maker Gladdris. If the Maker had been willing to cough up some Khutani secrets, maybe he could have sensed if they were in danger, and his Psy was being blocked somehow.

So what had awakened him? Tani stirred restlessly in his middle. Ah, the symbiont. <<Shalla, what's wrong?>>

<<I'm sorry I woke you, but I'm so hungry, Kasha. Or rather, we are so hungry,>> it amended. <<Can't you sense it?>>

Dunnagh considered. <<Yes, now that you've brought it to my attention, I can sense our hunger. But it's not of great importance; we can survive.>>

<<Can we?>>

Dunnagh slid his hands over his middle. Underneath his firm abdominal muscles, he could feel the symbiont's sinewy coils. Gently, he began to massage and stroke his inner companion. <<Yes we can—at least, I know the part of us that was only me once, can. Why, when I fasted for my manhood ceremony, I went without food or water for five days and nights.

<<Many times since then, while in combat, I have had to go without nourishment for long periods. It isn't comfortable to feel the hunger, but if it is not for too long we can manage.>>

<<Oh, I didn't know. Five days and nights! That's a long time, isn't it, Kasha?>>

<<Mm hmm. It is, but, Tani, we *have* eaten recently—it's just not as much as we were used to while in the pools. It may feel like we are starving by contrast, but we aren't.>> The symbiont was so young—too young maybe, to have its growth restricted by abstinence, Dunnagh thought. In the pools, they had been fed and nurtured like any child.

Their needs were anticipated, and taken care of, almost before they could think of them. Such security was every child's dream, and now, like a dream, it was gone. They were on their own now in a hostile world. Tani would have to grow up fast, and they would have to learn to rely on, and take care of each other.

Dunnagh had a sudden frightening thought. <<Shalla? I remember now, there are parts of your physical self that I don't share—*are* you all right? Can you cope with our new limited diet?>>

<<I think so,>> came Tani's hesitant mental voice. <<But, Kasha, can we please have some more to eat, just for tonight?>>

Feeling like a parent in spite of himself, Dunnagh chuckled softly. <<All right, a little. But not too much, OK? We don't know how long the formula the Khutani made for us will have to last us, remember.>>

<<OK, just a little—and I do remember.>>

As Dunnagh was trying to disentangle himself from the blankets and the sleeping woman beside him, Pela sat up. "Kashallan, what's wrong?"

He sighed and eased his other leg out from under the furry mantle. "Nothing, sweet. Sorry I woke you. I was still a little hungry. I was just—"

"I'll get it." He opened his mouth to protest, but before he could say another word, she was up and rummaging through the packs. Quickly finding the flask he had opened earlier, she returned and handed it to him, bowing.

"Uh—thank you." As he drank the thick, spicy liquid, he considered her thoughtfully. She was sitting atop their bed watching his every movement with an intense concentration that made his skin crawl. What was he going to do about this? Her anxious subservience was starting to drive him mad. When he had drunk all he would allow himself, he re-corked the flask and set it aside.

Sliding his legs back under the cloak they were using as a covering he said, "You didn't have to do that, you know, I could have gotten the flask myself."

"But I want to serve you," she insisted. "It's my duty, and—"

He stopped her with a finger to her lips. She stiffened, took a deep breath and relaxed. Gently he drew her down beside him and covered them both with the discarded cloaks. When she was nestled in the crook of one arm, he stroked her silky fur for a time, thinking. "Pela, we need to talk," he said finally. "Do all Avairei women act like slaves to their mates?"

"No, why do you ask?"

"Mm, that's reassuring. But, if it's not the custom, why are you behaving like that with me?"

"Because I-I—" Her voice trailed off in confusion. He could feel her warm slender body shudder under his hand. He continued the rhythmic motion, not wishing to upset her further by pressing her for an answer.

Finally she admitted, "I don't know."

Dunnagh caressed the velvety fur under his hand. So soft. Would he ever get tired of the feel of her? He took in a ragged breath, his heightened perception intoxicated by the musky scent of her warm body next to his. Mm, so sweet. "Pela, are you afraid of me?"

She shivered, but said nothing. Allowing the silence to lengthen, he continued his rhythmic stroking until she relaxed. At last he let his lips brush her forehead and repeated, "Are you afraid?"

"Maybe—a little," she conceded in a tiny voice. "But you are the Kashallan, and I honor and respect you, and I want to please you. It's my chosen duty, but—you are so , so—different."

"Mm." He ran a finger down one silky cheek. "Is it the alien, Dunnagh, part of me that frightens you?" She nodded. "I thought so."

Dunnagh had never thought of himself as particularly fearsome, and he found her revelation quite unnerving. Oh, as a professional soldier, he knew he was capable of generating fear in others when he was doing his job, but having a bedmate frightened of him—that disturbed him.

This situation was awful—he was no despot. He couldn't have someone near him who would cringe at his slightest unguarded look or word. All his Caldoni training and heritage rebelled at the thought. <<Tani, what should I do about this?>>

<<I don't know, Kasha, I taste your concern—and share it, but I just don't know.>>

There was a note of anxiety in the symbiont's mental voice that made him sorry he'd asked. Tani was so young—and he kept forgetting that fact. It didn't need his uncertainty on top of all the other frightening adjustments it was having to cope with right now. <<Well, don't fret about it, Shalla, we'll figure something out.>>

Dunnagh decided he needed more information, so he asked, "Pela, to think that someone is afraid of me makes me feel very sad. I know I am a stranger, you don't know much about me, and it's natural to be frightened of the unknown, but have I done something to give you cause to fear me?"

She shook her head, and murmured a muffled "No," against his side.

"Then why are you afraid, and why are you acting like a beaten-down slave around me? I don't expect it, or like it. Women of my own clan certainly wouldn't behave so, and you just admitted to me that the Avairei don't either, so why do you want to do this?"

Dunnagh felt her lift her head. In the dim firelight he could make out the reflected glow of her eyes watching him. "I thought it was how a warrior's mate *should* treat her man," she finally told him, in a tiny voice. "And, since you are a warrior, Dunnagh, I thought it was what you would expect—"

Dunnagh laughed softly, hugging her close. He kissed her on the forehead again, then said, "My silly sweet one, it is not that way with us at all. I don't know how the Warlinga here treat their mates. I never even saw a female when I was at Tragar Keep. Knowing what I do of Gormach, though, I wouldn't be surprised at anything that black-hearted devil would do, but it's not that way with my people—even those who choose to be warriors."

"It's not? Do your people choose what they will be? It isn't bred into them like it is for us?"

"No, it is not bred into us."

"Oh. Your home sounds so—different than here, I find it hard to imagine. That place must be so very strange. It feels *unnatural* somehow, and very confusing."

"It is different," he agreed. "Very different, but Timorna seems equally strange to me most of the time. When you grow up with certain customs, they seem normal to you, hmm?"

"I suppose. And what about your women," she asked shyly, "can they choose to be what they want too?"

"Yes. Some, like the women in my squad that are here with us, choose the warrior's path. But most decide to be wives and mothers, though they may do other things too, either when they are young, or after their children are grown."

Dunnagh's voice grew more confident as he explained his home to her, Pela put her arm across his broad chest and snuggled closer. He was so big and muscular, compared to the slimmer-built men of her own people. He was almost as massive as a Warlinga, truly!

Though she had to concede that he'd always been gentle, with her and with others, she sensed the potential in him for violence. Maybe when she knew more about him, this Chosen, this creature who had come such a far way to be host to the Khutani, maybe then she could feel safe.

"Tell me more about the women of your people," she begged. "Are they like Avairei women? How *do* they treat their mates?"

Dunnagh considered, then chuckled at a recalled memory. "I think perhaps they *are* similar to Avairei women—at least, if Sagas and the old Ima are fair examples of your womenfolk. My mother and older sister, Shivon Ru'a, would probably get on well with those two." He chuckled again. "Or they would half kill each other. I'm not sure which. They are a lot alike, when I think about it."

Pela laughed with him, trying to imagine what his womenfolk would be like.

Dunnagh continued, barely aware of her now. His voice became distant and dreamy as he was caught up in his memories of home and family. "Like your people, we Caldoni claim our descent through the mother's line. This gives women a lot of power and respect among us. Most of the women I knew when I was growing up were beautiful—a blend of many traits. They could be generous and kind, as well as stubborn and strong-willed.

"No Caldoni woman would ever bow down to anyone, nor would a Caldoni man want her to. It would break her fine, wild spirit. Most of our womenfolk are wise and give good counsel, though a man may not want to listen at the time.

"There are rules, of course—she certainly wouldn't speak disrespectfully to an elder—but, other than that, a girl learns early to speak her mind whenever, and to whomever, she pleases. And the Gods help the man or boy with whom she is displeased, for he's in for a tough time of it."

Dunnagh smiled to himself. "Yes, Caldoni women are fierce in both their loves and hates. A man learns to treat them with respect and mind his ways, or be sorry for it." He gave a small bark of a laugh as he remembered something, his voice in the darkness bubbling up with amusement. "Why, I remember the time my Da came home drunk once too often for my mother's liking. After giving him the sharp side of her tongue, and a good piece of her mind, she hauled off and punched him, hard as she could.

"Then she chased him around the kitchen with a broom-handle, screaming and swearing loud enough to wake the whole house. My aunt and an adult cousin finally pulled her off the poor man, or the Gods alone know what she might have done to him."

He laughed again. "Gave him a black eye she did, and a terrible headache next morn. Though it could have been the uiskia that did for his head as much as her blows, I guess. After that episode, my father was a mite more sensible about his drinking—or at least more discreet," he amended. "Da wouldn't even bother to come home at all if he got too drunk. He stayed at my uncle's place instead—said it was healthier for him.

"Yes, Caldoni women can be fierce, but they can be gentle and very loving too. I remember my mother's face and soft touch when she tucked me in at bedtime, or nursed me when I got sick. They are a mixture of so many things, and very beautiful."

Eyes closed and seeing only his inner visions, he sighed. Then, in a voice barely above a whisper, he said, "My Sairsa is like that, fierce and loving. She—" He stopped abruptly, the ache of her loss rising up to choke him. Dunnagh swallowed hard several times, feeling his eyes begin to sting. "Never mind," he muttered, then fell silent, lost in a flood of painful memories.

Gone. Caldon, his home and family—even his love Sairsa—they were all gone. They were stranded on this primitive world, and with the symbiont in his middle and the kavay running through his veins he could never leave Timorna. Never—even if someday a rescue ship found them.

Caught up in the tide of homesickness that the memories awoke in him, Dunnagh wasn't aware how distressed Tani was becoming in response to his grief, until Pela's startled gasp, as she felt the Khutani's agitation, finally brought him back to the present moment.

Dunnagh groaned and rubbed the symbiont's coils. <<I'm sorry, Shalla, sorry, oh so sorry. I didn't mean to drag you into my wallowing in homesickness and self-pity. I'll try harder to shield, next time.>>

<<Kasha, are we going to die? I feel so strange—what is happening to us?>>

Dunnagh sniffed, choking back his own emotions as he focused on his bondmate's fear. *Tani was so young. Stupid, stupid, you've got to remember; it's only a child—an infant really—you've got to be strong, for both of us.* <<Tani, easy now, we aren't going to die. Don't be afraid. What you felt was my homesickness. I was thinking of my family, and I let my emotions get out of control.

<<You and amla Gladdris helped me with my feelings before, remember? Unfortunately, it's one of the disadvantages you are going to have to get used to, having a human for a host. We are an unstable lot emotionally, not always knowing, ourselves, what our feelings are, or how to cope with them. So have patience with me, Little One.>>

<<Yes, all right, I will try to understand and not be afraid. But I'm amazed constantly by how little you do know about yourself,>>Tani said.

<<However did your people's breeding program get so out of control? It's a wonder your species survives at all.>>

Dunnagh breathed a sigh of relief—another crisis passed. <<True enough, Shalla, it is a wonder. True enough.>>

Opening his eyes, Dunnagh suddenly became aware of Pela, propped up on one elbow, watching him anxiously. He gave her a reassuring smile, reached up and caressed her cheek. "I'm sorry, did I upset you too? I was just offering my apologies to Tani—it was feeling my emotions and got frightened."

For answer, Pela touched a tear on his cheek with one slim finger. "Sairsa, was she your mate?"

Gods, why was she doing this to him? He didn't want to risk frightening her again too, but damn, he didn't want to talk about Sairsa. Not now, and especially not with her. "No, but we were promised to each other before—before I was brought to Sulas."

"You miss her, I think. What happened? Is she at the base waiting for us, or did she die?"

Startled, he tried to see her expression, but her features were only a dark blur in the dying fire's glow. Why was she so interested in another woman—his old love?

After a moment's hesitation, he said, "The day I was captured by the Begta she was supposed to come down for a visit. What has happened to her, or to the rest of my people left on the mesa, I don't know. Since nobody came to look for us, I can't help worrying that they are all dead." Dunnagh fell silent, feeling the sadness welling up again.

"Maybe not," Pela said. "Your people didn't come for you because you had agreed to the bonding. The Gods would not have let them interfere, but that doesn't mean they are dead."

"Hmm. I hadn't thought of it in quite that way before."

"Dunnagh, when we get to your people's camp on the mesa, you must take me to our Sairsa," Pela insisted. "I will teach her about Timorna and take care of her; she will be my sister-wife. This is a good thing, I think, then you will be happy again."

Dunnagh drew her once more down beside him. He was shivering and didn't want to think whether it was the cold, or his grief that was causing the tremors. He took in a deep breath and tried to lose himself in the sensual feel of Pela's warm furry body against his naked skin. His hand absently stroking her back and buttocks, he said, "Pela, I appreciate your concern for my happiness.

"The offer is a generous one, and truly noble, but things are different with us. The women of my people don't—uh—share their mates. Sairsa—well, it doesn't matter now, anyway. I'm not the same—and I have you now, and many new responsibilities. She probably thinks I'm dead by now—and she may even have found someone else—if they are still alive up there."

He hugged her desperately, burying his face in her braided hair. His voice muffled, he said, "I have a new life now, since the bonding. I can't go back to what I was, and I won't ask her to—" His voice trailed off leaving the rest of his thought unspoken.

Pela felt his trembling, and Tani stirring once more in response to his emotions. She reached out and stroked him, murmuring soothing nonsense to both bondmates, trying to comfort them.

What twisted fates the Gods have woven for us both, she thought. She hadn't understood most of what Dunnagh talked about. But his grief and sense of loss for a promised beloved she could clearly comprehend. It mirrored her own situation.

With some surprise, she realized she was not afraid of him anymore. He had come alive for her. He was a real person, not just a Holy One to be respected and served. And, he was also a man with fears and desires, and a need for compassion and love.

"It will be all right, Dunnagh-Tani," she said. "I will pray to the Great Mother for our Sairsa, and for all of us. It will be good. You'll see."

Chapter Eight

Half asleep, Nathan sighed with contentment. His turn at sentry duty had just ended, and it had been so good to crawl under an already-warmed blanket next to a willing bedmate again. Then he felt Tessa stir beside him. She raised herself up, and began crawling over him. Putting his arms around her, Nathan pulled her flat against his chest. He groaned dramatically, whispering into her ear, "Oh, not again, my love, you'll wear me out."

She giggled and pushed at his chest. "Let me up." Her breath against his neck, and the warm scent of her body, made his loins stir in spite of himself. He was tired, but he felt her hardened nipples tickle the hairs on his chest. Well—maybe...

Tessa gave him a brief kiss, then tried to push herself up. "No, silly, not that, I have to pee. Now let me up, or you're going to get awfully wet," she warned.

He chuckled, and hugged her tighter—now he was definitely interested. If she chose to pursue it— "I'm already wet—you saw to that a few minutes ago. What's your hurry?"

Tessa buried her face on his shoulder, stifling a laugh. "Let me up, beast!" she breathed, trying hard to control herself. "Let me up, or you'll be wetter, I promise. And this time it won't be so pleasant."

With one last kiss he released her. "Don't wander too far, love."

She slid the rest of the way over him, and stood up. "I won't. It's too dark to go very far. I'll be right back. I'm just going over there by those rocks, see." Tessa pointed to a cluster of boulders tossed up against the cavern's wall.

Nathan swiveled around to look, grunted, then settled back within the warmth of their bed. Moments later he was jolted fully awake, by Tessa's piercing scream. Throwing off the blanket, he leaped to his feet, snatching up spear and knife as he rose. He glanced around wildly.

What he saw froze him into momentary immobility. Tessa was struggling with two monstrous creatures, trying to drag her farther into the shadows. It was impossible to see them clearly in the dim light, but what he could see was like the worst of nightmares. Hideous things, they were, with large eyes and gleaming fangs arranged asymmetrically in their distorted faces. Their long, sinewy arms wound around their struggling prey, wicked claws already biting deep into her soft naked flesh.

"NATHAN!" she screamed again, and the sound of that cry unlocked his frozen reflexes at last.

"Lann Gheal! We are under attack!" he shouted, then charged after the fleeing beasts.

DUNNAGH JERKED AWAKE at the first scream, coming up into a fighter's crouch. Beside him Pela sat up wide-eyed, their blanket clutched protectively about her shoulders. Around him the camp exploded into a cacophony of panicked cries. He could hear snarling, Marti's foghorn bellow, Nathan bawling orders and the sounds of the armachda in armed combat.

But all he saw was a confused jumble of distorted shadows. Had the Warlinga from Sulas found them? No impossible! This was something else—some unknown danger—the hostile eyes he'd felt at his back. Dunnagh stepped away from the bedding. He heard Pela call to him but ignored her. Damn, all he could see was frightened Avairei racing for the rocks and panicked Loti kicking and running about aimlessly.

Then, a large sinewy form glided out of the rocks in front of him, blocking his path. Dunnagh froze, a cold chill ran down his spine. The creature was grotesque. Tall as a Warlinga, it had a lizard-like body with an elongated neck, and long whip-like tail. The beast's hindquarters were strong and compact, but in front its two sets of ropy arms were longer, sporting wicked claws at the ends of its four-fingered hands.

Its head was shaped something like that of a Warlinga, but when the monster turned to face him, it revealed a twisted, visage that was nothing like that of the lizardmen. It hissed at him and displayed its fangs in a lethal threat.

<<Umwira,>> Tani spoke into Dunnagh's mind, instinctively recognizing the ancient enemy. The Kashallan snarled, and bared his own teeth in a display of aggression to match the monster's.

THE GREAT AVENGER PAUSED, eyeing the defiant mutant crouched before him with contempt. These creatures had no real magic. They would have attacked his warband before now if they had. This male's puny defenses could be overcome with a casual flick of his powerful tail, or a mere scrape from one of his long-clawed hands. This one would be dead in another moment, and then he would take for his prize the fine young Avairei female.

The Great Avenger grunted and staggered as an unexpected blast of mental energy slammed into his mind. He growled deep in his throat and hastily through up a mental shield. Now wary, he studied his opponent with more respect. The creature's strange blue eyes were alight with his hatred, yet he hesitated, seemingly unsure whether to press the advantage he had momentarily gained.

"So," the leader hissed, "This is the way of it, hmm? You wish to fight me with the magics, do you, little mutant slime? Well, let us see how well your master has taught you, then. Let us see if you are good enough to defeat the Great Avenger, first war leader of the Ghostlands." Without another word, he launched his own merciless mental assault.

Through the long centuries, the Ghostlanders had become masters at using the mental war magics. They attacked unprotected minds mercilessly with their weapons of torment. With frightening images of torture and pain they shattered an enemies resistance. When the enemy was helpless, the Umwira either slaughtered them, or broke them to their will so they could be used as slaves.

Just the sight of the physical bodies the Ghostlanders chose for themselves struck terror into the hearts of the Avairei and the other species the Khutani had created.

As he had done so many times before, the Avenger flooded the mind of this impudent male with his hatred. He made the weakling feel, in exquisite detail, all the tortures that were waiting for those who chose to defy the Ghostlander's might.

DUNNAGH MENTALLY WRITHED, sweat pouring off his shivering body. Even with his Caldoni warrior's training, and with the Khutani's added mental powers to help, the bondmates were barely holding their own against such a powerful and experienced foe. Tani's instinctive hatred of this ancient enemy coursed through their blood, demanding vengeance and spurring on their efforts.

Sadly, Dunnagh recognized, however, that it would not be enough. The Khutani was still young, and too inexperienced to handle such a skillful adversary. There was something missing; they needed something more—but what?

Then, in a rush of insight, he knew what was wrong. Though two heritages and two intelligences made up this strange new creature called the Kashallan, they had been fighting this battle by only tapping into one wellspring of power—that of the Khutani—and it was not going to be enough.

Dunnagh had never felt more than adequate in his abilities to use the ancient powers that were the birthright of his own race. Although his teachers praised his skill, they insisted that he had the potential to be far better than he was. They chastised him often for wasting the full scope of his natural Psy abilities, but his lack of self-confidence held him back.

Now, once more, he stood before that closed inner door behind which the untapped power of his heritage lay. He felt his Shalla weakening as it tried bravely to fight, alone, the battle for both of them. He couldn't delay much longer. They would die here, if he didn't do something. And with their death would die the hope of so many. All the prayers and patient work of centuries gone, ripped apart and thrown away by his cowardice. It was too much to bear.

Dunnagh prayed for strength. Surrendering himself to the will of his Gods, he begged for help, not only for himself, but for all those who needed him, and whom he had sworn to protect. At his heartfelt request, the Ancient Ones answered, enveloping him in the ecstasy of their strength and power.

Feeling safe and protected in the Gods' might, he allowed himself to look within and name the terrors that had been tormenting him most of his life. With relief, he denied their claim upon him, and tasted freedom for the first time. Icy calm now, he stepped to that mysterious portal and opened it.

Body vibrating with the sweet ecstasy of his Gods, Caldoni war songs pounding in his head, he screamed a blood-curdling cry of challenge and defiance to the Umwira, hammering blow after blow at the hated one's mental shields.

Dunnagh gathered the strength of the ancient Caldoni battle fury around both himself and the symbiont, merging the two halves of the Kashallan together into a single weapon of revenge. The berserker rage sang in their blood. Heedless of self-preservation, the world narrowed its focus to the despised Umwira and the need to utterly destroy him.

Dunnagh drew upon his mercenary combat experience to form terrifying images of bloody war, fought with the devastating weapons used by the nations among the stars.

He chanted a war song from the legends of his boyhood to the ancient Caldoni Gods of battle. They accepted his offering of terrifying images and forged a new and deadly weapon. The Umwira leader staggered as a rush of unfamiliar, alien, and frightening memories flooded into his mind.

Pressing the attack with ruthless satisfaction, Dunnagh showed him the horrors of *civilized* warfare. He trapped him in a snare of fear against which the monster had no defense. Nothing the Umwira had ever experienced or imagined could compare with this assault. Over and over the Kashallan attacked, showing the creature that he, too, could be a master at this deadly game.

Shields down, defeated, shaking his head in a futile attempt to clear away the pain, the war leader backed away. Intent only on the combat and oblivious to any thought of personal danger, the Kashallan leapt atop his fleeing enemy. Unable to get a grip on the scaly hide, he slipped off the Umwira's back. Missing the vital spot in the neck for which he was aiming he sank his teeth instead into one of the creature's arms.

Frightened even more by the unexpected physical attack, the Umwira roared and lashed out with his tail, knocking his adversary to the ground as he lunged away into the darkness.

The Kashallan hit the stone hard, its flinty surface knocking the wind out of him. Gasping for breath, he sat up. The Gods' presence, and the battle fury they had lent him had drained out of him along with his lost breath. He wiped a hand across his mouth and spat, trying to get the taste of the enemy's blood out of his mouth. Ugh, it tasted vile. He spat again.

"Kashallan! Oh, Kashallan, are you all right?" Pela was beside him then, helping him up. He leaned on her heavily for a moment then steadied himself, pulling her to him. "I'm all right, but what about you, sweet one, are you hurt?"

She shook her head. Still trembling, she flattened herself against him. Over her head, Dunnagh looked around; what else had been going on while he fought the Umwira war leader? He could hear Nathan bawling orders, but with their leader in retreat the Umwira's attack seemed over. Dunnagh let out a long sigh of relief.

He felt mentally drained, like a vessel scoured clean. He wanted nothing more than to lie down and sleep for a week, but he knew he didn't dare relax even for a moment, not yet. They needed to assess the damage and get out of here before the enemy had second thoughts and came back.

From out of the darkness he suddenly heard Moraga screaming for medical help. Damn, that's all they needed, a medical emergency now! Releasing himself from Pela's grasp, he hurried to find her, the frightened Avairei at his heels.

Chapter Nine

As they fled into the blackness, the Great Avenger tried to brush away the remnants of unsettling fear caused by the stranger's attack. The creature was good, yes; he had been trained well by his wizard—that was certain. The terrifying images he had projected still haunted the leader's mind. He thrust them aside angrily; he had been caught unaware, that was all. Next time he would be ready for the creature's tricks.

Then we shall see who is the coward. Yes, we shall see—next time. The Avenger ground his teeth in frustration. Curse those two misbegotten spawn. Curse them to the hottest poisoning fires of the wastes for disobeying his orders, and attacking the female. It was a good thing for those two, that the big mutant male had killed them when he did.

After another failure, on top of all the others, the leader would have liked to do it himself. He would have made sure, however, that their punishment at his hands would have been much slower, and exquisitely painful. They'd been lucky, very lucky indeed, to meet such a quick and kind death.

Stupid fools. He supposed, in fairness, it wasn't totally their fault. If he had been younger and less careful, he might have done the same thing.

Blissfully unaware of their presence, the female had approached too near the young scouts' hiding place. Flaunting her delicious odor almost in their faces she had been irresistible. The added smell of her fresh urine, combined with the scent of the male's semen still wet upon her thighs had been an overpowering goad, forcing them into the unplanned attack.

That wonderful, ripe, sexual smell, oh, the reek of it! He had inhaled its compelling musk and trembled, even from where he lay some distance away. Like a defiant challenge, its presence here, at this time, declared the mutant males of this warband's contempt for the Ghostlanders as clearly as if they had spoken their defiance out loud.

The Great Avenger gnashed his teeth in helpless fury. The insolence of these rival mutants was intolerable. How arrogant, how sure of themselves and their master's powers they were. To bring favorite *breeding females* along to toy with, on a raid into what his people considered *their private* hunting territory. It was insufferable!

These strangers acted as if there were no possible danger down here, to themselves or to their property. They seemed to think they could do as they pleased, and the Ghostland clans were too weak to protect their own territory. Such an unbearable insult could not be ignored. It must be avenged.

The Master, Barak, must learn of this. His rivals to the west were becoming far more of a threat than he supposed. The Avenger hoped this information would be enough to stave off the punishment he feared for his failure. They had little to bring home for all their trouble, and the Master would not be pleased.

The females they had taken, he supposed, would make the trip. They seemed healthy enough, thank the fires, but the young Avairei male they had just snatched was so badly wounded that he would probably end up being eaten on the way north.

The old one would not be pleased with the Great Avenger's failure. It had not been his fault, of course, but he wasn't sure Barak would see it that way, and the thought of the Master's punishment terrified him.

Gliding up beside him, his Second spoke. "I have brought something that will please you, Great Avenger." He showed his fangs in a self-satisfied smirk, then opened a leather pouch around his neck and displayed the gruesome object it contained to his leader in triumph. "It is proof, yes? The Master and the others cannot blame us for our failure if another rival wizard has been meddling, can they?"

"Hmm, maybe not," the leader admitted.

They would have to conceal the truth, of course, make it seem as if the rival band stole their captives—well, they had, in a way, hadn't they? Yes, it might work, if they were lucky.

The Great Avenger eyed his subordinate speculatively. That had been very smoothly done, he mused. This one was getting entirely too clever for his commander's liking. The creature would take some watching, in future, to make sure he knew his place and kept it.

Chapter Ten

When the Kashallan found the source of the cries for help, Moraga was desperately trying to stop the blood spouting from the stump of Taliesh's arm. "Here, let me help." He grabbed the injured limb and held it above the man's head. "Now, tie that strap as tight as you can, just below his elbow." He nodded his approval as the red flood slowed to a trickle.

The Kashallan eased the injured man down into a more comfortable position. Pela handed him their folded blanket and he placed it under the man's head. "What happened?" he asked, his eyes going from Taleish's contorted face to Moraga.

Taleish licked dry lips, swallowed, then said, "It's my own fault, Sir. I got careless there at the end." He shuddered at another spasm of pain. When he could speak again he said, "I thought they were all running away. I dropped my guard for just a second. Then one of the big ones jumped me. It knocked me over, grabbed my arm, and—and just bit my hand clean off."

Taleish stared up at the Kashallan confusion and pain haunting his eyes. "Then it put my hand in a pouch it had around its neck and ran off. Why, Ce'awn? I don't understand; why did it do this to me?"

The Kashallan sat back on his heels, mouth agape. Why indeed. What an odd thing to do. He supposed the act had more significance than the horrid creature just wanting a bedtime snack, but neither bondmate could puzzle out its meaning. "I don't know either, Taleish, but don't try to puzzle it out now. Just try to keep calm while we get this arm of yours taken care of."

"Yes, I'll try. Ah, Ce'awn, it hurts!"

"I know, Armachd, I know." Turning to his new wife, he murmured, "See if you can find Ata Temog for me, Pela, I will need his assistance."

Dunnagh was worried; Taleish had lost a fair amount of blood before he showed up, and the primitive tourniquet they had applied couldn't stay on forever. <<Tani, is there anything we can do to help him? I would hate to lose another of my kin now. Are you mature enough, and strong enough, Shalla, to attempt a healing?>>

<<Don't worry, Kasha, if Temog doesn't have what your kinsman needs, I'll make up something,>> the symbiont assured him. <<You are right; we can't let him die.>>

The Kashallan looked up hopefully as someone crouched down near him, but it was Singey, not Temog. "I was coming to see if you could help Tessa. She's badly cut up, and very frightened." He glanced down at Taleish. "But I can see she will have to wait."

The Kashallan nodded and returned his attention to Taleish. Damn, where was the priest?

Singey studied the wounded man his expression grave. In an aside to Dunnagh he said, "I can't say I particularly like Taleish, but this maiming is a terrible disaster for the man. Even if we managed to save his life, what kind of life could he look forward to as a cripple on this primitive world?" He sighed. "I know you have told us that there is no way for us to leave Timorna now that the alignment is complete, but truly, I hope you are wrong. There's got to be a way to reverse the process."

Dunnagh dropped his eyes. The hopeful longing he read on the other man's face mirrored the secret yearning of his own heart. He glanced at Taleish, and his emotions writhed with the certainty of his fate. No, there was no escape for Taleish or any of them.

Cripple....

"I suppose it would be possible to cauterize the stump by fire," Singey suggested tentatively. "It may save his life, but—"

"What is it, Kashallan?" Temog said as he crouched beside him.

Dunnagh pointed to the wounded man's stump of an arm. "Have you anything for this?"

Before answering Temog applied green salve to his fingertips and touched them lightly to the bloody stump. At last he looked up and shook his head. "I have simples in plenty, but many of the more complicated mixtures from the pools I wasn't able to carry away with me. I was too closely watched by Combaron's apprentices before we left Sulas." He looked down unhappily at the pain-racked face of the wounded human. "I am sorry for my failure, Kashallan."

<<I was afraid he would say that. Kasha, I think I can manage, but I'm going to be very hungry after this, so no rationing. Just give me a minute to create what is necessary.>>

Out loud the Kashallan said to Temog, "I'm not really ready for this, but if you don't have what we need, I'll have to make something to seal the wound."

Temog gave him a worried frown, then asked, "Is that wise, Holy One? You are still very young."

"Maybe it isn't wise for me to attempt this, but if you can give him something for the pain so I don't have to do that part, I'll manage the rest."

Temog hesitated. "Holy One, I am shamed by my failure, but perhaps it would be best to let him—"

"No," Dunnagh said, blue eyes fierce. Then recalling that it was a Timornan custom to let a maimed Warlinga die; he curbed his annoyance. And spoke more gently. "I know it isn't the usual way these things are done, but I must try to save him. There are so few of my human kin here on Timorna—I won't let the Umwira have him."

Temog nodded. "Ah yes, I understand, Khutani. You will need his genetic patterns if your host's species is to survive and reproduce itself. I hadn't considered that factor."

Dunnagh gave the priest a withering look. Neither had he actually. Was that why the symbiont was being so obliging? Did it only care about Taleish's genes rather than the man himself? Would Tani tell him the truth if he asked?

Ah, all of this was so hard—so hard, and now wasn't the time to figure it out. Dunnagh saw the priest give him a confused look and inwardly sighed. He laid a hand on Taleish's shoulder, and said, "Taleish, can you hear me?"

The armachd opened his eyes. He licked his lips, then said, "Yes, Ce'awn, I hear you."

"Good. We need to fix that arm. Ata Temog is going to give you something for the pain then I will seal the wound. It will hurt, but we'll do the best we can, all right?"

"Yes, Sir, I understand."

"Moraga, watch him and keep him steady," the Kashallan said, then motioned for the priest to apply the painkiller. Temog made a few long scratches along the upper portion of the wounded man's arm. Into these he rubbed the orange colored kavay. Within a few moments, Taleish gave out a long sigh and relaxed.

The Kashallan laughed softly at Singey's startled expression. "Yes, it works fast, doesn't it? Could your doctors do any better, hmm?" He held up one of his own hands and examined it ruefully.

"To finish answering your question from our earlier talk—what is forming at the ends of these two fingers are the retractable tentacles I will use to diagnose an ailment and administer medicines." He sighed and brushed the damp hair off Taleish's forehead. The man had his eyes closed again and was breathing more normally.

"Unfortunately until the adaptations are completed, I'm going to need someone to help me—like now."

Singey glanced at the Kashallan's hand and asked, "How long before they are completed?"

"It's definitely a priority for our growth, but having to leave the pools so soon—" He shrugged. "With a rationed food supply, I can't say."

When Temog began to put away his things, Singey stopped him. Looking from the Kashallan to the priest, he said, "I understand, from earlier talks with Ata Temog, that the green salve was given to the Avairei to help with diagnosis. I believe it is intended to approximate what a kashallan would experience during a similar exam. Is that correct?"

Temog and the Kashallan both nodded. Taking a deep breath, he ventured, "Would it be possible for me to, uh, try it? As a scientist, I'm quite curious."

With a mischievous gleam in his eye, the Kashallan looked at the priest. Temog seemed startled at first, then bowed his head in assent. "If it is your wish, Holy One."

The Kashallan nodded. "Yes, it is my wish, Ata. Not all of my human kindred are suited for a warrior's life, as you may have guessed." His eyes flicked to Singey then back to Temog. "I would appreciate it if you would teach any who are willing to learn."

Temog bobbed his head in a slight bow. "As you wish, Holy One. I would be honored to teach San Singey and others of your kin."

"Good." Dunnagh gestured magnanimously to the Ata's bag. "Go ahead and try it. We have a few minutes while Tani is making the medicine it will need." Temog reached in and pulled out the green salve and thorn needle, and offered them solemnly to the scientist.

Singey stretched out his hand, then hesitated. "Now that I have your permission, I'm not sure I want to go through with this." Giving him a lopsided grin, he said, "Dunnagh, you're looking at me like a cat that's just swallowed the cream—what have I gotten myself into?"

Dunnagh laughed,. "Nothing," he said, but when Singey still hesitated, he sobered and added, "I hope you know me well enough to believe that I wouldn't intentionally do anything to hurt you, Philip. Go ahead and try it. What you experience will be—interesting, but it won't harm you—I promise."

Singey shrugged and took the offered jar and thorn from Temog. "Ah well, I asked for this, didn't I?" He made the required punctures in his fingertips as he had seen the priest do. Next, he applied a coating of the salve to them and handed the instruments back to the priest.

Suddenly he gasped as the world around him exploded into a kaleidoscope of unfamiliar pattern and color.

"The green kavay is designed to open up the awareness of the user," the Kashallan said. "What you are seeing are the patterns of energy that surround all living things. They are fascinating, hmm? With just that little bit on your fingers you haven't much time to explore, so don't waste it." He pointed to Taleish's arm. "Lay your fingers on the wound and *taste* it. Savor what impressions you get."

The scientist glanced at the wounded armachd; then he placed his fingertips gingerly atop the bloody stump, and closed his eyes to blot out other stimuli. At last, he opened them again and looked at the healers in astonishment.

"I don't quite know how to explain what I've just experienced," he murmured. "I could—feel—taste? He's lost a lot of blood, he's very weak—and still in some pain, though that is less now with the application of the orange salve." Turning to the Kashallan, Singey asked, "Do you experience this, all the time?"

"Not all the time; mostly we see the world through Dunnagh's eyes as you would see it, but, when needed, we can do naturally what you are using the salve to achieve."

<<I am ready, Kasha, we can seal the wound now,>> Tani informed Dunnagh. Nodding to himself, the Kashallan raised Taleish's arm to his mouth. "Tani says that it's time. Someone please hold him still. This will hurt."

While Moraga and Singey shifted their positions the Kashallan addressed the injured man directly. "Taleish." He waited. Finally the man's eyes opened and focused on his face. "I'm going to seal the stump now. I'll be quick, but it will hurt, so be prepared." Taleish nodded, then closed his eyes again.

Placing his mouth above the bloody stump, the Kashallan regurgitated a gelatinous brown liquid over the top of the gaping wound. The armachd bucked and then let out a piercing scream. "Hold him," the Kashallan snapped, raising and steadying the arm in his grasp. Taleish writhed. "Easy, I know it's painful. When the seal dries it will be better."

"Sorry, Ce'awn, but it hurts so—" his words ended in a groan that seemed to come up from the depths of his soul.

Unable to stop himself, Dunnagh shuddered. During his transformation into Tani's host, he had made sounds like that—when he wasn't screaming. Pushing that unpleasant memory aside, he returned his attention to the situation at hand.

Taleish was trying his best not to fight them, but while he was in so much pain, he wasn't able to control his responses. And the more he struggled, the weaker he was becoming.

<<I don't think he can stand this much longer—I will have to help him a little more>>

"I'm going to sedate him," the Kashallan announced. Once more he glanced wistfully at his useless hands, then, shrugging, he bent and bit into the man's arm. This time he regurgitated another substance into the bite, and moments later Taleish gave out a long sigh, his body going limp as he slipped into unconsciousness.

Letting out his own sigh of relief, the Kashallan looked around, his eyes widening with surprise. He had been so intent on his patient's needs that he hadn't been aware of Nathan and the audience of Lann Gheal armachda gathered around them. As he saw Nathan's horrified expression. Dunnagh shied away, unable to meet his eyes. Somehow he would have to tell him—have to explain—but not now, he was too exhausted.

Testing the hardness of the seal with a forefinger, the Kashallan nodded to himself. It was ready, he could leave the rest of this to another. "Will you finish this for me, Ata Temog? I'm tired. Moraga, if the Ata isn't around will you give Taleish as much water as he can drink as soon as he wakes up." Looking a bit glassy eyed, Moraga nodded.

Dunnagh stood, leaning on Pela for a moment to get his balance. "Come, Kashallan," she whispered. "I'll get you something to eat, then you must rest."

But as they started off across the camp, Nathan blocked their way. "Oh no you don't, not this time! I know what you're up to—"

"Nathan, please, I'm too tired for this now." Dunnagh tried to push past him, but the big man put a hand on his shoulder.

"What I'm *trying* to tell you is that you don't have to keep running in the opposite direction every time you see me coming. Singey has already told me about the symbiont.

"And, if I hadn't exactly believed him before—well, what I just saw..." At Dunnagh's astonished look, he gave him a mirthless laugh. "Right. I guess it's true then?"

"It's true." Dunnagh sighed and tried not to put his full weight on the slim Avairei watching him with a worried frown on her face. He was so tired, but he'd better finish this. "I guess I should be grateful to Philip for telling you. I'm sorry I let it go so long. It wasn't fair but—I was afraid of how you would react when I told you, and—"

"Damn you!" Nathan's face contorted with emotion. "Why did I have to hear that from him? Why not from you? By all the Gods of our ancestors, Dunnagh, don't you know how much that hurt me? After all that we've been to each other—after all we've shared—how could you do that to me?"

Dunnagh looked away, feeling very ashamed. In a small tight voice he said, "I'm sorry, Nathan, I didn't mean to hurt you. I was just so afraid—so afraid you wouldn't understand about Tani."

"Well, you're right, damn it. I don't understand. How could you do it—how could you?"

"Because they needed me," he said. Nathan snorted in disgust. "Damn it, Nathan not now—I'm too tired for this! They needed me, and I have sworn the Caldoni warrior's oath of service. What could I have done? You've taken the same oath—what would you have done in my place?"

Nathan rubbed a blood-streaked hand across his face and thought about that for a long moment finally he said, "I don't know, Dunnagh, I honestly don't know."

"Nathan, even though I'm the new host for a Khutani symbiont, I'm still the Dunnagh you know too." Dunnagh reached out a hand and traced the line of Nathan's jaw, forcing him to look into his eyes. With a strangled noise Nathan reached up and covered the hand then removed it from his face. Nathan stared in fascination at Dunnagh's elongated fingers. He shuddered and then let go of the hand and looked away.

Almost under his breath, Dunnagh said, "Don't be angry with me, Mo Cri, please. I was afraid if I told you I'd lose you, Nathan." He took a deep breath, then blurted out the rest of it. "I was afraid you would think I was some kind of monster."

"Shit!" Nathan shook his head in disgust. "You're a real ass, you know that? How anybody can be heroic and stupid enough to agree to this bond thing in the first place, and yet be such a craven coward not to be able even to tell me, your Battle Companion, about it—"

He folded his arms across his chest. "I don't know about who else is in that body with you, Dunnagh, but if I needed any proof that *you* are still in there, this *stupid* little trick would convince me. You are such an ass!"

Relieved, Dunnagh chuckled. "True enough. Tani has been after me constantly to tell you. I guess it was right."

Nathan's face clouded at the mention of the symbiont. "Tani. That's its name?" Dunnagh nodded. "Mm. Seriously, Dunnagh, I meant what I said about staying on Timorna with you—no matter what the rest of the armachda do when we get back to the base.

"But all this isn't easy for me, either. I need time to—" He shivered, swallowed hard, then continued, "To get used to all this."

Then, changing the subject, Nathan said, "And don't expect me to call you Holy One, or some such, like those fool Avairei priests do. Because I won't! I just can't—we've gotten drunk together in too many sleazy drinking houses for me to do that. I just can't."

Dunnagh laughed. He put a hand on Nathan's shoulder. "Fair enough, Mo Hara, fair enough." Then, sobering again, he said, "I want to get moving as soon as we can. Have you had a chance to discover the extent of the damage since the attack?"

Nathan nodded, returning likewise to the important matter at hand. "I was coming to report to you when— Anyway, the civilians are pretty badly frightened. Several are wounded, and a few of the younger Avairei are missing. I'm not sure at this point if they are just frightened and hiding, or if those creatures carried them off."

Startled, Nathan gaped as the being beside him snarled in a most un-Dunnagh like manner, baring his pointed triangular teeth. "Umwira filth, they dare much!" Tani hissed, then the Kashallan uttered a string of colorful Caldoni curses to emphasize his point.

Nathan blinked, then, clearing his throat, he continued, "Right. Uh, the rest of our Lann Gheal bunch is OK—a few scrapes, but Taleish there is the only one seriously hurt. The Begta—" He made a face. "Haven't seen the little furballs since the attack started."

"They'll be back." the Kashallan assured him. "And when you see them, send Dado to me immediately. We must find that side passage and get out of here, before the Umwira war leader has a change of heart and comes after us again. We're too poorly armed to fend off a serious attack from them."

He snarled again in frustration, Tani stirring restlessly at the mention of the Hated Enemy. Out loud the symbiont complained, "I know they're up to something—and it galls me to let them take our people without pursuing them." It sighed. "But my Kasha Dunnagh is right. We can't go after them in our present condition. I see the logic in that."

Nathan shivered, suddenly realizing it had been the Khutani talking to him, not his friend. He swallowed. "This is really going to take some getting used to," he said. "Gods, I'm not even sure who I'm talking to anymore. So what do, uh, either of you want to do about this?"

The Kashallan blinked, then gave him a sheepish grin. "Sorry. It is confusing for us too sometimes."

Nathan grunted, the corners of his mouth twitching. "So, I repeat, what do you want to do?"

"What I *want* to do is go home to the pools at Sulas, have a really satisfying meal, and sleep for a week, but since that is out of the question... We had best get packed up and moving."

Suddenly, Dunnagh let his face show how drawn and haggard he truly was. Dropping the teasing facade, he said, "Nathan, I'm sorry to put a lot of the organizational work on your shoulders, but I'm going to have to let you see to it. I'm exhausted right now. It wasn't a good time for me to leave Sulas. Tani is still too young, not really mature enough to be doing work like we just did with Taleish. I am dependent now on my bondmate to digest our food. I wasn't even weaned before we had to flee Sulas. The Khutani sent with us a formula they hoped would sustain us till we could reach another sanctuary, but it's very hard for us—and there are still adaptations in our shared body that aren't completed.

"Combine all of that with my fight with the Umwira leader—I've got to feed and rest, I just have to, old friend. I want to see to Tessa, and I know there are others that could use my help, but I *must* rest first."

"Go on, I'll see to it. Pela there has been giving me dagger eyes long enough for keeping you until now, so you better do what she wants and go, or she's liable to take after me with one of those little Avairei knives of hers."

"Yes, I must." Trying not to lean on the Avairei woman for too much support, he staggered off into the darkness.

Nathan watched him go with growing concern. He'd been so wrapped up in his own troubles, that he hadn't really noticed how weak his friend had become. Now that he saw it, he resolved to keep an eye on him, and also to ask Sagas what he could do for his friend, because, if anyone knew just how stubborn Dunnagh could get, it was him.

Chapter Eleven

The Kashallan sat obediently on the flat rock where Pela placed him, and closed his eyes. His whole body was trembling with weariness and the aftershock of the healing. He felt totally drained. Suddenly dizzy, he bent over, put his head between his knees, and took several deep breaths.

At last, becoming aware of a pair of furry feet standing directly in front of him, he straightened. A grim-faced Sagas, with tangled braidlets, folded her arms across her thin chest and confronted him. "So," Sagas said. "You have drained yourself, and you have put your very life in danger by your foolishness." Beside the Ima stood two young Avairei and a nervous Pela, with a flask of his formula and a bowl in her hands.

He started to protest, but she cut him off. "You have, and you know it. The Elders gave you into my care, young one, and I *am* going to fulfill my oath and take care of you. So you *will* stop all this nonsense and accept the blood gift, along with this flask from the pools."

Dunnagh glared at her stubbornly. "No!" in his middle Tani stirred. "No," he repeated, "we're a little tired that's all. We don't need—"

"Stubborn, willful child." Sagas took the bowl from Pela, and before he could stop her, she gashed her arm and held it up. Clenching and unclenching her fist she forced a stream of her own blood into the empty bowl. Tani writhed hungrily in Dunnagh's middle. Involuntarily, the Kashallan let out a low whimper as the delightful fragrance filled his nostrils.

<<Kasha, please, I am so hungry, and the formula in the flasks is already going stale. Please, Kasha, I'm sorry I frightened you that first time back at Sulas when we tasted the blood gift. But it's not usually that intense, and the part of us that is just me needs the blood gift right now. I feel so weak. Please, Kasha.>>

Sagas smiled with satisfaction at his reaction. "Smell good, hmm? You will drink it, yes?" He made a strangled, noncommittal noise, but his eyes followed her every movement. When she judged there was enough blood in the bowl, she motioned for one of the priests to sprinkle the clotting agent on the wound.

Sagas next filled the bowl to the brim with his formula, and held it out to him. Addressing the host directly, she said, "Chosen, I don't know how things are done on your home world—or why you have such a reluctance to accept our offerings, but here it is a natural thing to make the Blood Gift.

"We Avairei were bred to do this and have always offered our blood to the young Khutani. It is both our duty, and our joy, to serve you so. Let us feed you, for the sake of the Shalla. Don't be stubborn."

Tani squirmed, pouring into Dunnagh's awareness its desperate need. Dunnagh hesitated a moment longer then nodded. With trembling hands he took the bowl and drank. When the bowl was empty, one of the young men wordlessly stepped forward, bowed to him, then, made the blood offering. When he had finished he filled the bowl with fluid from the flask and returned it to the Kashallan, who took it without further protest

The second priest repeated the procedure once more, then, like a full and sleepy child, he allowed them to ease him down upon the pallet they had made for him. As he drifted off into exhausted sleep Dunnagh had a vision of his mother, her hair in tiny braidlets like the Avairei, tucking him in bed at night. He smiled and sank into oblivion.

IN THE OTHERWORLD OF dreams Dunnagh floated on a dark river of fear and exhaustion. So many responsibilities, so many lives depended on him, his human warriors, the Timornans who had followed him into exile and especially the young symbiont that had been entrusted into his care. Sulas. If he could just go back there...

Suddenly his private musings were interrupted by such a cry of loneliness and despair that he sat up to see where the noise was coming from. The sound came again and when he looked in that direction he saw a small silver eel-like creature swimming away into the darkening mists.

<<Tani, wait up! Where are you going, little one?>> with powerful strokes, Dunnagh swam after the crying symbiont, still shouting for Tani to wait for him—stop.

At last the symbiont seemed to become aware of his frantic attempt to catch up and slowed, then stopped. Swimming up to his bondmate, Dunnagh pulled the young Khutani into his arms.

With a whimper, the symbiont coiled itself about his torso and laid its head on his shoulder. <<Tani, what's wrong? Are you hurt?>> Dunnagh asked, running a hand over his bondmate's glowing coils.

<<I'm not hurt, Kasha. I just want to go home—back to Sulas. The Umwira—I'm afraid—I want our amla,>> Tani wailed.

Sulas. Had Tani been picking up his private thoughts—or had his own desire to return to Sulas come from his bondmate? *So young,* Dunnagh thought, *poor creature having only me to rely on, isn't very comforting, is it?*

The recent Umwira attack had shown him how much he still didn't understand about his new home. He wished there'd been more time to learn about this planet from the Khutani elders, before they'd been tossed into the river of alien politics and war, to sink or swim.

<<I know, little one, and you are being very brave, but going back to Sulas isn't possible right now. We have to get out of these underground passages before that war band comes back.>>

<<I know, but I was hoping if I called to our relatives in the Dream-Time they might come—>>

<<That will not be possible in future, Little One,>> a rumbling, yet familiar voice said. A large sinewy body appeared out of the gloom, enfolding both bondmates in its coils. <<To swim the dark rivers of the otherworld alone are dangerous. The Umwira are hunting—>>

Dunnagh barked a mirthless laugh. <<They are hunting in the physical world as well. We were just recently attacked by the River Magre by a Ghostlands war band, Amla Gladdris.>>

Tani wrapped a coil of itself about the Maker's neck, its mouth tentacles brushing over the sleek gray skin. <<It's true, Amla. And my Kasha was so brave. When their war leader attacked us, he fought off the monster with his powerful mind magic. The Ghostlander was so afraid he and his war band ran away.>>

Tani squeezed Dunnagh's chest. <<I love my Kasha. He saved me. He saved everyone. But the Umwira bit off Taleish's hand—and then Ata Temog didn't have the right medicines—so I had to help—and now—I'm so afraid. Can't we go back to Sulas, just for a little while? Please, Amla.>>

Making soothing gurgles deep in its throat, Gladdris nuzzled the young symbiont until it lay quiescent and content. Raising its head to look Dunnagh in the eye, Gladdris said, <<This news is very disturbing. We have been aware ever since your bonding, that the Umwira have been hunting the passageways of the otherworld with a renewed vigor.

<<We had assumed—hoped, that if we were vigilant, guarded your dreams, you would be safe. This doesn't appear to be so. Tell me of the attack, Chosen, and what are your plans.>>

Dunnagh began his report from the time they left Sulas and entered the underground pathways. He laid out his reasoning for going west to the humans' base to pick up weapons, supplies and any of his former comrades remaining there, before heading through the Great Swamp to Ticca.

He concluded his recital by saying, <<Our injuries concern me, but if we can find the side passage into the Broken Lands soon, and avoid both another Umwira attack and discovery by Warlinga, I believe we can make it to Ticca, before the Sorin Storms.>>

<<Hmm. I hope you are right. Heading directly into the Yeyen Banai Valley—no that would be most unwise. I understand your reasoning, but I'm not happy about it. We can offer you little direct help while traveling.

<<There are other problems in the Yeyen and elsewhere needing the attention of the Elders Council, but I will have to see what can be done for your continued safety.>> Gladdris tightened its coils in a gentle squeeze. <<We will not abandon you, never fear.>>

<<Can't we go back to Sulas for just a little while, Amla,>> Tani pleaded. <<Ima Sagas killed Combaron Dingay. Surely we would be safe there now.>>

Gladdris nuzzled the young symbiont again. <<No, Little One. You can't go back to Sulas, because Sulas is no more.>>

Tani let out a despairing wail. In response, Dunnagh stroked his distraught bondmate, trying to calm it. There was no time for childish fretting; they needed more information if they were going to survive. To the Maker, he said, <<No more? What happened? Did the Umwira destroy—>>

<<No, Chosen, the Umwira have not destroyed Sulas. We did it ourselves.>>

<<But why, Amla,>> Tani cried.

<<It is as I told you before. If these misbegotten, ungrateful Avairei were to deny a bonded kashallan—and try to kill you—then we will deny them—and destroy what we have created.>>

The Khutani had bred the four intelligent species introduced to repopulate a wounded world. But in doing so, they had made their creations dependent on them for their very survival.

Without the red kavay, there could be no fertile matings, and without all the other medicinal compounds the Khutani produced in their bodies and stored in containing pools at places like Sulas the Timornan peoples and their society couldn't survive.

Dunnagh's aura trembled at such a dire pronouncement. If the Khutani abandoned their creations and retreated into the "Long Sleep" what would that mean for him, and the other humans now stranded on this world, too?

<<What do you and the Council of Elders plan to do now, Amla Gladdris?>>

<<That hasn't been decided, Chosen.>>

<Please don't decide anything so important until Tani and I have a chance to better assess what is happening upon the surface. I'm sure there are many who are true to their breeding and haven't forgotten the path laid out for them by you Makers.>>

<<I hope you are right, Chosen. I will bring your words to them—and add my own admonitions as well.>>

Gladdris settled the bondmates more comfortably in its coils. <<Lie back now and rest while you can. I will watch over your dreams and give the young one what life-force I can spare.>>

The mental voice suddenly stern, Gladdris added, <<I will give you a lesson on how to shield your dreams better, but in future you must protect yourselves better. And don't travel the dark pathways of the Dream alone. It is too dangerous.>>

Chapter Twelve

Still uneasy about a possible threat from the Umwira, Nathan posted a few sentries while the rest of the camp cared for the wounded and packed up their scattered supplies. As Dunnagh had predicted, the Begta returned, so he sent them ahead to try and find the side passage that would get them out of here

Of course, once they left the underground river for more traveled passageways, they would be forced to worry about more enemies than the Umwira. The Tragar hunting pack, or another Warlinga pack sent from Riath, might be searching the Begta warrens on the off chance the fugitives had sought refuge there.

Oh, well, no sense in troubling his head about the future; there were too many other concerns that demanded his attention at present. Nathan sighed. Yes, there *were* too many other things to worry about, and one of them was standing at his elbow still looking lost and frightened. The young priest he'd coaxed out of the rocks was Ata Temog's apprentice, but he was also one of the lads who had been sent to the slave pens to collect Nathan and the armachda the night they escaped Sulas.

Before the Umwira found them some of the armachda had been teasing him about the young priest. They call Timma his furry shadow because the youth had taken every opportunity he could to follow Nathan around. He patted the youth on his shoulder. "How you doing, lad?"

Timma stared at him out of haunted dark eyes. "All right, San Nathan."

But he wasn't all right, and that was the Gods' own truth. They had almost given Timma up for lost, but on his last sweep of the campgrounds, Nathan had found him curled up in a small crevice among the rocks. The boy had been so frightened that he had been unable to move, even though he heard people calling him.

Timma told his rescuer that the monsters had almost taken him too, when they caught his best friend, Orlan. It was only at the last moment, that he managed to wedge himself deep enough into the crevice that they couldn't get at him.

Timma's eyes pleaded with Nathan not to send him away. Affecting a jovial tone, Nathan said, "Right. Then I guess you best come with me while I make my rounds."

As the youth fell in step beside him, Nathan decided that he would let the lad sleep with him for a while. Timma probably wouldn't rest otherwise. Tessa wouldn't mind, he knew. Gods, there was another one to worry about. *Tessa, oh love, I'm so sorry.*

His love was another victim of the damned Umwira's terrifying mental and physical attack. By all the powers, his own dreams would be haunted by the horrid things too. He could imagine how bone-chillingly awful it must feel to have been helpless in their grasp.

But with the battle going on around them, he hadn't had time for Tessa's clinging hysterics after he killed the creatures that caught her. He'd left her with the old Ima as soon as he could and returned to his armachda.

"Rhys," he shouted to his laconic Second, "Make sure all the water jars that didn't get broken in the fight get filled before we leave." The man saluted and Nathan continued his walk about the camp. "Damned stupid Loti," he muttered to himself as he surveyed the shattered food baskets and trampled bedding. Their supplies were scattered everywhere. The silly creatures had caused almost as much damage in their panic as the monsters had.

He glanced out of the corner of his eye at the youth trailing behind him. He wished he dared ask Dunnagh's advice about all this, but after observing how physically weakened the Kashallan seemed to be, he was afraid to add more worries to his friend's pile. He just didn't know enough about this bond thing, or even whether the strange new healing powers his friend seemed to have acquired would be of any use in treating emotional traumas.

SOME TIME LATER THE Kashallan was awakened by the sounds of a fierce, whispered argument. He listened a moment, then, recognizing the combatants' voices, he said, "Stop arguing, I'm awake."

The voices fell immediately silent. Without opening his eyes the Kashallan continued, "And stop glaring at him, Sagas, I told Nathan to come to me when we were packed and ready to move on."

Startled, the Ima glanced down at him. The Kashallan opened his eyes, and sat up, giving her a lopsided grin.

"How do you feel?" Nathan crouched down beside him. "Gods, you look like you've been on a two week drunk in Behdyar."

Dunnagh grunted. "I wish I had been. I'd probably feel better than I do right now." He grimaced and rubbed a hand across his face, trying to wipe away his fatigue. "So what did you wake me up for? I assume it's to tell me we're ready to move."

"Yeah, that, and to tell you the Begta came back. You were right—they snuck into camp not long after the fighting stopped. I knew what you wanted to see Dado about so I didn't wake you. I told the little furball to go find that damn side passage, or I wouldn't wait to feed him to the Umwira, I'd eat him myself."

Dunnagh laughed. "Thanks, that was what I wanted. Are he and his bunch back yet?"

Nathan smirked, "I don't know if it was my threat, or we were just that close anyway, but he's back. Came in a few minutes ago, telling me not to eat poor little Begta, and yes he had found the passage for nice starmans and Kashallan."

"Anything else I need to know right now?" Nathan considered, and then shook his head. "Good." Dunnagh held out his hand. "Help me up, and let's get going." Catching sight of Sagas's disapproving frown, he paused. "I know, I know, I need more rest, but I can sleep on Berren's back while we travel. Nathan can tie me on. We have to get out of here, before the Umwira decide to come back."

"I don't like this—you need more rest, but I have to agree with your reasoning." Sagas picked up his bedding and began folding it as Nathan called over the Loti.

Part Two: The Base

Chapter One

Sairsa took the empty bowl from the big armachd and smiled. "I think you're starting to feel better, aren't you, Tarla? You were able to finish all your meal today."

The armachd beamed. "I think maybe I am, Sairsa. Least, I hope so." He sighed heavily. "I never been sick like this before. That little native gave me a pretty bad bite, but I never thought any wound would make me so sick, especially 'cause it never got infected."

Sairsa patted his arm. "Well, don't worry about it, Tarla. This is a strange world. And you're getting better anyway."

"True enough, and you and the doctor has been real good to me, and I thank you for it." He glanced over at the other occupied beds in the sickbay.

Sairsa saw his gaze shift, and knew what he wanted to ask. Plastering a cheerful smile on her face she said, "They'll be all right too, Tarla. Dr. B will fix them up—you'll see. They'll be back on duty in no time."

He smiled tentatively, but more to please her than out of belief in Bennett's ability, she suspected. Before he could ask any more difficult questions, she took his meal tray and left.

It had been more than a standard month since that awful night when Sairsa's world turned upside down. All her happy dreams had been shattered by the reality of Bennett's ship being destroyed, and the refugees stranded on this primitive planet, with only the barest hope of rescue.

Sairsa's stomach churned. She leaned against the wall and wiped the icy sweat from her brow. Oh, it grieved her to remember. Her mother and stepfather, dead when the Creggan ship blew up the Chance. And her Dunnagh was still missing—oh, it was too awful. Eyes blurring, she blinked back the tears that she knew would start falling again any moment.

Then, a calm feminine hand touched her shoulder. "Sairsa, you all right, honey?" Gail asked.

Sairsa nodded, blinking.

"Dr. B just sent word that he needs that report now. But if you're not up to it, honey, I'll—"

Sairsa shook her head. She knew what Gail was referring to, her pregnancy. But her condition wasn't the problem. Her morning sickness was gone, the native virus hadn't come back, she felt fine—damn it, she *did*.

Catching Sairsa vomiting up her breakfast one morning, Gail had been certain that she had caught the strange disease that was going around the camp. When Sairsa assured her that wasn't the problem, she kept pestering her until Sairsa finally admitted that she was pregnant.

Of course, that had started more trouble, because then Gail told Dr. Bennett, and he insisted on examining her. At Sairsa's request, they agreed to keep her condition a secret for now, but, ever since then, Gail had been so protective, and it was starting to get on her nerves.

Gail had been wonderful, helping Sairsa through the worst of her grief for her parents and her worry for Dunnagh, but she had to admit to herself that the woman was a little too over-bearing for her comfort. She didn't want or need another mother. She just wanted a friend.

"Gail, stop worrying. Did you say Dr. B needed that report now? I told you I would take it over to him for you."

"Yes, but are you sure you're up to it? You've been working so hard."

Sairsa patted her arm, interrupting the flow. "I want to keep busy and make myself useful. It keeps me from thinking too much about—" She broke off, blinking away tears.

Gail sighed, handing her the report. "Here it is. And when you're done don't come back here, understand? Go get some rest."

"All right, you've made your point. I'll go lie down, I promise."

AT HQ, A GRINNING ARMACHD waved her to a back room where the sounds of a heated discussion were well under way. In the tiny room to which she'd been directed, Commander Tizu, Dr. Bennett, the Dymarian councilor and her aide Sadrew sat in folding chairs around a polli-plastic table. Computator pads lay on the table beside each of the newly appointed

"Camp Committee" members and in the center a bottle of water and a few glasses sat on a tray.

Plump and motherly, Counselor Arishim was saying, "Commander, there is a very good chance that Captain Jakison managed to send out a distress call before Dr. Bennett's ship was destroyed. And you yourself admit that your communications officer picked up a signal from a cruiser that was in pursuit of the Creggans. It is highly likely that the ship logged that distress call and will come back here to investigate. It is only a question of time before we are—"

"But in the meantime, Councilor," Commander Tizu said, "I need to—"

"Ah, Sairsa, here you are," Bennett said, an expression of relief crossing his tanned patrician face. "Did you bring that report I asked Gail to prepare and send over?"

"Yes, doctor." Sairsa blushed, and handed Bennett the pad. She was about to leave when the black-clad Lann Gheal commander smiled, and pulled out a chair for her next to him. Sairsa gave him a tentative smile and sat, waiting while Bennett skimmed through the report.

"How bad is it, doctor?" Tizu asked into the silence.

Bennett frowned, and set the pad down on the table between them, blanking the screen. "Today there are five more of your people in sickbay affected by the native virus. There are four Dymarian refugees as well."

"Doctor, are you having any luck in discovering what is causing this illness?" Arishim asked.

Bennett sighed. "The disease, if disease it is, seems to have a viral component, but it acts differently from anything I have ever seen or heard of before. I would recommend that we have as little contact with the native environment as possible, until I have a chance to study it further."

Tizu snorted. "That's going to be a bit hard to do, doctor, considering we're stranded here."

"But not for long," the cadaverously thin Sadrew reminded him.

Tizu rolled his eyes. Glaring, the aide's voice snapped with irritation, as he added, "The doctor and Councilor Arishim are very important people. The U.G.W. will not just let us rot on this barbaric planet—"

"Which brings me back to my point, Citizen Sadrew," Tizu said. "I need to send out another patrol to see if they can find out what has happened to our missing people."

"Commander," Arishim said. "As the doctor and I have told you before, we can't afford the risk of losing any more of your troops down in those canyons. The safety of the personnel on this base is your first priority at the moment, not Dr. Singey's party, or your missing armachda."

"If you had done a better job of checking out this planet, no one would have been lost in the first place," Sadrew sneered.

"And if you were so worried about Kai and his squad, you should have taken more care with that native your men caught, instead of killing him. Who knows what the savages will do now? If this base gets attacked by hundreds of screaming—"

"If this base gets attacked by the locals, I'll deal with it," Tizu snarled, half rising out of his chair. "Don't try to tell me my job, Sadrew—"

"Well, somebody ought to," Sadrew shot back, "Because you're obviously making a proper mess of it right now!"

"Gentlemen, please, this isn't getting us anywhere," Bennett shouted over the rising clamor. When the two men subsided he continued, "I am as worried about the missing members of this camp as anyone, believe me, but this type of behavior won't solve our problems. It will only create more of them. So let's put aside our differences for now, please."

Bennett gave each man a stern look, the echo of his wealth and position commanding their acquiescence. Taking a deep breath, he continued, "Commander, we have to think about what's best for the group as a whole, not just any one part of it."

"I can see that, doctor, but—"

"Commander, please, we don't know anything about the native population on this world—especially how they feel about our presence on their land. Or what they will do about the unfortunate incident that led to the death of one of their tribesmen.

"There is also an unidentifiable infection out there that, with the medicines I have on hand, I can only *hope* is curable. Any more trips into the local terrain should be carefully considered, because of the risk of contracting this disease and spreading it to other persons on the base.

"And lastly, we need to stay put in case a rescue ship does appear. When it does, we can locate our missing people much more efficiently, with the aid of the modern technology on board such a vessel, than we could blundering around on our own."

Tizu opened his mouth to protest, but Bennett cut off further discussion by picking up his materials and getting to his feet. "As the chair of this committee, it is my recommendation that we stay within the confines of the camp as much as possible, and wait for our rescue."

Meeting over Sairsa remained huddled in her chair, shocked and trembling. So they wouldn't even let Commander Tizu send out a search party for Dunnagh. She felt the tears running silently down her face, unable to stop them.

Oh, Dunnagh, love, where are you? And what will I do now about the baby? Oh, please, don't leave me alone, don't be dead like everyone else I've loved. Oh, please!

She looked up as a hand touched her shoulder. "Are you all right, Sairsa?" Tizu asked, his expression suddenly gentle.

She sniffed and nodded. "Sorry, I seem to be bursting into tears at the slightest little thing these days."

He patted her shoulder awkwardly, his dark eyes alive with a strange emotion of his own. "Try not to worry. I'll watch out for you and take care of you, no matter what, so don't be afraid."

Sairsa nodded, confused by the intensity she felt behind his words. Before she could reply, however, Arishim stuck her head around the door frame. Seeing the Commander bending over her, the councilor frowned. "Sairsa, aren't you coming, dear?"

"Thank you for thinking of me, Commander, I appreciate your concern for my welfare." Sairsa rose hastily and giving the Commander a shy smile, she followed the older woman out of HQ.

BENNETT SAT BEHIND the portable desk in the outer room of the med-pre-fab. It was getting late; he should go to bed, he told himself, but made no effort to move. From one of the desk drawers, he pulled out a bottle of expensive whisky and topped up his drink. He sipped, feeling its warm glow filling his middle and relaxing the tense muscles of his shoulders and neck.

From the next room came the sound of someone retching. He started to rise, then flopped back into his chair. The Lann Gheal medic, was in there; he could handle it. He took another drink, trying to ignore his growing feeling of helplessness.

Contrary to what the others believed, Bennett himself knew that he had no idea what was causing this strange infection, or how to treat it. Without a proper lab, and modern equipment at his disposal, he felt unequal to the task, and more than a little resentful that everyone expected him to solve all their problems.

The great Dr. Bennett, he thought ruefully. What a laugh—if they only knew. Never in his life had he felt so powerless and so unsure of himself. How could this be happening to him? Things like this happened to other people—the poor, the unfortunate—not someone like him. A Bennett, a son of one of the oldest, and most wealthy and respected, families in the U.G.W.—it couldn't be happening to him, not to him.

God, this was some kind of horrid living nightmare. Stranded here, his ship destroyed, and no way of communicating with that distant civilization from which he came. What if the Councilor was wrong—what if that cruiser thought they had all been on board Freedom's Chance, and been killed, along with the rest of its passengers and crew?

Oh, surely, they would come and look, not leave them here to rot on this God-forsaken world. Sadrew was right; he and Arishim were important people. Surely, the cruiser would come back.

Bennett shivered and took another sip of his drink to drown such morbid thoughts, then looked up as the door opened.

"Ah, here you are," Arishim said, coming in and closing the door quietly behind her. "Nurse Gail said I would probably find you over here, instead of resting, as you should be."

He grinned at her sheepishly, and, holding up the bottle, lifted an inquiring eyebrow.

Arishim shook her head, but walked over and took a chair near his desk. "Thanks, but no, I have a low tolerance for that stuff." She smiled companionably. "But I am glad to find you relaxing, at least, and not wearing yourself out in that makeshift lab of yours."

Meldra Arishim was a woman in her middle years. She had the typical dark eyes and golden skin of most Dymarians. With her long gray hair worn piled atop her head she was an elegant woman, who in spite of the primitive conditions in camp dressed as if she were ready to attend a civic function at any moment.

Bennett chuckled, then asked, "Did you need something, Meldra, or did Gail just send you over to spy on me?" Then, as another thought struck him he asked, "You're not getting sick, are you?"

She shook her head and laughed. "No, Hyram, it isn't that. I feel fine." Then, sobering, she added, "I wanted to talk to you about my aide, Sadrew. He's been acting so difficult lately. He hardly listens to me anymore, and I'm afraid his constant baiting of Commander Tizu is going to lead to trouble.

"I don't know much about these things, mind you, but even I can tell that the Commander is a dangerous man, and not one to antagonize, as Sadrew is doing, yet he won't listen to me. I was hoping you might have a word with him." Her voice trailed off. She shrugged her shoulders expressively, her eyes expectant.

Bennett sighed. Another problem dumped in his lap that he was expected to solve. But Arishim was right—Sadrew was walking on dangerous ground. Tizu, or any of the Lann Gheal, were not people to be trifled with. "I'll speak to him and try to talk some sense into the man, because you're right about our Commander."

He hesitated, then asked, "Meldra, this isn't really any of my business, but, however did you happen to acquire such an obnoxious fellow in your retinue? Is he really that good at his job in the Assembly?"

Arishim grimaced. "Not really. Oh, he's competent enough, but I sort of inherited him, you might say, from my predecessor. And his family connections—well, it seemed politic at the time to keep him."

Bennett was about to ask more when the door opened and his assistant entered. Closing the door, she folded her arms across her chest. Arishim stood. Bennett rose as well and took the councilor's hand. "I'll have a talk with him in the morning, I promise," and walked with her to the door.

"Then I won't keep you further, and thank you."

Bennett opened the door for her, then turned to face his other female guest. He sighed, unable to meet her eyes. “I know I promised, but—”

Gail was tall for a Dymarian woman. In a land where rounded curves were admired, her slim build added to the impression of height. She wore her dark hair pulled back in a severe bun, and right now that unflattering hairstyle added to the worry and discontent plain upon her golden face.

She scowled at him a moment longer, then her features softened. Stepping closer she reached up and kissed him lightly, wrapping her arms around his neck. “You did promise, and I’m here to see that you keep it.” She kissed him again. “You need your rest as much as any of us. Please, won’t you come to bed now?”

He nodded, and allowed her to lead him out into the night

Chapter Two

Eyes closed, Dunnagh rode with his cheek against Berren's shaggy back and breathed in her pungent, doggy smell. After the long journey underground he was content just to ride and doze, feeling the warmth of Timorna's red-gold sun on his back once again. Mm, it felt good.

Since daybreak the fugitives had been traveling through one of the reed choked canyons that led to the humans' base. Tawny rock walls hemmed them in; the ever-present, tall, brown reeds slowing their progress. The air was close, pungent with the clawing stench of broken foliage—and so damned quiet.

Everyone was thankful to be out of the gloom, but traveling through these reeds still made Dunnagh feel like a rabbit caught in an unmoed hay field. Even atop Berren, he could barely see over the waving brown mass.

Here and there the monotony of the landscape was dotted with the dark silhouettes of kavalpa thickets. The black leafed, willow-like trees offered the promise of shade and refreshment, but the travelers ignored them. They dared not take their good fortune for granted. If a hunting pack of Warlinga were to discover them before they reached sanctuary...

They must keep going. Their only hope for rest and safety lay on the mesa—if the camp was still there. Ah, but was it? No, Dunnagh told himself, he wouldn't think about that—not now. The day was too fine. Whatever they found—they would cope—somehow they would cope. Would they? Without better weaponry and more food and medical supplies, would they? *Stop it, damn it stop it!*

Shit! Now that he'd opened the worry barrel he couldn't help looking inside. They were so weak and vulnerable—him most of all. Could his bedraggled band of castaways and outlaws heal and survive?

The physical wounds that they'd suffered during the attack, even Taliesh's arm, would heal in time. The emotional traumas suffered by many were a different matter, however.

The fear the Umwira inspired was their most effective weapon. The creatures were masters at projecting a lasting terror into the minds of their helpless victims, and the effects lingered long after their physical attack was over.

Fresh air and sunlight were powerful medicines, already making a difference in everyone's outlook. He was grateful for that, but inwardly he writhed at his personal failures. The healing Timma, Tessa, and some of the others truly needed, was too complicated for the young symbiont to manage.

Dunnagh stopped himself from going down that mental pathway. If he continued he would only alert Tani to his mood and what good would that do. The poor creature already felt bad enough about its failure. It was too young, and nothing he or his bondmate could do would change that fact, no matter how hard they wanted to relieve suffering.

Gods! Maybe if he could just go to sleep...

<<Kasha.>>

<<Hmm?>>

<<Don't try to sleep now; I want to see.>>

<<See what? There's nothing but the liru reeds to see, and if you've seen one, you've seen them all.>>

<<Please, Kasha, I really do want to see them.>>

Dunnagh sighed. Tani had been after him constantly since they'd come out of the tunnel's gloom to let it observe every aspect of the surface world within their range. Tired of the boring monotony of the landscape, Dunnagh on the other hand, wanted nothing more than to forget his worries and sleep. <<Shalla, let me rest—and besides, it's boring.>>

<<No, it's not. Please, Kasha!>>

<<Mm, later.>>

There was a long pause, then Tani asked, a hint of worry in the mental voice, <<Kasha, are you feeling all right?>>

Oh shit, was Tani picking up on his worries again? He didn't want that; the symbiont might sicken if he shared too much. But it was hard to remember to constantly shield. And yet even shielded, if he allowed his negative emotions to intensify, his body's chemistry would alert Tani, no matter how good his mental barriers.

Dunnagh mentally stuffed his worries back into the barrel and slammed down the lid. He chuckled. <<I don't know—am I? All that inner working of our body is your department, remember? I'm just the poor suffering beast of burden that carries you around from place to place, and opens my eyes at your every command.>>

<<Ha, ha! Very funny. Besides, you're not doing much carrying at the moment, Berren is.>> Then, more hesitantly, the inner companion asked, <<You are teasing me, Kasha, aren't you?>>

<<Yes, I am teasing,>> Dunnagh patted his middle. Good, Tani hadn't noticed his laps.<<But, Tani, I am tired of doing this, and I do want to rest and enjoy the warmth of the sun. So let's compromise—I'll keep our eyes open a little longer, because I know how excited you are, but then you've got to let me rest, fair enough?>>

<<Oh, all right.>>

NATHAN PUSHED THROUGH the reeds and fell into step beside the Kashallan. After offering a greeting to Berren, he fell silent, studying his friend. He was doing something un-Dunnagh-like again—probably conversing with the symbiont. Gods of his ancestors, would he ever get used to this bond thing? Nathan shivered.

Unable to watch any longer, Nathan cleared his throat to get their attention. Speaking in Caldoni for the sake of privacy, he asked, "What are you doing?"

Without turning, Dunnagh countered, "What does it look like I'm doing?"

Nathan brushed a sweaty clump of brown hair off his forehead and frowned. "Uh... you're swinging your head from side-to-side looking at the reeds."

"Mm hmm, that's exactly what I'm doing."

"Uh, I'm not sure if I really want to know this, but—uh—why are you doing that?"

Dunnagh turned to face him, and said with a twinkle in his eye, "Because I have to."

"You have to." Nathan scratched his ragged beard. "Thank you for sharing that—I guess. Dunnagh, what are you talking about?"

Dunnagh laughed, his new pointed triangular teeth reminding Nathan once again of that alien other that shared his friend's flesh. Nathan felt a shiver run down his spine and ignored it.

He was still Dunnagh damn it—still Dunnagh, his friend, his battle companion—his love.

As if sensing his friend's discomfort, the mischievous gleam in Dunnagh's eyes faded. "I'm talking about Tani looking at the surface world for the first time through my eyes. Even when it's these very boring liru reeds, Tani won't let me alone. It's about to drive me crazy."

<<Kasha!>>

"Mm, well, you two can stop staring at the vegetation and stare at me instead, because I need to talk to you."

Dunnagh straightened; all traces of amusement erased from his expression. "What's wrong?"

"Dado just came back from a scouting trip. He talked to some of his relatives. There definitely are people at the base camp, which is good to know. But unfortunately for us, while we were—uh—away, some of the little furballs got too greedy for 'pretties' and took to raiding the camp.

"I don't know what the Begta did exactly, but it must have rattled Lann Gheal pretty bad, because now they've tightened their security. They're more apt to fire on anything coming out of the canyons, than wait to talk."

"So what's that got to do with us? We'll just keep the Begta at the back of the line till we have a chance to explain things."

Nathan gaped. Then at Dunnagh's raised brows he swore in exasperation. "I hope this brain lapse of yours isn't a permanent part of this kashallan thing. Dunnagh, you and your bondmate want to see something more interesting than the weeds? All right, open those big blue eyes of yours and look at us! I mean really look at us, then tell me what you see.

Do we look like the kind of folks to inspire confidence in a bunch of trigger-happy armachda? Or do we look like we just might be more of the same native scum that have been scaring them half to death?

"Look at me, Dunnagh. I've changed—shit, we all have, you most of all. Too bad you can't see yourself. You're naked, with pointed teeth and the purple brands of the kavay alignment all over your skin.

You're wearing bone necklaces and a fur cloak, your hair's braided like an Avairei priest, your face is covered with one of the scruffiest beards I've ever seen, and you're sitting up there on Berren's back like some native Ce'awn traveling along with his retinue. Gods, would you recognize yourself, or any of us, if you were in their place?"

"Hmm, you do have a point. Over the course of our ordeal I've become accustomed to how we look. It seems perfectly normal to me now. But you're right; that isn't how the armachda left back at the camp—who haven't shared our experiences will see us."

He sighed and rubbed a hand across his face, "I hate to think about it but maybe you're right about them shooting first before asking questions."

Nathan grimaced, and let out a bark of mirthless laughter. "To be shot down by 'friendly fire" after everything we've been through—wouldn't that just tear it wide open."

"Yeah. That would be a laugh, wouldn't it? Save the hunting packs chasing us the trouble."

Nathan gave him a crooked grin, then sobered. "Well," he pressed, "got any smart ideas on how to handle this?"

"No. And besides, why are you asking me? Aren't you the one who keeps reminding me how 'stupid' my ideas have all been lately? So—you're my new Hunt Leader, you think of something for a change."

Nathan grunted, and gave him a disgusted look. "Thanks a lot."

Dunnagh's lip twitched but he said nothing further. They continued on for a while, each lost in his own morbid thoughts, until Dunnagh finally said, "I can't see any way to handle this other than just to go up there, as openly as we can, and hope for the best. If it's bright daylight, and we take it slow, so as not to frighten them we should be all right.

"I don't know what else we can do, Nathan. We have to try and make contact. We need better weapons and supplies or we may not make it to the sanctuary at Ticca."

Nathan sighed, "Right. I'll go up to point position. I'll send someone back to let you know when we start up the trail to the mesa."

"Take care of yourself; don't do anything foolish."

Nathan snorted. "Me?"

"Yes, you. I'm not the only stupid ass hero around here, you know?" Nathan laughed and loped off without answering.

<<He will be careful won't he, Kasha?>>

<<Yes, Shalla, I'm sure he will. Don't fret. We were joking with one another. We tease and joke with each other all the time.>>

<<Oh. But the danger is real.>>

<<Yes, Shalla, it is. I won't lie to you, but we'll be fine.>>

When Nathan was gone, Berren paused, then turned her head around, an anxious expression on her heavy-featured face. "Kashallan, is something wrong?" You and your Hunt Leader, San Nathan, were speaking in the Chosen's language, but I could tell that something was troubling you. Have the Umwira—or the Warlinga found our trail?"

Dunnagh shook his head and patted her shoulder reassuringly, then urged her forward again. "No, it isn't as bad as all that; the Umwira or the Warlinga haven't found us. Nathan was just telling me that the Begta have been causing trouble for my kin up on the mesa, that's all. There's nothing to worry about."

Under her thick brow ridges Berren's yellow eyes narrowed. "The Begta are always causing trouble, that is true, but if that's all that you were saying, why were you speaking in that alien language so I wouldn't understand you?"

The Kashallan chuckled. "All right, there is a little more to it than I was saying, but it's nothing that Nathan can't handle, truly."

Berren considered a moment, then she said softly, "You are very precious to us, young one, I hope you are right about your Hunt Leader. We would not want to lose you, all Timorna needs you."

Addressing her with the term of respect for her people, he said, "I know Timornshaya, it will be all right, you will see."

As Berren continued up the trail, Dunnagh leaned forward, and rested his head once more upon the Loti's shoulder, and hoped that what he just said to her was the truth. He closed his eyes.

This time there was no protest from his Khutani bondmate; they both had a lot to think about and watching the scenery was a distraction.

Chapter Three

Hesitant to mull over their current situation for fear of upsetting the symbiont further, Dunnagh determined to focus his mind on more pleasant reveries. The day Commander Tizu had ordered him to take his squad and go after the missing scientists, his fiancé Sairsa had been scheduled to come down from the orbiting ship to spend some time with him.

Sairsa. An image of her wavy dark blond hair, sparkling green eyes and lovely, strong featured Caldoni face, rose up in his mind's eye to delight him. Gods of his Ancestors, how he missed her...

Where was she now? Was she waiting for him on the base as Pela assured him? Or had she left the planet—or found another?

How could he blame her if she had. He had Pela didn't he?

The Ima Sagas, with the approval of the Khutani Makers, had given Pela to him as wife. It was the custom on Timorna for the Avairei matriarch and the Khutani elders to make all the breeding alliances. Pela was a gentle creature, and with Tani's biochemical goads to spur his interest, he had agreed willingly enough to the mating.

Sairsa. Oh, my love, I thought you were dead—what have I done—did I give in to these aliens' designs for me too easily?

NOT LONG AFTER HIS unit of the Lann Gheal mercenaries had been assigned to the planet Dymar, he'd met her. It had been a lovely evening, promising romance.

Tired of the sleazy drinking houses the armachda usually frequented, he and Nathan took a city transport across town to the university district, looking for a different kind of amusement. At the second hostelry they'd entered, Nathan caught the attention of a pretty student with a mischievous gleam in her eye. Not long after that, he abandoned Dunnagh to his own devices, he and the girl going back to her place.

Dunnagh hadn't minded. Alone, he'd continued on to the university, preferring to walk its shaded paths, smelling the bright flowers and listening to silvery water fountains, rather than being cooped up indoors in another drinking house on such an evening.

As he walked aimlessly around the campus, his mind slid without conscious thought, into the Caldoni religious disciplines that were part prayer, part relaxation exercise. Time seemed to stand still. He drifted through the green twilight, letting go the tension of combat, enjoying the beauty of growing things again.

Startled out of his reverie at last, Dunnagh realized that it was almost dark. He was tired, hungry and hadn't a clue where he was.

Then, around the next corner, he found a quiet little hostelry and decided to go in. The place was about half full, couples and small groups sitting around dark wooden tables in comfortable, brightly colored chairs. In the back was a small dance floor with a local band warming up for an evening's entertainment.

Dressed all in black, Lann Gheal insignia on his shoulders, his long, red-gold hair rippling down his back, he created quite a stir as he walked to the bar. Taking a seat near the end of the counter he ordered a beer.

The clientele seemed to be older than the group he and Nathan came across earlier. For the next few minutes he sat, half turned to the room, gazing at the artwork on the walls and making his own quiet survey of the premises. Firm yet polite, he discouraged conversation with his fellow patrons, content to drink his beer and watch these Dymarians without becoming involved in their concerns.

Dunnagh was considering leaving to find something to eat, when a woman in a newly arrived party seated near the door caught his attention. She was dressed in a long wine-colored dress, and like himself, her fair skin was an exotic contrast to the amber-skinned Dymarians in the room.

She was pretty enough to make any man smile, but what really caught his eye wasn't her looks, but the silver torc she wore at her throat. He had seen such jewelry before, many times. Its curving spirals and twisted knot work pattern screamed Caldoni workmanship, of a type worn by the women of the clans.

It was definitely not a piece that tourists, no matter how much money they offered, would be allowed to purchase. Such a torc was too bound up with Caldoni religion and family tradition to be so abused. Wherever did a woman on Dymar come by such a thing? Intrigued, he decided to stay a while longer. Food could wait. Maybe he could have a private word with the pretty stranger and find out who she was.

Dunnagh got his chance a short time later, when the two couples she came in with, went off to the dance floor. Seizing the opportunity, he walked quickly over to her table. When she looked up, he smiled.

Then deciding to take a chance, he said in Caldoni, "My name is Dunnagh Kai. May I join you?"

In the same language she said, "My name is Sairsa Basheya; please sit down, Armachd."

Dunnagh continued the conversation in Caldoni, but it didn't take him long to realize her difficulty with that language. His first few questions she hesitantly answered, then with an embarrassed laugh she switched to Standard.

"I'm sorry, Armachd Kai, I left Caldon with my mother when I was only eight. I've been here on Dymar so long, I'm afraid I've forgotten much of the language from home. So, if you'd like to talk about something a little more complicated than the weather, would you mind if we used this language?"

A pity, he thought, but smiled politely and switched languages. "No need to be so formal, please call me Dunnagh." She blushed, then nodded. "I couldn't help noticing your clan torc. I was curious to know what such a prized family heirloom was doing here so far from home."

Sairsa touched the warm silver at her neck. "This was my grandmother's. My mother gave it to me when I came of age."

They spent the rest of that first evening getting to know one another, and over the next few weeks, they saw as much of each other as Dunnagh's schedule would allow.

As often happens, the immediacy of a possible war escalated their relationship towards intimacy. He ended up in her bed before the first week was out, and by the time of the evacuation, they were tentatively speaking of marriage and a return for them both to Caldon.

When Dunnagh discovered that Sairsa had delayed her own evacuation to be on Dr Bennett's ship to be with him, he'd had mixed emotions about it. In a way, he'd been glad, but at the same time, he'd been furious with her for risking her safety by waiting so long to leave.

And now? If the Creggan warships hadn't followed them and destroyed their base, she might be still alive—trapped as he was. Doomed, like all the humans stranded on Timorna, to spend the rest of her life in hardship and danger on a primitive, forgotten world.

Chapter Four

Nearing the path up to the mesa, Nathan halted their progress and sent word back down the line for all his armachda to join him at the front of the column. When they'd gathered, he led his squad away from the Timornans, then turned. Expression grim, he said in a low voice, "All right we're going up now. Take it slow; we don't know what we'll be facing."

"Do you know if anyone's still alive at the base, sir?" Oglas asked.

"According to the Begta yes. But Lann Gheal's had some trouble with the locals and may not be friendly to strangers coming up from the canyons. Don't do anything stupid.

"We'll lead the column so Commander Tizu's sentries can see that it's humans coming up the trail, before they catch sight of the Timornans. That may make things a little easier for everybody."

"But what if it doesn't?" Chang asked.

Marti gave him a withering look but before she could respond Nathan held up a hand and said, "If there's trouble, get everybody back down the path as quickly as possible. Our first priority is to protect the Ce'awn and the rest of the Timornan civilians. Spears can't argue with beam rifles. We'll go back down and try to communicate with them later."

By their grim faces, Nathan could tell they didn't like it. Well, he didn't much care for the prospect of getting shot either—but what else could they do? "All right, let's get this over with. Move out." Guts in a knot, Nathan started up the slope.

From Temog he'd gotten a piece of cream-colored bandage cloth at their last rest stop. He'd tied it to his spear, hoping those fool sentries would take it for a white flag of truce and not start shooting before he had a chance to say a word.

At the top of the cliff, Nathan's squad fanned out, flanking him. Marti gave him a lopsided grin and crossed her fingers. He winked, then held up his makeshift flag and started forward.

They were halfway to the base when a shouted command of "Halt!" rang out from the rocks up ahead. Slowly Nathan raised his flag, and called out in Caldoni, "Don't shoot. It's me, Patrol Leader Nathan Derek and the missing squad. We have the scientists with us, too."

Four black-clad figures rose from the boulder, their beam rifles aimed directly at them. Nathan swallowed hard, but held steady under their scrutiny. No one in either group moved.

When he could stand it no longer, Nathan swore under his breath, and lowered his flag. "Well, you pack of mangy dogs, what are you staring at? Haven't you ever seen naked people before?"

When he still got no response, except that now the beam rifles were trained directly on him, Nathan swore under his breath, and said, "Ross, if you don't stop pointing that rifle at me, I'm going to come over there and make you eat it."

Beside him, Marti gave out her sultry laugh and, addressing one of the other sentries, added, "What's a matter, McLaren? You been after me for months to let you see my tits." She cupped one cinnamon-colored globe, lifting it for his inspection. "Well, here's your big chance, boyo."

The other sentries laughed and lowered their weapons, as McLaren turned bright red. "P-Patrol Leader, is that really you?" Ross stammered. "W-we thought you were dead."

"Yeah well, we aren't dead. It's me all right. We're alive, not ghosts, so the lot of you quit looking at us like that."

At that point Dunnagh guided Berren through the armachda, stopped the Loti beside Nathan and dismounted. Surveying the sentries with a critical eye, he nodded his approval.

"We heard that you have been having trouble with some of the natives. Good work. You kept your heads and didn't do anything foolish. You're to be commended for that, Armachd Ross."

Ross snapped to attention, keeping his eyes determinedly focused on Dunnagh's face. "Yes Sir, we have, but—"

"Armachd," Dunnagh cut in, "you can give me the details later. Right now, I suggest you have Goronwy over there use his communication-link and tell Commander Tizu that we've returned. Tell him we have the two scientists with us and a number of natives. We will all be needing a safe refuge for a while."

"Yes, Sir."

Chapter Five

Commander Tizu wished he could just walk out of this tedious meeting and do something useful for a change. Instead, he reached for the water pitcher in the center of the table and poured himself another glass. The other members of the "Camp Committee" sat around him discussing the usual tripe.

The wind rattled the roof, dishes clattered in the mess and outside someone laughed. Outside. Gods, how he wished he was out there—anywhere else but here.

The base was a cluster of pre-fab buildings and large tents hastily erected around a central quadrangle of yellow moss-like vegetation. The base had never been intended as a permanent habitation, though in the long weeks that followed their arrival on this primitive world, it had become one out of necessity.

When Dr. Bennett's ship, the Freedom's Chance left Dymar, the ship had been dangerously over-crowded with war refugees. The Chance was damaged during the escape, and they had been forced to create this camp as a temporary refuge for the passengers while repairs were made on board the ship. Unfortunately, a Creggan warship followed them away from the blockade of Dymar. The last communication they had received from the Chance was that she was under attack and moving away from the planet.

His eyes slightly unfocused, Tizu took a sip of his water and listened to Councilor Arishim drone on. How these Dymarians loved to hear themselves talk. It seemed like ever since the Creggans had blown up Bennett's ship, the politicians had done nothing else.

And what was the bloody point? Without the ship, they weren't going anywhere. Why should they go on tormenting themselves with false hopes? No rescue ship was coming to take them off this God-forsaken rock. They were stuck here to rot.

He shifted his position as another spasm of pain twisted through his gut. Concentrating on keeping his expression bland, he fished around in his pocket for one of the pills Dr. Bennett had given him for this little problem and popped it into his mouth.

Though he'd tried to be discreet, he saw Bennett take note of his action. Damn. Then he held himself rigid as another spasm hit. He had told Bennett that he was over the native virus. Now, of course, the doctor could see that Tizu had been lying to him. More than half the camp was down with this strange malady, to one degree or another. They had even had a couple of deaths.

Gods, if he ever felt it getting to him that bad, he would just end his pain quickly with a shot in the head like armachd O'Shea. He would prefer a nice quick suicide rather than face the painful spasms that accompanied such a death.

Tizu took a deep breath and let it out slowly. Ah, that was better. The pain had passed for now; the pill was taking effect. His morbid outlook placed on hold, he returned his attention to his surroundings. Not much had changed during his lapse. Sadrew was speaking now, but it was the same useless drivel.

Tizu glanced across the table at Sairsa. Now there was a more pleasant subject for his attention. Creamy skin and fathomless green eyes, she was a tall full-figured woman. An exotic to his people's way of thinking, but after joining Lann Gheal, and being stationed on Caldon for so many years, he'd grown to appreciate the big-boned, strong-featured beauty of Caldoni women.

At the moment this particular flower was sitting beside Bennett, hunched over a portable computator terminal, a slight frown of concentration on her lovely face. There was a wisp of long hair that had come loose from the ribbon tying it back. It fluttered a moment in a slight breeze, then curled around to caress her chin. What would it feel like to take off that ribbon, sink his hands up to the wrists in that ash blond wavy cataract? Ah, someday...

As if somehow aware of his regard, Sairsa brushed back the offending strand and glanced up. Their eyes met. Tizu put down his glass. A shy smile curved her lips, then she lowered her eyes and returned her attention to taking notes for the endlessly boring meeting.

She's pushing herself too hard again, he thought. In spite of her own bouts with the local virus she was volunteering to help care for the sick, and acting as Bennett's secretary.

Beautiful, stubborn Sairsa, he worried about the dark circles under her eyes and the feverish intensity with which she was going about her work. Was she grieving again for her dead parents aboard the Chance? He wished, not for the first time, that she would accept the reality of their situation, face the fact that Dunnagh was dead and let him take care of her. But every time he had suggested it, offering his love and protection, she thanked him, then insisted with quiet certainty that she just knew Dunnagh wasn't dead. He would be coming back for her.

Dunnagh had asked him to take care of her when he'd headed up the patrol to find the missing scientists. At the time, Tizu had casually agreed, then dismissed the incident from his mind. But later, after the ship was destroyed and Dunnagh's squad disappeared, he realized that fulfilling that promise meant a lot to him.

She had lost so much, her home, her family, her lover, and yet she bore all these misfortunes with a quiet dignity and courage that won his heart. Much to his own disgust, he found himself falling hopelessly in love with her.

And that was another worry and frustration to add to the growing pile laid upon his back. What would happen to her if he couldn't fight off this thing? Or what would he do if he lost her to the virus? Damn, he had to stop this, or he'd drive himself insane.

Deciding finally that he'd had enough, Tizu was about to get up and leave, when one of his armachda burst into the meeting, gasping for breath. Without waiting for permission to speak, she blurted, "Commander Tizu, he's back!"

Sairsa blanched, a hand flying to her mouth to stifle a cry. Tizu glanced at her anxiously, then growled, "Calm down, Ellis, you're not making any sense. Who's back?"

Still panting, she went to attention and saluted. "Sorry, Sir." Ellis glanced around the table and blushed. Taking a deep breath, she continued.

"Sorry to interrupt, but Armachd Ross just sent in a message over the communications-link. He says Unit Leader Dunnagh Kai and his squad have returned. Unit Leader Kai says he has the scientists with him, and a bunch of the natives, sir. Armachd Ross wants to know if he should let them come into camp."

"Why would he want to know that, Armachd?" Bennett inquired. "I should think that would be obvious. Of course they should be let into camp."

Ellis blushed and explained. "It's because of the natives they have with them, doctor. The Commander's orders were not to let any natives into camp." Returning her attention to Tizu she said, the Unit Leader and his armachda say they won't come into the base unless they can bring all their party with them. Armachd Ross wants to know what he should do, sir."

Tizu sighed. "Tell Ross to let them pass if Kai will vouch for the natives' good behavior." The woman saluted and hurried out.

Glancing at Sairsa, Tizu could see how her eyes sparkled with excitement. His guts suddenly spasmed and he wasn't sure if it had been caused by the native virus, or something else that he didn't want to think about right now. Rising hurriedly, Tizu made his apologies to the group and followed Ellis out.

Chapter Six

Bennett rose as well, straightening the pleats of his embroidered tunic. "This is wonderful news." A golden-skinned man, slightly thick in the middle, he gave them one of his famous Bennett smiles. Addressing Councilor Arishim directly, he said, "Meldra, I think we should adjourn this meeting, don't you agree? I know our devoted secretary here has been looking forward to this day for quite some time. It would be most unfair to keep her at her post any longer."

Councilor Arishim gave the impression of being nothing more than a plump motherly woman with warm brown eyes and a coil of graying hair atop her head. Behind the soft exterior, however, was a sharp intelligence that her political enemies had learned to fear.

Immaculately dressed in a cream-colored robe and dark-blue over tunic, she smiled kindly at Sairsa, and nodded. "I do agree, Dr. B. And perhaps we should all go out to the quadrangle to welcome them back."

Addressing Sairsa directly, she said, "Run along, dear, I know you'll want to pretty yourself up for that handsome young Unit Leader of yours. Go on now—you must be very excited."

Sairsa blushed, laid the computator terminal on the table and laughed. "Oh yes, thank you."

The news of the missing squad's return spread quickly through the camp. Excited Dymarians and off-duty Lann Gheal armachda hurriedly gathered in the central square to observe the missing party's return. His shoulder-length graying hair tied back with a ribbon, his patrician features animated, Bennett stood beside Arishim and a scowling black-clad Tizu at the front of the crowd.

When the lost party came into view, however, Bennett gaped open-mouthed along with everyone else. The vision heading into the quadrangle was so bizarre, he could hardly believe his eyes. Beside him Tizu swore angrily under his breath. Bennett glanced his way and their eyes met.

"Well, I can certainly understand your Armachd's hesitation to let them pass," he murmured. Tizu grunted, his black eyes smoldering; then tight-jawed, he turned back to watch the entering cavalcade.

The humans of Kai's squad looked like naked tattooed savages. With tall bone-tipped spears in their hands and crudely carved bone necklaces around their necks, they marched protectively alongside a variety of somewhat humanoid furred creatures, also wearing primitive ornamentations.

Bennett studied the newcomers with interest. The scene was so bizarre—straight out of some anthropological text on primitive cultures, he thought. What had happened to these people?

And the natives were examples of the local inhabitants they'd not encountered before. Dr Farris and Dr. Singey should have some fascinating tales to relate about their adventures when they got back to civilization.

He frowned as he scanned the group for a glimpse of his young protégées. Tessa was nowhere to be seen, but he did see Singey's tall ebony figure walking beside a couple of the furred natives wearing kilts made from a coarse home-spun cloth. He smiled as their eyes met, but the young scientist's grim expression never changed.

Confused, Bennett looked away, his attention next captured by the tall, naked human riding one of the shaggy, centaur-like natives in their midst. Decorated more elaborately than the rest, he was obviously their leader. Bennett blinked in astonishment, finally recognizing that personage as none other than Unit Leader Kai.

What game was the man playing here? There were galactic laws against the exploitation of primitive populations. If Kai had been abusing his status as a civilized man on this planet, he could be arrested and charged for it. And, Bennett decided, he would enforce that law if necessary.

Next to him he could hear Tizu's muttered cursing in Caldoni. Bennett let out the breath he hadn't realized he'd been holding. "Talk about someone going native," he whispered to his companion. "My God, Commander, what has happened to these people?"

Tizu snorted without taking his eyes off the approaching band. "I don't know, but I damned sure intend to find out."

As Bennett continued to watch their approach, his doctor's professional eye took note of the bands physical condition. None of them looked in good shape. They were all battered, bruised, and dirty. All of the armachda and many of the natives also sported long, half-healed claw wounds. What kind of creature had claws like that—and more to the point why hadn't Lann Gheal found out about them on their initial reconnaissance?

Another hideous surprise this world had in store for them. God, when would the rescue ship come?

Divining his unspoken thought, Tizu said, "Well, well, looks like they've been in a scrap of some kind."

"Yes, I noticed that too—but with what? Look at some of those claw marks." Bennett shuddered. He gave Tizu a worried frown. Damn, was Sadrew right about the man's incompetence?

Eyes still focused on the on-coming group, Tizu grunted, fingering his sidearm. "It does make you wonder."

In a wary silence Kai's band passed between A barracks and HQ, and stopped in front of the welcoming committee. By this time everyone waiting in the quadrangle had seen the odd company's approach and were shocked into silence. No one spoke, each side looking at one another, waiting for someone else to initiate contact.

A strange thought popped into Bennett's mind as he watched Kai slowly looking around the quadrangle. Kai gave him the impression that he was seeing this place and the people gathered here for the first time. But that was impossible; the man had helped build the base.

Bennett banished such a foolish notion and glanced at his companions. Meldra was the politician here; it was her idea to welcome them back in such a public manner, therefore she should begin.

For once speechless, Arishim had a phony smile plastered across her face, but she was avoiding eye contact with anyone. Poor Meldra, this definitely wasn't what she'd had in mind when she suggested this little welcoming ceremony.

Next to her, the narrow face of her aide Sadrew was turning a dangerous shade of purple as he choked down his rage. On Bennett's other side, Tizu seemed nearly as close to exploding as the aide, scowling murderously at everyone.

Do something, he ordered himself, but he continued to stare speechless along with the rest.

Finally, Kai dismounted. He touched the centaur-like creature on the shoulder and spoke to it in a low voice. The native said something to him in return, than turned and trotted back to stand among the other waiting natives. *How very interesting*, the scientific part of Bennett's mind thought. These creatures were obviously far more intelligent than horses or other riding animals.

The Lann Gheal armachda and his protégées weren't ignorant savages. What had happened to change these people like this—and where were their clothes—and weaponry for that matter?

Some of the armachda like Kai, seemed untroubled by their tattooed nakedness, and the affect they were having on their onlookers. Others like Singey and Tessa were more modest—as was proper for civilized people. They seemed to be trying to hide behind their furred companions.

Well, no matter, there was probably a perfectly good explanation for all of this. So, they'd best get this over with as soon as possible. But if word of this lapse in propriety got out it could seriously damage Philip's career. And poor Tessa, her marriage prospects would definitely be limited if galactic high society learned of this. He would have to caution Meldra to keep her staff under control—for the sake of everyone's good name.

The silence was beginning to drag on painfully, when Kai spoke, breaking the tension. "I am glad to see that you are still alive up here. When no one came to rescue us after the first few days, I assumed that either the ship had been repaired and you had left us to our fate, or that the Creggan warships had found you."

Avoiding traveling down that road of inquiry, Bennett cleared his throat. "Welcome back, Unit Leader Kai, we are all relieved, I'm sure, to see you safely returned."

Before he could say more, an excited female voice cried out from the back of the crowd. "Dunnagh, oh, Dunnagh!"

Turning, Kai saw Sairsa pushing her way towards him through a knot of bystanders and held out his hands to her. "Gods of my Ancestors, Sairsa, love, you're safe."

When she was almost upon him, she jerked to a stop, eyes widening as she actually saw him for the first time. Unable to hide her shock, her face paled and a hand flew to her mouth. For just a moment, Kai's face contorted with a mixture of raw emotion painful to behold, then he regained control, his features sliding into a neutral mask.

His voice barely above a whisper, he tried again. "Hello, Sairsa," When she continued to stare at him speechless, he dropped his hands to his side and looked away. At his back a tall armachd muttered something encouraging, but he ignored him.

Kai started to rub his stomach, then thought better of it and returned the hand to his side. Closing his eyes his lips moved in a murmured communication of some sort. Though Bennett strained to hear Kai's words were too low for him to make out.

Opening his eyes again, he noticed Commander Tizu glaring at him. Kai dropped his eyes, looking even more confused and miserable. Bennett cleared his throat and spoke into the strained silence, changing the subject.

"Unit Leader Kai, you mentioned our lack of response in coming to your aid. I can see by the wounds many of your folk have suffered that you have had a hard time of it, but we've had our share of trials to contend with as well. While you were gone, we've had trouble with some of the natives. They've stolen or damaged several things on the base. One of the articles destroyed soon after you left was the hover sled."

Dunnagh gave Bennett a grateful look and nodded. "Yes, we just heard about that. The raids were done by some of the Begta living in the warrens under the cliff. We were told by the Begta with us, that while we were in the mountains, some of their relatives had been up here searching for 'pretties,' as they say.

"The Begta are incredibly curious and resourceful little folk. They are totally fascinated by anything shiny. I gather some of them didn't like how their headman distributed the spoils they had from capturing us. So I suppose they got greedy, and came looking for more—"

He broke off his explanation as a new thought struck him. "But surely you could have brought another sled from the Chance?"

Bennett shook his head. He would have preferred to wait till they were rested before giving them the tragic news, but there was no help for it. And, like lancing a boil, maybe it was better to get it over with quickly. It would be cruel not to tell them. They would find it out soon enough.

"Unfortunately not, the ship is gone, Unit Leader. The Creggans did indeed find us, the night after your squad disappeared, in fact. We are all stranded here for the moment."

"But not for long, doctor," Councilor Arishim said. "As I keep reminding you, that Creggan ship was followed by a galactic vessel. They would have picked up our distress signal by now. As soon as they are able, they will be back to rescue us."

She smiled at Kai, keeping her eyes determinedly focused only on his face. "And now that you and your people are safe, Unit Leader Kai, when the ship comes—"

"No. I'm sorry, Councilor, that won't be possible. Even if a rescue ship does return, I cannot leave Timorna." His eyes lingered for a moment on Sairsa's confused face. "This is my home now—forever. I have been bound by my warrior's oath to serve the peoples of this world. No matter what happens to the rest of you I must stay."

The Councilor looked puzzled, but both Tizu and Bennett knew enough of Caldoni custom to know exactly what he was talking about and he saw it in their eyes.

"I came here to ask for weapons and supplies, before we continue on to another sanctuary. My people and I can't stay here long, but I do need to give you some important information about this planet. Until such time as we can get all this sorted out, I ask the gift of Caldoni hospitality," he said, bowing formally to Bennett and the Commander.

Totally flabbergasted by this turn of events, Bennett hoped his expression didn't convey the confusion he was feeling at that moment. To give himself time to think, he glanced at Tizu, hoping for inspiration. No help there, Tizu's expression displayed a barely contained hostility.

What was wrong with the man? He'd expressed only the highest regard for this officer in the past to Bennett. Perhaps he was angry about losing him to some ancient Caldoni tradition that no one in their right mind would honor these days.

Before things could degenerate further they needed to end this charade and get Kai and his people settled. Later they could talk further and perhaps persuade the man to give up such a foolish notion as remaining on this primitive world.

Turning back to Kai, Bennett bowed in the manner of one Caldoni chieftain to another. In heavily accented Caldoni, he intoned, "Ta shiv cuj milla faltia, Ce'awn. (You are most welcome, chieftain.")

Kai's mouth twitched, then he answered with similar formality. "Go ra myi get, mo Eirla. (Thank you, my Lord.")

Bennett was breathing a sigh of relief when the Caldoni ritual of hospitality was suddenly shattered by the sound of high-pitched laughter.

Chapter Seven

As startled as the rest of them, Dunnagh swung back to his followers. Chang was standing, head thrown back, tears streaming from his eyes, and laughing hysterically. Rhys was trying to calm him, but Chang pushed him roughly aside, almost knocking Rhys over in his manic frenzy.

"It's gone," he kept repeating, flinging his arms around wildly. "It's gone kabloom!" He laughed that crazed laugh again. "The ship went boom! boom! kabloom! and this nightmare will go on, and on, and on, 'cause nobody's going home—ever." Chang choked, ending with a sob.

Ignoring the onlookers, Dunnagh seized the hysterical Chang and pulled him into a confining embrace. "Stop this, Armachd, right now, stop it!" At first Chang fought the restraint, then, recognizing who held him, he suddenly quieted.

"It doesn't really matter now what Dr. Singey finds in the lab, does it, Ce'awn?" His face a mask of despair, Chang looked up, his dark eyes pleading.

"I'm sorry." Dunnagh shook his head and released him. "It never did matter, armachd, not for you, or any of us. I wasn't lying to you, Ma Lu Chang; I told you the truth. The kavay alignment is irreversible."

Chang thought about that for a moment then said, "My wife and son must think I'm dead by now."

At the tone of hopelessness in the man's voice, Dunnagh's own heart lurched. The Maker Gladdris had used its tremendous Psy and blessed him with a final leave-taking of his loved ones, but when reminded like now, the loss still hurt. His mother, his sister Shivon, his Da, he would never see them again either.

His voice heavy with regret, he said in Timornan, "I suspect all our families have held our wakes by now."

With a strangled cry Chang drew the bone knife from the belt around his waist and began to push the blade into his exposed abdomen.

As if anticipating something of the kind, Nathan's meaty hand clamped down on Chang's arm just above the wrist and pulled it backwards. Chang writhed trying to force the blade in deeper. "Stop fighting me you little shit, stop," Nathan growled.

"Let me go, damn you," Chang cried. "Let me finish it! I'm dead to them already—so let me die!"

Chang had been like a volcano ready to explode for quite some time, Dunnagh chided himself. He should have expected this. "Damn you, Chang, why did you have to do this now, in front of the whole camp!" Then, "Rhys, Oglas, give us a hand," Dunnagh snapped as he reached for the man's kicking foot.

Screaming curses Chang fought desperately to hang on to the weapon. It took all their combined effort to wrestle the knife away from him and confine him.

When the grieving man had finally exhausted himself and hung limp between Nathan and Rhys, Dunnagh breathed a sigh of relief. Rhys had a nice new bruise on his left cheek, Oglas was muttering under his breath and holding a hand to his side and the long claw wound on Nathan's right arm had reopened and was dripping blood down onto Chang's shoulder. Gods, what a mess!

Nathan looked down at the blood and grimaced. "The little shit fights like a devil from the black pit," he complained.

Dunnagh's lip twitched. "Well, he *is* one of our best hand-to-hand combat experts, you know."

"Yeah, I know, but does he have to practice so enthusiastically on his friends?" Nathan gave the man a disgusted shake. "Hear me, asshole? We're your friends, so ease up next time."

Dunnagh motioned for his captors to set Chang on his knees in front of him. Chang knelt, head bowed breathing heavily. "Chang, look at me," Dunnagh said, Chang looked up. In his eyes was a naked longing that tore at Dunnagh's heart.

No, damn you, I can't let you do it. I need you, I need all of you. In a stern voice, he said to the distraught man in Timornan, "Ma Lu Chang, I am not going to let you shame me, or yourself and your ancestors, by giving up and dying like a coward.

"I know it hurts, but you have given your fealty to me, and by all the Gods of Caldon and Timorna, I will hold you to it."

Chang glared at him angrily, but Dunnagh held his gaze, waiting. At last, Chang bent his head in submission, and in a low voice said, also in Timornan, "Your will, Kashallan."

The Kashallan's expression softened, he could imagine how hard this news was for the man. His wife had given him a son only a few months ago, and now the boy would grow up never knowing his father. "If you want me to, Chang, I can ease the hurt for a while like I've been doing for Tessa and some of the others. Do you want that?"

The armachd considered, then nodded. Dunnagh glanced around at the bystanders, suddenly self-conscious again.

We are none of us what you expected, are we?

<<If they plan on surviving on this world, they will have to deal with Timornan realities, Kasha,>> Tani said. <<Let them watch. Chang needs our help; that's what matters.>>

<<Yes, you're right, Shalla.>>

Addressing Chang once more, he held open his arms. Still speaking in Timornan, he said, "Then come to me, my warrior, and I'll give you what peace I can."

Chapter Eight

At the first sounds of hysterical laughter, Dr. Bennett's medical instincts urged him forward. Before he could take more than a few steps, however, he felt a hand on his arm. Annoyed, he tried to shake off the grip, but it only tightened. To his surprise his former protégé Philip Singey was the one holding him.

A grim expression on his face, he shook his head. "No, Dr. B, let the Kashallan—uh—Unit Leader Kai deal with this."

"Philip, have you gone mad? I'm a doctor for heaven's sake! Kai's a military man, not a physician; how can he possibly know what is best for that traumatized man?"

Singey's lip curled into a sneer, the lines of his face hardening. "Perhaps, doctor, you don't know as much as you think. I can't allow you to interfere. The Ce'awn will do what is needed."

A shiver ran down Bennett's spine as he stared into Singey's dark eyes. Philip's odd behavior was sorely testing his composure. What had happened to these people?

He opened his mouth to argue, when someone else took hold of his free arm. Unsure whether to be irritated or frightened, he swung his head round and met the hard-eyed stare of a tall, brown-skinned woman. Continuing to hold his arm in a vice-like grip, she said, "I know you mean well, doctor, but Mr. Singey is right—it is not your place to interfere. Chang is one of us."

Effectively restrained by his "guards," he had no choice but to comply—unless he wanted to involve Tizu in this little struggle. He sighed and relaxed. There was no point in doing that. If they thought they knew better than a highly trained doctor, then on their heads may disaster fall...

"All right, if that's what you want, I'll let you people handle this—for the moment." They nodded, but to Bennett's disgust didn't release him.

Out of the corner of his eye Bennett stole a look at his former protégé. He's changed, Bennett thought. There was a new severity to his features that hadn't been there aboard the Chance. The marks of pain and hardship were etched deep into the lines around his mouth and nose. Whatever had happened to him had left some deep scars.

Returning his attention to the tableau, Bennett observed that Kai's people, both native and human, had gathered around the struggling men, blocking with their own bodies the spectators' view as much as possible. When Bennett could see again, the screaming man had quieted and was kneeling on the ground in front of Kai.

He wished he could understand what they were saying, but they were speaking in the native language now. Then Kai opened his arms, and the armachd rose and stepped into his embrace. As Bennett stared, Kai placed his mouth over the other man's.

Was Kai kissing him? No, he was doing something—else. Bennett strained to see, but Kai's men were shielding them more effectively now. The ludicrous image of a mother bird feeding one of her young popped unbidden into his mind. He tried to dismiss it, but it kept returning.

"Philip," he whispered in spite of himself, "what is he doing?"

Singey fixed him with that cold expression he had so recently acquired. "I'm sorry, doctor, but I can't tell you that. If you truly want to know, you must wait and ask the Ce'awn. He will probably tell you, but it is not my place to do so."

Bennett felt a cold chill run down his spine again. Suddenly he wasn't so sure he wanted to know. This was all so strange—so alien.

He turned back to face the group shielding Kai. Whatever had been going on was almost over now. Kai raised his head and released the other man. Just for a moment, before he wiped it away, Bennett saw a bright orange liquid dripping out of the corners of the troubled man's mouth. Now he stood glassy-eyed, swaying slightly. An olive-skinned woman was talking to him, her hand a steadying presence on his arm as Kai moved away from them.

Bennett blinked, not sure what he had just witnessed. If he didn't know better, Bennett would have sworn that the poor man had just been given a very powerful tranquilizing drug. But that was impossible.

Trouble over, and Kai's people now talking among themselves, his temporary guards released him and joined their comrades. Bennett hastily stepped back to his original place among the welcoming committee.

Catching his eye, Tizu motioned him away from Arishim and Sadrew. When they were far enough from the others not to be overheard, Tizu asked, "Doctor I saw you talking to your protégée. What's this all about?"

"I wish I knew, Commander. These people have obviously suffered emotional and physical traumas while lost in those canyons, but I can only guess as to the nature and severity of their injuries."

Tizu frowned. "So, what should we do with them?"

"Do with them. That's a very good question, Commander." Bennett sighed, rubbing a hand across his face. "If you press me for an answer, my advice is that we watch them carefully until I determine what has happened to them. By then, we should know better what should be done."

Hand on his sidearm, Tizu turned squarely to face him. "Dr. Bennett, if you think they are dangerous, either my lost armachda or their native allies, I will force them to leave. For the sake of our security, would you like me to do that?"

Bennett considered, then shook his head. "No, I don't think that will be necessary. They are obviously in need of our assistance. Look at them, Commander. They have almost nothing, no clothing to speak of, no shelters, and I would guess little in the way of food. Wherever they came from, they left in a hurry.

"And, judging by their wounds, they've been running from something quite dangerous. It would be inhumane to turn them out now when they are injured, exhausted, and probably frightened."

Then, as another thought struck him, he added, "Besides, they are the only ones among us who know anything about the people and conditions off this mesa. I fear we may need them. They know the country, and can even speak the local language. I think it would be most unwise to turn our backs on such a source of knowledge, no matter how strange they seem to us at the moment."

Tizu looked dubious, but at last grunted his agreement. "So where do you want me to put them?"

"I think they will want to stay together—and that will be for the best. We can watch them better that way, too. Isn't D barracks nearly empty?"

"Of people yes, but not supplies. We've been using it as a storeroom."

"Can it be cleared?"

Tizu sighed. "Yeah, I suppose so. I'll see to it." He glanced once more at Kai's bedraggled band and his expression hardened. "But I'm also telling you straight out; I don't like this. If I decide they are a threat to the security of this base, out they go."

Chapter Nine

Though in different ways, their reception on the base had turned out to be an unsettling experience for all of them, native and human-Timornan alike. By the time he and Pela retired to have some privacy, Dunnagh was wishing that there had been another way to get their needed supplies and warn the base without coming here.

Trouble started not long after the Commander's men had readied D barracks for them. Dunnagh had expected the native Timornans to be anxious, even frightened by all the new things they were going to encounter, but he hadn't expected the experience to be quite so intense.

There were so many small, everyday things that he and the other humans just took for granted—things that were new and disconcerting to his other followers. Mundane items like showers, chemical toilets, mirrors, bright indoor lights, pre-cooked and packaged rations, all both delighted and sometimes horrified them.

There were also many wonders made out of metals to exclaim and marvel over. Everything on the base was new to them and their functions needed patient and repeated explanations.

Bombarded by questions from the natives, Dunnagh had yielded to the squad's insistence and sent Nathan with them to get their belongings—the gear they'd left on the base while on their mission into the canyons.

Not long after the squad left, however, Nathan and the rest came storming back, faces menacing as thunderclouds. They were returning with duffel bags in hand, so Dunnagh at first couldn't figure out what was bothering them. He looked from one angry face to another, then asked, "You've got your things, what's the problem?"

"We got our gear all right—all but our weaponry," Marty growled.

Grim-faced, Nathan nodded. "Yeah, all but our weapons."

His own temper igniting, Dunnagh felt a flush heat his face. They would need those weapons when they headed on to Ticca—they might not survive without them. "Why?"

"Who knows, really," Nathan grumbled. "I didn't believe the brainless story Tizu told us about trouble in the camp, and him needing to keep the extra weaponry locked up—I didn't believe that shit for a moment."

Knowing he'd better find out the reason for this unheard-of behavior, or there would be trouble, Dunnagh immediately followed Nathan and Rhys back to HQ.

Entering HQ, they found Tizu reading a report at his desk. As Rhys closed the door behind them, the off-duty armachda lounging in the room straightened. Was it his imagination, or were their hands really hovering a little closer to their side arms? Dunnagh's jaw tightened; they were definitely alert and hostile.

What was going on—why were they being treated like this? Nathan and Rhys on either side of him Dunnagh stopped in front of the desk and stared down at his former commander.

Ignoring them, Tizu continued to read. Dunnagh's temper simmered nearing the boil. He took in several deep breaths, trying to calm down. Tizu and the armachda seemed to be deliberately trying to provoke them into doing something rash, but why? Was the commander looking for an excuse to circumvent Bennett's hospitality and drive them off the base?

Dunnagh glanced at his two companions, wondering if they had come to the same conclusion. Nathan gave him the briefest of shrugs; Rhys remained expressionless.

But he wasn't imagining the provocation. As an added goad, someone behind him made a rude comment about his braided hair. Another man snickered and said something too low for him to hear. More laughter followed. This situation couldn't be allowed to continue.

Having no luck getting Commander Tizu's attention, Dunnagh slowly turned, glaring at the offending men. Some of the armachda dropped their eyes—embarrassed, but others answered his challenge with a hard stare of their own, as if daring him to take the confrontation further.

To his dismay, Dunnagh realized that trying to pull off a really menacing glare, when you were naked in a room full of clothed, well-armed men, was next to impossible. His effort fell a little flat. They didn't take him seriously—and why should they?

Gritting his teeth he at last gave in and spoke first. "All right, Commander Tizu, what's this all about? Why won't you give my people the rest of their belongings. Their beam rifles and other weaponry are there personal property. They have a right to them."

Tizu ignored him for a while longer, then put down the report and fixed Dunnagh with hard eyes. "Like I told your Second Derek there, we had a bit of trouble while you were gone. It's a new rule. Nobody goes around camp armed."

Beside him Nathan snorted. Dunnagh could feel the heat flushing his own cheeks and clenched his jaw to hold back the angry words that were threatening to spill out. Losing his temper right now wouldn't solve anything, but why was the man doing this?

Dunnagh looked pointedly at the armed Lann Gheal armachda in the room. "If this is a new rule, then why is Goronwy and the rest over there wearing their side arms, hmm?"

Tizu gave him a wolfish smile. "The rule applies to the civilians in camp, not to Lann Gheal. It's our job to protect the camp from all enemies."

"Wait a moment, are you trying to tell me you think me and my people are this camp's enemies?" Dunnagh demanded.

Tizu's smile widened. "No, but you and your people aren't under my command either. You made that very clear when you came in, Kai. So, that makes you all civilians in my book.

"You asked for shelter and protection, and we'll give you that—while you're here. You also said you want to meet with us before you 'leave.' Well you can do that too, Bennett will set up the meeting; we'll let you know when. Until then, you'll follow the camp rules—or get out—understand?"

Tizu leaned back in his chair, and smirked. "In the meantime, why don't you just go back to D barracks and relax."

Unable to hold his silence any longer Nathan blurted, "And what about when we leave? You going to send us back down into the canyons with no weapons to defend ourselves? What kind of shit is that—"

Dunnagh made a cutting off motion and Nathan subsided. Turning back to Tizu he said, "Nathan has a point, Commander, what about when we leave? There are a lot worse things to contend with on this world than the Begta. If you send us away without adequate means to defend ourselves, we will surely die. Do you really want that?"

Tizu's face became expressionless while he thought about it. At last he sighed. "No, I guess not. When you people leave, you can have your weapons back—and what supplies we can spare. But until then, you obey camp rules and no weapons."

After that pronouncement there was nothing else to say. They left, but later a discreet, yet visible, guard was stationed outside D barracks. Everyone noticed of course, and that had almost started a small war right then and there.

Dunnagh's squad couldn't understand why they were being treated like hostiles. Throughout all those long weeks of slavery and hardship, their dreams of coming back to be among friends had been all that had kept them going. And now they were here, and it was all so wrong. Their former comrades mistrusted them, treating them like enemies or alien crazies, and it hurt. It hurt very much.

Fearing that violence would break out if he didn't step in and say something, Dunnagh called his human followers to him, and ordered, "Let it be, for now—all of you."

'But, Ce'awn," Taleish protested.

"I said drop it," Dunnagh snapped. "When I meat with Bennett and this camp committee we'll get all this straightened out so just relax for now, and don't start trouble. You'll get your gear back so stop worrying."

His hunting pack hadn't liked it, but at last gave him their reluctant agreement to stay calm.

They'd carried on their little "discussion" in Caldoni, but when the Kashallan tried to reassure the Timornans that all was well, his words lacked conviction—and they sensed it. He couldn't blame them for their skepticism. The Dunnagh part of himself was just as disturbed by Lann Gheal's behavior as the rest of his human followers.

Maybe they all needed to take Tizu's advice and just relax and let him be in charge for a while. The Sorins and his dwindling formula supply wouldn't permit a long stay. But in the meantime, the Gods alone knew they could use the rest.

Chapter Ten

Pela ran her furred hand down the Kashallan's naked flank, still humming a wordless hymn deep in her throat. She could feel his taut muscles soften as he drifted into exhausted sleep. She sighed. Good, he was finally resting. For a time after they had retired to this tiny room, she wondered if he would ever settle.

The day had been filled with a series of frustrations, which Dunnagh tried to hide from her without success. She knew in spite of his refusal to translate for them, that Dunnagh and his hunting pack hadn't expected the hostile greeting they'd received.

Pela didn't understand why the Chosen's kin were so frightened, or why he insisted they had to stay. Pela hated it here. The base was a terrible place, with all its frightening contraptions and alien machines. She hoped they would leave soon.

In his sleep, the Kashallan had turned his back to her, and now lay snoring softly, his head cradled on one muscular arm, his unbraided hair spread out like a russet shawl over his back and shoulders. Pela smiled to herself. She had to admit that, though his alien half was often unpredictable, she was starting to become quite fond of her unusual husband.

Leaning forward she brushed the hair from his forehead, then yawned. Life with him was certainly different, she thought, as she nestled down next to his warmth and drifted into sleep.

...PELA LAY IN A WARM, dark, womb-like space, protected and safe. Mm, so good...Then without warning, her pleasure was shattered by the far-off sound of a baby crying. The child sounded so lonely and afraid; its cries tore at her heart. Within the darkness and the echoing distortions of her dream, she couldn't tell where the sounds were coming from.

Was this some kind of sending, a warning from her Goddess of danger to come? Could this crying infant be her own unborn little one? *Oh, Holy Mother, no, please.*

Looking deep within herself, she brought her awareness to bear on the tiny life nestled safely within the confines of her expanding womb. No, it was not her little one. He swam peacefully in his watery home, happy and content, and a bit startled by his mother's anxious regard when aroused.

Swimming further into the darkness, Pela searched, listening to the crying, growing more and more frantic, but it wasn't the Goddess who finally answered her heart-felt pleas.

It was her own child. From within his warm nest, Jorran spoke. <<It's my brother Tameh, mama. He is crying because he and his mother are dying. You must save them. Please, mama, you must go to them. They need you and my father, or they will die.>>

Suddenly the sound of the baby's terrified wailing became deafening, his screams shredding the very fiber of her soul. Terrified now herself, Pela cried out, then felt herself falling into wakefulness....

With a gasp, her eyes flew open. Breathing raggedly, she glanced around the tiny room momentarily confused by her strange surroundings. Through the window across the room the artificial light from the quadrangle outside showed her the solid bulk of the man sleeping beside her. She breathed a sigh of relief—now she remembered where she was. They were at this strange place he called "the base."

Her dream's urgency once more flooding her mind, she glanced wistfully at the tiny altar she had set up in a corner of their room. She wanted to pray, she needed to understand what she should do—but she didn't want to disturb the man beside her either.

Early in their relationship, Pela had been amazed to learn the power she had over her new mate when she used the red kavay and enticed him with her feminine charms. All the Avairei had been shocked, however, when, after her conception, the Kashallan had still maintained his interest in his lovely young bride.

Pela would have denied him after she'd conceived, as was the custom, but her mentor, Ima Sagas had warned her not to quit taking the red drink.

When he's being stubborn you can use his continued sexual interest in you, to help him relax and get the rest he desperately needs.

Staring at the ceiling, she held herself perfectly still while she considered what to do. Deciding at last that she desperately needed the counsel of her Goddess, she would have to risk awakening him.

Moving slowly and carefully, Pela slipped out of bed, crossed the room, and knelt beside the tiny altar. Sprinkling a bit of the burning powder into the votive lamp, she watched the green flame rise. Then, making a small offering of her blood, she composed herself for her prayers.

"Pela, sweet, are you all right?"

Startled, Pela looked around. The smell of her blood offering, however small, must have aroused the ever-hungry Tani. Maybe in future she should forego this part of her devotions. She would ask Ima Sagas in the morning. "It is nothing, Dunnagh-Tani. I just wanted to pray. I am sorry that I disturbed you. Please go back to sleep."

The Kashallan studied her thoughtfully for a moment longer, then nodded and closed his eyes. She wasn't sure he'd believed her, but no matter, she would make it up to him later. Right now she needed to pray....

Finishing her prayers some time later, Pela rose and returned to the bed. She would have walked around to the foot and crawled in behind him, but he pulled down the blanket in front of him and patted the mattress.

She hesitated, then crawled into his warm embrace. He settled the blanket over them both, then, kissing her gently, he asked, "Pela, I know being here must seem very frightening to you. We will go soon, but for now, I must stay. Can you understand, sweet, and not be too worried?"

She reached up and stroked his cheek. "Of course you must stay; we will need your kindred to come with us." Then she snuggled deeper into the sanctuary of his arms.

He kissed her again and would have drifted back to sleep, with her slim, furry body held close, but her next words shocked him awake.

"Husband, why don't you bring me to my sister-wife? I saw her today, I think. Why didn't she come to us?"

Dunnagh sighed. "Pela, do you remember, when I told you that things were different among humans? Our women—they don't usually want to share their mates. And Sairsa—well, you saw how she looked at me. I think it would be better if I just let her go."

Hoping to distract her, no doubt, he kissed her. "I have you and many new responsibilities. That is more than enough for me now."

"But Dunnagh," Pela protested, "she is my sister-wife. I must go to her, she—"

"You forget yourself, priestess," Tani snapped. "My Kasha has told you to stop. This is painful for him, and you are making things worse with your meddling."

Pela gasped. "I-I am s-sorry, Holy One, I didn't mean to displease you." Trembling, her voice trailed off uncertainly.

Muttering to himself, Dunnagh pulled her closer. She buried her face against his chest, and sobbed. He stroked her silky back rhythmically, and crooned to her in Caldoni till she quieted.

"Pela, sweet, I'm sorry. Tani was feeling my distress. It is still quite young, and it was frightened by my emotions. The Shalla is sorry too; it isn't angry with you. I know you mean well, and want me to be happy by having Sairsa with us, but let's just forget about it, please, sweet?"

Solemnly she nodded. "If it is what you wish, husband, then so be it."

"It is what I wish, yes."

Pela closed her eyes, and began to breathe rhythmically, feigning sleep. Soon she felt him relax and drift back into an exhausted slumber.

Oh, Holy Mother, Pela prayed silently. You told me in my prayers just now that I must go to my sister-wife—that I must take care of her and the baby, or they will die. If that should happen, it will be very bad for all of us. But how will I find her in this alien place if he won't help me?

Chapter Eleven

Tattooed savage. The words rang in Sairsa's mind like discordant chimes. That's what the people on the base were calling Dunnagh, a tattooed savage—or worse.

Standing in the violet evening shadows, she looked across towards D barracks. A moment ago noises in the quadrangle had driven her out of the sickbay to investigate. She couldn't see much from here, but she'd been warned not to go over there.

Suddenly a number of the furry natives ran out of D barracks screaming, and some of the Commander's armachda rushed to investigate. The two groups mulled about for a time, then one of the Lann Gheal armachda laughed.

After that both groups of armachda began trading increasingly more heated insults at each other, while the frightened savages huddled together against the barracks wall.

Sairsa had no idea what had started the uproar—this time. But judging by the amount of Caldoni profanity being traded back and forth, things were definitely getting out of hand.

Suddenly dizzy, she leaned against the pre-fab wall for support, and clasped her hands together to stop them from shaking. This was so terrible; she wished they would stop—stop before somebody got hurt. Why were they doing this to each other? She swallowed down bile, her stomach churning. This whole mess was so awful!

Then, Dunnagh push past the natives by the doorway and stepped between the opposing factions, Nathan not far behind him. Sairsa's heart lurched. Dunnagh...

He was clothed in bone necklaces and a kilt, rather than the black Lann Gheal uniform he should be wearing. Like some of the natives, his long red hair was platted in dozens of tiny braidlets that hung down his naked tattooed back. Then the image of her lover blurred—and she was crying again.

Oh, Dunnagh, my love, what happened when you took your squad after the missing scientists? What have the natives and this horrible planet done to you?

Seeing him decked out like some alien primitive when he first arrived had been a shock—it still was—and she couldn't understand why he was doing it. She desperately wanted to go to him, but had his affection for her changed as much as his physical appearance? Maybe he didn't love her anymore? No, she wouldn't believe that, because if that were true, then what was she going to do about the baby?

His baby...

All the weeks when he was missing she'd kept praying for his return. Finding him again should have been the answer to all those supplications, but instead it was turning out to be a nightmare come to life.

It's all gone wrong—all my dreams are melting away in the reality of this forbidding world.

Startled out of her reverie, Sairsa heard the door to HQ slam, and Commander Tizu came striding across the quadrangle, a murderous expression on his almond-eyed face. Dunnagh and Nathan stepped forward to meet him. The three leaders talked for a while, then after a few more shouted exchanges by the quarreling armachda, the dispute was resolved and the two groups dispersed.

Sairsa breathed a sigh of relief, grateful that no violence had broken out—this time.

Still unwilling to return to her project inside, she pressed herself further into the shadows, and continued to watch, her eyes wistful, her heart aching. Dunnagh too seemed to hesitate before returning inside. He stood near the entrance looking around the quadrangle as if searching for something—or someone.

"Sairsa?"

Sairsa straightened, blinking back her tears. She rubbed a hand across her face, pushed back her hair and said in a choked voice, "I'm right here, Gail. Is something wrong?"

Coming around the corner of the sickbay Gail, stopped and peered into the shadows. "Sairsa? Honey, what are you doing out here—are you all right?"

A tall angular, woman who wore her dark hair pulled back in a severe knot when working, Gail was the older sister of a school friend, and Dr. B's assistant. Ever since she had discovered Sairsa's pregnancy, the woman had been mother-henning her till sometimes Sairsa wanted to scream.

"I'm fine, Gail," she said, "I just came out here to see what all the noise was about."

Gail scowled, glanced over at the closed door of D barracks, then stepped closer trying to make out Sairsa's expression in the gloom. "You've been crying. Sairsa, you're not thinking again of going over there, to see him, are you?"

Sairsa sighed, did they need to go through this again? A note of impatience coming into her voice, she said, "I don't know. I haven't decided yet, but he is my fiancé. I'm carrying his child, I can't just walk away and pretend otherwise."

"Honey, please, remember what the Commander told us? Promise me you won't do anything foolish, please."

"Gail, Dunnagh wouldn't hurt me. No matter how much you, the Commander and Dr. B think he's changed, I know he wouldn't—"

"You don't know anything of the kind," Gail said firmly, hands on her hips. "We have no idea what's happened to those people. Look at them, for God sake—do they look like sane, rational human beings to you?"

Sairsa dropped her eyes and sighed. She was too sick and too tired to argue, especially since a tiny voice in her mind agreed with Gail, in spite of all her protests to the contrary.

Seeing she'd made her point, Gail changed the subject. "Come back inside and wash your face, Dr. B is at HQ now, but he will be along soon to escort us to dinner."

Sairsa had just finished repairing the damage her tears had made to her appearance, when Bennett entered the waiting room of the sickbay to collect them. Gail looked up from the book she was reading and smiled. Then seeing his worried expression she sobered. "Sairsa and I heard the commotion a few minutes ago. What was it this time?"

Bennett gave her a forced smile. "Another minor misunderstanding that's all. Nothing to worry about."

When her expression remained dubious he relented and explained, "It started when the natives became frightened by some of our technology. A few of the Commander's armachda thought it was amusing. Kai's bunch was offended. Well, one thing led to another and..."

Gail snorted. "Caldoni armachda, they're all a bunch of barbarians; not much difference between them, and the ignorant savages Kai brought back with him."

Sairsa could feel the flush darkening her cheeks. Growing up on Dymar, she'd heard such sentiments—and worse all her life. It hadn't gotten any easier to bare—especially when people who should know better expressed them. Hearing the tightness of her own voice, she said, "My stepfather may have been a Dymarian, but I'm Caldoni too, Gail, have you forgotten that?"

Gail looked away, but made no effort to apologize.

Stepping in smoothly to ease the tension between the two women, Bennett said, "Gail meant no offence to you Sairsa, I'm sure. We're all just a little on edge these days that's all. Don't take it to heart, please." Bennett gave his assistant a stern look and she reluctantly apologized.

Sairsa sighed, she knew Gail's feelings about the Caldoni, she'd heard it all before. There was no point in getting upset about it now. What did it matter—they were going to be stranded here forever anyway.

Deciding to change the subject back to what was most important to her, Sairsa asked, "Dr. B, you told me earlier that you wanted me to wait until you had a chance to talk to your protégées' Dr. Farris and Dr. Singey before I went over to see Dunnagh. Have you spoken with them yet? Have you found out what you needed to know?"

"No, my dear, I'm afraid I haven't."

"Hyram, she wants to go over there—to him."

Seeing his shocked expression, Sairsa pleaded, "Dr. B, he's my fiancé—can't you understand that?"

"Yes, of course, but—"

"I know what you and Commander Tizu told me, doctor. But I'm also pregnant with his baby. He has a right to know that. He isn't going to hurt me—I'm sure of it."

Bennett rubbed a hand across his haggard face, walked behind his desk, pulled open a drawer, brought out a bottle and poured himself a drink. Glass in hand he sat down heavily, and took a large swallow. "Sairsa, my dear, I'm sure you want to believe that, and so do I. Under normal circumstances I would agree with you.

"But think, my dear. This is an unknown, alien world that we're stranded on at the moment. We know almost nothing about it. We have no evidence or experience on which to base our assumptions.

"We don't know what happened to them after their capture by the natives. And we don't know what those natives are capable of, for that matter. All the people who were lost have changed a great deal—why, they are almost unrecognizable. Until we do know a little more, it's only prudent to wait and see what develops before we make any rash moves.

"I've promised Unit Leader Kai to arrange a meeting so that he and his people can tell us their story and we can acquaint them with the problems we have been having in their absence. That meeting will take place as soon as possible. After that, we'll know a little more about what has happened to them, and then—we can make some plans."

"But—"

Bennett held up a hand to stop her. "I know the waiting is hard on you my dear, but I'm only concerned about your welfare. You mentioned your baby. Its welfare is an important consideration for all of us. Don't jeopardize your own or the child's safety, by doing anything foolish, please. Be patient just a little longer."

Sairsa could feel the tears gathering behind her eyes once again. What the doctor said sounded so right and sensible, but her heart cried out for a different response.

Recalling that haunted look that came into Dunnagh's eyes when he saw her shocked face—oh, Gods, how could she stand it? He was her love. How could she just sit here and wait? Every fiber of her being craved to go to him.

Before she could argue further the sickbay door opened and Commander Tizu stepped into the room. Tizu glanced at the assembled group, then focused his attention on Sairsa. "Sairsa? Is something wrong?"

Sairsa dropped her eyes, refusing to answer. She didn't want the Commander involved—it might only start more trouble. She felt sick and wished she could just go lie down, but if she tried to excuse herself, Gail would insist that the doctor examine her and then they would start in on her again.

She sighed, suddenly too exhausted to argue. "All right, Dr. B, I'll do like you want me to do and wait."

Bennett smiled, finished his drink and stood, taking Gail's arm. "A wise choice, my dear. I'm glad you agree with me."

Tizu raised an inquiring eyebrow but when no one offered an explanation, he shrugged. Coming over to Sairsa he smiled and held out his hand. Sairsa returned the smile half-heartedly, slipped her arm in his, and allowed him to escort her to the mess for dinner.

Chapter Twelve

Looking into the mirror, the Kashallan stared intently at the Caldoni features of his face. He took note of the strong, firm jaw, the high cheekbones, straight nose and full, curving lips. Brushing the red-gold hair back from his forehead, he moved closer to his reflection and gazed into a pair of deep blue eyes.

<<Ha, the kavay really is the color of our eyes, as the Avairei say, Kasha.>>

Dunnagh chuckled. <<I never thought of my eyes that way before coming to Timorna, but I suppose in a poetic sort of a way, there is a resemblance in the colors.>>

<<Mm, I like that—having eyes the color of the kavay.>>

Growing impatient with his bondmate's regard, Dunnagh begged, <<Shalla, please, I'd like to finish shaving sometime this morning. You can look at our face again later.>>

<<Oh, all right.>> Tani watched its host's reflection as he applied the soapy foam and began to slide the razor across his cheek.

<<Can we take a shower again soon? I like the shower. That was almost as nice as being back in the pools. I like the feel of the water on our skin. Can we?>>

<<Mm, maybe later, but not now,>> Dunnagh said, trying to be patient. He chuckled. <<Is it the shower you want, Shalla, or just to gaze into the big full-length mirror that's over in the bathhouse?>>

<<I do like that mirror better than this little one,>> Tani admitted. <<It's interesting to see what we look like to everyone else. Can we go back there today?>>

<<Maybe, we'll see,>> Dunnagh hedged.

He worked on his beard a little longer. Then suddenly his bondmate asked, <<Kasha, are we considered handsome among your people? The

Avairei think you're ugly, but what about your own people? Are we pleasing to them?>>

Dunnagh rinsed the foam from his blade, then paused, considering. "I suppose we are thought of as handsome.>> He patted his thicker middle. <<Yes, even though my body has changed its shape a bit, I think we would still be considered attractive by the women of my species.>>

<<That's good. And Pela is making us some new clothes. She was very happy when you gave her your little sewing kit with the bright, sharp needles. She and Ima Surrel are already taking apart some of your old things and making us something new to wear. I'll like that, won't you, Kasha?>>

<<Yes, that will be very nice.>>

There was silence from his internal companion as the shaving process continued. People came and went around him, using the facilities, but left him alone. Dunnagh had decided that Tani was tired and would finally give him a little peace, when the symbiont asked, <<Kasha, why do you want to do that?>>

Dunnagh sighed, obviously not. <<Do what, Shalla?>>

<<Cut our face like that.>>

<<It's called shaving, and—well, I'm just used to having a smooth face. I've shaved for so many years that it just feels more comfortable to me than having a beard, that's all. It's just a custom with some of us.>>

<<Mm, Marti. Moraga and Tessa have smooth faces—do they have to shave?>>

<<No, they're women, they don't need to.>>

<<Mm, I don't have anything in my encoded memories about the females of your species. When we get our tentacles, I could taste them and then, maybe I could adapt us so you wouldn't have to do that—>>

<<NO!>>

<<But—>>

<<NO! Tani, don't you dare. That is one adaptation we can definitely do without. The difference between males and females in my species is caused by substances we call hormones. Women have smooth faces because of these chemicals.

<<If you start messing around with the male hormones in my body, I may not have to shave anymore, but along with that change will come other things.>>

<<Like what, Kasha?>>

<<Like a higher voice, and larger breasts, to name a couple of examples. I'd rather shave than have that happen to me.>>

Tani was quiet for a long moment, pondering this new information, then it said, <<Pela has very tiny breasts because that's the way the Avairei were bred to be. Marti and Tessa and Morag have very big breasts. It would be kind of nice to play with ones like that, if we—>>

Dunnagh dropped his razor in horror. <<NO! Oh, Gods, Tani, please. Promise me you won't do anything like that to our body, please.>>

<<Oh, all right, Kasha. If you're that upset about it, I won't do anything. I just thought you might like it, and having big breasts would be kind of interesting and fun, that's all.>>

Relieved, Dunnagh picked up his razor and continued his shave.

He was almost done when a high-pitched screaming began in the barracks' main living area. "Shit! What now?" Putting his shaving gear away, he sprinted for the door.

Coming out of the washroom, he glanced around the barracks, trying to locate the source of the trouble. At the front door, two of their "guards" were just stepping in to see what all the noise was about. Sunlight behind them, he couldn't tell from their silhouettes who they were. The large one was probably Tarla, and the other—Owyn, maybe. Well, whoever they were, he'd better settle this quickly, or half the Commander's troops would be over here again.

The last time the "natives" had gotten frightened over some of the humans' technology, most of Lann Gheal had rushed over, thinking there was some kind of fight going on.

There hadn't been, of course; it was just something stupid, like somebody forgetting to warn the Timornans before turning on the indoor lights after dark. The light had been so bright and such an unusual color that they had been frightened.

Between Tizu, Nathan, and himself, they managed to get everyone settled down before any violence occurred, thank all the Gods. But the incident had left a bad taste in everybody's mouth. They didn't need a repeat performance today—not with the mood his armachda were in.

Ignoring Tizu's men he scanned the room and at last found the source of the disturbance. In the far corner a large group of his followers, humans and Timornans alike, were clustered round something, or someone, all shouting at once. It was definitely a someone, as a Begta's high-pitched shrieking could be heard above the clamor.

Pushing through the crowd, he came to the center of the commotion. Rhys, Marti, Chang, and a couple of the young Atas were holding on to a struggling Dado. From their actions, it wasn't clear if they were trying to restrain or murder the poor creature.

Out of the corner of his eye, he saw Nathan coming through the back door at a run.

"ALL RIGHT, THAT'S ENOUGH. STOP IT!" he bawled at the top of his voice. It took a moment, but at last they heard him and fell silent, except for a low whimpering from the cowering Begta.

Aware of Tizu's guards right behind him, the Kashallan glared at his followers angrily and demanded, "What's this all about?"

Quivering with rage, Marti pointed to the vid machine, its mangled insides scattered all over a nearby table and floor. "The slimy little furball broke it, and we're going to break every bone in his mangy little carcass, just to see how he likes it."

Around him, the Kashallan heard a chorus of angry agreement. "Dado, remember I told you—you couldn't have any pretties unless you asked me or Nathan first?"

Dado looked up, his yellow eyes wide with fear. "I-I remember, I no take pretties—"

There was a warning growl from the group around them. Dado cringed, covering his head with his arms. "No eat poor little Begta," he whined. "I not take pretties."

The Kashallan pointed at the trashed vid machine. "Then why is the vid broken?"

Dado peeked out from between his fingers at the wreckage. "I wanted to find where little starmans live. I wanted to see where they sleep at night."

Over the heads of the others, Dunnagh glanced at Nathan, raising an inquiring eyebrow, but Nathan only rolled his eyes in exasperation. No help from that quarter.

Coming up beside him, Tarla surveyed the wreckage in admiration. "Those little guys are sure curious, aren't they. That's about how the inside of the sled looked when we caught some of them in there. Armachd Ross sure was pissed when the Commander made him try to fix it too."

"Mm."

Waking up from a nap yesterday afternoon to the sounds of gunfire, Dunnagh had hurried out into the main room, only to find everyone engrossed in some stupid war vid. Entranced, humans and Timornans alike were staring wide-eyed at the screen.

Tani too had been interested, so reluctantly he had sat and allowed his bondmate to view the program. But Dunnagh found as he watched the vid that he had mixed feelings about showing this kind of mass-produced garbage to the unsophisticated Timornans.

It was natural for his armachda, now that they were back among familiar surroundings, to amuse themselves with such entertainments. It was what they had always done before, while awaiting an assignment in base camp.

But was it right for the native Timornans to see what was depicted in these vids? There would be so much they wouldn't understand—especially since they didn't speak the language.

Privately, Dunnagh worried that the vids might do a lot of harm, filling their minds with disturbing images that the more sophisticated humans took for granted.

Though he hadn't said much at the time, he had been glad when Tani's need for rest had overridden its desire to explore new things. Now it would seem that the Gods, and the ever-curious, ever-resourceful Begta, had taken matters out of his hands. There would be no more vids for his folk—period!

Still looking at the damage, Tarla said, "Unit Leader Kai, Sir, I could go to our barracks and bring over our vid machine for you to use for a while."

Dunnagh shook his head. "Thanks, Tarla, I know you mean well, but we don't need it."

"But, Ce'awn—" Oglas protested.

"If you want to watch the damn vids so bad, Oglas—or any of you—then go to C barracks and watch them over there. I want no more of it in here. It's just going to cause trouble, so forget it."

Marti faced him, hands on her broad hips, her bold eyes flashing. "But Ce'awn, you know we can't do that. They don't want us over there." Angry murmurs of agreement from his followers echoed her complaint.

Tarla looked at his former comrades, then back at Dunnagh, a bewildered expression crossing his placid face. "I don't understand, Sir. You guys are still a part of the outfit, aren't you? Why wouldn't you be welcome at C barracks?"

Of all the Lann Gheal left on the base, this simple, kind-hearted giant had been the only one who seemed to be glad to see them when they returned. Tarla had treated them the same as always, coming over to their barracks when off duty, as curious about the Timornans and their adventures as any of the Begta were about the base and its pretties.

At first the Kashallan's followers had been wary of Tarla's friendliness, but he was so good-natured that secretly Dunnagh was sure that his people were glad for his continued camaraderie, even though most of the armachda considered Tarla to be slightly retarded.

Looking at the big man kindly, Rhys said, "It's all right, Tarla, don't worry about it. If we get bored, we'll come over and visit. But the Ce'awn will probably have lots of things for us to do here."

Face a grim mask, Owyn, who had also come up to the group, took the big man's arm. "Come away now, Tarla, we're supposed to be on duty. The trouble's over, and if the Commander catches us in here visiting we'll be on report." Still troubled Tarla allowed himself to be led back outside.

When their guards were gone, Dunnagh motioned for his human followers to gather round him. Speaking in Caldoni for privacy, he said, "There's no point in getting used to things from our old life. It will just make it that much harder for you when we leave.

"You're going to have to accept this new life, with all its differences, and right now that includes finding other ways to amuse yourselves, when not on duty. In the Great Swamp or Ticca there won't be any vid screens for you to stick your faces in, so get used to it."

As the group dispersed he stared down at the still-cowering Begta. What was he going to do with them? He'd better think of something, before someone killed one of the little troublemakers out of sheer frustration. Tensions were building, and he couldn't understand what was causing the delay.

The Sorin Storms were coming; they needed to get out of here. Yet every time he or Nathan asked about having the promised meeting with this "camp committee," they were given only excuses, the meeting postponed.

Trying to ignore other frustrations, he crouched beside the frightened Begta. One problem at a time. "Dado, look at me."

The Begta peeked out again through his fingers. "Kashallan mad, Kashallan eat Begta?" he asked in a tiny, frightened voice.

"No, I'm not going to eat you," the Kashallan promised, "but I am angry with you. Dado, you have got to be more careful. I know you didn't mean to break the starmans' machine. I know that you were just curious, but you did break it, and that made everybody angry, including me.

"So what you have to do from now on, is not take something apart till you have watched long enough to see how to fix it again after you look at it. Then nobody will be angry with you, or want to eat you, all right?"

"Begta be good. Begta remember—no eat poor, little Begta."

"No eat Begta." Then the Kashallan smiled as an idea occurred to him. "Dado, you told me there was a spring nearby with a rich supply of kavay in its water. Can you find it, if I have Nathan assign some of my hunting pack to go with you?"

Dado grunted eagerly.

"All right, I'm sending you and your kin to get some of its water for us—we'll need it soon. We'll have to start mixing more kavay with our base rations or we're going to get sick. It would be very helpful to me if you would do that. Just be careful, in case Gormach's Warlinga are around."

Dado shuddered, then brightened again. "I am happy to help Kashallan. I get plenty of good kavay for everybody."

The Kashallan stood up. "Good," he said, then, looking at Nathan, he added in Caldoni, "See to it, will you? We do need the kavay, and it's probably a good idea to get them out of the barracks for a while, till everyone has had a chance to cool down."

"Yeah, you got that right. I'll take care of it." Then he took hold of the Begta. "Come on, furball, let's get you and your kin out of here before somebody gets hungry."

Chapter Thirteen

Surveying the Kashallan critically as he approached her, Sagas's mouth tightened. He was rationing himself too severely again; she could see it in his flat alien face. When he was beside her, she said, "You are waiting too long between feedings, young one. You must come to us more often. You will injure your health if you do not stop this."

He gave her a thin-lipped smile. "I'm here now, and I see Ima Surrel standing there waiting for me. I assume you have arranged for her to give me the Blood Gift this morning, so I'd best not keep her."

Before he could go, she put a hand on his arm to stop him. "I see that your pet Begta have caused more trouble. What is it this time?"

He blinked, then gave her a thoughtful look. At last, he answered, "Dado took apart the vid machine because he thought there were little people inside. He wanted to see where they slept at night."

"And what do you plan to do about this broken machine?"

He shrugged. "Nothing." Noticing her continued frown, he smiled, and added, "If you mean do I plan to get another machine so that everyone can still watch the vids, the answer is no."

Sagas couldn't help letting out a long sigh of relief. The Kashallan's smile widened. "I didn't like everyone watching them, either. And now it would appear that your prayers to the Mother have been answered. The ever-curious Begta have solved that little problem for both of us."

"I am glad. That is one less thing to worry about—I didn't like them. But that is a minor issue. Holy One, the storms are coming and your formula—"

"Sagas, enough. We've been over this before. I'm not sure what is the hold-up with the meeting, but I can't leave without warning my kin about the dangers that await them if they stay here.

"A little longer isn't going to make that much of a difference, either to the coming of the storms or the depletion of my formula. I'm doing as you want—I'm taking the Blood Gift. I'm not going to starve if I wait a while longer."

She snorted. "And, what good will it be if we wait around to warn these people, and then get caught in the open by the storms ourselves?"

"I'm not leaving here without speaking to my human kindred," he snapped, "I can't just abandon her—them here to die! I have to try to convince them to come with us."

Sagas stepped back a bit, surprised at his vehemence; his face was darkening like the clouds of the Sorins themselves. Before she could carry the argument further, Surrel stepped in, took the Kashallan by the arm, and led him away.

When they had disappeared into the tiny room that he shared with Pela and closed the door, Sagas sighed. What was she going to do with this stubborn, willful and totally frustrating creature? She had sworn to the Khutani that she would take care of him. He was making it unbearably difficult for her to keep her vow. But she could be just as stubborn and willful—and she would be, too.

Ah well, at least the destruction of that damned machine was a small blessing. In matters concerning his health, she would argue with him relentlessly. But among his other kin, she had felt hesitant and shy, unwilling to criticize the alien technology from the Chosen's home, in spite of her unease.

Like everyone else, Sagas had sat spellbound yesterday, watching the pictures on the alien machine. Seeing the images of the world from which the Dream-Chosen and his kindred came, both fascinated and terrified her.

Like the images the Maker had shown her in her dreams before Dunnagh was brought to the pools at Sulas, Sagas was awed by the power this alien race had under its control. She had remained sleepless for much of the night thinking about it.

Truly, it was as old Ima Nansa had told her more than once. Because of her people's failure, the Khutani had allied themselves with a powerful alien race that would change their world forever. And with such mighty and versatile companions now sworn to them, what need had the Khutani for the Avairei? Sagas thrust that horrible thought back into the shadows where it belonged.

Coming out of her reverie, she looked around her with a start. How long had she been standing here like a stone—had anyone noticed? In the large, rectangular room that made up the bulk of the barracks, the morning's activities were going on as usual.

The Loti were sweeping, and laying the mattresses and bedding in tall stacks along the walls for the day. Outside the far door, she could hear Ata Loran drilling his students in their lessons. Their melodic voices were a comforting reminder of normality in this alien place.

Everyone seemed to be trying very hard to ignore the growing tension by keeping busy, but Sagas caught the exchange of frightened glances now and then among the people still in the room.

Noticing Ata Temog and Ima Nansa sitting on the floor by the room's makeshift altar, watching her, Sagas crossed to them and sat down heavily beside them.

Temog gave her a sympathetic smile. "Have you been arguing with him again, Ima?"

Sagas scowled, glancing over her shoulder at a knot of the Chosen's kin, talking in low voices by the wall. "This place is very bad. The Sorins are coming. We should be leaving—"

"Never mind that for the moment," Nansa said. "Is he going to bring in another one of those horrible machines that show the pictures?"

"No," she said slowly. Nansa smiled, displaying her toothless gums. Sagas frowned, giving the old Ima a measuring look. "Nansa?"

The old woman cackled. "Well, you weren't going to do anything about it. I could see that, so I merely happened to wonder—out loud of course—where all those little people went when the box was turned off."

Temog chuckled. "And you just happened to do this wondering out loud where the Begta could hear you. Ima, truly, you are a sly one." He slapped his knee and chuckled again.

Nansa maintained an innocent expression, but her eyes were sparkling with mischief, "Why, Ata, I don't know who was listening. It's a big room; anyone could have heard me." Temog and the old Ima laughed companionably.

Then, noticing Sagas's shocked face, Nansa's voice took on a note of exasperation, "And what's wrong with you, child? You look like you just sat in a puddle of pee."

Sagas blinked. "That was a very dangerous thing to do," she hissed, glancing over her shoulder once more. "He could have—"

"Be quiet, girl," Nansa snapped. "He might *have to* become angry if his hunting pack hear you and complain.

"I saw the Chosen's face last night—he didn't like those things being shown any more than we did. And you said yourself he wasn't going to get another one—so just forget it."

Sagas pushed back her braidlets, letting out a heavy sigh. "I wish our other problems could be solved so easily."

"What do you mean?" Temog asked, becoming serious again.

She glanced over at the small altar, saying a silent prayer. "What I have said before, and will say again and again till he hears me. His formula won't last forever, even with the blood gift as a supplement. We need to get out of here."

"Sagas," Nansa said, "you're a good enough breeder to know that we can't leave without trying to take some of these others with us. The Chosen may be staying out of sentiment, but the Khutani would know that, if there are to be future generations of hosts for its kind, these people must have a large enough population from which to breed. We need them."

Sagas snorted, her braidlets jangling with her agitation. "If they are too foolish to arrange this meeting and leave with us, then they are too stupid to breed anyway. So what's the point?"

"Sagas, please," Temog begged, "just give him a little more time."

Sagas scowled, then relented. She would wait, but in her heart she prayed that the Mother would protect them, for she still had a bad feeling about all these delays.

Chapter Fourteen

Bennett groaned, his stomach spasming once again. Someone held out a basin and repositioned his head, so that the stream of acrid liquid he was vomiting hit its intended target. A strong arm held him steady until the spasms passed, then laid him back upon the cot and covered him with a light blanket. When he recovered enough to talk, he stammered, "T-thank y-you, I-Ian."

Lifting one of the doctor's trembling hands out from under the covers, Williams, the Lann Gheal medic, took his pulse. When he was finished, he asked, "Bad this time, sir?"

Bennett nodded. Right now, he felt so ill, he wished he could just roll over and die. Every muscle and bone in his body ached, and he knew, in spite of all his cheerful assurances to his frightened companions, that he was getting worse, not better.

They all were.

"What was my pulse?"

"Same as before, sir."

Bennett sighed and turned away. In a moment he heard Williams move off to check on another of his patients. He lay perfectly still, knowing by now that any movement on his part could set off the vomiting again. He felt so helpless.

The great doctor Bennett—ha! If my enemies could see me now, they would all have a good laugh.

With nothing to do but lie on the sickbay cot and brood, Bennett felt the pressures of his position and his self-imposed responsibilities crushing the life out of him. He had to get out of this bed. Too many people were counting on him. The longer he lay here, the more things would fall apart.

Meldra Arishim couldn't control her aide Sadrew by herself—that was becoming all too clear. Thank God that Tizu was not sick again. If he were to contract the virus while Bennett was still ill...

The stress of their confinement was making Sadrew insane. He was becoming a real threat to the stability of the base, in Bennett's opinion. But if the aide wasn't careful, Tizu would kill him someday. And the idiot didn't even seem to be aware of his danger.

Born and raised on pampered, politically liberal, and non-violent Dymar, Sadrew had no conception of what kind of trouble he was courting by baiting the Lann Gheal Commander. Used to the verbal bullying of Dymarian politics, he believed that his family and his position would protect him no matter what he said.

The aide seemed to dismiss the idea that there were men in the galaxy who would actually follow through with physical violence when verbally attacked. It was a wonder that he was still alive.

So far, Bennett had managed to restrain or cajole both combatants into keeping their thrusts only verbal, but how long would that last if he remained in this bed for any length of time? He had no idea, and didn't want to consider it—he would just have to get better—and soon.

Now that his mind had climbed onto the treadmill of his worries, there were Kai and his bunch to think about. Williams had told him, reluctantly, when he'd pressed him, that the Unit Leader had been pestering Tizu for that promised meeting. He wasn't at all happy about the delay. That was another reason he needed to get on his feet.

Tension was growing between Kai's squad and the Lann Gheal who had remained at the base. Tizu would like to see them gone, but they couldn't let Kai leave—not yet, anyway. He was the only one who had information about this planet.

And in spite of himself, Bennett was starting to wonder if Kai, or some of the natives with him, could help him cure this terrible virus. It obviously had a cure, because none of them were sick. But if Kai was forced to leave, would they survive till the rescue ship arrived?

Sadrew, of course, was fanning the flames of that fire, as well, spying on D barracks, and demanding that Tizu get rid of them before everyone caught a plague again and died. He was stirring up trouble talking to the Dymarians and to disgruntled members of Lann Gheal.

But who knew—Sadrew might even be fool enough to try harassing Kai himself if something weren't done soon. Bennett wouldn't put it past him. But there, too, Sadrew didn't realize his peril. Crossing the red-haired Caldoni wasn't wise either—if he intended to stay alive.

Thinking of Kai made him wonder, not for the first time, what had happened to change the man and his band so much. How could they just go native like that? Even Tessa Farris and his protégé Philip, who both should have known better, had lost all sense of reason.

Why, Philip was wearing bone beads and primitive tattoos, like the rest of them. It was absurd. The man was in need of professional help, and Bennett would see that he got the best psychiatric care he could afford, when they got back to civilization. Until then, he would do the best he could, if Philip would let him, of course.

Singey was from the wealthiest, most educated class of galactic society. How could he just abandon everything for this primitive, backwater world? It made no sense. He was a promising young scientist with a bright future in front of him, not a half-barbaric Caldoni.

Bennett did appreciate the Caldoni as honorable fighters he could hire for his philanthropic projects. And he was curious about—some might even say obsessed with their culture and traditions. But he didn't really see them as his social or intellectual equals. Nor were they Philip's, or Tessa's, for that matter.

Commander Tizu was right; Kai was definitely putting on airs—but that didn't explain why people like Singey were letting him boss them around as if they were no different than the ignorant savages with whom they were traveling.

Bennett groaned, and held himself perfectly still. This worrying had almost triggered his vomiting reflex again. How he hated this! When the urge passed without incident, he relaxed with a grateful sigh and returned to contemplating his protégées.

Tessa, what was he going to do about Tessa? If she stayed here with Kai's bunch, how could he ever face her parents again? He had been furious with her for sneaking aboard his ship—even if she did have a grant to study the Caldoni. But when he finally discovered her, they'd been nearly to Dymar.

He hadn't wanted to turn back; there had been so much at stake. In hindsight he wished he had. This barbaric world was no place for a young society woman like Tessa.

Blithely she had boasted to him of her anthropological studies—but that was just it—they were nothing more than academic studies. She hadn't had any real field experience in primitive conditions.

Until now that is, he reminded himself. Was the woman cracking under the strain as well as Singey? She shouldn't be here, and he felt deeply responsible for her.

While they had been waiting for D barracks to be readied, Bennett had approached Tessa, and suggested that she return to the quarters she had previously shared with Gail. He had assumed after what she had gone through, she would prefer to be back among her own kind.

To his surprise, however, she had refused. And when he had kindly but firmly insisted that it wasn't proper for someone of her social standing to share a barracks with a bunch of wild Caldoni armachda and some local savages—she had laughed.

Tessa had laughed and laughed, until tears ran down her face. Then she began to cry. Before Bennett could say or do anything to help, Kai's Squad Leader was beside her, enfolding her in his arms. He glared at Bennett angrily, fixing him with those steely gray eyes of his, and told him quite forcefully to leave "his Tessa" alone.

Before things could get out-of-hand, a blond Caldoni woman and one of the four-footed natives came over and took Tessa away. When he turned back to the big Caldoni Squad Leader, more of Kai's men had joined him. They formed a solid wall against his intrusion.

Reluctantly Bennett decided to drop the matter before Tizu could get involved. The woman was of age, and if she wanted to have a Caldoni lover for a while, well, that was her business. When the rescue ship arrived, however, she would be leaving with him, and that was that.

Round and round his mind raced, and always there was another problem rising up to meet him. Bennett sighed. He was getting so tired. But he would just have to get himself out of this bed, no matter what.

Cracking open an eye, he peered around to see if Gail or anyone else was watching. Gail was talking to someone in the other room, and Williams? He was busy helping another patient in the far corner. Good. Reaching into the drawer in the nightstand beside his bed, Bennett pulled out a small vial of pills and took one. Trembling with the effort, he replaced the vial, and closed the drawer.

In a part of his mind, a small voice warned him that what he was doing was very dangerous. The medication he had just dosed himself with was slightly toxic and highly addictive.

It might enable him to be up and out of this bed by tomorrow, as he hoped, or it just might kill him instead. He was risking everything, but if Kai had the answers he needed—well, it would be worth it, even if he himself didn't survive to benefit from the cure.

Chapter Fifteen

Standing in the inner doorway, Tizu surveyed the sickbay with a jaundiced eye. The emergency facility consisted of two rows of cots lining the side walls with cabinets and a sink along the back. Less than half the beds were occupied at the moment, and that was a relief.

Was Bennett still in here?

Williams was helping one of the Dymarians puke into a basin. Watching made his own gorge begin to rise, so he quickly turned away. Scanning the room again, he searched for Bennett, and at last found him.

"Shit!" Tizu swore under his breath. The man looked as white as the sheet he lay upon. Feeling his own knot of worry tighten, he wondered what would happen if Bennett were to die. Damn it, he wouldn't think about that, not the way he was feeling today.

Suddenly he recognized the head of ash-blond hair in a bed nearby, and froze. Oh no, not Sairsa! His heart in his throat Tizu hurried over to the cot. How bad was it this time?

She didn't look sick only peacefully sleeping. Damp hair curling around her pale face, she lay with eyes closed, the blanket rising and falling with her slow even breathing. Beautiful, gentle, Sairsa. Damn Kai why did he have to come back—he didn't deserve such a flower.

Sairsa opened her green eyes. When she saw who it was, she smiled. "Hello, Hukiyo."

Reaching blindly for a chair behind him, Tizu snagged it and sat down. "Sairsa, I didn't realize you were sick again. How are you feeling?"

"Oh, it comes and goes. I didn't think I needed to be in here, but Gail said she couldn't be running back and forth to check on me, so I'd better stay here instead of in my own quarters." She made a face. "It seems so silly, but I was too tired to argue with her."

Reaching over, he took her hand, clasping it tightly and looking deep into her eyes. "It's not silly. You need to take care of yourself—need to get better." He squeezed her hand. "I don't know what I'd do if...

"Well, you just stay right here and do what Gail and Dr. Bennett say and you'll be fine."

"Thank you, Hukiyo, you've been very kind to me." She yawned. "I'm sorry. Gail just gave me something to make me sleep."

He released her hand. "It's all right. Go to sleep, and get well soon."

She nodded, her eyelids heavy. "Would you ask Dunnagh to come see me? I have to tell him..." Her voice faded out, and she was soon fast asleep, unaware of his continued presence beside her.

For a long time, Tizu just sat there, staring blindly into space, trying to control the mixture of jealousy, fear, and love that was threatening to overwhelm him. Damn Kai for leaving her here for him to fall in love with. And double damn him for coming back. But if she were to die—brave, lovely Sairsa...

With a muttered curse, he rose, and, catching sight of Williams over by the sink, washing out the basin, he walked over to him. Turning his back to the room, Tizu leaned against the counter and fixed his subordinate with dark, smoldering eyes.

Startled, Williams looked up. Turning off the water, he said, "Sorry, sir, I didn't see you come in."

"Never mind that," Tizu growled impatiently. "And keep your voice down. What I want to know is, how bad is Bennett?"

Still facing the sink, Williams murmured, "Bennett's pretty bad, I think, sir. He keeps denying it, but this attack is the worst he's had yet."

Tizu swore softly. If Bennett died... Thinking of Sairsa, he muttered, "And the rest of them in here—"

Williams shrugged. "It's hard for me to say, sir." He glanced over wistfully at the sleeping Bennett. "I'm not a doctor, but I'm doing the best I can," he muttered, "I just don't know."

Tizu started to get angry, then nodded. What was he getting mad at him for? Williams wasn't a doctor, and the man looked exhausted. If the medic didn't watch it, he'd be down with the virus next—and then what would they do?

Tizu lowered his voice even further, and said, "I know you're doing the best you can. I'm just worried, that's all. Look, Williams, you may not be a doctor, but I'm hoping you can help me out a little here.

"See, I'm starting to get sick again, and, with Bennett in the bed over there I can't afford to get sick too. So, I need some more of those pills—the ones Bennett gave me before."

Williams froze, then faced Tizu squarely and shook his head. "Commander, I told you the last time, that drug is very dangerous. I can't—"

"Look, Armachd," Tizu snarled, "I know what you told me, and I'll have to risk it. This base is falling apart, and just who do you think is going to take over around here if both me and Bennett are lying flat on our backs in here, hmm?

"Miss hoity-toity, let's-all-be-friends Dymarian Councilor Arishim? Or her shit-for-brains aide? Or maybe you would prefer our own tattooed, bone-bedecked, gone-native Unit Leader, hmm?

"Come on, which would you like? 'Cause if I'm not here, or Bennett, one of them is just exactly who you're going to be taking your orders from next. So what's it going to be?"

The medic studied his commander thoughtfully. Tizu could see he didn't like the idea of giving him the drug, but the alternatives didn't appeal to him either. At last he nodded, reached in the cupboard over the sink, and gave him what he'd asked for.

JUST OUTSIDE THE SICKBAY, Councilor Arishim hailed Tizu. She gave him a politician's smile, but Tizu saw the worry in her eyes. Catching sight of the cadaverously thin Sadrew coming up beside her, Tizu braced himself for more trouble. He was willing to maintain the brittle facade of courtesy if the Dymarians would do so as well.

"Commander, I was just coming to see Dr. Bennett," Arishim said. "Since you've just come from sickbay, I assume you know how he is. I thought I'd ask you, in case he was resting,"

"I didn't talk to him directly, Councilor, because he was asleep, but I did speak to my medic. He says that the doctor is doing fine, and should be back on his feet soon."

Sadrew snorted, but said nothing further when Arishim gave him a sharp look. "That's good to know. I'm anxious to hear what Unit Leader Kai and his people learned about this planet, so I hope we can have that meeting soon."

Tizu said something meaningless in agreement. Out of the corner of his eye he saw Sadrew roll his eyes and smirk at a few of his cronies who had wandered over to see the show. Tizu gave them a hard look, and they covered their mouths to hide their smiles.

Unaware of this little by-play, Arishim continued, "Commander, I know your Unit Leader has said he won't leave this primitive world, but surely, when he sees the rescue ship, he'll change his mind.

"I've always heard that the Caldoni were very clannish, so I can't believe he's truly serious about staying on this primitive world."

"I wouldn't care to comment on what Kai would or wouldn't do."

"Speaking of Kai, Commander," Sadrew interrupted, now that he had an audience, "We've been keeping an eye on him and his bunch of renegades. There's something strange going on over there in D barracks, and I don't like it. For the sake of the safety of the people on this base, it's time you got rid of him and his savages."

"Citizen Sadrew!" Arishim said. "We've been over this before, and I told you Dr. B has his reasons for not wanting Kai to leave yet. When the doctor is feeling up to it, we'll meet with the Unit Leader and his people, and then—"

"And I told you, Councilor, that we all could be dead by then. Kai and his bunch brought that virus back to the base. Now everybody's getting sick again. The man's a menace and I want him out of here—or dead."

Arishim gasped. "Jakis Sadrew! What are you saying? The virus has been here all along, and this talk about killing—"

"Oh, shut up, Meldra, you're ignoring the facts. Kai is trouble and I've had enough—"

"No, *I've* had enough," Tizu snarled, and, grabbed the startled aide by the collar and slammed him up against the sickbay wall. The force of the blow knocked Sadrew's head hard against the prefab siding, the sound echoing like a clap of thunder. Twisting the man's tunic collar firmly, Tizu waited for the aide's eyes to focus. When he saw that Sadrew was aware of him again, Tizu tightened his grip. "Now you keep a civil tongue in your head when addressing a lady, or I'll cut it out for you, understand?"

When he received a strangled agreement, Tizu continued, "Get this through your shit-for-brains head, Sadrew. I don't like Kai being back here any more than you do. But Bennett's right. We need to know more about this place if we're going to survive, and Kai's the one who has that information.

"So for now we play it the doctor's way—get it? If you're so worried about your precious carcass catching something—then stay away from D barracks, asshole."

Tizu gave him a feral grin, tightening his grip a little more. "And remember this too. If there's anybody needing to be killed, you're right up there at the top of *my* list, got that?"

Releasing the man, Tizu stepped back and looked around. Arishim stood, eyes wide, hand over her mouth. Behind her, the other Dymarians looked equally shocked and frightened.

At his back, he felt the presence of some of his armachda. They stood, grim-faced, hands near their side arms, eyeing Sadrew and his cronies with a feral intensity. *Good*, he thought. *This will give these people something to think about. Maybe now they'll stop playing their little games with me, and let me do my job.*

Chapter Sixteen

The Kashallan sat cross-legged in the yellow moss a few paces from the outer wall of D barracks. A couple of scrubby thorn bushes shielded him from the off-duty armachda in the tents beyond. Behind him in the barracks one of the Avairei chanted an ancient ballad to the accompaniment of a bone rattle and rhythmic clapping.

Interlacing his fingers, he raised his arms over his head, and stretched. Mm, that felt good. As he leaned back, he stole a quick look over his shoulder.

As he'd expected, a young Avairei priest and one of Tizu's guards were watching him. At least they weren't pestering him—so let them watch.

A few minutes ago, he had had enough. Storming out of D barracks, he had angrily told all of them to shut up and leave him alone for a while. If Sagas badgered him just once more to leave the plateau, he thought he might go crazy. He would go when his business here was finished—and not until then, damn her.

In spite of his other worries, he had to admit that it felt good to relax his constant vigilance, and let someone else do the guarding for a change. He trusted the Commander completely to keep the camp safe from the demons that still haunted his own nightmares.

Ah, trust—that was a whole other issue.

Tizu's armachda could watch and follow them all they wanted. None of his folk were planning a massacre—or anything else dangerous. The base personnel's suspicions would pass with time, Dunnagh kept telling himself, and he kept repeating that to his hunting pack, too.

"We've all changed. They don't know what happened to us—what we suffered. Give it time. they'll come round," he kept insisting.

The bone beads of their death strands, their new language skills and the tattoo-like brands, caused by the kavay alignment, all set them apart physically from other humans. But those changes were only the tip of the iceberg. There were other changes that they couldn't share with these "outsiders." Dark, haunting things that had left horrible unhealed wounds upon their souls.

He doubted if their former comrades could imagine what it had been like to live through a slavery in which the Warlinga of Tragar Keep had dined on them like animals. And, they would definitely be shocked if they knew about the cannibalistic Timornan funeral rites that he and his squad had adopted during their enslavement. And then there was Tani and his new vampiric diet to explain as well...

No, their secrets were best kept to themselves, at least for now. Someday, those humans who went through the alignment process and joined him would have to know, but, not right now when the atmosphere of fear and mistrust was so heavy in the air.

<<Kasha, stop it. Don't waste our time alone by brooding again,>> the symbiont complained. <<It frightens me when you do this—and there's no point. Think of something more pleasant.>>

Dunnagh stroked his middle. <<I'm sorry, Shalla, I didn't mean to upset you—and you're right there's no point to my brooding.>>

The Kashallan lay back, gazing up into the mauve sky. Yes, this was better—this felt good. No more dark musings. He had just fed recently. He allowed himself to feel delightfully lazy and very self-satisfied. He yawned. Maybe he would take a little nap right here in the sun.

But first, he wanted to see them—just once more. He was so proud of his new acquisitions. A smile curving his lips, he sat up with his back to the barracks, and placed his hands palms down on both knees. He stretched out the two middle fingers on each hand and extended his newly grown tentacles once again.

Would he ever get tired of looking at them? They were so beautiful. This morning was the first time he had been able to extend and retract them, and even though they were getting a little sore from overuse, he was still very excited.

The Kashallan ran one hand experimentally up his own smooth thigh. He shivered deliciously, as a wealth of undreamed-of sensory stimuli flooded his dual awareness. Under his kilt, he felt his sex begin to harden, and moaned softly with the thought of an unanticipated pleasure.

Tempting as that course of exploration was becoming, he glanced once more over his shoulder. He decided not to indulge in such a private pleasure at the moment. Instead he allowed his hands to slide down his leg and into the moss beside him. Here too was a treasure box of information available for the symbiont part of himself to study.

Becoming so absorbed in his examination of the moss, he was startled when Nathan spoke from just behind his shoulder.

"What are you doing?"

The Kashallan jerked erect, hastily retracting his tentacles before he brought his hands up from the moss. He smiled, and patted the ground beside him. "Come sit with me, Nathan. I want to show you something."

Nathan shrugged, than sat down cross-legged in front of him. Like the rest of his armachda, Nathan had gone back to wearing his old uniforms, minus the Lann Gheal insignia.

The Kashallan had not, however. He was still attired more or less as the Avairei chose to dress him. They had decked him out like one of their own high-ranking members, in kilt, cloak, and many of their own treasured necklaces and hair ornaments.

Nathan studied his friend carefully for a moment before reporting, "I have a message for you from Bennett."

"That's nice."

"Nice. Yeah, right." Nathan scratched his jaw looking bewildered. "Uh, you don't seem very excited; I thought you were anxious to here from the man, so we can get this meeting over with."

"Mm. I am excited."

"Could have fooled me. What's wrong with you today?"

"Nothing." The Kashallan dropped his eyes and went back to running his hands through the moss, a faint smile curving his lips.

"Hmm. I'm not sure if I really want to know this, but I'm going to ask anyway—what are you doing out here by yourself?"

The Kashallan tucked his hands under the folds of his kilt. "I'm hiding."

Nathan sighed. "All right, I'll play, what—or should I say who, are you hiding from?"

The Kashallan laughed. "Mostly from Sagas and her nagging, but really I just needed some peace and quiet away from all of them for a while." Nathan started to rise, but the Kashallan stopped him. "No, don't go, your company is most welcome. If Bennett's message isn't urgent, tell me later, all right? I don't want to spoil my hard-won peace by thinking about our problems for a while. And I do want to show you something."

"The message can wait a bit. Uh, Dunnagh, I'm not sure I like that mischievous gleam in those big blue eyes of yours. Do I really want to see this—whatever it is?"

"It's mostly Tani you're talking to right now, Nathan, though Dunnagh is hearing what I'm saying to you, and you to me. I don't know if you want to see, but please, Nathan, let me show you anyway. My Kasha and I want you to be the first one to see them—we are so excited."

NATHAN SUPPRESSED A shiver. Would he ever get used to this? It was so unsettling, never even knowing who he was talking to. Damn, he hated this. No matter how hard he tried for Dunnagh's sake, he still felt uncomfortable talking directly to the symbiont.

Taking a deep breath he said," All right, Tani, if you and Dunnagh are that insistent, I guess you should show me whatever it is that's more important than my message from Bennett. I'm—uh—honored that you want me to be the first one to see this, whatever it is. Should I be impressed?"

"Oh yes, see?" He held out his hands and extended his new pink tentacles. His blue eyes eager, he studied Nathan's expression. When Nathan didn't respond Dunnagh's face crumpled—like a child ready to cry. "You're not impressed," Tani said, "I was hoping you would like them too."

Seeing that expectant child-like expression on his old friend's face stabbed Nathan to the heart. Gods! Not for the first time since all this began did Nathan feel torn almost in two by his conflicting emotions.

Taking a deep breath, he said, "Ah, Tani, I'm not impressed yet, because I'm not exactly sure what I'm looking at. If you explain, then I'll probably be more enthusiastic."

"Oh. Well, what you're seeing is our new tentacles. This morning was the first time we've been able to extend and retract them." To demonstrate the Kashallan retracted and extended them again. "See?"

"Mm. I see. That is quite impressive, I got to admit, but—uh—what do you plan to do with them?"

The Kashallan gave him a long-suffering look. "Why, taste with them, of course. What else, silly?"

"Taste, hmm. Care to explain that a little further?"

Tani made an exasperated sound in Dunnagh's throat, then the Kashallan closed his eyes. When he opened them again, Tani said, "I'm sorry, Nathan. Dunnagh has just reminded me that there is nothing like this on your home world, and so of course you wouldn't know about how we plan to use them.

"With these," he held up a hand and extended the pink appendages once more, "I can make direct contact with the world outside my Kasha's body. Mostly I will use them for diagnosing and treating my patients when I'm healing, but I can also use them to find out other information about the world around me. Do you understand better now?"

Nathan nodded. "I think I do. And you're right, I am suitably impressed."

"Oh good, that's very good. Knowing the love Dunnagh has for you, I have wanted to do this for such a long time. Let me have your hand now, so I can taste you for myself."

As the Kashallan reached for a hand, Nathan barked a nervous laugh and thrust his hands behind his back. "Oh no you don't, your Snakiness, no way. As Dunnagh can tell you, I have this thing about pain—I don't like it!"

"Oh, don't be such a big baby about this. I'm not going to hurt you. Come on, Nathan, please," it coaxed, "Give me your hand!"

Nathan hesitated, not sure what to expect, and definitely not sure he wanted to find out.

"Please?" Tani begged, fixing him with Dunnagh's sorrowful blue-eyed stare.

"Oh, all right, if it's that important." He held out his hand palm up.

"Not like that. Turn your hand over, palm downward." Nathan reversed it, then held out his hand again. Tentacles extended, the Kashallan wrapped his own hand, palm down, over the back of Nathan's and curled his two elongated middle fingers around the big man's wrist. Filaments from the sensitive tips of those newly acquired organs sank into his friend's flesh.

The link was formed for the first time in living memory.

"Hey! You said this wasn't going to hurt."

"Sorry, I'm just learning how to do this." As Nathan continued to scowl, the symbiont said, "Oh, come on, it didn't hurt that much—just a little pinprick. Dunnagh says it isn't any worse than the vaccination needles you two used to get at school, whatever that means."

"Hah! Well, ask him how much I used to like those needles, why don't you, hmm?"

"He says you were a big cry baby about them."

"I was not!" Nathan protested indignantly. "Dunnagh, I was not!" The Kashallan only smiled. "I was not," he grumbled under his breath, then, "Well, not all the time anyway. Besides, Dunnagh, you cried, too, sometimes over nothing.

"And as long as we're going to dig up old skeletons from our childhood, don't forget to tell your bondmate about the time Shivon Ru'a made you eat her mud cakes, or that time when you were plugged up, and your ma took you to the old Gran and she made you drink—"

Tani laughed.

"All right, all right, Nathan, you've made your point," Dunnagh said, still chuckling. "I'll tell my Shalla later. Now shut up and let us taste you."

Nathan grunted. "You'd better, or I will—"

"Nathan."

He shut up. The Kashallan closed his eyes, and sank deeper into the link. Nathan gazed at his well-loved features, recalling for a time pleasant memories they'd shared as children.

Then he happened to look down and saw his hand, resting against Dunnagh's thigh, with those so-alien tentacles jabbed into the veins of his arm. Nathan's stomach lurched and he looked away.

Beyond the camp with its familiar human sights and noise, lay the thorn bush and moss-covered mesa. Still farther off he could see the tawny peaks of the Rim Wall Mountains. Alien. This world looked nothing like Caldon—nothing like home.

Suddenly he felt so lonely, frightened and confused. Oh, Dunnagh, what have you done to yourself—and to me?

Unable to stand it anymore, he turned back to his companion and blurted, "Well, what do I taste like? Beefsteak, colcannon, pizza, what?"

The Kashallan opened his eyes, and grinned. "How about kavay."

Nathan snorted. "Figures."

The Kashallan gave a short bark of a laugh, then sobered again. "Seriously, Nathan, it's not like that," Tani said. "I use the word 'taste' because I can't think of any other word to use, but it's different from what you mean by taste. It's more like—a knowing. I know a thing, but I do it by tasting its different flavors." Tani sighed. "You are confused, I know, but I don't know how else to explain, I'm sorry."

"All right, so when you do this to somebody, what do you learn? What do you know about me now, that you didn't a few minutes ago?"

The Kashallan looked away, suddenly unwilling to meet Nathan's eyes. "Tani, what did you taste?"

At last, taking a ragged breath, Tani said very softly, "I didn't know it would be like this—so intense, I mean. I don't know if I want to tell you, or if I even should."

"Oh no you don't, Your Snakiness. You started this, and I want to know—so out with it."

"All right, so be it. The most dominant flavor I savor, is your deep, long-lasting love for Dunnagh, of course. But at the moment that love is spiced with the many worries you hold all knotted up inside you.

"And, I can also savor your confused feeling towards me. I taste your fear, and your anger, and your loneliness, because you're afraid I've taken Dunnagh away from you forever. Though that last isn't true, you know. I would never do that."

Ouch! This was cutting too deep for comfort, Nathan decided, sorry now that he had pressed the issue. Feeling very uncomfortable, he shook his head in denial and tried to pull back his hand, but the Kashallan only gripped it tighter.

"No, Nathan, you pushed this, so let's finish it. Don't pull away and don't try to lie to me, because you can't, not when we're linked like this. With a lie, your taste changes, I would always know. And I in turn, won't lie to you, either. I'm not surprised by what I taste in you, but it does hurt—a little—no, more than a little. Because Dunnagh's feelings for you are so strong, I have learned to care for you, too."

Nathan rubbed his free hand across his face. Gods, this was so terrible. Aware that the symbiont was still reading his feelings, if not his thoughts, he said, "I'm so sorry, Tani. I don't want to hurt you, but it's hard for me. It's going to take time for me to get used to this bond thing.

"Dunnagh and me—we've been so close, for so many years—ever since our childhood together. And now there's you. It feels sometimes like an eavesdropper, some stranger I hardly know, is always there listening in on what we say to each other. We're never alone, and it's hard for me to get used to that."

"Alone? I've observed that humans spend a lot of energy wanting to be alone, and then when you are, you complain about being lonely."

Nathan blinked. That was a very profound and painfully accurate statement. Just another one of those disconcerting ambiguities that came with this bond thing. In actual age the symbiont was a child, but as Dunnagh had explained to him, Tani also had the encoded memories of its elders to draw upon as well.

"As much as you might want it to be otherwise, our sharing is part of the nature of the Kashallan bond. We share the same senses. I see and hear through Dunnagh's eyes and ears. And he can taste and touch through my tentacles, and some other adaptations I have made to him."

"I'm not asking you to stop what I know you can't change," Nathan said. "I'm just saying that sometimes it's difficult for me. I've got no other experience to draw upon to make it easier, and it's so—."

"Alien," Tani supplied.

"Yeah."

"I'm not sure if you have ever considered this, but it's not always easy for us, either, you know. We have to get used to this kashallan bond, too. And, personally, I find humans very confusing."

Surprised, Nathan blinked, his mouth dropping open. Tani chuckled. "Hadn't thought of that, eh? Well, it's true. Dunnagh and I are learning to adjust and compromise with one another, too. I think it will take time for all of us to adjust. Will you give me that time and be my friend, too, Nathan?"

Tani released his hand, breaking the link. He thought about it for a while, then said, "I'll try, yes. For Dunnagh's sake—and for yours, I'll try."

"Thank you." Tani gazed with adoring admiration at Nathan's sensuous mouth, his clear gray eyes, and his long brown hair framing his rugged features. The Kashallan reached out a trembling hand, and with tentacle tips slightly extended, he traced the lines of Nathan's face.

"I'm so glad, we can share so much love—all of us," it whispered. Tani cupped that well-loved face between Dunnagh's palms, bent forward, and gave Nathan a deep, lingering kiss.

Startled Nathan froze, then he found himself surrendering to the other's will and returned the kiss in kind.

Oh, Dunnagh, don't—please don't—stop...

At last the Kashallan released him. Sitting back, with one hand still caressing Nathan's cheek, he stared deep into his old lover's eyes. Trembling, Nathan reached up and removed the hand from his face. "Don't do this to me," he breathed. "Oh, Gods, Tani, Dunnagh, please, don't do this to me."

"But why, Nathan?" Tani pleaded. "I think I love you too, and you and my Kasha used to—"

"That was a long time ago—in the distant past," Nathan said in a strangled voice. "We were—things are different now."

"But, you still want us. I know, I tasted it in you. We all want—"

"Oh Gods, no!" Nathan shook his head, but that kiss had opened up something he had thought safely hidden away deep inside him. Damn the symbiont, how had it known? "Please, Tani. Just let it be."

Nathan stood up. Chest heaving, he stared down at the Kashallan, wanting to run, but unable to move. Dunnagh's beloved face stared up at him, anguish and confusion looking out at him from teary blue eyes.

"I'm sorry," Tani whispered. "I don't want to hurt you, I love—"

Nathan groaned. "Oh, shit, don't look at me like that, damn it."

"Like what?"

"Like that! Ever since we were small, when you look at me like that, Dunnagh, I feel so—" Nathan groped for words. "Oh, Gods—" His voice trailed off in confusion.

"Maybe I can help you," Tani offered. "Half the time my Kasha doesn't understand what he's feeling, either, so I have to help him. If you give me your hand again, I could—"

Nathan let out a strangled sound, somewhere between a laugh and a sob. "Oh, Gods—no." He began to laugh hysterically, tears streaming down his face. When he finally got control of himself enough to talk, he said, "Oh, Tani, just leave it be, all right? Thanks, but I don't want you to help me, not right now."

The symbiont sighed heavily, then said, half to itself, half to its two human companions, "Sometimes I wonder if I will ever understand humans."

"Probably not," the two humans chorused almost in unison.

At that moment a hail from one of their Lann Gheal guards over by the barracks brought the Kashallan to his feet.

Nathan glanced around them, the sun was sinking behind the barracks wall. It was getting late. "That's probably our escort. I was coming to tell you that Bennett had set up that meeting we've been waiting on. He said he would send someone for us when it was time."

Chapter Seventeen

When the Kashallan and the Timornans arrived at HQ, they found to their chagrin that the talk included dinner as well. It was the kind of event that Bennett was famous for throughout the galaxy. A nice relaxed get-together where, over drinks and dinner, peoples from different races and cultures could mingle informally and discuss their problems.

Secretly amused, Dunnagh supposed that they should feel pleased. He and his people were being treated by the good doctor as if they were ranking Timornan dignitaries, rather than the ragtag bunch of hounded outlaws that they really were.

Knowing that Bennett was trying to honor him didn't make the prospect of the coming meal any less daunting. Dunnagh discreetly sent Temog back to their barracks for a small flask of the thick, blue kavay that the Begta had been bringing up to them from the canyons.

Though his people had been forced to draw on the base's stores of food and other necessities, they had been taking their meals in the privacy of D barracks. No one at camp was yet aware of the liberal doses of kavay they had to consume with each meal to make the food edible. But the people on the base would know soon enough if they planned to survive on this world.

While they waited outside the mess hall for the priest's return, he noticed Sagas staring off to the west. Stepping to her side, he asked, "What's wrong?"

For answer, she pointed to a dark line of roiling clouds near the far horizon. Narrowing his eyes he looked in that direction and felt a shiver run down his spine. "Is that a Sorin storm coming already?"

"No, Kashallan, it is only a rainstorm—this time. But this means that the Sorins won't be long in coming." She turned to him, a desperate look coming into her eyes as she struggled to convey her urgency to him. "Now do you understand why I want us to leave this place? We must be out of this high country before they hit. We may die or suffer the mutations as the Umwira do. Do you want that?"

He shivered again. No, to suffer that kind of mutation was not a fate he wished to contemplate. "How much time do we have?"

"As to how long we have—I can't say exactly; it varies from year to year. The rains come first; the storms can be quite violent, and very dangerous. When they stop, the air will dry out very suddenly as the winds shift to blow out of the dead lands to the north, then... "

"I see." He studied the horizon more closely. The storm was some way off, but it was coming fast. If those flashes of green and purple fire lighting up the massing clouds were any indication, it was going to be a rough one.

"I know we need to be away from here—and we will go soon—but do you know if we will be safe in the Swamps if the Sorins find us before we reach Ticca?"

"You will have to ask your pet Begta that question. I don't know. The little ones never come to the keeps during the storms, so they must have ways of keeping themselves alive. But do you really want to spend the storm season down in a stinking Begta warren?"

"Not particularly."

"Then you had better start thinking of getting out of here soon, or that is exactly what we will be doing."

"Unit Leader, is something wrong?" Turning, he saw a smiling Bennett was hurrying over to them.

Dunnagh indicated the far horizon. "The Ima here was just pointing out to me that the seasonal rains are coming. I suggest the Commander have his people secure the base. That front looks bad."

Bennett looked where Dunnagh pointed and frowned. "Ye-es," he agreed, "I think you may be right."

Joining them at that moment, Tizu saw where they were looking. He nodded then loped off, bawling his orders as he went.

"Ah, Unit Leader, I see that fellow of yours has returned. Shall we go in?" Bennett invited.

PELA WRUNG HER HANDS in frustration; this was not good, not good at all. The Great Mother Goddess had bidden her find and take care of Sairsa and her unborn child. She wanted desperately to go to her sister-wife, but there had been no way to do so before now. No one would risk the Kashallan's anger and help her.

Pela had been near the front of the group when they first arrived on the base. She had seen her sister-wife then. Sairsa came running up, all excited. The Kashallan called her by name, but then things went all wrong, and Pela didn't understand. Why hadn't Sairsa come to them. This morning when she awoke, she knew that she must go to the alien woman soon, or something very bad was going to happen.

Temog and Ima Sagas had gone with the Kashallan this evening. She must take this unwatched opportunity to search for her, but the base was a frightening place to Pela. In order to find her sister-wife, she would have to take one of the Kashallan's hunting pack with her.

And that was where the difficulty lay.

A storm was coming; she could hear the wind rattling the doors and windows of the big drafty room. Pela glanced surreptitiously around her. Most everyone had come inside to get out of the weather. The place was crowded, and reeked with the smells of alien chemicals, incense, and musky fur.

People sat around in small groups on mattresses, talking and working on craft projects. By the altar in the far corner Ima Surrel and several of the senior Avairei were kneeling in prayer.

Good. No one was paying her any attention. It was time. But who could she ask? Most of the Kashallan's hunting pack and some of the Begta were huddled together in a corner playing a bone game. Their shouted curses and boisterous laughter caused her to smile. If Ima Sagas was here they wouldn't dare be so noisy. Should she go over there and ask one of them to help her? Hmm...

San Oglas was sitting by himself, sharpening one of his blades for the hundredth time today. He looked bored. He was very friendly to her and the other Avairei; he would help her this time—he must.

As she approached, Oglas looked up and smiled. "Ah, 'tis yourself, is it? And what can I be doing for you, My Lady?"

Trying to copy one of Sagas's famous stern looks, she said, "San Oglas, I need to go find Sairsa. You must help me."

He sighed and picked up his whetstone again. "I can't, and I told you that, the last time you asked me. The Ce'awn wouldn't like me interfering in his business like that. I won't do it. And besides, there are guards out there, who won't take kindly to us wandering around by ourselves."

"The storm has driven the guards inside."

"The answer is still no. I'm sorry."

Pela stamped her foot and growled in frustration. "No, you will take me, or I'll go by myself. This is not man business, or Kashallan business. This is sister-wife business. I *must* go to her."

Saying nothing further he shook his head, then went back to his work. Pela remained where she was, determined not to be put off this time. Finally he said in a gentle voice, "I can see that this is important to you, but I don't understand why it is. Most women that I know wouldn't want to meet their man's old lover—"

"But, it's not like that for us, San Oglas. Sairsa is my breeding sister-wife," Pela insisted. "I am carrying the Kashallan's child, she is carrying Dunnagh's child; we are sister-wives. Sairsa needs me. She is all alone and in great danger. My Goddess has told me that I must go to her—

"Please, San Oglas, you must come with me. She and the baby will die if I don't help her. I must find her!"

In mid stroke, Oglas's hand froze. Putting down his blade and stone, he gave her a searching look. "Does Dunnagh know about the baby?"

"I-I don't think so."

"Then, how—"

Pela impatiently stamped her foot again, cutting him off. "I just told you. My Goddess sent me the warning in a dream. I must go to my Sairsa—please believe me."

Oglas shuddered and made a hand sign that Pela had been told his people used to ward off evil. "Your Goddess told you about the baby and Sairsa needing help?"

"Yes."

"I don't understand. If this is true why haven't you told the Ce'awn?"

"I tried, but the holy symbiont has forbidden me to speak of Sairsa, because my talk upsets its chosen host." Pela looked at him with pleading brown eyes. "Please, San Oglas, our Sairsa will die. She needs the Kashallan's help."

Oglas hesitated a moment longer then stood, replacing the knife in the sheath at his hip. "All right, My Lady, don't worry. We'll find her."

Outside, a blast of cold wind hit them full in the face as they rounded the corner of the barracks. They heard an ominous roll of thunder, and several flashes of green lightning split the darkening sky to the west. Pela shivered, wrapping her cloak more tightly around her shoulders. This storm was going to be a bad one. Then she whispered a little prayer to the Mother, to keep them all safe and to let her find Sairsa.

Chapter Eighteen

Still hugging the wall of D barracks, Oglas scanned the quadrangle to see if they'd been noticed. All the Commander's men were fully occupied with the task of securing the base. No one was paying any attention to them for once.

That was a good sign. Bending close to the priestess, he shouted over the rising wind, "Did that Goddess you've been talking to give you any idea where to find this sister-wife of yours?"

Pela made a negative gesture with her hand.

Figures, Oglas thought. Isn't that always the way with the Gods. They give you only enough information to serve their purpose, but not enough to make it easy to carry out their commands.

Where might Sairsa be? Assuming she wasn't in that meeting with all the camp leaders, she would probably be in her quarters, the sickbay—or somewhere else out of this wind.

She could be almost anywhere, but a good place to get some information was the sickbay. They would try there first. Someone was always supposed to be on duty there, so if Sairsa wasn't around at the moment, whoever was on duty could probably direct them to where her quarters were.

A plan of action in mind now, he took Pela's hand and they headed in that direction, bracing themselves against the rising wind.

THIS WAS AWFUL! NATHAN stared glumly down at his plate. They were sitting at a long table in a partitioned off area of the larger mess hall. Beyond the barrier he could hear the sounds of quiet talk and clinking cutlery as the Dymarians and off duty armachda ate their own meals.

All during their captivity, he had tormented himself with thoughts of the wonderful meals he would enjoy when they escaped and got back to the ship. He had big plans. He would gorge himself on big juicy steaks, colcannon, oatcakes fresh out of the oven and dripping with melted butter, tender, flaky apple pie and ice cream—all his old favorites.

And now here he was, with one of those dream meals set out before him—and, damn it, it tasted like sawdust in his mouth. It wasn't fair. By all the Gods, it just wasn't fair. He raised the forkful of steak to his mouth, then set it back on his plate again, swearing under his breath.

Glancing up he caught the Kashallan watching him. "What's the matter, Mo Hara, doesn't it taste good?"

Nathan made a face. "It's not fair, damn it, it's not fair!"

The Kashallan's mouth twitched. "I know what you mean. Before I acquired my interesting new dining habits, the host part of me also had such fantasies. It's the kavay alignment, you know. It changes how everything tastes."

"I figured it was something like that, but it still isn't fair," he grumbled.

The Kashallan handed him the flask of kavay. Frowning, he took it, then looked around furtively to see if anyone was watching. And, just his luck, he saw Tizu staring right at them.

"Shit." Nathan sighed and started to hand the bottle back, then decided, what did he care if Tizu watched. Everybody on the base would be craving blue puke juice soon enough.

Taking the top off the flask, he poured a generous portion of the thick blue liquid over his food and resumed eating. Hmm, it did taste better. Tizu stared, obviously revolted at the blue sticky mess on his plate. Nathan grinned. "It's a local native sauce. It's quite delicious—and addicting, once you get introduced to it."

Tizu made a face, then turned and glared at Dunnagh. "I see you're not eating. Camp rations not good enough for you anymore?"

Keeping his voice even The Kashallan said, "I'm sure the food is fine, but I'm restricted to a liquid diet, for the present."

Tizu snorted. "On a diet, eh? Yes, I've noticed that in your role as leader of this merry little band, you're the only one who seems to have put on weight."

Nathan froze, his fork halfway to his mouth. Oh shit! Dunnagh's face had taken on that white-lipped, blank expression he got when he was really, really angry. Gods, what was wrong with Tizu anyway? Ever since their return, Tizu had been giving Dunnagh hostile looks—and being a real pain in the ass. Something was obviously bothering the man, but Nathan hadn't a clue what it could be.

Tizu's insult had not gone unnoticed by others at the table; a shocked silence followed his outburst. Dunnagh closed his eyes and took several deep breaths. He was probably trying to talk Tani out of some murderous idea, no doubt.

When the Kashallan opened his eyes, he said in a cold, dangerous voice, "Commander, my dietary restrictions, or the reasons for them, are none of your concern. But that isn't the point here, is it? If you have a problem that you need to discuss with me, let's deal with it later. Now is hardly the appropriate time or place to be trading insults—or worse."

Tizu's swarthy face reddened. He glanced around, saw Bennett's shocked expression and dropped his eyes. A moment later he sighed, and met the Kashallan's eye. "You're right, Kai, this isn't the time, and I do owe you an apology. That remark wasn't called for."

The Kashallan gave him a stiff nod of acceptance and Nathan popped the piece of stake in his mouth.

Chapter Nineteen

"Good evening, I'm Gail Pointe, Dr. Bennett's assistant. The doctor isn't here right now, so unless it's urgent, I would suggest you come back tomorrow."

Oglas hesitated in the shadows just inside the door, getting his bearings. Sickbay seemed deserted except for the woman in white reading at a desk near the far wall. The woman was trying to hide it, but she was obviously frightened—but of what—them?

Damn! His jaw tightened as his temper ignited. What did she think they were going to do to her? What kind of lies had Bennett or Tizu been telling to make this woman react so unfavorably, just because they came inside her door? He growled a curse under his breath.

A soft touch on his arm reminded him of their reason for coming.

Realizing they were making things worse by huddling over here in the darkness where the nurse couldn't see them clearly, he took his companion's arm and stepped boldly into the light near the reception desk.

With what he hoped was a friendly expression plastered across his face, he drawled in his thickest Caldoni accent, "And a good day ta ya, Missus. It be a powerful storm a-comin' in out there, and right col', ta be shoor."

"Yes it is. As I told you, the doctor isn't here. Come back tomorrow."

A small man with sparkling green eyes and freckles, Oglas gave her a boyish smile. "I thank ya, but it not be the good doctor we be a-needin' at the moment. Ya see, this fine lady and me, we be a-lookin' fer a kinswoman o' mine. We be a-hopin' you kin help us ta be a-findin' her. One Sairsa Basheya be who we want. Do ya be a-knowin' wheer we kin fine her?"

Gail gave him a hard look. "What did you say your name was?"

"I didn't, sorry, Missus, an oversight on my part. I be Shemu Oglas at your service, Missus," and he gave her a theatrical bow.

"Hmm. As it happens, I know Sairsa quite well. She went to university with my younger sister. I don't recall her ever mentioning a Shemu Oglas, or any Oglas at all. What would you like to speak to her about, hmm?"

Oh shit! Just my luck to meet up with an old friend of the family, Oglas thought. Ah well, I've gone this far, might as well play it out. "Well now, ya see, I'm her father's mother's sister's boy twice removed," Oglas invented hastily. "Sairsa and me, we be close, to be shoor. I know she'll want ta be seein' me. And as ta why I'm a-wantin' ta see her—well, it's kinda parsonal-like. Family stuff, don'cha know. So if ya would please ta tell us wheer ta fine her, we be most grateful."

Outside, a gust of wind slammed into the building, making the doors and windows rattle. A flash of green lightning lit up the interior of the room, followed almost immediately by a booming clap of thunder. The woman shuddered, the frightened look coming back into her eyes.

Oglas saw the expression and could guess at some of the wild fancies rolling around in her head. Her terror was almost thick enough to cut with a knife, and the storm outside wasn't making his job any easier.

Did she think he'd been sent to kidnap Sairsa while everyone was in the meeting? Probably. By all the gods, this was terrible! The woman obviously knew where to find Sairsa—but how to make her tell them without scaring her further?

"Please, Missus, we'er not gonta hurt nobody—we just wan ta talk—"

Gail closed her book with a snap and stood up. "I'm sorry the doctor doesn't want me giving out information about our patients. Please leave."

"Patient! Is she sick then?"

Gail shook her head. "I'm not at liberty to give out that information. You must go now."

Then a sleepy voice from the inner doorway made them all turn in that direction. "Gail? What's going on?" a drowsy voice asked.

"Go back to bed, honey. Dr. B told you to rest, remember?" She gave the intruders a hostile glare. "These people were just leaving."

At that moment another flash of green lightning lit up a row of cots in the room behind the swaying figure in the doorway. The thunder rumbled, and she caught hold of the doorframe for support.

She blinked, then pronouncing her words carefully, she said, "I know Dr. B told me to rest, but I heard s-somebody calling my n-name out here and—I"

With a startled cry Pela threw off her cloak and crossed to her, taking her hand. "Sairsa—sister what is wrong?"

Gail made a move to stop her, but Oglas was beside her then, all pretenses gone. He put a restraining hand on her arm and shook his head. "Let it be, Missus, the lass isn't going to hurt her; no need to be afraid."

But she was afraid. Staring into his eyes, she began to tremble. Oglas's jaw tightened. Gripping her arm firmly, he led her over to her chair behind the desk and set her in it. With his hand still on her arm, he positioned himself to keep an eye on both Gail and the two standing in the inner doorway.

Bending close to her ear, he murmured in a low voice, "Now, it's like I been try'in' to tell ya, Nurse Gail, me and the lady here don't mean you or Sairsa any harm, so just sit quiet-like, and don't make me do anything that either of us may regret later."

Sairsa looked down at the slim, furred woman with the ornamented braidlets. "Hullo. You're one of Dunnagh's people, aren't you?" She gave her a sleepy smile. "Did he send you to get me—"

Sairsa broke off clutched her stomach and doubled over. Pela caught her before she could fall. When the spasm passed, Sairsa leaned heavily against her, and Pela helped her back inside the other room.

Noticing the unmade cot in the row closest to the door, Pela laid her down upon it, and anxiously looked into the woman's unfocussed eyes. Lifting Sairsa's cold hand, she felt her pulse. It was rapid, and uneven. Next Pela opened her gown and placed a hand over Sairsa's lower belly. Pela hissed. The rounded mound felt hard, and contracted under her touch. The child was in danger, and the mother too, if she was any judge.

She was about to close up the gown when her eye caught the curve of a faint purple line. A Kavay brand, was that possible? She pulled aside the garment again exposing the whole of the woman's creamy torso. Sairsa moaned and tried to pull the gown closed.

Pela grabbed her hand and crooned to her in a soothing sing-song while she studied the marks more closely. Yes, they were kavay brands—she was sure of it. She'd seen them many times before. Like Dunnagh, this woman's skin was sort of pink in color. The brands were just beginning to manifest, a vivid blue against her paleness.

Sairsa was going through the kavay alignment process, but in this case there was something badly wrong.

Leaving the sick woman for the moment, Pela returned to the doorway. "San Oglas, I think my sister-wife is going through the kavay alignment process. But these ignorant people have done something to her. She is very sick and the child is in danger. You must get our husband."

Taking the nurse by the arm, Oglas followed Pela back into the sick room and sat Gail down in a chair away from the door. Affecting a dangerous tone of voice he said, "Now you just stay where I put you, Nurse Gail, don't make me have to chase you."

Keeping an eye on her, he moved closer to Sairsa's cot and glanced down at the sick woman. Pela pointed to the emerging kavay brands. Oglas took a good look and swore.

He pulled the blanket up over Sairsa and rounded on the nurse. "You stupid, ignorant fools! Why didn't you come tell us about this?" the nurse cringed, her eyes rounding in fright. Pela put a hand on his arm and he subsided. "You're right; there's no point in yelling at her. I'll get him, My Lady, don't worry. My Ce'awn or Ata Temog will know what to do for her."

Then he paused, another thought coming to mind. "Lady, if I am to go, I will have to leave you alone with this woman—" He jerked his head towards the frightened Gail huddled upon the chair.

"It doesn't matter, go! I will be all right. She will not touch my Sairsa; if she tries—" Pela bared her sharp teeth. "I will kill her."

Oglas nodded. "I believe you mean that. But let me talk to her before I go, and maybe I can prevent any trouble."

Standing once more in front of Gail, Oglas gave her what he hoped was a stern look. "Missus, I think you will agree that Sairsa needs some doctoring right now. I'm going to go over to the mess hall and get help. Do you understand me?"

Gail bobbed her head, her eyes never leaving his face. "Yes, that would be a good idea."

"I'm glad you agree." He hesitated a moment as if gathering his thoughts, then he said, "I don't know if you are a religious woman or not, but this lady with me is a priestess. She has had a sending from her Goddess. She was told to come here to help Sairsa and the child, so just let her be. She isn't going to do anything to hurt them.

"I wanted you to know that, because I'd like your word that you'll not do something foolish while I'm gone, or I'll have to tie you up before I go."

The woman gaped when he mentioned Sairsa's pregnancy

"How did you know about that? Only myself and the doctor knew about the baby."

"I just told you. The priestess's goddess sent her a vision."

Gail hesitated, then in a shaky voice, she said, "All right, you have my word. You don't have to tie me up, just go get the doctor."

Oglas gave her a toothy smile as he fastened his coat. "Oh, I will; you can be certain of that."

But it won't be Bennett I'll be bringing back with me, that's for sure.

Chapter Twenty

Thank all the Gods of Timorna and Caldon, the meal was finally over. Caught between Tizu's angry scowls and Nathan's deliberate attempts to bait the man, the Kashallan wondered if they would finish eating before war was openly declared between the two factions.

When the after-dinner drinks were being served, Arishim suggested that they take their chairs and move to the main part of the mess hall. He could hear people gathering in the room beyond the partition. It was time.

This news would affect the entire camp, so at Dunnagh's request, Bennett had agreed to make the proceedings public. When they were settled and the room quiet, Bennett stood up and formally introduced the audience to the Kashallan and the other members of his party.

Then turning to him, he said, "I'm sorry, Ce'awn, for the delay, but certain things came up that needed to be taken care of before I—uh—we could devote ourselves fully to your news. We are all here now, however, so please begin."

"Just a minute, Dr. B," Councilor Arishim said. "Citizen Kai, before you convey information about this planet, could you please give a brief summary of what has happened to you and your party since you left us? I'm sure I, and the rest of the people listening, would appreciate that."

"That is a reasonable request, Councilor." He glanced pointedly at Tizu. "I am surprised that no one else has thought to ask us that question since our arrival."

Evidently she was, too, because her eyebrows rose as she confronted Bennett and the commander.

Dunnagh continued, "I myself, Dr. Farris, or Dr. Singey will be happy to tell you what we can. We would also like to know what has been happening up here as well."

"But of course," Bennett chimed in, "there was no slight intended here, Ce'awn. That is the main reason for this get-together, to bring us all up to date on what has been happening to our two groups."

Dunnagh turned to the two scientists, hoping one of them would begin the tale. He hated talking in big groups like this. Singey saw his pleading look, but his eyes flicked to Tessa. "The study of primitive cultures is Dr. Farris's expertise. Perhaps she should begin."

Well, well, Dunnagh wouldn't have expected the scientist to be so inhibited about speaking, but Singey seemed as reluctant as he was himself, now that they were in front of an audience. They waited, all eyes focused expectantly on Tessa. Only the moan of the wind outside punctuated the silence.

During the preliminaries, Tessa had been translating mechanically for the Timornans. Eyes slightly unfocussed, she was staring at nothing, waiting for the talk to resume, unaware of the looks being directed her way.

Finally Temog touched her arm, and whispered something to her. She started visibly at his touch, listened to him, then turned pleading eyes on the Kashallan. "I can't," she begged in Timornan. "Please, Kashallan, I can't talk to these people right now, the dreams—" Her voice trailed off, the haunted look once more coming into her eyes.

"Do you want Nathan to take you back to our barracks and stay with you till I can come to you?" he asked in the same language.

She glanced at Nathan considering, then shook her head. "No, I want to stay. I want to do something useful—I want to help."

"All right," he said slowly. "Do what you think best, but tell me if you need my help to keep the Umwira's magic away."

She nodded, looking down at her hands.

Bennett looked from one to the other of his guests, a worried expression clouding his face. "Tessa, are you all right, my dear? Can I do anything to help?"

She looked at him then, a strained expression in her dark eyes, but she only shook her head no.

Bennett might have pressed further, but Singey cleared his throat. "Excuse me, Dr. Bennett, I think perhaps Dr. Farris is still a bit worn out from our ordeal, and finds it too tiring to speak to groups yet. Perhaps I should begin."

Diverted, Bennett blinked, gave Tessa one last concerned look and smiled at Singey. "By all means Dr. Singey, we are listening."

"Before we talk about the events of our capture, I should explain a little about Timornan society."

The Kashallan watched the faces of the people around the mess hall as Singey, with a little help from the priests, explained about Timorna and the events of their capture and escape.

Without prior arrangement, Dunnagh noted that the scientist became deliberately vague when speaking about the torments they had suffered while being held by Gormach of Tragar—torments that ended in cannibalistic funeral rites.

Singey mentioned the Umwira attack, of course, to impress upon his audience this world's danger, and explain the wounds they had had upon their arrival. But he didn't go into much detail about the monsters and their terrifying mind magics. Philip was also very cagey when he spoke about the Kashallan himself, a fact for which the bondmates were grateful.

What Singey told them was that Dunnagh had been chosen and bound, according to the terms of his Warrior's Oath, by a council of Elders on this world. Now known as the Kashallan to his followers, Dunnagh was committed to a life of service to the peoples and land of Timorna. And, because of this bond, he had access to certain ancient lore that made him very knowledgeable about his new home.

Singey assured his listeners that what the Kashallan had come here to tell them was not based on Dunnagh's limited knowledge, but came from the learning that had been gathered by these Elders through countless centuries.

Inside his mind, Dunnagh heard the symbiont's mental murmur of approval, and the host had to agree. The story had been very cleverly told. Singey was telling them the truth, to be sure, but in a way that left out what the human-Timornans were hesitant to share with their former comrades.

When he was finished, Singey looked to his chieftain for approval. The Kashallan nodded and the scientist beamed.

Around them in the hall there were whispered conversations, as the content of Singey's talk was discussed in low voices. Even though Singey had glossed over much of what had happened to them, he had told enough to shock them. There were a few questions that Singey and the priests answered, but at last the hall fell silent again, all eyes turning to the Kashallan.

Outside thunder boomed and the green lightning flashed. The wind had picked up and was now rattling the door and window frames as the storm broke around them. The Kashallan sighed. The Dunnagh part of himself hated speaking to groups like this, but it couldn't be put off any longer; Tani's special knowledge was what was needed now.

He rose, making eye contact with the waiting audience. "Thank you for coming. As I told Dr. Bennett upon our return to camp, we hoped for rescue after we were captured. When that didn't happen, we thought you were all dead, or you had repaired the ship and left.

"Later, when we realized that people might still be up here, it was our duty to come tell you our story and give you certain facts about this world. After I have finished, you will have to decide whether to come with me and my people when we leave, or stay here and take the chance of being rescued.

"Each of you must choose for yourselves, because your very lives will depend on your decision. That is why I requested that this meeting be open to everyone, and not just for those you have chosen as your temporary camp leaders."

There was a murmur of surprise at that. When they had quieted again, he went on, raising his voice slightly to be heard over the storm outside. "It is my hope that you all will come with me, because this plateau is going to become a very dangerous place soon." He gestured to the storm, a flash of green lightning giving emphasis to his next words.

"These violent thunderstorms precede a weather condition known here on Timorna as the 'Sorins.' When the rainy season is over, the winds will shift their current direction and come down straight out of the North.

"These winds will blow across the wastes of the northern continent, picking up a lot of poisonous debris as they come south. These storms are full of radioactive dust and other toxic particles. They are in large enough quantities to cause horrible mutations or death to any living thing caught in their path.

"During this time on Timorna, life here has made certain adaptations. Plant life goes dormant, and all other living things seek shelter underground until the storm season has passed. This camp is right in the path of those storms, and these prefab buildings will be no shelter whatsoever from the high winds and fallout of the Sorins." The Kashallan paused, the raging storm outside giving an ominous urgency to his words.

In the silence that followed, Arishim spoke out loud the question that must have been on the minds of many. Turning to Bennett, she asked, "Hyram, did the ship's computator have any information to verify or refute his claim?" when Bennett made no reply, she repeated, "Dr. B?"

Bennett started, an expression of pain crossing his face for a moment before he controlled it. Giving Arishim an apologetic smile, he said, "Sorry. What was it you asked?"

The councilor gave him a concerned look, then repeated her question. Bennett took another moment to collect himself before answering. "You must understand that we only had the ship's secondary backup computator system on which to make any assessments before we landed. But the Kashallan—as we should now begin to call our former Unit Leader—is correct in saying that to the north there is a large, barren continent that is indeed still marginally radioactive.

"It's possible that, if the wind's direction were to change and blow out of that quarter, it could bring with it harmful particles." He nodded his head. "Yes, it is quite possible."

"But we can't leave here, not now!" Sadrew protested. "The rescue ship may be back for us at any time, and they aren't going to find us if we're stuck down a hole somewhere with a bunch of primitives. We have to stay."

There were murmurs of agreement from around the hall as he finished. The Kashallan's jaw tightened at the implied insult to him and his people. Oh, yes, the host remembered this man all too well from his stay on board Bennett's ship. Arrogant little prick.

From somewhere in the crowd, a voice asked, "If it isn't going to be safe for us up here, then can't we just go with the Unit Leader, and come back here later after these storms are over? We could leave a message telling the rescue ship that we had to go to a safer place, and—"

The Kashallan shook his head. "I wish it were that simple, but it isn't. Timorna is a possessive mother, to be rather poetic about it. Once claimed as her own, she will not allow her adopted children—meaning us—to leave."

"What are you talking about?" Sadrew snapped. "Forget about being poetic, damn it, and make sense."

"All right," the Kashallan said. "Have it your own way, Citizen Sadrew. The doctor has verified my claim that there is toxic debris on this planet. Do you accept that as a fact?"

Sadrew hesitated, giving Dunnagh a suspicious look. He thought about it a moment longer, then nodded. "If the computator said it was so, then I'll accept it."

"Good. Then it would seem logical to assume that since living beings do exist on this world, something has to have been created to counterbalance those poisons, hmm? This something would have to either filter out and dispose of those dangerous substances, or attack and destroy any toxic materials entering the living creatures to which it has been introduced. Can you agree with my logic so far?"

Sadrew scowled. "Is this a trick?"

"No trick, Citizen. I am deadly serious."

Suddenly alert to the new possibilities, Bennett blurted, "Yes, I can see that possibility. Such a substance introduced into the environment would make perfect sense. But how was it accomplished?

"Your hypothesis implies that a highly intelligent and sophisticated species, with a superior technology would have survived that holocaust you told me of. We've seen no evidence of that since our arrival."

Inside the host's mind the Shalla made a pleased sound. <<I like this human, Kasha, he seems very intelligent,.>>

Dunnagh grunted, meeting Singey's eye. "Not necessarily, Doctor. Tool making and technology is the path that humans chose for their evolution, but it is not the only way a species could evolve.

"Timorna is a world that is extremely poor in metals, Doctor, especially since the Great Wars. The technology of its inhabitants is very limited compared to what your own people have achieved.

"What you haven't discovered yet, is that Timorna is a world where biochemistry and genetic manipulation has reached a degree of sophistication that far surpasses that used, or even dreamed of, by humanity."

Bennett set down his drink and stared incredulously. "But that's impossible!"

<<Not as smart as you thought, eh, Shalla?>> To the doctor the Kashallan said, "It isn't impossible at all, for that is exactly what has happened. The Elder race, practically the only species to have survived the destruction, created the kavay, which is just such a substance. Part biochemical, part viral organism with limited instinctive intelligence, it was designed and produced by the Khutani to meet this planet's unique needs."

"But how?" Bennett interrupted. "Without a lab or proper equipment—" He shook his head. "I can't see how—no—that would be impossible."

"Yes, for you it would be, but the Khutani are not human, Doctor, so don't judge them by human criteria. They created the kavay as well as other helpful and healing compounds within the 'chemical laboratories,' if you will, of their own bodies.

"When the original dominate species of this world nearly destroyed themselves and all life on the planet, the Khutani, this ancient species I speak of, retired to the waterways deep within the bedrock of this world, where only they could survive."

"Later, after the worst of the destruction was centuries in the past, the Khutani created the kavay and bred the plants and animals, as well as the intelligent races to re-populate an entire world."

He held up the flask of blue liquid Temog handed him. "Here there is a saying: With the kavay there is life; without it, there is only death."

Tizu grunted. "Get to the point, Kai. You and Bennett can trade interesting scientific trivia later."

There was that hostility again, Dunnagh noted. "Ah, but, Commander, kavay is the point," he said. In spite of himself, the man was starting to get on his nerves. "No life can exist on Timorna without it. When we were captured, we were forced to eat native foods that quite naturally contained the kavay.

"Because we were not aligned with it, we got very sick at first. When the alignment process was finished, we returned to our normal health. I, myself, and all who were with me, like all other Timornan species, are aligned to the kavay now." Holding up a brawny arm he pointed out the kavay brands, like swirling tattoos upon his skin.

"But we paid a high price for this gift of life, for, in order for the kavay to do its job, it made permanent changes within our bodies. These changes go far deeper than an addiction to an alien drug; the adaptations made to our metabolisms are far more fundamental and are irreversible.

"We live, and may even prosper, here, but we can never leave this world, because after the alignment occurs, a constant source of kavay must always be present in the diet, or that person will die."

The Kashallan sighed, and looked at his audience with tenderness. "I am sorry; I know many of you are desperately hoping for the ship to come back and save you. But unless it comes very soon, that can't be. The longer you remain here, the more likely it is that you will begin the alignment. It is inevitable.

"The substance is everywhere—a cut exposed to the air, a drop of rain upon your tongue, anything, could begin the process. And that is why I tell you: If you agree to go with me to Ticca, there is no turning back.

"Timorna needs you, so I hope you will choose to follow me. I can offer you a new and fulfilling life, if you come with me, but if you choose to come, you must swear your fealty to me as the Kashallan, and make a commitment to your new home. Those are my terms.

"If you choose to stay here, and if the ship comes back for you soon, you may have a chance. If it doesn't come, then you will surely die. Is that plain enough for you, Citizen?"

Sadrew stood up, his face contorted with rage. "I don't believe a word of this crazy story. Tizu is right. You're either a puffed-up little despot who expects us to fall in and be your groveling slaves, or you're totally insane! What a bunch of lies. You're no scientist; you can't prove any of this. I don't know what your real game is, Kai, but if you think the rest of us are going to believe such drivel, you're badly mistaken!"

Fists clenched and eyes blazing, Nathan rose slowly to his feet. Across from him Tizu rose as well, a challenge to the bigger man plain on his face. Around them the hall exploded into chaos as people shouted and argued. Bennett bellowed for order, but for the moment he was being ignored.

In the midst of the turmoil, Oglas slipped in and strode quickly to the Kashallan's side. Bending close, he gave him Pela's message.

When Oglas finished the Kashallan put a restraining hand on Nathan's shoulder, and drew him away from the others. "Never mind that now. I need you to come with me."

Nathan started to protest, but something in Dunnagh's expression changed his mind. "What's wrong?"

"I don't know exactly. Oglas just brought me a message from Pela. I'm not sure what she's doing over at the sickbay, but she says I must come, because something's wrong with Sairsa."

The Kashallan glanced around him. The hall was still in confusion, and now was a good time to escape. He motioned for the other Timornans to join them.

When they had gathered around him, he said, "Oglas has just brought me a message. I've got to leave. Philip, I'm sorry to have to do this to you, but you and the Avairei are going to have to take over for me, at least for a little while. I've told these people all I can anyway. Just do your best. If they don't want to hear it—" He shrugged.

Sagas snorted. "These people are too stupid to let breed. Chosen, how could you ever have such unworthy relatives?"

Dunnagh chuckled. "These people are not all my blood kin, dear Ima. Just as the Dingay and other Avairei clans are not all your kin, humans are of different clans as well."

"So even among those who come from the stars, there are clans like the Dingay? I would not have thought it. But where are you going?"

"Pela has sent word to me that someone I care about very much is ill. I am going to see what the problem is."

Sagas clutched at his arm. "Be careful. I know she wouldn't send such a message if it wasn't important, but—"

"I'll be all right; stop worrying. I'll take Nathan with me—maybe it will keep him out of trouble," he added. "San Oglas can stay here with you. He will bring you back to our barracks when you feel you've had enough."

Then, wrapping his cloak about himself, he motioned for Nathan to follow him.

Nathan hesitated; torn by his loyalties, he glanced worriedly at Tessa.

"Go with him, San Nathan. I will take care of her," Temog promised.

Nodding his thanks, Nathan followed the Kashallan out the door and into the storm.

Chapter Twenty-One

The minutes seemed to crawl by. Gail sat in her chair, listening to the raging wind rattle the windows and never taking her eyes off the alien priestess in her sickbay. The woman didn't seem to be doing Sairsa any harm, merely holding her when the spasms came and talking to her softly in her weird tongue.

The priestess was keeping an eye on her though, she knew, for each time Gail shifted on the chair those hostile dark eyes glared at her.

Gail wasn't particularly religious; she considered most faiths to be superstitious drivel. But knowing that the savage had divined the child's existence when Sairsa wasn't visibly pregnant—and they hadn't told anyone—made her skin crawl. What kind of powers did these people have?

She glanced up at the clock again. It seemed to her that the Caldoni was taking an awfully long time, but it probably was just her imagination.

Suddenly Sairsa began to choke and retch. This had happened before. Gail looked up at the clock. Yes, it was time for another dose of the medication doctor B left for her.

While the priestess was occupied helping Sairsa vomit into a basin, Gail rose quietly, went to the wall cabinet, and prepared another injection. By the time she had finished, Sairsa was resting once more upon the bed, eyes closed and breathing raggedly.

Determined, yet still a bit frightened, Gail cautiously approached the bedside, hypo in hand.

As she neared, the priestess glanced up. She saw the needle, and hissed, shaking her head.

Gail gritted her teeth and came closer. "Now listen, you little savage, it's time for the medicine Dr. B left for her. You can see how sick she is; this will help her get better."

She growled, just like an animal. Then, in halting Standard, she ordered, “No! No touch. No give my Sairsa.”

Gail sighed. As a nurse she was used to dealing with difficult patients and their families. She was also used to getting her own way in the end. Speaking in a soothing voice, as if to a child, she told the priestess that if she really wanted to help Sairsa, she would let Gail do what was best for her patient.

“No,” she warned, “no come closer—you come, I kill.” Glaring at the nurse, she bared her teeth.

Gail halted, taken aback by the woman’s ferocity. *Ignorant savage, she probably doesn’t even know what I’m talking about.* Her lip curled in disgust. The alien was smaller than she was herself. Gail had often had to wrestle unwilling patients into doing what she wanted. So, she reasoned, she should be able to physically force this little barbarian, if necessary, into letting her do her job.

Gail stepped to the bed, reaching for Sairsa’s arm. In spite of her experience, Gail wasn’t prepared for the violence of the furry woman’s attack. Without warning, the priestess launched herself at the nurse.

In one swift motion she knocked the needle out of Gail’s hand, then, with claws extended and teeth bared, she went for the woman’s throat.

Unnerved by the vicious attack, Gail screamed, praying that someone would hear her over the roar of the storm. Desperately, Gail struggled to fend off the other woman’s teeth and claws, but in spite of her larger mass, she suffered several deep gashes along her neck and cheek before she could get away. Shoving the priestess from her at last, the frightened nurse raced through the doorway.

In the other room, Gail leaned against the wall, her breath coming in ragged gasps. Outside, the storm seemed worse. Rain hammered against the metal roof, its din punctuated by loud crashes of thunder and bright flares of the eerie green lightning.

What should she do? She was trapped in here, alone with a madwoman! The noise of the storm had obviously prevented anyone from hearing the sounds of their struggle. She hated to leave her patient, but she must get help.

Trying to be as quiet as she could, Gail crossed to her desk and slipped on the coat that was draped over the back of her chair. Keeping an eye on the inner room to make sure the priestess wouldn't attack her unexpectedly from behind, Gail tiptoed to the door then flung it open.

Head down against the sudden blast of the wind, she rushed out the door and ran into a solid, immovable object, knocking herself breathless. Strong arms caught and steadied her and when she glanced up, a pair of concerned blue eyes gazed down upon her. "Are you all right?"

For just a moment, the blazing green lightning lit up the cloaked figure in the doorway, giving him an eerie, otherworldly look. Gail let out a strangled cry and lurched backwards inside out of reach.

Oh, Heaven save her. She'd recognized who was cutting off her escape. It was the mad Unit Leader, with one of his men right behind him. She was trapped. Breathing raggedly, Gail slowly retreated into the room.

THE KASHALLAN STEPPED into the sickbay, Nathan yanking the door closed behind them. The woman in front of them drew back until her progress was halted by the mass of a large desk. With eyes wide she clutched the edge of this piece of furniture with white knuckled hands trembling violently.

The woman was obviously terrified—and of him, it would seem. Why? Then he noticed the long scratches along her cheek and neck.

Hearing the outer door open and close, Pela got up and hurried into the other room. "Oh, Kashallan, thank the Goddess you have come at last."

Glancing from one woman to the other, he asked in Timornan, "Pela, sweet, what has been going on here?"

Pela folded her arms across her chest, in unconscious imitation of Sagas when she was being stubborn. Her eyes flicked to the nurse, then she returned her attention to the Kashallan. "She wouldn't listen to me. I spoke to her in your own language, Dunnagh, and she still wouldn't listen."

When he continued to watch her, without comment, she looked down at the floor and said more hesitantly, "Are you angry with me, husband?"

"Should I be?"

Pela looked up. "No. I am sorry I cut her face like that, but she wanted to give our Sairsa more poison and I wouldn't let her. I—"

Pela broke off as if unsure of him, then gathering her courage she blurted. "Oh, please, husband, come! It's our Sairsa. She is very sick, and I think she may be going to lose the baby if you don't help her soon."

Baby? Gods, what was she babbling about? Throwing aside his cloak, the Kashallan hurried across the reception area and followed her into the other room.

Seeing that the way to the door now lay open for her escape, the nurse bolted for the entrance. Once again strong arms caught hold of her and drew her away from the door.

Panicked beyond reason, she fought him. Finally in disgust Nathan applied pressure to a nerve point in her arm. When she had quieted sufficiently to understand him, he said, "Now that's better."

Not giving her time to recover, he guided her towards the doorway through which Pela and the Kashallan had gone. "You don't want to go out there in that wind and rain," he confided.

Inside the inner room, he pushed her down onto a chair. "No, it's damn cold out there. And if you sit here and be very good, nobody's going to hurt you. Do you understand me?"

She licked her lips and nodded. "I understand. If I don't do what you want you will kill me." Nathan gave her a toothy smile.

Dunnagh crossed to the cot and looked down at his beloved. His heart gave a lurch. Oh, Gods, his Sairsa, lying here so pale and suffering. He reached out a trembling hand and touched her sweaty forehead. Her eyes had been closed, but at his touch she opened them.

When she recognized him, she smiled. "Dunnagh?"

"Yes, love," he murmured, "It's me."

She let out a long sigh. "I knew you would come for me. Are we going home to Caldon now?"

Dunnagh choked on a sob. "No, love, we aren't going home, but I'm here to take care of you," Sliding his hand under the blanket he took up one of her hands. The Kashallan extended his tentacles, and slipped them into the veins below her wrist. "Just rest now and everything will be all right, love, I promise."

Sairsa murmured something, then closed her eyes, drifting back into her drug-induced confusion. The Kashallan too closed his eyes, the host allowing his bondmate to use its unique talents without any distractions.

At last, Tani said, <<She is very bad, Kasha. The alignment has begun, as San Oglas told us, but the medicine Dr. Bennett has been giving her is interfering with the process.>> The symbiont writhed. <<Yuck! That stuff tastes horrible. It is so alien to Timorna, I can understand why the kavay would be attacking it so fiercely. To the kavay, this medicine would seem like one of the poisons from the old days.>>

<<What can we do for her?>> Dunnagh asked. Then, in a frightened mental voice, <<Tani, she won't die, will she?>>

Tani sent filaments of its tentacles deeper into the woman's unresisting flesh, testing, tasting. At last it said, <<Kasha, I know this is hard for you, but, at this point, I don't know. We must get her back to our barracks as soon as possible, and begin giving her the kavay. I will do all I can for her, I promise. After that we can only pray.>>

<<I never doubted that you would, Shalla.>> Then recalling Pela's other revelation he asked, <<Tani, what does Pela mean about a baby?>>

<<Pela is right. I don't have any encoded memories about your species to draw upon, and you, of course, aren't a lot of help in this case, but as best I can determine it would seem she is pregnant.>>

<<But—>>

<< Oh, Kasha, we'll talk about that later, right now this drug is making me sick. I'm going to drain her of some of the poison, then I'm breaking the link.>>

<<You're right, we need to get her back to our barracks.,>> the host agreed. <<But, Tani, be careful—I can feel the taint now, too. Don't try to do too much.>>

<<Don't worry, I won't. Now get ready, in a moment we are going to be very sick.>>

The Kashallan retracted his tentacles, and opened his eyes. They were watching him intently. The nurse stared wide-eyed in horror and fascination at his hands.

Dunnagh started to explain what they needed to do, when Tani's prediction about being sick came dramatically true. Rushing to the sink in the corner he bent over it, violently spewing up what Tani had collected from Sairsa's body.

Frightened, Pela was beside him in an instant, holding him and steadying him. At last he straightened. Drawing a cup of water from the tap he rinsed out his mouth.

"Are you all right, husband?"

"Yes," he murmured. "Or I will be in a moment." He pushed himself away from the sink and crossed to stand in front of the nurse. The Kashallan saw her eyes flick down to his hands again, then look quickly away. He had no wish to alarm the poor woman further, but there were things he needed to know.

"What happened?" Nathan asked quietly in Timornan.

"Tani was just draining off some of the drug from her system," he explained in the same tongue. "Whatever Bennett's been giving her has been interfering with the alignment process. That's most of the reason she's so sick. We need to get her out of here, though, and back to the barracks, where we can start giving her the kavay that she needs to complete the alignment."

Nathan nodded, then followed Dunnagh's gaze as he returned his attention to studying the frightened nurse. "What's your name?"

She swallowed, then replied, "Gail Pointe."

"Hmm. I seem to recall Sairsa mentioning you on the ship as a friend of hers." The woman bobbed her head in agreement. "Well, Gail, as you are aware, Sairsa is quite ill at the moment. She has begun what we Timornans call the kavay alignment process. I have already told Dr. Bennett about this adaptation, but I don't have the time to explain it to you now. What I do need to know so I can treat Sairsa properly, is how long she has been ill with these symptoms."

"Sairsa, like most of us, has had it for a while. The symptoms come and go. We thought she was over the illness. It's only been in the last day or so that she's gotten worse again—"

He held up his hand to stop her. "Just a minute—are you saying that there are others who are going through the alignment process too?"

"If that's what you call it, then yes. The symptoms seem to come and go, but more than half the base has been down sick with it at one time or another.

"Listen to me, Gail, this is very important. You must not give your patients any more of these drugs. They are doing more harm than good. The people in this camp who are affected must complete the alignment. It is the kavay they need now, or they will all die."

Frightened of him as she was, she still resisted; he could see it in her eyes. Catching her attention, he deliberately held up a hand and extended his tentacles. "I am not telling you this as Unit Leader Dunnagh Kai. I am telling you this as a Timornan healer, who knows about these things.

"On this planet I am the doctor, not Bennett. I will have to see all the sick ones eventually, but right now my first concern is for Sairsa."

He reached down and, before she could resist, he picked up her hand and slipped those alien tentacles into her flesh. She cried out and tried to pull away. Nathan reached out to hold her steady.

The Kashallan looked into her terrified eyes then sent a tranquilizer down the link into her bloodstream. When he saw her eyes glaze, he gave her a lopsided grin. "Feeling better?"

"Wh-at are you do-ing to m-e?"

"I'm giving you a tranquilizer, Timornan style. I know you're very frightened of me right now, and believe me, I'm sorry for that, but I am a healer, as I told you. I want to treat those claw marks on your face before we go. I knew you wouldn't let me unless I sedated you."

Raising his other hand to his mouth, he spat a thick, yellow, gelatinous substance into his palm, then began plastering it over the scratches on her face and neck. "Pela says to give you her apologies. She didn't want to hurt you, but she couldn't make you listen.

"And, though I wish it could have been otherwise, she was right to stop you from giving Sairsa any more of that medication."

The Kashallan surveyed his work with satisfaction. "There, I think that's got them all," he announced. "This stuff will harden in a few minutes. Leave it on a day or two, and the cuts will heal without any scarring."

Glassy-eyed, Gail nodded slowly. “Good.” Then guiding her to an empty cot he helped her lie down. Giving her a last dose, a sedative this time, he released her from the link.

Covering her with a blanket, he turned to Nathan. “We have to get Sairsa out of here so I can treat her.”

“I’ll get your cloak to wrap her in, and I’ll carry her. You save your strength—I have a feeling you’re going to need it.”

The Kashallan barked a mirthless laugh. “You’re right about that, and thanks.” Retrieving his cloak, they bundled up the sick woman and hurried out into the storm.

Chapter Twenty-Two

The assembly finally agreed to table any further discussion, until some experiments could be done in the base's lab. At Bennett's insistence, Singey reluctantly consented to help him. That seemed to satisfy everyone and the meeting was adjourned until the scientists had something to report.

Singey had agreed to help, both as a lab assistant and subject for their study. As a fully-aligned human, his blood would be as good as any for their experimentation. Though he didn't believe for a moment in the return of a rescue ship, he was curious, and welcomed the opportunity to study the Kashallan's assertions about the kavay.

The doctor wanted to get started on those tests as soon as possible, so Singey parted from the Timornan delegation outside the mess hall and followed Bennett to the sickbay. Tizu trailed after them for his own unspoken reasons.

Wrestling open the sickbay door, they piled inside and Tizu slammed it hard behind them. Bennett sighed with relief. He unbuttoned his coat and hung it up to dry. "What a storm! If this is any indication of what we have to look forward to, I confess your chieftain has a point, Philip. It probably would be better to get off this high mesa."

Tizu snorted, his face darkening at the mention of his former armachd. Singey studied him warily out of the corner of his eye. He hadn't particularly paid attention to the man on board Bennett's ship, but now the Commander's attitude made him nervous.

"Gail?" Bennett glanced around the outer room and frowned. "Odd," he murmured. "She should be here. Sairsa wasn't feeling well, and—"

With a strangled oath, Tizu brushed past them and hurried into the other room. Just inside the doorway he halted, flicking on the light switch. He looked around, swore a vile Caldoni oath, then bolted from the sickbay back out into the night.

Bennett stared after the man, his mouth agape. Singey stepped around him and into the inner room. An empty, unmade cot caught his eye, and then on the opposite row, he noticed Gail asleep on another bed.

Crossing to the bed, he stared down into her tranquil face and reached out a hand and touched her stained cheek; his lips twitching into a ghost of a smile. Yellow kavay. A gasp from Bennett made him turn.

"My God, what's happened to her, Philip?" Bennett glanced anxiously around the room and noticed the empty cot, "and where's Sairsa?"

Singey let his hand fall from Gail's cheek. Taking the doctor's arm, he guided him into the other room and set him down in a chair near the desk.

Rummaging in one of the drawers, he brought out a bottle and a glass. He poured Bennett a stiff drink and handed it to him. Then, propping himself on the edge of the desk, he said, "There's nothing to worry about, Doctor, Gail is fine."

Bennett stared up at him, blinking in confusion, a shiver rand down his spine as he became aware of the grim expression on his protégé's dark face. New lines of pain had been etched deep into those features.

Such a pity, Bennett thought. This man was so unlike the old Singey he had known before the capture. Perching there before him now was a different man, with different loyalties and different dreams.

"Drink your drink, Doctor B," Singey suggested. "As I said, Gail is fine and Sairsa is with the Kashallan. Based on what Oglas told us, my guess is that he'll be treating her for the alignment sickness, and there's nothing you can do to help with that. It's a Timornan problem. It needs to be handled by a Timornan healer."

"But—"

"Leave it be, Doctor," he warned. "She's not your patient anymore." When Bennett finally nodded, he continued, "As to your nurse, there's nothing wrong with Gail really; she's just been given a Timornan sedative, and is sleeping. She'll be fine in the morning."

"But what about her face?" Bennett protested. "What happened?"

Singey shrugged. "I don't know, but whatever it was, it's nothing serious. He treated her with the yellow kavay before he left. The old Avairei doctor, Temog, has been teaching me their healing techniques. I've used that particular compound before on patients myself; it does wonders."

Suddenly, he pushed himself off the desk, a feverish light coming into his eyes as he began to pace in front of his old mentor. Behaving more like the old Singey that Bennett remembered, he said, "Doctor, this world is a fascinating place."

He waved his hand in dismissal of Bennett's perceived objection. "Oh, it can be harsh, even unbelievably cruel at times, but it's a biochemist's dream. The Khutani have taken biochemical science and genetics far beyond what humans have done, even with all our so-called superior technology.

"This Elder race, well, they are both frightening and amazing creatures. They have accomplished miracles here. With no technology to help them, only their innate intelligence, and what substances they can produce in their own bodies, they have created an entire world of life.

"They are trying to rebuild a whole ecosystem, with nothing to go on but the genetic patterns they salvaged from the destruction. Oh, it's far from perfect, and there are lots of gaps, but, considering what they had to work with, it's incredible what they have achieved."

Bennett leaned forward, his anxiety for the moment forgotten, caught up in spite of himself, in the young scientist's narrative. "Philip, do you mean to say that you have actually seen and talked to these creatures—these Khutani? Tell me about them!"

Singey froze, a closed expression coming once more over his ebony features. He surveyed Bennett through narrowed eyes.

He's said too much, Bennett thought. *He got carried away talking to me, like we used to do. But he doesn't trust me—I can sense it.*

There's some big secret surrounding the Khutani—something all of Kai's people know about, but don't want to share it with us. And now he is afraid he's let something slip out in his excitement, but I haven't a clue what it could be.

"Philip," Bennett said, his voice low and soothing, as if speaking to a nervous patient. "I'm not your enemy, you know. Before all this," he waved his hand in an encompassing gesture, "I thought we were friends as well as student and mentor. Can't you trust me?

"I know it must have been hard for you among all those savages. You've had a bad time of it. I would like to help you, if you'll let me."

Singey came back and sat down on the edge of the desk. For a long time he watched his old mentor, his expression guarded. At last, coming to some inner conclusion, he sighed. "It's not that simple, Doctor. Things are not the same between us any more. The kavay flows in my veins and Timorna is my home.

"And you? You are an outsider, an alien creature to me now. True, I called you both friend and mentor once, but not now. I'm sorry, Doctor, that is just how it is."

Bennett sat back stunned. He raised the glass to his lips and took a large swallow, suddenly needing the liquor's comforting warmth. He hadn't expected this honest yet passionless rejection.

Had this kavay substance changed this man that much? How could Philip see a fellow human as an alien? For goodness sake! They were of the same species—or were they? He shivered, feeling suddenly uneasy for the first time, knowing he was alone in Singey's company.

Singey saw the fear come into his eyes and grimaced. Nodding to himself, his lips curved into an ironic smile. "Doctor, should I repeat your own words back to you? I am not your enemy, either.

"There are things that have come between us, but I too want to reach out and help you. And whether you realize it or not yet, if you are going to survive here on Timorna, you will need my help—and that of the Kashallan.

Bennett's expression must have betrayed his disbelief. When Singey spoke again his voice had hardened. "Don't believe me, eh? The Great Dr. Bennett, savior of the galaxy. You've always seen yourself as the giver of help. A man who, because of his wealth, his family's position and his quick intelligence, was able to reach out and give succor to those less fortunate than himself."

Singey let out a bark of brittle laughter. "I wonder if you can see the unbelievable arrogance in that attitude. I couldn't see it in myself, you know. I look back at my life before coming to Timorna, and realize what an incredible fool I was."

Bennett sipped his drink, eyeing the man over the rim of his glass. "I'm not sure I understand what you're trying to tell me, Philip."

"No, perhaps not. I'll explain it to you, if you like, but I wonder if you have the courage to hear me, or the strength needed to survive here."

"Go on, I'm listening."

"All right. A few minutes ago you implied that you wanted to know my pain, so you could help me." His voice hard edged again, he laughed. "You stupid shit, how could you possibly help me?"

Singey saw Bennett's jaw drop at his use of one of Nathan's favorite epithets. He laughed. "Yes, Doctor, I've been consorting with the wild Caldoni armachda and it's rubbing off.

"But the point I'm trying to get across to you is this. Your money and position mean nothing here. You know nothing here. You can't help me or anyone. You're the one who needs help, and you don't even see it yet."

"Philip, calm down. I'm sure if we work together, we will be able to help each other."

"Don't patronize me, Doctor B," he snapped. "You think my Ce'awn and I have gone-native or just crazy. You feel superior to us, don't you? Oh, you're more polite about it than the Commander, but we know what you're thinking."

"All those long, agonizing days when we were so sick, we prayed for rescue, or the strength to escape, so we could return here to our comrades. And when we get here, we're treated almost as badly as we were during our slavery."

"Philip, I know your ordeal as a slave to some savage alien race must have been terrible, but I only want to help, can't you see that? If we pool our knowledge, surely—"

"No!" Singey cut him off with an impatient hand gesture, his black eyes smoldering with rage. "You still don't understand." Speaking very slowly as if to a stupid child, he repeated, "We—don't—need—your—help. You can't help, because you have nothing to give us that would help.

"Slavery. What do you really know about it? Are you going to tell me what you read in a book? Well, let me tell you, it is a very humbling experience.

"And so is knowing that you are nothing more than a piece of meat to grace your masters' dinner table any time they so choose."

At the doctor's shocked expression, Singey laughed bitterly. "You haven't asked me about my assistant Gemma."

"What happened, Philip? Though I didn't see her, I assumed—"

"Three of those who left that day didn't make it back, Doctor, Gemma and two armachda." His harsh laugh again, "To the Timornan way of thinking meat is meat; we eat slaves, enemies, even our own dead."

Bennett gasped.

"I left that out of my little tale, didn't I?" Singey unconsciously fingered the bone beads around his neck. His eyes took on a haunted look, as if seeing other visions in his mind.

At last he returned his attention to Bennett. "Such experiences strip away all facades, even the arrogant facade of our ridiculous belief that as humans we are superior to all other forms of life."

He leaned forward, eyes ablaze. "Now, really, Doctor. Knowing what I've just told you, can you, with all your money and education help me?" He shook his head. "I think not. You can't offer me anything but empty words and platitudes.

"No, on Timorna, Dr. B, you are like a young child, and just as ignorant. But what I wonder is, do you have the courage to swallow that Bennett pride of yours, as I had to do with mine.

"Can you accept that you are nothing—not wise, not rich, not even a good doctor. On this world you are just a man, who must relearn everything anew. Can you let go of everything from your old way of life, even this stupid notion that you are going to be rescued?"

Bennett was quiet for a long time after Singey finished, staring into his glass, shocked and still a little frightened by the man leaning upon the desk, eyeing him so critically.

Philip was right though—what could he offer people who had gone through such experiences but empty words and platitudes. And Philip was right about other things as well. He wasn't doing any good at treating his patients, so letting Kai try—especially if he had access to indigenous knowledge was probably better than what he, himself, was doing for them.

It was a hard pill to swallow; Bennett's skill as a healer was something he had always taken pride in. Starting over with nothing—could he do it? He didn't honestly know, and right now he was too tired to think about it.

The pain in his gut was returning; he would need another dose of the drug soon.

Singey continued to watch him, waiting for some kind of answer. Finally he sighed, rubbed a hand across his face and said, "I don't know, Philip, I truly don't know. And right now I'm getting too tired to figure it out."

Singey nodded. "At least you're honest about it; that's a good start." He stood up and stretched. "It's getting late. I'll come back in the morning and we can get started on those tests."

Chapter Twenty-Three

Tizu flung himself out of the sickbay and back into the night. The storm that raged around him was nothing compared to the turmoil that was roiling inside him. Bracing himself against the force of the wind, he plowed through the rain, heading for his own quarters.

He'd get Kai for this. He'd kill him for what he'd done tonight—he'd kill him. Around him green lightning flared and great peals of thunder boomed. He laughed, feeling the wild power of the storm calling to him, knowing that it matched the fury that had been building within him ever since Kai's return.

The wind tore at him, the rain drenched his clothing and plastered his hair across his face. Tizu brushed it out of his eyes and shook a clenched fist at the uncaring sky. Sairsa was his, damn Kai, she was his! And he wasn't about to let that degenerate Caldoni have her.

Oh, the man thought himself so very clever, getting them all stirred up with his tales of gloom and doom. Then, when no one was paying attention, he snuck off with Nathan Derek to abduct her.

Stealing her out of the good doctor's care, taking her away when she was so sick she couldn't resist—and doing God alone, or the devil, knew what to her. Well, not for long—Tizu was going to get her back and kill him. He'd take care of Kai for good, and any other crazy who tried to stop him.

Reaching HQ at last, he wrestled the door open and stepped inside. Ellis and Ross looked up from a card game, startled. Scrambling to their feet they saluted. Ignoring their shocked faces, he returned their salutes automatically, then, without a word, headed for the small alcove in the rear that was his private quarters.

A few minutes later Tizu reappeared. Fully armed, with beam rifle in hand, he headed for the outer door. Looking alarmed, Ross stepped in front of him. Clearing his throat, he asked, "Is there trouble, sir?"

Tizu halted; he had been so intent on what he was going to do to Kai that he'd forgotten about his two armachda on duty in the outer room. "Nothing I can't handle myself, now get out of my way. You're dismissed."

"But sir—"

"That's an order, Armachd. Go to bed," Tizu snarled. Black eyes smoldering, he dared them to question him further. When they didn't he stepped around Ross, flung the door open and headed back into the storm.

NATHAN TURNED OFF THE overhead lighting in D barracks and crossed to the mattress on the floor that he and Tessa shared. The barracks was quieting down, everyone settling in for the night. In the far corner a few green-flamed votive lamps burned on the makeshift altar, giving a soft, now-familiar and comforting glow to the darkened room. Sitting down on the side of the pallet, he put a hand on his sleeping companion's shoulder.

Temog told him when he returned that he'd given her something to keep the nightmares away and let her sleep. But, Gods, he hated to see her like this. He'd rather have her at her most difficult, arguing with him over anything and everything, than the way she was at the moment.

That scared, haunted look in her soft, dark eyes made him feel so helpless—and so guilty—if he had only....

Nathan was just about to lie down when the door to their barracks crashed open. A shadowed figure stood framed in the doorway, green lightning outlining his silhouette and the leveled beam rifle in his hand.

The man stepped inside and closed the door with a jerk, never taking his eyes off the people in the room. In the eerie half-light, Nathan could see the crazed look in Tizu's eyes, and rose slowly to his feet.

Stepping across the laid out mattresses, he edged slowly closer to the door. Now the focus of Tizu's attention, he halted just out of reach. "Commander. How nice of you to drop by, but it's a little late for a visit; we were just going to bed."

"Shut up, Derek. Quit the crap, and tell me where he is. I want him."

"Who?"

Tizu swung the barrel of the rifle around, aiming it directly at Nathan's chest. "Don't play games with me, Derek. I'd enjoy killing you almost as much as I'm going to relish killing him, so don't push me. You know exactly who I mean."

Nathan edged a step closer. Out of the corner of his eye he saw Chang and Marnez, inching along the wall on opposite sides of the door. Keeping Tizu's attention focused on him, so as to give them time, he admitted "Yeah, I know who you mean. He's gone to bed. What do you want him for?"

Tizu let out a mirthless laugh. "Yeah, I bet he has, and with her, no doubt. And it isn't sleep he has in mind either. Well, he isn't going to take advantage of her. Sairsa's not well, and I'm taking her back to the sickbay where she belongs so Bennett can—"

Suddenly the door crashed open behind him. Tizu turned. At the same instant two shadowy figures leapt at him from the darkness on either side of the doorway.

Tizu spun around and lashed out with a sidekick that brought Chang to his knees. Throwing off Marnez who made a grab for him from behind, he raised the rifle. Nathan took hold of it, and they wrestled for control of the weapon.

With a strength born of desperation, Tizu fought the bigger man like a demon. Back and forth they swung, the rest of the armachda watching helplessly. The gun discharged with a loud boom, blowing a hole in the ceiling, sending a shower of white sparks cascading down into the room.

The Timornans screamed. In a panic they sprang away from the sparks raining down among them. Backing into the far corner they watched, round-eyed, as the men fought. Once more the weapon discharged into the ceiling before Nathan saw his opportunity and hit Tizu hard on the point of the jaw.

Before Tizu could recover, he wrenched the weapon out of the man's hand, and tossed it to Marnez. Then Nathan hit him again—just to relieve his pent-up frustrations. Tizu dropped like a stone at his feet.

Sighing with relief, Nathan looked down at his former commander and muttered a curse under his breath. What had gotten into the man? Tizu had always been hot-tempered—but not crazy.

Glancing at the door, where a bemused Singey stood motionless he grinned. "Nice timing, Philip, did you have to practice very much to get that good?"

Singey blinked. "It's a talent I never realized I had, but I'm glad to know I have it." He pushed the door shut behind him and surveyed the room.

Bedding and supplies were scattered everywhere like a chaotic carpet. Marti and a one-handed Taleish were trying to smother a flaming mattress with the fire extinguisher. Moraga was talking to a frightened cluster of Avairei huddled by their altar." What's going on?"

Nathan followed his gaze and made a face. "I'm not sure exactly." He glared down at Tizu, stretched out unconscious in the growing puddle of rainwater on the floor. "He came boiling in here a few minutes ago, wanting Dunnagh and spoiling for a fight."

Turning round he called. "Hey, Rhys, go in my pack over there and find those handcuffs of mine. Put them on him before he wakes up, I'm not in the mood for any more exercise tonight." Then he looked up in disgust at the gaping holes in the roof, and sighed, "Good thing you came back when you did."

Singey followed his gaze. "Mm." Turning back to Nathan, he asked, "When he's, uh, safe, would you mind if I have a look at him? I can't help wondering if this irrational behavior doesn't have something to do with the kavay alignment process. Ata Temog told me that people can do strange things when the alignment goes awry."

Nathan snorted. "Anything for an excuse to put that green goop on your hands, eh? Sure, go ahead—you may be right. And you're probably the only one in here with medical knowledge who will touch him, after the stunt he just pulled."

Nathan's eyes flicked to the Timornans venturing out into the room. "I'd better try to get everybody settled down, and go report. The Ce'awn has heard the fuss, and he'll want to know what happened."

Chapter Twenty-Four

When the first explosion from the beam rifle sounded, Pela cried out in alarm and pressed herself against Sairsa's sleeping body. "What was that, husband?"

"I don't know, sweet."

Damn it, what was going on out there, he wondered. Dunnagh shifted restlessly on the bed, all his warrior's instincts screaming for him to go find out what was happening in the next room. When the gun went off again, Dunnagh jumped, then swore. <<Tani,>> he pleaded.

<<I can't leave her now,>> Tani said. <<You're not a warrior any more, Kasha, We'll have to let Nathan and the hunting pack handle it.>>

Dunnagh reluctantly had to agree. Whatever it was, Nathan would have to take care of it. Sairsa's health was more important. He scowled at the closed door for a moment longer, then plastered a reassuring smile on his face and turned to his Avairei wife.

"Don't be afraid, sweet. I'm sure my Hunt Leader will handle the problem. Pela gave him a dubious look, but made no further comment.

A few minutes later, there was a soft knock at the door. "I'll see to it, sweet. Don't worry; just stay where you are, and keep an eye on Sairsa, while I find out what's been going on." The Kashallan retracted his tentacles. He was finished and could leave her now.

On the other side of the door, Nathan was just raising his hand for another knock when Dunnagh opened it. Nathan grimaced and dropped his hand. "What's been going on out here?"

"We had a late night visitor," Nathan said.

"Mm?"

"Yeah, Tizu dropped by and decided to do a bit of interior decorating for us. Guess he figured the property values in the neighborhood would go up if he put a few skylights in our accommodations."

Dunnagh looked up and noticed the gaping holes in the roof for the first time. Green lightning still lanced the sky, but the wind and rain seemed to be abating. He surveyed the damage for a moment longer, then his eyes lowered to the confusion going on in the rest of the room.

"Too bad he couldn't wait till it stopped raining. Anybody hurt?"

Nathan turned, eyeing the small group of frightened Timornans still huddled in the far corner and the growing puddles on the floor. "Hey, Chang, Moraga, Timma—somebody over there," he shouted. "Get a couple of buckets under those leaks and mop up that mess. Do something about it before we all drown in here."

When he saw his orders were being obeyed, he turned back to the Kashallan and continued, "Nobody is hurt. There are a few minor burns from falling debris, but most of our people are just shook up, that's all. They'll settle down in a bit."

"And how about the Commander?"

Nathan shrugged. "He's out cold but otherwise all right. Remember those handcuffs I kept after that free-lance job we did a year ago? Well, the Commander now has some new jewelry to wear. He's not going anywhere for a while."

"Do you think any of his armachda heard the noise and will be over here to investigate?"

"Maybe, but the storm is pretty bad out there—and it's late. If someone on duty heard the racket and comes to investigate, I'll talk to them. In the mean time I posted Marti as sentry. She'll let me know if there's trouble coming."

"Good. Sounds like you covered everything, thanks." Nathan gave him a pleased look and saluted. Dunnagh returned the gesture. He knew Tizu was angry about something, but this angry? It was hard to believe that whatever was bothering him, he would have taken it this far.

"Before you jumped him did he say what this was all about?"

"Sort of," he admitted. "He babbled some stuff about Sairsa and how you had taken her away from him and how he was going to kill you for it."

Dunnagh's mouth dropped open, this new revelation hitting him like a thunderbolt. Suddenly all the hostile looks and odd behavior were starting to make sense. The man was in love with her!

Gods, what a tangled web we have created for ourselves. "Should I go to him?" The Kashallan asked.

"No. Don't bother, at least not tonight anyway. He'll be fine. Singey thinks part of his irrational behavior is due to the alignment sickness. Philip is happily daubing that green goop on his fingers right now. He's delighted to have another victim to practice on. Singey or Ata Temog will do what needs doing, so don't trouble yourself."

Nathan was right; Tizu could wait, and he was getting so very tired. "How about Tessa? Do I—"

A troubled expression crossed the big man's face, but he shook his head. "She'll keep too. Temog gave her something when they returned from the mess hall. Whatever it was kept her asleep right through the fight. She's still sleeping."

Nathan stretched his neck and peered over Dunnagh's shoulder. Unable to see much, he finally asked, "How is Sairsa?"

Dunnagh swayed with weariness and steadied himself on the doorframe. He rubbed a hand across his face, and said, "Tani says a bit better, but it's still too early to tell."

Nathan surveyed him critically through narrowed eyes. "You don't look so good yourself. Hadn't you better go lie down?"

Dunnagh grimaced. "Yes. I'm going to, but I'm going to have to feed before I do. Could you find someone who is willing—"

Nathan put a hand on his shoulder and gave it a reassuring squeeze. "Yeah, I know what you need," he murmured. "I'll get somebody."

Nathan had started to turn away, when Dunnagh stopped him. "Nathan. Make sure it's someone who hasn't made the gift for a while, will you? I'm very hungry."

"Yeah, sure." Then, without turning to look at him, he said, "I'll take care of it."

Part Three: The Kavay

Chapter One

Timma's patient opened his eyes and tried to sit up, then fell back with a groan. When the pain subsided, he tried once again to sit up, then he became aware of the rope and handcuffs confining him. Cursing, he struggled frantically, then flopped back, at last recognizing the futility of further attempts to free himself.

"Please, San Tizu, don't fight or you will become sick again."

Lying back confused and gasping, the alien hunt leader happened to glance up. Through the gaping hole in the roof, he saw the russet light of a Timornan dawn. Timma saw his expression change as the memory of last night's events came rushing back into his mind.

Then he choked on another curse as the muscles in his gut spasmed, and he felt an overpowering urge to vomit. As the urge became uncontrollable, a pair of furry arms helped him turn on his side, and placed a bowl under his chin.

Tizu retched again and again, straining to relieve himself of the foul, unwanted mess that was cramping his gut. When it was over he lay back, exhausted, and glared at Timma as if somehow this was all his fault.

Pushing back his braidlets, Timma set down the brimming bowl, and wiped the human's sweating face. "There, there," he soothed in Timornan. "The Kashallan says this part of the alignment process won't last too much longer. You'll feel better soon."

The alien couldn't understand his words, but Timma hoped his tone of voice sounded reassuring. Timma sat back on his heels, but he saw only hostility in those dark eyes. He sighed. In this case his bedside manner definitely lacked something.

The young priest glanced up at the holes in the roof. This alien warrior wasn't much taller than Timma was himself, and he had no fangs or claws—not even small ones like Timma had.

If he had had a beam rifle when the Umwira attacked them in the caverns, maybe his friend Orlan wouldn't have been taken.

Avoiding the man's angry glare, Timma's eyes flicked to the front door. San Nathan had gone to someplace called the "HQ" to tell some of his other kin about the Commander's illness, and that he would be taking charge for a while.

In spite of the great honor San Nathan and the Kashallan had paid him by entrusting this man into his care, Timma would have preferred to go with San Nathan. Maybe, if he was finished here by the time San Nathan returned, he could tag along on other errands.

In spite of what this man had done, both the Kashallan and San Nathan wanted him treated, rather than killed. They claimed that this "Commander Tizu" was an experienced Hunt Leader, and should be given the chance to swear his allegiance once the kavay alignment was completed.

The problem at the moment was that most of the Avairei were afraid of his patient and wouldn't tend him. This was why Timma had been forced to stay behind when San Nathan left.

Picking up a flask of kavay-enriched water, Timma poured a large cup and held it up to the Commander's mouth. "Drink it," he coaxed. "The sooner you get used to the kavay, the sooner the alignment will be completed and you will feel better."

His patient grimaced and turned his head away. "Get that shit away from me, you furry savage. What are you trying to do, poison me?"

Timma didn't understand most of the words, but the tone was plain enough. "No, no, you must drink it. Please, San Commander Tizu, drink."

He offered the cup several more times, but always the man refused, growling at him in his strange language.

Frustrated, Timma sat back on his heels; what should he do? The man must have the kavay. Should he ask one of San Nathan's hunters to help him?

"What's wrong, young Timma?"

Timma looked up, then lowered his eyes in shame. Ima Sagas was staring down at him, arms folded across her chest. "I'm sorry, Ima, but I am having trouble fulfilling my duty. The Kashallan and San Nathan wish me to take care of this one, but he won't drink his kavay,"

Sagas transferred her baleful stare to the bound man lying on the mattress at her feet. She snorted. "I can't imagine why the Kashallan and Hunt Leader Nathan want to bother with this loathsome creature—especially after what he did. Who can understand these aliens. Here, give me that," she said and snatched the cup out of the startled Timma's hand.

Pushing the cup into Tizu's face, she commanded loudly in his language, "Drink!"

Tizu gave her a defiant look, and kept his mouth shut. "Stupid alien Warlinga, I said drink it," she growled in Timornan.

"Ima," Timma ventured, "he doesn't speak our language. He doesn't understand, he—"

"Oh, he understands me all right," Sagas said through her clenched teeth. "He's just being willful and stubborn, like the rest of his kind."

"But, Ima—"

Ignoring Timma, Sagas jammed the cup once more into Tizu's face. "Drink it, you ugly, flat-faced creature." When he still wouldn't comply, she reached over with her free hand and pinched his nostrils closed. Letting out a gargled protest, he bucked. "Hold him still, Timma. He is going to drink his kavay—or else."

When Tizu finally opened his mouth, Sagas poured the kavay down his throat with a satisfied smirk.

SPLUTTERING AND CHOKING, Tizu swallowed, then glared at her angrily. "You skinny cat-faced old witch, if you want to kill me then just do it, but stop fooling around trying to make me drink that disgusting blue slop."

A quiet chuckle near them made Tizu look up. Singey grinned. "It's not blue slop, Commander. It's blue puke juice. At least that's what Nathan dubbed it when we went through the same alignment process.

"Its actual native name is kavay, and it's what your body's been craving for some time now. The Ima here wasn't trying to poison you, but to help you."

Tizu grunted. "You couldn't prove it by me," he grumbled. He eyed the kilted figure with her arms folded across her furred chest. "So what was she saying to me?"

Kneeling down beside the bound man, Singey reached in his pouch and took out his jar of green kavay and his thorn needle. He chuckled. "In spite of the language barrier, you two were doing a pretty good job of insulting each other."

"Oh yeah? What did she say?"

Singey pricked his two middle fingers and dabbed some of the contents of the jar on the punctures. "You have to understand that the Avairei don't think any of us are very good-looking. She called you an ugly, flat-faced, stupid Warlinga."

"Warlinga?"

"Yes, a Warlinga is what they call a warrior on this planet."

Tizu scowled. "Well, I never thought I'd win a beauty contest, but ugly? And calling me stupid? Ooo, just who is this old bag, anyway?"

"It's a bit hard to translate her rank into galactic terms, Commander, but the Ima Sagas here is something like a cross between an abbess and a general. Everyone around here does what she says. Even the Ce'awn."

Tizu snorted, studying the native woman more carefully this time.

"What is this stupid Warlinga jabbering about, San Singey," Sagas asked, still keeping an eye on the repulsive male.

"Nothing much, Ima," he hedged.

Sagas returned Tizu's scowl. "Mm, Stupid Warlinga. Well, he can insult me all he wants in his jabbering tongue, but he will do what I say, and you can tell him that, too." Giving Tizu an imperious last look, she turned and stalked off, her braidlets swinging.

Watching her stiff-backed progress across the room, Tizu grunted. "Skinny old witch. She isn't going to push me around," he muttered.

Turning back to the scientist, he watched Singey touch his green-coated fingertips to an unhealed scratch along his left arm. "And just what do you think you're doing to me with that green glop on your fingers?"

For a long moment, Singey remained silent, eyes closed. At last he removed his fingertips from Tizu's arm and opened his eyes. "The alignment is coming along fine, but the injury to your head is still bothering you. I'll have Timma give you some orange kavay for the pain."

Tizu gaped and the scientist laughed softly. "It's not the type of medical exam that either of us is used to, Commander, but it's how things are done here on this planet. I'm checking on your condition for the Kashallan."

At the mention of Dunnagh, Tizu grimaced. "I'm fine. At least, I would be if you and the rest of these savages would leave me alone."

Singey's eyes flicked to the brimming bowl of vomit on the floor, then returned his gaze to the commander's. The bowl's smelly contents was a pungent testimony to the contrary. He shook his head. "Commander, you and I both know that's a lie.

"As I mentioned earlier, your symptoms are those of the kavay alignment. We all went through it during our captivity. As your body adapts to life on this world, these symptoms will go away—provided you continue to ingest the kavay."

"That's a bunch of superstitious drivel, and I'm surprised that a man of your education would believe in such nonsense. It's just a stupid native virus. It comes and goes. Bennett's been treating us for it for quite some time.

"And if I am sick with the damned virus again, then I demand to be treated by a real physician, not by you and a bunch of native witch doctors sticking green paste on your fingers and giving me blue crap to drink."

Singey opened his mouth as if to speak, then thought better of it. His hands moved with quick, angry gestures as he busied himself putting away his medical supplies. When they were packed he returned his attention to Tizu. "Commander, it's because I am a scientist that I am telling you this. Believe me, I was just as skeptical when I was first told about the kavay, if not more so."

Tizu grunted, unconvinced. Deciding to change the subject, he asked. "What's happened to Sairsa? She was sick, but Bennett was treating her. If anything happens to her, I'll kill him."

"Yes," Singey said, "You've already tried to do that." He glanced pointedly at the handcuffs. Following his gaze, Tizu scowled.

"For your information," Singey continued, his tone of voice hardening, "Sairsa is very sick as you say. She is going through the alignment—same as you. There are certain complications in her case, but she is receiving the best treatment this planet can offer. Everything is being done to save her life, believe me."

"But she needs a doctor!" Tizu pleaded. "Damn it, man, I don't care what Kai and you bunch of psychos plan to do with me, but she needs proper medical care and—"

"And you just don't seem to be getting the picture here, Commander," Singey interrupted. "Sairsa is being treated by a doctor, a Timornan doctor, trained to recognize and treat Timornan conditions. On this world, Bennett doesn't know what he's doing!

"Oh, I'm sure Dr. B has tried his best, but he doesn't have any idea how to treat the alignment, and you know it as well as I do."

Unable to answer, Tizu looked away. Yes, damn him, Singey was right. Bennett's own failing health was clear testimony to that. He sighed. "Yeah, maybe you're right. So, what do you and your 'Ce'awn' plan to do with me?"

"I have no idea at the moment what will be done with you. You're quite ill, and you'll need to rest, but a lot of what happens from now on will depend on you." He looked pointedly at the cuffs again, then added, "Nobody wants to keep you chained up like this, but, on the other hand, this barracks doesn't need any more interior decorating. And innocent people don't need to be scared half out of their wits either. You think about it.

"I'm going to go over to sickbay and talk to Dr. B. You'd probably be more comfortable over there. If there are others who need to be treated—well, it would be best to have all the sick in one place. But that's not my decision to make."

He smiled. "That will be up to the senior healers and the Ce'awn to decide. I'm just the apprentice, like Timma here."

Singey motioned to the young Avairei squatting patiently nearby. "Timma will stay with you for now and help you. But don't give him any more trouble about taking your medication, or he probably will call his Ima back over to help him."

"All right, all right, I'll drink the damned stuff for now," he muttered.

Singey stood up. "Good, I'll tell him." Shifting languages, Singey said, "Stay with him, Timma. He's promised to take his kavay without causing trouble, but if he forgets, get the Ima to help you." He winked and the youth gave him a faint smile in return.

Chapter Two

The rest of D barracks' occupants had arisen while he'd been occupied with his patient. Rhys and Chang stood in the center of the floor gazing up at the holes in the roof discussing repairs. Around them, the Loti and Begta mopped the floor, stacked the mattresses along the walls and carried outside armloads of damp bedding to hang on the thorn bushes to dry. On a long table near their altar, the Avairei set out food and sorted through their damaged belongings.

Unlike the usual morning clamor, the Timornans were going about the daily routine with troubled expressions on their faces, and when they spoke to one another it was in low frightened voices. Singey saw them glance up often at the holes in the roof and then at the Kashallan's closed door.

Inwardly he raged. Damn, these poor people didn't need this again. Everyone was just getting over the Umwira attack—and now this. Swallowing his annoyance he wandered over to the long table in search of something to eat.

The red-gold Timornan sun was well over the horizon and sending soft golden light into the barracks windows by the time Singey finished breakfast and was ready to face Bennett and the laboratory. Did Bennett know about Tizu's illness? It would be all over camp soon enough.

Many people would be troubled by the news. Perhaps it would be a kindness to warn him before he was bombarded by questions from Arishim and the Dymarians.

Just as he was about to head over to the sickbay, Ata Temog hailed him. "San Singey, if you will act as my translator, perhaps I should come along. I would like to see this 'sickbay' and talk to your Doctor Bennett myself. Do you think that would be all right?"

"I see no reason why not, Ata, and I would be honored to translate for you." He motioned to Rhys standing by the door to join them.

Rhys opened the door and allowed the elder Avairei and Singey to precede him out into the quadrangle.

Outside the sky was clear and raindrops sparkled in the purple thorn bushes. Singey took in several lungfuls of the vibrant air; it smelled of copper and vanilla, and a pungent, peppery scent, for which he had no name. They stepped around blue-tinted puddles in the Quadrangle, already shrinking in the morning light. Near HQ a couple black-clad armachda followed their progress warily, but made no move to stop them.

When they arrived at the sickbay an ominous silence and the stench of souring vomit caused them to pause in the doorway. The place seemed deserted. Bennett or his assistant Gail should be here. He called out, but received no reply. Could they be at the mess getting breakfast? Maybe, but that smell. It hadn't been here last night. They waited, ears straining. Singey called Bennett's name again.

He was about to send Rhys to the mess to look for Bennett when the door to the lab was opened a crack and an eye peeked through the opening. In the next moment the door was flung wide. An ashen -faced and trembling Meldra Arishim leaned against the doorframe. "Oh, Philip, I think he's dead!"

Singey was beside her in an instant, grabbing her as she swayed. "What are you talking about, Councilor? Who?"

For answer, she stepped aside and motioned to a crumpled body lying on the lab floor in a congealing pool of vomit. Brushing past her, Singey knelt beside the prone man, reaching for a hand to take his pulse.

"I found him like that a few minutes ago," Arishim explained in a quavering voice. "I-I came here to get Dr. B. Briya is down with the virus again, and—" She choked, back a sob.

Temog crouched beside Singey, helping him slide Bennett away from the noxious puddle and turn him over. "As best I can tell, Ata, his pulse is weak, but he is still alive,"

Temog took out his jar and thorn. "Mm. I take it that this is your Doctor Bennett."

Singey nodded, then reached over, rolled up Bennett's sleeve, and made the required scratch for the diagnosis. Temog placed his green-daubed fingers over the cut and closed his eyes.

Singey looked up; Arishim was staring down at the priest, her eyes wide with a mixture of horror and fascination. "He's not dead, Councilor, but he's very weak." Suddenly wondering if another one was sick too, he said, "Where's Gail?"

"S-she's asleep in the other room. I tried to wake her, but I couldn't rouse her. Dr. Singey, Gail has this yellow stuff all over her face—I thought they were both dead—"

Singey eyed the priest; he wished Arishim would shut up. What was taking Temog so long? "She's not dead, and the yellow stuff is nothing to worry about. She was given a strong sedative last night and must be still sleeping it off. Don't worry about her for the moment."

"Will Dr. B be all right?"

Singey made an impatient cutting gesture and returned his attention to the priest. When Temog opened his eyes again he said, "How is he?"

"Not good. He has the alignment sickness, but he has also been dosing himself with something that is very bad. The kavay has almost killed him in its efforts to get rid of the alien drug."

"What can we do for him?"

Temog sighed. "We can give him the kavay, of course, but he is very weak. His body can't stand much more of the violent spasms that accompany the alignment." A note of regret coming into his voice, Temog said. "I don't have the kind of medications he needs with me. If his life is to be saved, we will have to ask the Kashallan for help."

Singey sat back on his heels. He knew what Temog meant. The young symbiont's strength was already being overtaxed. But if they didn't tell the Kashallan, and the man died—well, that would create its own set of problems. "We will have to tell him," Singey agreed, "but not just yet."

"Yes. Sagas isn't going to like this, but it is clear that these people are beginning the alignment, whether they like it or not, so we will have to care for them as best we can."

Addressing Rhys, Singey said, "Help me get Dr. Bennett settled in a bed in the other room, then go to D barracks and bring us back some kavay. If the Ce'awn is awake, tell him he'll need to look at this case, but if he's busy, or resting—I'll come and tell him later myself."

WHEN BENNETT WAS SETTLED, and the armachd had gone, Singey left Temog to watch their patient, and led Arishim into the outer room and set her down in a chair. Reaching into Bennett's desk, he pulled out the doctor's bottle and poured the woman a generous drink. She took it gratefully, downing half the glass in one long swallow.

Singey could see the mistrust in her eyes as she watched him put away the bottle. He sighed and turned back to face her. "Councilor, listen to me. I know you've been warned about my Ce'awn and me, but we are not crazy or dangerous. Can't you see that we are the only ones who know this planet and can help? Won't you try to have some faith in us?"

Arishim sighed, and sat down her empty glass. "Maybe you're right, Philip, but it isn't easy for us."

"Councilor, the man in there with Dr. B is an experienced Timornan doctor. For treating a Timornan condition, like the kavay alignment, he is far more experienced than someone trained in galactic medicine. We learned last night that there are others here who have been sick. The medications Dr. B has been prescribing have been masking the symptoms, but the alignment is still trying to proceed.

"Both Citizen Basheya and Commander Tizu are ill with the kavay alignment as well. It's not just Dr. Bennett. We need these people to come forward and be treated or there will be deaths—and no one wants that.

"Meldra, I need your help with this. Talk to your people. If they have had any kind of symptoms, they must come for treatment. Do you understand? They will die otherwise."

Singey watched Arishim's expression change when he mentioned Tizu's illness. He hoped his expression conveyed the seriousness of his words. "Yes, Councilor, there will be no support from that quarter. Please believe me. We only want to help."

She thought about it a moment longer then sighed. "All right, Dr. Singey, I will do what I can to assist you. I'll talk to my people. I don't know if I believe everything you and your leader said last night, but I won't work against you, either. I'm sure you're right—those who are sick need to be treated.

"I have a responsibility to my people—and you and your chieftain seem to know what you're talking about. If you can cure this illness and prevent a death, that's more important than anything else at the moment."

Chapter Three

The Kashallan lay back on the bed and closed his eyes. He was exhausted, every bone and muscle in his body ached. He had to sleep; his sweet Sairsa, Bennett, Tizu, so many were sick—needed his help—but first he just had to rest.

Within Dunnagh's middle Tani stirred restlessly, their hunger a nagging goad, making it difficult for it to settle. They had fed recently, as much as he could allow himself, but it wasn't enough. Their formula was nearly gone, and even with the blood gift to supplement their dwindling food supply, it was becoming clear to both bondmates that they couldn't continue on much longer as they were.

Dunnagh was worried. Tani had been trying to shield him from knowing its true condition, but its dwindling strength bled through the bond. He, alien that he was, could 'taste' the life-threatening strain of the healings the symbiont was forced to conduct, if these people were to be strong enough to leave the mesa in time to avoid the storms.

Feeling very discouraged, Dunnagh wondered if he had done the right thing in coming here. Yet what other choice had he? He'd had to warn the base—save as many as he could. Not to mention that his own hunting pack of human warriors needed better weapons than bone-tipped spears before they headed into the Great Swamp.

The notion shocked him, but he missed the interfering presence of the Makers. Where were the big worms when he needed them anyway? Ensnared in its coils he could relax, have a satisfying meal and let the big worm solve his problems....

Dunnagh stifled a laugh. No chance of that happening anytime soon, so he'd better stop feeling sorry for himself and get on with solving his own problems. Maker Gladdris had entrusted the young symbiont into his care. Against the advice of some of the others, Gladdris had allowed him/them their independence. He valued Gladdris's high regard, but on the other hand he/they needed help.

Gladdris had warned him upon their last meeting, not to swim the spirit pathways of this world unaccompanied. After nearly dying entrapped in an Umwira illusion, he had some idea of the dangers awaiting him should he ignore that admonition. He'd given the matter careful thought, but still saw no other solution.

The night outside was quiet. A dim glow from the solar-powered lights in the quadrangle cast wavering patterns upon the opposite wall. In the bed behind him, his wives slept, almost as worn out, as he was himself. Tani at last lay quiescent as well. Dunnagh took a deep breath and closed his eyes. The Caldoni invocation of opening, singing in his mind, his awareness sank deeper into the trance....

Another breath and Dunnagh allowed his spirit body to rise from his physical form and drift into the void. The silver tether to his living flesh trailing out behind him, he swam deeper into the dark passageways of the otherworld.

Unfortunately, it wasn't long before Dunnagh found himself hopelessly lost. Humans being such visually orientated creatures, even the inner world of the spiritual plane was interpreted by his people in visual imagery. This alien otherworld of the Khutani was another reality all together, however.

His eyes here were useless. About him was the stink of ozone, fish slime and burning copper. All sound was distorted in the blackness. Taps and loud booms, then what might be the groan of ponderous rocks falling down about him.

Dunnagh shied making a hasty retreat from he knew not what. A little farther he was assaulted by an icy vibration and heard what he thought was the roar and hiss of water cascading through the channel of an underground river.

He was hesitant to attract attention to himself by calling out for Gladdris, in case the Umwira were near enough to also hear. But he was lost, and had to do something....

Before he could make up his mind what to do, Dunnagh heard a frightened wail. The cry was indistinct as if he were hearing it underwater. Then the silver cord of his tether quivered, bringing with each vibration a sense of urgency. Dunnagh readied himself for attack. Maybe the Umwira had found him....

No it was only Tani. The dreaming symbiont had discovered him missing. Following his tether, it had swum into the void in search of him. Using the cord as a guide, Dunnagh traced his way, hoping to discover his bondmate before anything dire happened to either of them. Tani shouldn't be swimming the void alone. Neither should he, maybe, but too late to worry about that now.

It wasn't long before Dunnagh caught sight of a glowing silver eel-like being, streaking towards him through the gloom. Relief flooded his awareness; it was Tani, in its natural Khutani form. Sensing his nearness at nearly the same instant, Tani hurled itself into Dunnagh's outstretched arms, wrapping its coils about his chest.

<<Kasha, oh Kasha, I found you.>> Tani rested its head on his shoulder, its mouth tentacles anxiously exploring his face.

Dunnagh put up a hand and stroked the distraught symbiont. <<Calm down, Tani. Don't take on so. Why did you follow me? What are you doing here?>>

The symbiont reared back its head, mouth tentacles quivering. <<What am I doing here? Shouldn't I be asking you that question? We were warned not to swim the dark rivers of the void. Maker Gladdris will be very cross with us for disobeying—>>

<<Maybe, but I had to risk it.>>

<<Why, Kasha?>>

<<Because I'm worried about you. And we need help.>> Tani started to protest, but Dunnagh interrupted. <<Tani stop. I remember what the elder said. I know it's dangerous. But I also know you can't hide from me what a strain so much healing work is having on you. We need help and that means finding Amla Gladdris or one of the others. And we need more formula before we journey on to Ticca.>>

<<I taste your reasoning and find its flavor—palatable—though I don't like to admit it,>> Tani grumbled.

Dunnagh chuckled. <<I wish you'd let me do this myself, but since you're here—and I know won't go back without me—got any ideas how to

find one of our elders?>> He waved a hand encompassing the gloom. <<I can't see anything in this blackness.>>

Tani made a noise that sounded to Dunnagh's spirit-ear like a snort. <<You're not supposed to see anything, silly. You have to 'taste' the way.>>

<<Mm, I was afraid you were going to say something like that. All right, can you 'taste' one of our elders nearby?>>

<<I'll try.>> uncoiling a portion of its mass from around his neck and chest, Tani stretched out its head with mouth tentacles waving, savoring the ether through which Dunnagh propelled them.

<<This is why you need me to always come with you, Kasha, as an alien on this world you don't understand how to—>>

<<Tani, instruct, or scold me later. Keep searching.>>

<<All right, I'm searching. I'll find the spoor.>>

Dunnagh swam blindly through the darkness, allowing his bondmate to focus on the task at hand. He had no concept of time passing in this other realm, but it seemed like they'd been searching for a long time—and the longer they remained, the greater would be their chance of discovery by an enemy.

But Dunnagh also had become aware of Tani's frustration. It, too, was equally aware of their peril, but was unable to detect any sign of a Khutani presence. Had they swam in the wrong direction? Direction? There was no direction in the void. Intent was the key to location, or finding what one wanted.

All right, if they weren't going the wrong way, then maybe the Makers were shielding, because they didn't want to be found. They wouldn't be expecting a visit from the bondmates; it was possible. Or it could also be that an enemy was blocking them. Enemy—Umwira Psy. Dunnagh's aura quivered with that latest revelation.

He was just about to suggest to Tani that they turn back and try again tomorrow night, when a sphere of blinding orange light engulfed them.

Tani screamed, its head wreathed about with flames.

Battle-trained reflexes springing into action, Dunnagh pulled Tani out of the flames and hugged it close to his chest. As the sting of the etheric fire licked at his own exposed feet and legs, he hastily swirled a geyser of blue water around them.

The orange flames exploded into clouds of rolling steam, whining and moaning like a teapot on the boil. From beyond the cloud, he could hear the frustrated roars of their attackers. Dunnagh bared his teeth in a silent challenge. Umwira Filth.

Still maintaining his shield, he diverted some of his attention to his bondmate. Against his chest he could feel the symbiont trembling. <<Oh, Shalla, I'm so sorry—I should have been paying more attention. Tani, how badly are you hurt?>>

Tani hugged him tighter, but it answered bravely enough. <<Not bad I think. My fault, not yours, Kasha, I should have been more careful—>>

The mist was dissipating, the sullen orange light revealing the hulking forms of a pack of misshapen monsters. They were somewhat simian in appearance with heavy upper bodies, long muscular arms and lethally clawed hands. Like Warlinga, they had scales rather than fur covering their bodies. Also like Warlinga, they sported whip-like tails and heavy jaws bristling with long fangs.

With a gurgle of a laugh the one appearing to be their leader lumbered through the last shreds of hot mist. The rest of the pack fanned out to cut off any possible retreat. <<What have we caught trespassing, cousins?>> the leader growled. It's voice was deep and gravely, sending a tremor through Dunnagh's aura.

Another let out a chortling laugh. <<An infant slimeworm and its mutant slave.>>

<<By the Power of the Poison Fires, our hunt has been blessed. We shall feast well,>> a third monster cried with glee.

Dunnagh would have liked to create a beam rifle out of his etheric matter and blast those toothy grins off their hideous faces, but he doubted if he had the strength to shield and create such a complex weapon. <<Leave while you still can, Umwira Filth.>>

He settled for a sword and lashed out at a pack member who ventured too close, but even so, he was aware of the dimming of his protective shell.

With a snarl the creature leapt out of reach, but returned to taunt him almost immediately. The Umwira, too, must have sensed his growing weakness. They howled and laughed as they surrounded him in ever narrowing circles.

<<Growing tired, mutant, want to rest?>>

<<Let us caress you with the fire. When the pain dies you may sleep forever.>>

<<Traitor.>>

<< No, traitor, your death will not be restful!—not at all.>>

<<My Kasha is no traitor, Unnatural Beast,>> Tani cried

<<Oh, ho, the infant speaks!>> their leader laughed. <<Have no fear, little one, once we kill the traitor we will enjoy playing with you as well.>>

<<Come play with us, infant slimeworm. Yes play with us. We want to teach you a new game—very painful—very delicious.>> The pack howled, their threatening attacks increasing with each taunt.

Dunnagh was having a hard time keeping them all in sight, and deflecting their fiery attempts to smash through his shield.

<<Tani, it's probably not a good idea to antagonize them further. I'm barely holding on here.>>

Tani wasn't listening. Goaded by its instinctual hatred and the pack's taunts the symbiont gave as good as it got.

Then, he felt Tani squirm loose from about his chest. Dunnagh made a grab for the symbiont, but it eluded him and flung itself at an attacker Dunnagh hadn't noticed. The scaly creature had snuck behind them and had seized the bondmates' tether within its powerful jaws.

<<Oh shit,>> Dunnagh muttered, <<that's torn it.>> He shouted a Caldoni war cry, banished his shield and took the offensive with his sword. If the cord was severed, their spirits would be trapped in the otherworld and their body would die in the physical realm.

Dunnagh missed his target, but he had no time to renew his attack on the Umwira gnawing at his tether. Barrier gone he was mobbed by the rest of the pack. <<Tani leave me. Get away! I'll keep them busy as long as I can!>>

Heroic words, a noble gesture, but stupid, he realized in the next moment. Tani couldn't survive without him. They were doomed....

Tani ignored or hadn't heard him anyway. Focused on its prey, it lunged towards the monster holding their lives in its jaws. Coiling like a striking snake, Tani opened its mouth and spat out a stream of dark light. The somber violet glow encircled the head of its adversary, penetrating like acid.

The creature screamed, dropping the tether. It staggered away, clawing at the melting features of its face.

In the momentary confusion that followed, Dunnagh lopped off the arm of the nearest attacker, snatched up his dazed bondmate and fled blindly into the darkness.

<<Tani, what did you just do?>>

<<I made the otherworld equivalent of black kavay,>> came the weak reply.

<<Black kavay, eh? Well, you can explain that one to me—later.>> Still running flat out, he hugged the symbiont tighter, praying that "later" wouldn't be in the halls of the dead.

He could sense bubbles of hysterical laughter threatening to rise up and choke him. <<It's maybe nice to know that I'm not the only one in this partnership that Nathan would curse out for being heroic and stupid.>>

<<Are you going to tell him?>>

<<Probably not.>>

<<That might be best.... Kasha, I'm very tired.>>

<<I know, little one. Be brave. Don't fade on me—we'll find the Makers—somehow.>>

Though he'd been joking with the symbiont, trying to distract it, inwardly he was cursing himself for a fool. Making that—whatever it was—had cost Tani vital energy.

He could see the dullness of the symbiont's blue tether braided in with his own silver cord. He should have anticipated Tani coming after him, should have been more alert—where were the damned big worms when he needed one?

Somewhere in the gloom behind them, he could hear the pack baying in hot pursuit. Dunnagh poured more of his life-energy into speed. The pack had discovered their trail. The Umwira were gaining.

Then, jagged forks of lightning lit up the gloom at their backs, followed by a booming roar and howls of pain. Burning ozone stung his nostrils and a whirlwind snatched them up, spinning them about wildly. The bondmates clung to one another, helpless as leaves in a cyclone.

Then, in the next moment a glowing net snatched them from the chaos of the storm, dragging them to safety out of the wind. Dunnagh could see only the shadowy forms of several creatures pulling the strands of the net deeper into the void.

Fearing that another warband of the enemy had captured them, Dunnagh was about to conjure another etheric sword, to slash their way out of the net, when Tani stopped him. <<Don't hurt them, Kasha, I recognize some of our cousins from the Sulas pod. We are safe now.>>

Now that Tani had drawn it to his attention, he could see that their captors were indeed Khutani—and maybe a little familiar. But whether they were safe, that was debatable. The pod refused to answer Tani's greeting, and didn't seem happy to see them.

<<Where are they taking us, Shalla,>> Dunnagh murmured.

<<Silence, disobedient child. You will know soon enough,>> the largest Khutani growled.

<<Your foolishness has drawn Our Amla away from important matters and endangered us all,>> another spat.

Sensing Tani's weak and frightened body coiled tight about his middle made Dunnagh angry. <<Arrogant slimeworms! Our reason for coming is important, as well,>> Dunnagh shot back. <<Where is Maker Gladdris? The Maker is our Amla, too, you know. And we need to speak with it.>>

<<Patience, young one, >> came a gentle voice from the tangled gray mass hovering around him. <<The Maker will be with us shortly. It lingers only to make sure all the enemy is dead.>>

As the Khutani finished speaking, they arrived in a sheltered pool, glowing strands of fungi clinging to the walls of a shadowy grotto. Flung into the pool's center, the net was banished from around them. Still clutching his bondmate, Dunnagh tread water and surveyed the circling pod.

<<What now, Tani?>> Dunnagh murmured. He got his answer soon enough.

Rising up from the ebony waters beneath them, Maker Gladdris enfolded him in its heavy coils. There was a long gash, leaking ichor on the Maker's neck, a gift from the Umwira chasing them, no doubt.

Gladdris's hold was confining—almost painful. Dunnagh tensed as the Maker's mouth tentacles examined him and the symbiont. Unlike his other encounters, this probe stung—radiating Khutani displeasure.

<<Amla Gladdris, please don't be angry,>> Tani whined. <<We had to come. We need your help.>>

Finished with its exam, Gladdris loosened its coils and Dunnagh lay back relieved. Maybe it would hear them out, before deciding to discipline—or eat them.

<<Your flavor has a sour tang, young ones. I had hoped you would be well on your way to Ticca by now and under the protection of Maker Tinguss. But I taste that you are not. What has happened? Why have you risked so much to come in search of me?>>

With help from Tani, Dunnagh related what had happened to them since leaving Sulas. He explained about the sick humans and their desperate need for more formula. As they spoke, Gladdris's descendants twined themselves about the Maker's massive coils, the better to listen.

When the bondmates finished, the maker was silent for a long time, at last it said, <<This news is very disturbing to all of us. I taste your exhaustion and depletion of strength. Before escorting you back to the threshold of waking, we will share with you all the etheric power that we can spare. You will wake strengthened, if not renewed.>>

<<And what of our formula?>> Dunnagh pressed. <<Is there a pool somewhere in the Broken Lands where we could go to get help?

<<Knowing how the Avairei despise the little folk, I doubt if they would care for them without enslaving them should they come to them for medicine. What provisions have the Khutani made for the Begta?>>

Gladdris gurgled a laugh. <<You are a very clever being, Chosen. There are 'wild pools' in the Broken Lands, but their whereabouts has been kept secret. But you are correct we can offer you succor there as well.

<<I will send a few of my descendants as messengers ahead of you. You will be cared for. Send Begta with containers to the nearest pool and we will make what you need.>>

<<Thank you, Amla,>> Tani said.

<<Lie back now and rest. We will form the link and share our power with you. And after what has happened, don't venture these dark waters in future, unless you absolutely must,>> Gladdris warned. <<We will do what we can to shield you, but the tang of your spoor flavors the dark channels now. The Umwira will be searching for you.>>

Chapter Four

With eyes still closed, Sairsa took in a deep breath and let it out in a long sigh. It felt so good to be lying on a soft bed, safe, warm and free of pain. A dim light filtered through her closed eyelids; outside all was quiet. Was it morning yet? She savored the pungent smell of human male, and another more delicate, spicy musk nearby. She stretched, turned on her side, smiling as she recognized the pair of blue eyes gazing at her.

Rising up on one elbow, Dunnagh leaned over and kissed her on the forehead, his lips a soft caress against her skin. "Good morning, love. I'm glad you're finally awake."

It was morning, but still early yet. Through the slats in the window shade she could see a glimpse of russet sky. Over his shoulder near a closed door, leather packs and clay jars were stacked along a bare wall. None of this looked familiar. "Dunnagh? What happened—where am I?"

"We are in D barracks, sweet. You're here with me and Pela. You've been very sick, my love. The illness Dr. Bennett was treating you for wasn't a virus at all, but what Timornans call the kavay alignment. Your body has been going through the process and the drugs Bennett proscribed were poisoning you.

"Kavay? I don't understand."

"All life on this world is aligned with the kavay. My armachda and I went through the same sickness when we were captured. It's a painful process, but once aligned you will become healthy again, I promise."

His voice suddenly thick with emotion, he said, "Gods, I don't know what I would have done if Pela hadn't found you in time."

Time, time for what? Her head felt like it was stuffed with cotton. "Pela? Who is Pela?"

For answer, he reached across her and stroked another's velvety shoulder. As if aware of his regard, even in her slumber, Pela sighed and laid a possessive arm across Sairsa's hip. "Pela," he said, continuing to stroke the native fondly.

Turning her head, she became aware of someone at her back. She touched the woman's silky fur. One of the natives, and somehow vaguely familiar. But what was she doing here, in bed with herself and Dunnagh?

"She's been praying for all of us, ever since I told her about you," Dunnagh explained. "When we arrived here, she tried to tell me something about your illness and how her Goddess had charged her with your care.

"I didn't understand, more fool me. But my courageous dear knew your life was in danger, and she got one of my armachda to help her find you just in time."

He chuckled, remembering. "Poor Gail—I think she's almost forgiven us, but we did give her an awful time that night. Since we brought you back here, Pela has been nursing you constantly. I gave her a sedative a few hours ago so she would sleep; otherwise she'd be up right now mother-henning us both. She was so frightened for you, my love—but for now we'll just let her sleep, all right?"

Sairsa disengaged herself from the clinging woman and turned back to face him. "I still don't understand—if I was so sick why wasn't Gail taking care of me? And, why am I here rather than in the sickbay?"

"Sickbay is very crowded at the moment. Gail and Dr. Bennett are both very sick, too, my love. And I was being selfish," he gave her a faint smile, "I wanted you near me."

"How long have I been here? I don't remember anything after checking myself into the sickbay."

His face clouded as he thought about her question. Sairsa became aware of the dark circles around his eyes and the gaunt hollows under his cheekbones. *He looks as tired as I feel. Has he been sick too?*

"You've been here—four, maybe five days. I'm not sure exactly—there has been so much going on, I've lost track of the days too. Ask Pela later, if you really want to know."

Pela. Sairsa glanced over her shoulder at the sleeping native woman. She was so tired—and all this was so confusing—what was she missing here? Trying to curb her growing annoyance, she said, "Dunnagh, I don't understand. Why is she here with us in our bed?"

Ignoring her question, he closed his eyes; his lips moved, but she couldn't make out what he was saying. Sairsa leaned forward. "What did you say?"

Seemingly lost in his own internal dialogue Dunnagh made no answer. Sairsa shivered. He looked so odd; had Commander Tizu and Dr. B been right about him all along? "Dunnagh?"

Dunnagh jerked as if stung by a bug and opened his eyes; When she saw she had his attention again she said, "Dunnagh, are you all right?"

"No, I mean yes—" He chuckled and tried to hug her, but she stiffened and drew back. A pleading look came into his eyes, but he made no attempt to force the intimacy.

He took a deep breath, and at last said, "Sairsa, things have changed for all of us since we came to Timorna—perhaps for me most of all. I've been afraid that you wouldn't understand. There's so much I want—"

Ignoring his stammered explanation, Sairsa's stomach churned and her eyes blurred with unshed tears. Best get this over with quick; maybe it will hurt less that way. "Dunnagh, are you trying to tell me that you don't want me anymore? That you don't love me?"

"No, oh no!" Dunnagh made a strangled noise in his throat and gathered her to him. Unable to resist him this time, she buried her face against his chest, the hot tears beginning to flow. "Oh Sairsa, it's not that; I will always love you. It's just that—things are different for me now—"

He sighed, groping for words. "Sairsa, I have sworn an Oath to serve the land and people of Timorna. My bond and my new life bring with it responsibilities and obligations that I can't, and won't, break, because these ties involve more than the person of Dunnagh Kai."

He bent and kissed her gently, his mouth a yearning promise upon hers. Then he pulled back so he could look into her eyes. "I still want you and need you, Sairsa.

"But the life I can offer you now is a very different kind of life—a fulfilling one, I would hope, but it will not be like the dreams that you and the old Dunnagh made before leaving Dymar. Will you share this new life with all of us, love? For my sake, would you try?"

Sairsa didn't understand, but his words frightened her. All those weeks of waiting—of hoping and praying—all that time, knowing, somehow, that he would come back to her. Now—he was back, and he was right; it wasn't the same.

Suddenly she felt very alone. She had lost so much, her home, her family, everything. Would she have to lose him too? Dunnagh was her one anchor in this sea of nightmares. Oh, Gods, what was she going to do about the baby—his baby—if she lost him?

"What are you thinking about, love?"

She sighed, drawn out of her thoughts by his voice. "Dunnagh, I want to understand, but you're not making much sense. Tell me about this bond, and these obligations you're referring to, and," she took a deep breath, "tell me about Pela."

Dunnagh gave her a lopsided grin. "Yes, you're right—I'm not being very clear. Let me begin by telling you first about Tani, then I'll get to Pela."

Tani? Who's Tani—oh, Gods, not another native woman! "Tani?"

"Remember I spoke about my choosing to accept a bond?" She nodded. "Well, the bond is called a kashallan in the Timornan tongue. It is a bond between a host and a symbiont. In this case the host body is me, Dunnagh, and the symbiont who now shares my flesh is Tani, a child of the ancient race of this world, the Khutani."

Sairsa pulled away from him and stared incredulous. Was he serious? He nodded, his blue eyes solemn. She shuddered. Suddenly dizzy she closed her eyes, her mouth quivering. A symbiont? Had she heard him a right? She was so tired—and this was all so confusing.

"Sairsa? Don't be afraid, love—please I'm no alien monster; a part of me is still the Dunnagh you know. I won't hurt you. Though we share the same body now, Tani and I are two separate beings in many ways. The Khutani can't survive on the surface world except as symbionts. It's a partnership, you see. Together, as the Kashallan, we have obligations to fulfill on this planet.

"Tani is a healer, among other things. We have been charged by the Khutani elders to offer service wherever we are needed. If you choose to be with me, love, you must know that my bond and its duties, will sometimes have to be put first—before our personal concerns."

Never in her wildest dreams had she ever considered something like this. "This is all so strange, I-I don't know what to say."

"There is nothing I want you to say; you need time to get used to all this." Picking up her hand, he laid it across his muscular middle; inside Tani shifted its position. Her eyes opened wide as she felt the alien within her lover's body move under her hand.

"Tani?"

He nodded. "My bondmate. It was Tani who helped you when you were so ill, Sairsa."

She trailed her fingers over his pale skin, just able to feel the symbiont's coils deep within his flesh. "How?"

"You mean how can Tani do its work from in there?" She nodded. Dunnagh chuckled. "Well, that did present a problem. Certain modifications have been made in my body so that my inner companion can taste, as it puts it, the outside world."

Taking her hand once again, the Kashallan held out his other hand and extended his tentacles, then slipped them into her arm to form the link.

Sairsa let out a startled cry and tried to pull her hand away, but he held her firmly until she relaxed. "Don't be afraid. I won't hurt you—I promise. I just want to make sure the alignment is progressing well."

Dunnagh closed his eyes, suddenly absorbed in his diagnosis. Unable to stop herself, she stared at his tentacles. The experience didn't exactly hurt, but it made her feel queasy—it was so weird. When he finally opened his eyes, Sairsa could sense that there was something different about him.

"There," Tani said, a different timbre to the voice now addressing her. "Not so bad, is it? Actually, sweet Sairsa, I've been doing this to you for some time now—tasting you, so I could assure my Kasha that you were getting better."

Realizing that she was now talking to the symbiont, Tani, she tried once again to pull away.

"No, no, my sweet one, I can taste your fear, and there is no reason for it, I assure you. Try to remember—you have felt my touch before. Think back to when you were so ill. I tasted you many times then. I gave you respite from the pain, remember? And with my medicines, I am helping the kavay complete the alignment. I am a healer, I would not hurt you. My Kasha Dunnagh loves you very much."

Dunnagh's face took on a child-like eagerness. "Please don't be afraid of me—I want to be your friend and love you, too."

Vaguely she did remember something, but the events of the last few days were all a blur. Sairsa's heart gave a lurch. Unable to meet that expectant gaze, she closed her eyes. *Oh Dunnagh, this was so creepy—why did you do this to yourself?*

"Sairsa, this isn't good for you, in your condition. I will have to put you back to sleep if you become too frightened of me," the symbiont warned.

Sairsa's eyes flew open. Had there been a hint of menace in the alien voice? She glanced down at the pink, alien tentacles stuck in her flesh and shuddered. Healer. What other powers did the symbiont possess?

Tani gazed at her out of Dunnagh's sweet blue eyes, a concerned expression on that beloved face. That face—that face that was not just his face anymore. Oh, Gods, could she get used to this? Could she live with this—this creature that was part her lover and part alien stranger?

It was watching her intently now—could it read her thoughts too? Then it released its tentacles from her flesh.

"Give it time, my Sairsa," Dunnagh said. "Give it time. And, whatever you finally decide, I will understand, and I will always love you."

She sighed and nodded. Yes, it would take time, and the creature—Dunnagh, Tani, or whatever it was—was right; she was weak and tired. This whole situation was too much to think about just now.

Pela yawned, propped herself on her elbow and glared at Dunnagh-Tani with accusing eyes. "You made me sleep, didn't you?"

He gave her a toothy grin. "I did. You wouldn't listen to me when I told you to rest. You were wearing yourself out. I merely did what I thought best for you, sweet."

Sairsa stifled another shudder, noticing, for the first time, his sharp triangular teeth, obviously another alien adaptation the symbiont had made in her lover's body.

"Hah, and do you listen when my Ima, or the Ata, or even when San Nathan or I tell you that you need to rest, hmm?"

"No, not usually," he admitted, "but all of you have a way of making me pay for my disobedience in the end."

She laughed. "Mm, and you deserve it—you would drain yourself completely if we didn't stop you."

"Yes, my sweet, but sometimes—like now—it can't be helped; there are so many sick ones to look after." Dunnagh gave Sairsa a wink. "See what I mean about mother-henning? And she's not the worst of them; she's still taking lessons from her Ima."

Pela noticed that Sairsa was awake and smiled. "Ah, my sister-wife, you are awake now—I am so glad." She leaned over and brushed her tongue across Sairsa's cheek. "Are you feeling better, my Sairsa'meh?" Before she could answer, Pela looked at Dunnagh-Tani. "Is she better, husband, is she?"

He nodded. "She is better, little one, but still weak and needing rest—as do you, I might add."

"Later. My Sairsa must eat first, and have her kavay; then I will rest—maybe." Pela narrowed her eyes, examining him critically. "And you must feed too. You are hungry, I can see it in your eyes." Crawling out of their bed, she came around to his side and scowled down at him with a "give me no nonsense" look. "I will tell my Ima, and she will arrange it."

"What was I saying about making me pay for my disobedience?" he grumbled. Pela folded her arms across her chest. He smiled and relented. "All right, all right. I am hungry. Go arrange it, and tell San Nathan, that I want to see Dado before they go to the springs today."

With a last appraising look at him, she nodded, threw a cloak about her shoulders, and left.

Her emotions in turmoil, Sairsa watched the native woman leave the room. Pela had called him husband. Oh, gods, this was so terrible—what was she going to do now about the baby? When Pela had closed the door, Sairsa turned back to him.

Searching for a more neutral subject she said, "She speaks our language very well for one of the natives. You must have spent a lot of time teaching her."

He gave her a curious look, then shook his head. "No, love, I haven't. Pela knows very little Standard; it is you who has learned a new language." He gave her one of his disconcerting smiles, then the timber of his voice altering, Tani said, "While you were so ill, I also changed the taste of you so you could speak and understand the Timornan language. That is how my kindred helped Dunnagh and his hunting pack learn our language, too."

Suddenly afraid again, she wondered what other changes had this creature made in her body without her knowing. What kind of power did these Khutani have—could she really trust him?

As if he had divined her thoughts, he was watching her again, a sad look in those big blue eyes of Dunnagh's. Oh, Gods, this was so hard.

"There isn't any reason to be afraid, truly, I would never hurt you."

Sairsa sighed and dropped her eyes. She was so tired—what did it matter now anyway. He had found another; it was over between Dunnagh and her.

"You might as well finish it. You were going to tell me about Pela. She called you husband and me her 'sister-wife.' What did she mean?"

"Mm, yes, I should finish it." He settled once more beside her, pulling the blanket up over their shoulders. When they were comfortable Dunnagh began, "This is a different world, Sairsa, with different customs. When I took up the Kashallan bond it was necessary for me to accept certain obligations. Taking a mate was one of them. Pela is an Avairei priestess. Her superior, Ima Sagas, arranged for our mating."

Feeling suddenly very empty inside, she asked in a tiny voice, "Did you love her?"

He shook his head. "That was not a requirement of the pairing for either of us. In fact, Pela was quite frightened of me at first, at least of the Dunnagh part of me. Oh, by now, I am growing very fond of her; she is a beautiful person in many ways, and I think she is getting used to, and perhaps a little fond of me too. But this isn't Dymar or Caldon, and the same rules don't apply.

"She was given to me as the Kashallan, not as Dunnagh Kai. She is the mate of the Kashallan, not of Dunnagh Kai. Only you, if you so choose, can be the wife of the part of me that is still Dunnagh."

He lifted a lock of her hair, idly twisting it between his fingers as he continued, "When no one came looking for us, I thought you were dead, or that the ship had been repaired and you were gone. If I had known... Well, I'm not sure what I would have done, to be honest—red kavay is a powerful lure.

"But Pela does want you to share her life with me. Tani tells me it is the truth. No one can lie to Tani when in the link. She wants Dunnagh to be happy. She says she has prayed to her Goddess, and that the Mother has told her to take you as her sister-wife.

"I have explained to her that it's not a human custom, for the most part, and that you may not want this. But she still insists that it is what her Goddess wants, and I can't argue with her about it."

"Is it a native custom here for a man to take more than one wife?"

"No more so than it is for a woman to have more than one husband. It isn't a usual practice, but it is not unknown, and in my case—well, it would be different because of the bond.

"I know women in the so-called civilized world think differently about such things, but here there doesn't seem to be the concept of jealousy, or the competitiveness among women that spoils so many relationships between people out there among the stars.

"I would ask you to be kind to her; she is exactly what she seems, and she means what she says. She does love you, and wants you with us as her sister-wife. But of course, in the end, it is you who must decide what you will do.

"I know Commander Tizu would be good to you, if you should choose not to stay with us."

Sairsa gasped. "How did you know?"

Dunnagh let out a mirthless laugh, his expression suddenly hard. "The fool came over here, half-crazed with alignment deprivation, wanting to kill me because I took you out of the sickbay."

Sairsa blinked, her mouth dropping open in surprise. "He did what!"

He nodded. "I think he must love you very much. Do you want him, my Sairsa? He's a good man, and your life with him would be more, uh, conventional than what I can offer you."

Yes, life with Hukiyo would be more conventional, if she were to accept Tizu's offer and marry him. Their life as husband and wife would be as traditional, and as much like her dreams, as this primitive world could offer them.

But that life would be without Dunnagh. Was that what she really wanted? Hukiyo had been good to her, and she had grown fond of him, but she didn't love him.

On the other hand, was she really able to accept this new state of affairs? Could she live with Dunnagh like this, sharing him and their bed with another woman—and, Gods, don't forget the symbiont. Even Dunnagh wasn't wholly Dunnagh any more. The symbiont who shared his flesh would always be there, as yet another presence in their life.

She had no idea what it would mean to be in a relationship with two "aliens", symbiont and Avairei priestess, as well as her Caldoni lover. Sairsa honestly didn't know if she could live like that, even for Dunnagh. It was too much to think about when she was still so confused and tired.

All her ponderings were giving her a headache. She welcomed the distraction that Pela offered when she pushed open the door and entered with a tray in one hand, Nathan trailing behind her.

Dunnagh-Tani sat up, reaching for his clothes. Nathan glanced over at the bed, and smiled when he saw Sairsa watching him. "It's a good thing you sent Pela out when you did. Rhys was about to leave. Dado's waiting for you outside."

"Good." Dunnagh stood, making a final adjustment to the folds of his kilt. He picked up his cloak, then bent and kissed Sairsa. "I've got to go, love; try to sleep if you can. Pela will take care of you. I'll come back to see how you're doing later."

Pela put down the tray on the table beside the bed and turned to him. He took her in his arms and kissed her, then tapped his finger on the tip of her nose. "And you, get some rest too, or I will make you rest."

She giggled. "I will rest, with my Sairsa, and I will make sure you rest, later. Now go, see to your hunting pack. After that my Ima will be waiting, with someone to make the blood-gift." He nodded, kissed her again, then followed Nathan out of the room.

Sairsa watched the door close on him with a sinking feeling in the pit of her stomach. Now she was alone with this stranger—this native woman who called her "sister," and shared the man she'd thought would be hers alone forever.

"Let me help you relieve yourself, my Sairsa'meh," Pela offered. She pointed with her lips toward a covered bucket in the far corner.

Sairsa blushed. Suddenly shy, and a little nervous she looked away from the woman's eager face, and mumbled, "Thank you, but I can do it myself."

Sairsa swung her legs out of bed and tried to stand. Dismayed she fell back, shocked by her own weakness. She stared up at the other woman in confusion. Gods, she felt as helpless as a newborn. And, damn it, now that Pela had mentioned it she did have to pee.

Pela made a cooing sound in her throat and helped Sairsa to the bucket. When she finished she leaned heavily on Pela's shoulder and stumbled back to the bed. Pela sat down beside her. "Are you hungry, my Sairsa'meh?"

Sairsa nodded. "That's good; for it is time for you to have the kavay again." Lifting a bowl and spoon from the tray, Pela handed them to her.

Sairsa looked down at the contents of the bowl, and gagged. Native food. She guessed it was some kind of stew; there appeared to be lumps of meat and what could be vegetables floating around in the unappetizing blue-green mess.

She didn't want to offend, but did the woman really expect her to eat this stuff? Out of the corner of her eye, she glanced at Pela. Evidently she did, because she was watching her expectantly.

Sairsa blinked back tears—it was all too much to deal with. Her hands starting to tremble she handed the bowl back. "I think I'll wait a bit; I'm more tired than hungry."

Pela took the bowl before she could drop it. Then she laughed. "Oh, now I know what the problem is. I'm getting better at reading all your alien human features. I think your face is saying that you don't like it, because you aren't used to food being that color. It's the kavay that makes all we eat and drink that bluish color.

"San Nathan is always grumbling about how the kavay makes food look. His names for the kavay drink and for our food, in your language, are 'blue puke juice' and 'glop,' whatever that means."

She giggled. "I gather it isn't a very flattering comment, but I notice he always eats and drinks his share, nonetheless."

Sairsa had been thinking of Dunnagh's followers as the aliens, when in fact, she and the rest of the humans were the aliens. The outsiders.

This revelation made her feel odd, adding to her sense of loneliness and confusion.

Alien. Oh Gods, Dunnagh, what am I going to do if I lose you?

"You must eat, my Sairsa. No matter the unusual color; your body needs the kavay." Taking up the spoon, Pela coaxed, "Here, close your eyes and I will feed you; then you won't have to look at it—this time. You will like the taste better. Your body will know what it needs."

Sairsa sighed. She was hungry, and Dunnagh was right—the woman wasn't going to give up; she was a bit of a mother hen. Sairsa obediently closed her eyes and opened her mouth, like a baby bird waiting to be fed. Well, it wasn't great, but she had to agree—it did taste better than it looked.

When she emptied the bowl, Pela gave her a cup of the blue liquid to drink. Sairsa felt faintly dizzy and very tired by the time she finished it. She allowed Pela to lay her down upon the bed. Setting the tray aside, Pela crawled in beside her and pulled the covers up over them. Enfolding Sairsa in a silky embrace, Pela brushed her tongue lightly down Sairsa's neck.

"Dizzy?"

Sairsa gasped, faintly aroused by the woman's touch. Was that the native equivalent of a kiss? "Mm hmm."

"It will pass," Pela assured her. "The dizziness will end as the branding becomes more pronounced. It's the final stage of the alignment, so the Kashallan has told me."

"Branding? I don't understand."

For answer, Pela pulled down the blanket and lifted one of Sairsa's smooth white arms. She traced a livid bluish purple mark that ran spiraling down the human woman's arm and onto her breast. "It is the mark that the kavay has given to all Timorna's adopted children. Perhaps we have it too, but, if we do, it is hidden by our fur."

Dunnagh and the rest of his squad had such marks, but she had assumed they were caused by some sort of native tattooing process that the humans had been forced to endure while in captivity. She began to cry—this was so terrible—she was so ugly!

"Sairsa'meh, sister, don't cry." Pela made the cooing sound again, touched her tear-stained cheek with her tongue, and hugged her tighter. As if reading her thoughts, she said gently, "Don't be sad, my Sairsa, the kavay branding is very beautiful upon your pale skin. It's a sign that you and your kinsfolk are well loved by my Goddess. You are most favored and blessed in her eyes."

The woman's talk of her Goddess, and her affectionate demeanor, were disconcerting. They were arousing feelings within her that she'd never known she possessed, and wasn't sure she was comfortable with.

"Sairsa, you are trying too hard to think it out and understand." Pela soothed. "Let it wait. Now let's sleep some more, as our mate wishes us to do. Sleep, my Sairsa'meh, go to sleep."

Sleep, yes, it was too much to think about now—sleep.

Chapter Five

A blast of wind whipped the Kashallan's cloak out behind him as he and Nathan stepped away from the shelter of the barracks wall. Wrapping the cloak tighter around his shoulders, he faced into the wind and studied the horizon. Another bank of dark clouds was gathering. There would probably be rain again later. The weather was just another goad adding to the urgency of their situation.

When he returned his attention to the men waiting for him in the quadrangle, he was surprised to see that the foraging party contained some of Tizu's armachda, carrying empty containers strapped to their backs like the Loti. Dunnagh raised an inquiring eyebrow.

The big man shrugged. "If more go, we don't have to make as many trips, and we're less likely to be discovered by a hunting pack of Warlinga."

THE MORNING AFTER TIZU shot holes in D barracks, Nathan went to HQ to explain things. Ross had been worried about the Commander's absence, and was suspicious when Nathan told him about Tizu's attack. But when he saw the damage done to D barracks, and then saw how sick Tizu really was—well, it hadn't taken long for him and the rest of Lann Gheal to fall back into old patterns and accept the leadership that Nathan offered.

Dunnagh was glad it had ended so well. The Dymarians were still a problem, however. Most refused Dunnagh's suggestion that they begin the alignment process voluntarily. They were still hoping for an off-planet rescue.

After Bennett's collapse, Sadrew had bullied his way into a leadership position among the Dymarians, displacing the more moderate Meldra Arishim. He was openly hostile to Dunnagh and took every opportunity to speak against him to anyone who would listen. He claimed Dunnagh was a liar and a degenerate, and unfortunately many people were listening to the fool.

Sadrew, in fact, was becoming quite an annoyance. But the Kashallan was too preoccupied with the sick to worry about the man. As long as he kept out of his way, he chose to ignore him. And so far, that was exactly what Sadrew had been doing—especially after the Lann Gheal armachda accepted Nathan over himself as their acting commander.

In the pragmatic way of its kind, Tani had pointed out, <<The man is too stupid to be allowed to breed anyway. Timorna will have no use for him or for any who take him seriously.>>

In a way, it was like a process of natural selection, Dunnagh thought. Those who were flexible enough to set aside old ways and adapt to the new conditions on Timorna, would survive. Those who couldn't—well, their fates were out of his hands.

Catching the gleam of something shiny out of the corner of his eye, he located Dado standing among his relatives. All of them—especially Dado—were decked out like ancient gypsies, their necks and arms weighed down with the masses of pretties they'd collected.

The Kashallan drew Dado aside into a sheltered spot, out of the wind. When they were far enough away so that the others couldn't hear them, he squatted down beside the smaller man and looked deep into his yellow eyes. "I need your help, little brother."

"Begta will help. What Kashallan need?"

Tentacles slightly extended, he held out his hand in a now familiar gesture. Dado stretched out his own hand and allowed the symbiont to form the link. "Good, I was hoping I could count on you and your people. You see, almost all the formula I brought with me from the pools at Sulas is gone. We have had to stay here much longer than I expected.

"And now, with so many sick—I still can't leave. But I must feed. If I continue to take so much of the blood gift from my people, it is only a question of time before everyone is too weak to journey to Ticca.

"I know, from the memories of my Khutani kindred, that there are wild pools in the Broken Lands and the Swamp. I also know that the Begta use such pools. I will not betray your people's secrets to the Avairei, but I need you to take some of the empty flasks and go to a wild pool for me. You must ask my kin there to make more formula for me. Will you do this?"

Dado scratched his curly, round head, his face taking on a worried expression. "I want to help, but I don't know where Khutani pool is."

Forcing down the panic that was threatening to overwhelm him, he took a deep breath and tried again. "Dado, I really am going to need that formula. If you don't know where one of the pools is, does anyone else know who will help me? Please try to think, little brother, this is very important."

Dado scuffed a dirty clawed foot in the moss thinking. Then his eyes lit up, and he smiled. "Yes, yes I do know! Old shaman Umwa knows where is pool. He knows Kashallan too. He help Chosen get to Sulas. He will help me—he will take Dado to Khutani pool."

Dunnagh's mouth dropped open. "Wait a minute—do you mean that crazy old man who, when we were captured, tried to beat me to death with charms and somebody's arm bone?"

Dado nodded vigorously. "He is a great shaman. He got a dream, he knew about Kashallan bond. He not want Chosen to go back to mesa—must go Sulas. He used his big magics to fix everything."

<<Close our mouth, Kasha,>> Tani said. <<The Begta may be right. At least from what I can taste through the link, he believes what he is saying is the truth.>>

<<Is that possible, Shalla? I mean, Begta believe a lot of things that aren't necessarily true. Could the old fellow really have known about me?>>

The symbiont considered, tapping ancient memories. Finally it said, <<Yes, it is quite possible. The Begta were bred as a random factor in the Timornan pattern. Their development has been much more their own doing than the other races.

<<You said yourself that the old shaman stopped you from recognizing the Begta trap. Or contacting anyone back here when you tried the Cumarsaid trance. He obviously has what your people call the Psy power. It is quite possible that he knew of your coming and helped you get to Sulas for the bonding.>>

Ah, Gods of my ancestors, Dunnagh thought privately. *He may have known and helped me, but at what a terrible cost, both to his own people and mine.*

"All right take some of the flasks to this Umwa, and tell him to go with you to a Khutani pool. I am putting a message to my kindred within your blood.

"The old man must take you with him. When you get to the pool, cut your arm and put it into the water, like the priests do. The Khutani will taste my message to them, and make me what I need. Do you understand?"

Dado nodded. "I understand—I will get food for Kashallan."

The Kashallan released the link and stood. "I hope so, little brother, I hope so." Then, putting an arm around the Begta's shoulder, he walked with him back to the waiting party.

When the foragers were gone, a grim-faced Sagas approached him, a strong young Loti named Mashen at her heels. Ravenous, Tani stirred restlessly. Bowing to the Loti, the Kashallan motioned for the Timornan to follow him to a sheltered place where they could have a bit of privacy.

The Kashallan lay back in the moss, replete at last. On the other side of the building the cold west wind rattled the windows, but here against the poly-plastic wall, the sun's light was still able to give a bit of comforting warmth to the day.

Closing his eyes, Dunnagh wanted only to rest for a while in the warm sun while the Khutani part of himself digested their meal, and replenished the substances it used when healing.

When he finished with the Loti this time, Dunnagh was horrified. Mashen, may the Gods bless him, made no complaint, but he could barely stagger to his feet. Tani's needs were becoming insatiable, because of the demands of its still-maturing body, plus the doctoring. The blood gift was draining his people of their strength.

The Avairei were bred to recover quickly from giving the blood gift, but, even so, they were not bred to take this much of a strain. And what about the other Timornans he was draining? Yet what else could he do? Feed he must; there were only two of the precious flasks of formula left. So many lives depended on his abilities.

All his people knew his danger, and accepted that at some point he might have to take lives to save his own. If he couldn't find another source for the formula, he might have no choice. Oh, by the Gods, he didn't want that to happen!

Hurry back, Dado, Dunnagh prayed silently. Hurry back before I am forced to go too far, and kill someone.

Chapter Six

Next morning when he finished doing his rounds at the sickbay, Dunnagh decided that it was time to quit putting off an unpleasant chore, and go talk to Tizu. The Commander had recovered from the worst of the alignment sickness rapidly, once he began taking the kavay his body craved. But he still wasn't recovered enough to resume his duties as Lann Gheal's commander.

Not finding him at the sickbay, the Kashallan was told by a harried Temog that Tizu had insisted on returning to his private quarters at the rear of HQ. Nodding his thanks to the busy priest, he wrapped himself tightly in his cloak again and crossed the quadrangle.

When he entered the Commander's alcove, he found Tizu sitting up on his cot, with a very frustrated Ima Surrel trying to get him to eat his kavay-laced meal. The poor Avairei was speaking to him in a strongly accented Galactic Standard, but the Commander was ignoring both the priestess and the offered food. As the Kashallan entered, Surrel threw up her hands in frustration, muttering under her breath.

Trying hard not to smile, Dunnagh heard her say something about "ugly, flat-faced, stupid Warlinga." He didn't catch the rest, because at that point she saw him. Dropping her eyes, she gave him a deep bow.

"It's all right, Ima, you were doing your best. He's being deliberately annoying; he understood you. But leave him to me now. I'll see that he eats and drinks the kavay."

Tizu grunted with satisfaction as the priestess stalked out of his room. When she had closed the door behind her, he turned to face his new visitor. "You've got them trained real well, haven't you, just like an all mighty king and his slaves."

Dunnagh's jaw tightened, but he made no comment. Sitting down on the chair that the priestess had just vacated, he picked up the cup of kavay, and held it out. "She gives me her respect by her own choosing. I don't require or demand it of any of them. Now drink your kavay—I won't be so easily put off."

Tizu took the cup. He stared down into its depths, making a sour face at its unappetizing contents. "This shit looks disgusting," he grumbled.

"Your point?"

Tizu glared. "How do you expect me to drink this revolting mess?"

Suddenly impatient with the man's evasions and acid remarks, Dunnagh snapped, "Cut the crap, Tizu, don't try to jerk me around, too. I always figured you for a survivor. If you are, then you'll drink what's in that cup and quit complaining. Your play-acting, and your denial of the craving you're feeling right now, won't fool me.

"Just like the rest of us, you need the kavay; your alignment is almost complete. So if you want to go on living, you will eat kavay-laced food, and drink kavay-laced water, no matter what it looks like. If you don't—well a gun to the head is a far faster suicide."

Tizu remained motionless, glaring. When his visitor returned the look and waited, Tizu at last gave him a curt nod, then drank. When he finished the beverage, he put it back on the tray, picked up his plate, and began grimly to eat.

Dunnagh watched him eat, and made no attempt to make small talk. What needed to be said wouldn't be easy for either of them. They both needed the time to gather their thoughts.

Finally, Tizu set aside his plate and faced the Kashallan. "So what happens when I've recovered from this alignment—or whatever you call it? You've taken my command away from me—and everything else." His face twisted with the bitterness of his perceived loss. "What do you plan to do with me?"

Dunnagh sighed. "This isn't any easier for me, Commander, believe me. As to what I plan to do with you, I don't have any special plans. You, like everyone else in this camp, have two choices—give me your allegiance and come with me to Ticca, or stay here. It's that simple."

NO, IT WASN'T SIMPLE, Tizu thought bitterly, not simple at all. There were many things to consider. What had this creature done to Sairsa? And what would he himself do if Sairsa was lost to him forever? Could he give Dunnagh—or this Kashallan, what he asked for if that happened? He didn't know. Stalling for time, he said, "What about my command?"

"When you're fit for duty, your command will be returned to you. Nathan has taken over temporarily—at the request of your armachda, I might add. He will be quite happy to return it to you when the time comes."

That shocked Tizu. He had assumed that Dunnagh himself would jump at the chance to step in as commander of Lann Gheal. His surprise must have shown on his face, because Dunnagh grimaced.

"No, Commander, I don't want it, nor does Nathan. He has other responsibilities, and, as the Kashallan, so do I. Though they've been giving Nathan no trouble, I think your armachda will be glad to see you up and about again."

Dunnagh chuckled. "Way I heard it from Owyn was that, when Lann Gheal met to discuss what to do after your collapse, the armachda decided that, if all their former officers were either sick, crazy, or gone native, they'd rather stick to one of their own as acting commander than accept Sadrew and his bunch as their bosses."

Tizu grunted, giving him a crooked grin.

Dunnagh grinned back, then, serious again, he added, "Actually, truth be told, Commander, I need you. I have many obligations to Timorna and her people, but being a war-leader isn't one of them.

"In the future we may come up against very formidable enemies. Your experience at my side would be appreciated. I hope you will choose to join me when I leave."

When Tizu made no response he continued, "I know it won't be easy under the circumstances for you to accept my offer, but I hope you will at least think about it."

"After what I tried to do the other night I'm surprised you didn't kill me. I would have in your place. And now you expect me to believe that all is forgiven—just like that?" Tizu snorted.

"No, all isn't forgiven—just like that, but the attack the other night was partially the deprivation sickness. I have always held you in the highest regard. I would like to believe that under other circumstances, you would have tried to settle this thing between us without endangering the lives of innocent people."

Ashamed in spite of himself, Tizu nodded and looked away. Without turning to face him, he murmured, "We thought you were dead..." Choking on a curse, Tizu rounded on Dunnagh, eyes fierce and accusing. "Damn you, you asked me to take care of her, to keep her safe! I couldn't help—"

"I know, I figured it was like that. You're a good man, Commander, and she's a fine woman. It was only natural that you should fall in love with her. And, I know that, if she wishes to be with you, you would cherish her, and take care of her and the child to the best of your ability."

"Child?" Sitting up straighter on the cot, Tizu's mouth dropped open in astonishment.

"Mm hmm, my bondmate discovered it during the course of its treatment. I thought you knew."

"No. I never touched her, I—" He flushed. Suddenly Sairsa's repeated refusal of his offers, and her constant insistence that her lover was still alive, made sense. If she was pregnant with his baby, then of course she would be hoping and praying for Dunnagh's return.

With a sinking feeling, Tizu realized that he had probably lost her. His face crumpled and he turned away again. Damn the man, he'd won this round too.

"I wasn't sure if the child was mine, and Sairsa's been so ill—well, there's been no time to worry about the babe's paternity, when we might have lost both of them."

"How is she?"

"Doing better—so Tani says. She and the baby are recovering, but she's still weak and needs rest. When you're up to it, come see her for yourself."

Changing the subject, he gave Tizu a lopsided grin, then reached out and took his hand. Tentacles extending, the Kashallan sank them into the veins near Tizu's wrist. "Speaking of patients, we need to see how you are doing as well."

Tizu stared down mesmerized at his arm, trying hard to control the fear and revulsion he felt. The thought of Sairsa, the woman he so desperately loved, with him—Shit! The man wasn't even human any more—some strange mix of Caldoni and alien, bonded together in some fool mystical and physical union to help this God-forsaken world.

His guts twisted in revulsion as mental images of lovely, sweet Sairsa being held, and touched, by this—this unnatural monster. He inwardly writhed, seeing her white skin penetrated by the alien's loathsome, slimy tentacles. It was too much to bear...

Raising his eyes, he saw that Dunnagh was watching him intently, a knowing expression on his face.

As if reading his mind, Dunnagh said, "Commander, things are different on Timorna. Don't judge me until you know enough to understand how it is here."

Disconcerted, Tizu sighed. Putting aside the unwanted visions, he slowly nodded. "So what happens now?"

The Kashallan retracted his tentacles and shrugged. "You're almost over the alignment process. The dizziness will pass soon, then you must decide whether you will give me your oath or not."

"And what about Sairsa?"

"When she is feeling up to it, she will have to decide, just as you will. I won't lie to you, Commander. I still love her and want her, but when I made the kashallan bond, things changed. What I can offer her now is much different than what we had planned for our lives when we were on Dymar.

"I have told her about the kashallan bond. I've also told her that if she doesn't wish to share my new life, she is free to do whatever else she chooses. I will not stop her. Nor will I, as the Kashallan, do anything to influence her final decision. I give you my word on that."

Tizu grunted. Well that was fair enough. He studied Dunnagh's face intently. The man wasn't totally human any more, could he trust him? Shit! He would make himself crazy again if he started down that path.

"I also told her that I thought you were a good man who would love her and take care of her, should she decide she wanted a more conventional partnership. There is nothing more to say—the choice is hers, as is your own, Commander. And I wasn't lying when I said that I do want you with me when I leave for Ticca.

"But you will have to decide before then if you can put aside the anger and bitterness that you now feel towards me. Before we leave, you must be able to give me your wholehearted loyalty if you come with us. I will demand that of everyone who accompanies us, not just you.

"And, believe me, you won't be able to deceive me. If you harbor any ill-will or thoughts of revenge, I will know it, because I will take your oath while we are in the link."

He extended a tentacled fingertip to make his point quite plain. "Hear me clearly, and believe. I will know if you try lying to me, and I will punish such an attempted deception with a horrible and immediate death. Do you understand me, Commander Tizu?"

Tizu glared at him defiantly for a long moment. The Kashallan waited, as unyielding as stone. Shit. Tizu lowered his eyes and nodded. "You've made your point, damn it. If I decide I can give you what you want, there'll be no tricks; I'll be your man, body and soul. But right now—" he sighed, suddenly exhausted again. "I don't know what I want to do."

The Kashallan stood. "Fair enough. I will leave you to think about it."

Chapter Seven

When the Kashallan entered D barracks, it was clear that an argument of some kind was in progress. He started to ignore it, feeling wrung out after his talk with Tizu. Not in the mood for another confrontation, he wanted only to sleep, but then he noticed Nathan in the midst of the furor. Catching his friend's eye, Dunnagh mouthed, "What's wrong?" With a jerk of his head Nathan motioned him over.

<<I wonder what he's gotten himself into this time.>> Tani grumbled.

<<Knowing him, it could be anything. I suppose, Shalla, we had better go rescue him, if we can; he looks pretty desperate.>>

To his surprise the Kashallan found that it wasn't Nathan who was at the center of the turmoil. Temog's apprentice Timma, had that dubious honor. Several of the Avairei were shouting at once, and the gist of their tirade seemed to be that they were angry at the youth, and angry with Nathan for encouraging him in some disobedience.

Timma held himself rigid, his eyes cast down, not looking at anyone. But the Kashallan could see his clenched fists at his side and the determined set to his jaw.

There was something odd about the lad, but he couldn't place it... Ah, now he saw it. Instead of wearing his long Avairei mane in many little braidlets, as the rest of the Avairei wore their hair, Timma had braided his in one long warrior's braid like Nathan's.

When the combatants momentarily ran out of breath, he asked, "Is this a private disagreement, or can anyone join?"

Startled, they turned, but when they recognized him, the uproar began anew. Finally he'd had enough and held up a hand for silence. "That's better. Now, I can't understand anything when you're all yelling at once, so if you want my help with whatever is the problem here, you'll have to tell me about it—one at a time. And since I gather this all has to do with Timma, perhaps I should let him tell me his side of it first."

He nodded his encouragement to the young priest. Timma looked up, eyes unsure, mouth trembling slightly. "Go ahead, lad, don't be frightened. I do want to hear what you have to say, and I won't be angry, whatever it is."

Timma glanced over his shoulder at Nathan. The big man nodded, and the youth returned his gaze to the Kashallan. In a quiet but determined voice, he said, "Today I wouldn't go over to the sickbay to help, because I don't want to be an Avairei priest any more, I want to be a Warlinga like San Nathan. He said he would teach me but the Imas say no."

Timma straightened his shoulders, and clenched his fists. Staring defiantly at the Kashallan, he cried, "Even if they discipline me every day, like today, I still won't go back there."

Well, well, this is an interesting and unexpected development, Dunnagh thought. He glanced at Nathan. "Did you suggest this to him, or did you just agree to teach him?"

"The idea's his own, but I see no harm in it. He's quick and has a good eye. He's about Chang's size, so I figure Chang could probably teach the lad his techniques and—"

"No!" Sagas cried. "Timma is Avairei, and his duty is to the Khutani—that is what we have been bred for. This is a disgrace." She rounded on the young man. "Timma, you are a shame to your family and clan. You insult both them and the Kashallan by your disobedience. You are an ungrateful child. We are Avairei, not stupid Warlinga; our duty is to serve the Khutani and now the Kashallan—that is the way things have always been and will always be!"

Timma turned to him, eyes moist and pleading, and for just a moment the Kashallan saw the pain and fear hidden in their depths. Then, trembling, the youth looked down at the floor, his shoulders slumped with the weight of the Ima's accusations.

Growing angry in spite of himself, Dunnagh gritted his teeth and rounded on Sagas. "Those were harsh words to give one so young, Sagas. In future, Ima, let me decide for myself if I am insulted or not."

Sagas gasped, then looked down at the floor. He sighed. Softening his voice, Dunnagh began again. "Listen to me, all of you. Things are going to change on Timorna now; it is inevitable. And sometimes those changes won't always be predictable—or even to your liking.

"The Makers have indeed found a compatible host species in us, but humans aren't mindless beasts, with only enough wit to carry the Khutani. We are a tool-using race, with our own ways of doing things. When you got us, you got that too.

"We choose our life path; it isn't bred into us. And, because of our example, there will inevitably be those Timornans who will see our ways, and want something different for their own lives, like Timma here.

"There probably won't be many, but you might as well get used to the idea. It's unavoidable. It's the price that the Khutani and Timornan society will have to pay for our aid."

<<Kasha!>> came the shocked cry from his bondmate, as Tani added its voice to the growing din of outrage.

Dunnagh closed his eyes. <<But it's true, Shalla. I don't know if the Makers reckoned on this happening, but life here will change—it must.>>

<<But—>>

<<Tani, listen to me. What are my people supposed to do on Timorna, hmm?>>

<<Oh, I don't know, be Warlinga, I guess—I hadn't given it much thought.>>

<<Perhaps that's part of the problem here. You Khutani, for all your great knowledge, are very limited in your view of the broader picture. Think about it now, Shalla. Can you imagine Tessa or Sairsa, or even Singey, as a Warlinga?>>

<<No,>> came the grudging reply.

<<And among the Dymarians there are even more who are not suited to my old profession. They are scholars, artists, musicians, and maybe there are farmers and engineers among them too. These humans all have good things to offer this world, to help it grow and prosper, but not if we are confined to one small portion of society for which we may not be suited.

<<And what about being Warlinga? That may be fine for now, but we have no natural weaponry, remember. We rely on our tools to follow that profession. The weaponry we brought with us won't last forever. They will

wear out, like any made thing. Eventually there will come a day when we won't be able to repair them anymore.

<<Just like with the old technology left after the Great Destruction, our weapons and other tools will have to be abandoned. Then what will we do, Shalla? Are we to be kept like beasts or slaves in pens, bred only to serve as hosts for our Khutani masters?>>

<<Oh, Kasha, don't talk like that. No, of course not. That was never the Makers' intent, surely you know that. Why are you saying such hurtful things to me?>> the symbiont wailed.

Privately, Dunnagh suspected that a slave pen for his people, was exactly what some of the elders had envisioned, but there was no point in distressing Tani further with that bitter comment.

<<Shalla, I don't want to hurt you. I'm just trying to point out to you that there is going to be change. Whether planned or not, things are going to be different on Timorna. By our bonding we have already begun the process, and my species, and Timornans like Timma, are going to have their effect on this world, too.>>

<<Oh, I never thought—what do we do?>>

<<Perhaps, Shalla, our role should not be to stop it, because change can't ever really be stopped. I think it would be much better if we try to shape it, for the good of all.>>

<<Kasha, I understand what you mean, but this is very risky. What if there is another Great Destruction some time in the future, and it happens because of what we do now—>>

<<Yes, it is a risk, but what has already been set in motion can't be recalled, Shalla. No matter what we do or don't do, another Great Destruction may happen anyway. We can't worry about that; we can only do the best we can at the time, and leave the rest up to the Gods.>>

<<Yes, I suppose you're right—but we need to talk to the Elders about this, agreed?>>

<<Agreed, but until then, let's not make any quick decisions.>>

<<All right.>>

<<Will you help me? I want to put Timma in the link. Other than his admiration for Nathan, I want to know if there's another reason for his

decision to go against breeding and tradition to become a warrior. Then we will know better how to decide this.>>

<<Yes, a good idea, Kasha.>>

At last Dunnagh opened his eyes; the group was silently watching him. He gave them an apologetic grin. "Sorry, we were discussing this problem among ourselves. Tani, like most of you, was greatly shocked by my attitude."

"And what did you decide, Holy One?" Sagas pressed.

"That a final decision must wait on a talk with our Elders, but we both agree that a temporary decision should be made for now. Is that agreeable to everyone?" He looked around the circle, making eye contact, grudgingly winning their approval.

Finally he turned to Timma. The young man met his gaze defiantly at first, then, lowering his eyes, he nodded his agreement. In a gentle voice the Kashallan asked, "Will you come to me, Timma?" He held out his hands, tentacles slightly extended.

Timma hesitated a moment, then boldly stepped forward holding out his hands. The Kashallan took those trusting hands and inserted his tentacles to establish their connection. "Before I make any decision about whether to let you become a Warlinga, I'm curious. Why do you want to go against your breeding and tradition to do this?"

Timma shifted nervously, not meeting his eye. "Because I want to. San Nathan has shown me a few things. You don't have to be big or have strong teeth or claws to kill, and I'm smart; I can learn to use a beam rifle, I know I can—" His words were suddenly choked off by a sob.

Through the link, the bondmates felt the lad's pain, as the sensations he had experienced during the Umwira attack flooded their awareness. The youngster's fear and the grief he felt over the loss of his best friend at that time roared down the link.

And, along with that pain, came Timma's guilt. If he had only known how to fight, how to kill those evil creatures, maybe he could have saved Orlan. Instead he had hidden away in the rocks, like a coward, or a baby and watched them take his friend.

He had learned enough. When he felt the young one's emotional flood slow, he retracted his tentacles and broke the link. "I think I understand now, Timma, thank you." Turning to Nathan he asked, "Have you talked to Chang about teaching him?"

"Not really. Timma's been hinting, but he never came out with it until today. Chang would probably do it, though." He paused, considering, then nodded. "Yeah, he'd do it. He needs to be doing something besides sharpening his knives and brooding, anyway; teaching Timma would help take his mind off his lost family. Yeah, he'll do it. If I have to, I'll make it official, and order him, but I don't think I'll have to."

"Good, then arrange it with him. Tell Chang I said to concentrate on self-defense and unarmed combat techniques, with a bit of knife and small arms training thrown in for good measure. And teach him yourself anything you think appropriate for his size and the Timornan environment."

Nathan eyed the hostile Avairei warily, then shrugged and nodded. "All right. I'll tell Chang tonight. Timma can start with him tomorrow."

The Kashallan ignored the murmuring Avairei for the moment and returned his attention to the young priest. "Do you understand what I just told San Nathan, Timma?"

"Yes, Holy One."

"Well, understand this too. Whenever a band of human Warlinga go out to hunt the enemy, they always have with them skilled healers. Many more men would die if a medic, as we call them, wasn't there to help the wounded."

He gave Timma a conspiratorial wink. "So, along with your weapons training, I am requiring you to continue your studies with Ata Temog. My human Warlinga have only armachd Williams, and he isn't as skilled with Timornan medicines as you. I need several new medics. I want you to be one of them—do you agree? Are you willing to take up your Avairei studies again under these terms?"

"Yes, Holy One, I would be honored to be one of your new med-ics. I will study very hard. You will not be ashamed of me."

The Kashallan patted his shoulder. "Yes, lad, I'm sure I will be proud of you, because I already am. Now, may I suggest that you go see if Ata Temog or San Singey needs you? They have been at the sickbay all day, and they're probably very tired. Take them some food when you go. And tell them I said they were to rest."

Excitement once more alive in his eyes, Timma bowed and left. Grinning, Nathan also gave the Kashallan a slight bow and went to go find Chang. Turning back to the Avairei, he found Sagas was still scowling at him. "Are you still displeased, Ima?"

"I don't know," she admitted. "He is an Avairei, he should—"

"Sagas." He put an arm around her shoulder, and led her away from the others to a place near the altar, where they could sit down. When they were seated, he continued, "Timma is an Avairei, true, but he is also a young man who has seen his closest friend savaged by the Umwira. He knows now, because of his association with my hunting pack, that you don't have to be big and have sharp teeth and claws, in order to defend yourself and those you love against the enemy.

"When I tasted him I learned that he blames himself for Orlan's capture. He feels that if only he knew what Nathan knows, he could have saved him." The Kashallan sighed. "And he's afraid that the Umwira will come back again and try to take him, too.

"You have lived through two of their attacks. Can you honestly condemn him for wanting to try to defend himself and others from their murderous violence?"

She shivered, then admitted. "No, I cannot."

"Then let it be for now. The training I've ordered for him won't hurt. He will feel less frightened and more confident for it. And, I don't think he is serious about wanting to be a 'stupid Warlinga,' as you put it. You saw how his eyes lit up when I showed him how he could have both." He leaned forward and kissed her lightly on the forehead and smiled. "Timma won't forget his duty, so rest easy, dear Ima."

Chapter Eight

On the following evening, Dunnagh coaxed Sairsa and Pela out of the little room they shared. Together with Singey, they crossed the outer room, to sit with Tessa and Nathan on their pallet by the wall.

At first Sairsa held back painfully aware of the curious looks directed her way. Dunnagh seemed to sense her nervousness and put an arm around her waist, guiding her forward.

Once there, Sairsa wedged herself between him and Pela on the mattress. She listened to the others talk while covertly watching the activity in the big room. She was curious about the Timornans in spite of herself.

The room was crowded and bustling with activity. By the front door two armachda stood as if they were on duty, but the rest of D barrack's inhabitants clustered in small groups, mending gear, eating or just talking with one another.

The Loti fascinated her most; she hadn't realized before now, that they were more than just beasts of burden. In spite of their horse-like appearance from the waist down, they weren't as clumsy in such a confined space as she would have expected.

They walked around the room with a delicate grace and economy of movement that her poet's eye found delightful. Most stood chatting with other companions, but two of the young men sat with their legs tucked, playing a dice game with a few off-duty armachda. Fascinating! She felt more like her old self as the evening filled with unexpected marvels.

A short time later when she became engrossed in the conversation going on around her, Sairsa was surprised to learn that one of the books Singey had devoured, in his eclectic reading, was her book of poetry.

"Poetry, my sister-wife writes poetry; did I understand a right?" Dunnagh nodded. Pela beamed and gave her one of her exotic licking kisses. "This is very good," she announced to them. "When my sister-wife is well enough, I must begin teaching her how to read and write our language, so that my people can read a translation of her work."

Sairsa found herself feeling a warm glow inside at the woman's innocent praise. Dunnagh, damn him was right about Pela, she thought. She wanted to hate her—claw her eyes out for taking her man, but, Gods, it was so hard to dislike her when she was so open and kind.

"Thank you, Pela I would like to learn to read your language." Then she glanced hopefully at the bondmates. "I don't suppose—"

The Kashallan laughed, and shook his head. "Unfortunately, my sweet, you will have to learn the Avairei glyphs the old fashioned way," Tani said. "I have no encoded information I can give you through the link, as I did for the Timornan spoken language,"

"Ah, well, just thought I'd ask."

"Would you teach me as well, Pela?" Singey asked. "Ata Temog has told me that Ticca, where we are going, has a very good library, and I'm hoping they will let me study there. I feel quite lost sometimes without anything to read."

Dunnagh chuckled. "I think you may have a big class, sweet; all of my kindred will need to learn this new skill."

Pela looked shocked. She glanced sidewise at Nathan, then back at Dunnagh. "Do even Warlinga among your kindred read, Chosen?" she whispered.

Overhearing her, Tessa laughed. Nathan glared at them. "What? I can read, and not just porn mags and trashy novels either," he insisted indignantly. "Yeah, and I've even read some of Sairsa's book—so there."

"You did? When?" Dunnagh said.

"When you left your copy in the mess that time and you thought you'd lost it, that's when," he grumbled,

"Ah, so that's where it went. Took you long enough to give it back, too, didn't it?"

"So?"

Everyone laughed. Nathan folded his arms across his chest and glowered at them indignantly. At last Tessa had pity on him and quit giggling. Leaning over she kissed him. "Stop glowering, my fearsome warrior. We are just teasing you—don't take it so hard. And Pela didn't mean to offend you. On Timorna the Warlinga don't read, only the priests do. She didn't know our customs are different."

"I am sorry, San Nathan, I meant no offense. You are a very brave and good Warlinga." She gave him a slight bow. "If it is the custom among your people for everyone to learn the secrets of scholars, I would be most honored to teach you,"

Nathan grunted and returned the bow. Behind him someone cleared her throat. Sairsa glanced up along with the rest. A tall muscular dark-skinned woman saluted both Nathan and Dunnagh.

Addressing Nathan she said, "Excuse me for interrupting, Sir, but Armachd Ross wants you to come over to HQ right away." Nathan swore under his breath and stood.

"What's the problem, Marti?" Dunnagh asked.

"Don't know exactly, Ce'awn," Marti said. "That Dymarian councilor's aide, Sadrew and some of the Dymarians are outside HQ, demanding to talk to the Commander. Ross says they also want access to the arms locker."

Dunnagh started to rise, but a nip from his internal companion made him flop back with a startled yelp. <<Kasha, let Nathan take care of it. You made him your Hunt Leader—let him do his job.>>

Giving Nathan a lopsided grin, he settled himself again. "Sorry, old habits die hard. Tani just reminded me that it's your job now."

Nathan snorted, then grinned too. Giving his friend a final salute, he followed Marti out into the night.

THERE WAS STILL ENOUGH light to see by, but the sun had gone down, turning the mauve sky a deeper shade of purple and the camp buildings to shadowy lumps of charcoal gray. In spite of the gloom Nathan had no trouble seeing the angry crowd gathering around HQ. Before they were spotted, he motioned for Marti to follow him around the outer perimeter of the base, so they could enter HQ from the back door.

Once inside, they moved quietly down the hall towards the command center. Noticing the Commander's closed bedroom door, Nathan whispered, "Where's Tizu?"

Marti paused, her eyes flicking to the closed door. "Still asleep, at least he was when I left to get you. He was up earlier today, but about an hour ago he said he was tired and went back to bed."

Ross and several off-duty Lann Gheal armachda looked up as Nathan entered. From outside the closed front door he could hear people shouting for Tizu to come out. "All right, Ross, I'm here; what's going on?"

Ross saluted. "It's Sadrew, and a bunch of the Dymarians, Sir. They came here a few minutes ago with some fool story about the Ce'awn being a vampire. They say they need to protect themselves from the 'monster.' They want me or the Commander to give them some of our weaponry,"

Nathan froze, glancing sharply at Marti. She returned his look with a worried one of her own. Now how had that trouble-making shit learned about Dunnagh's exotic new dining habits? Damn the man! They didn't need to deal with this, on top of everything else.

Nathan swore under his breath, checked the handgun on his hip and yanked the front door open. He stepped outside. Marti and Ross flanked him, their hands held near the butts of their own weapons.

There were about twenty of them. Sadrew, of course, was right up front. The group consisted mostly of men, but there were a few women as well, scattered throughout the group. At the back, Councilor Arishim stood, wringing her hands and looking frightened.

On sight of him, the group fell silent. "All right, Sadrew," Nathan said, "What's this all about?"

Sadrew stepped forward. "Get out of the way, Armachd Derek, we want to talk to the Commander."

"The Commander's busy. I'm in charge at the moment; you'll talk to me, or nobody. I repeat; what do you want?"

"You? Hah! I'm not talking to you. I demand to see Commander Tizu. We need to protect ourselves from you human degenerates, and that vampire you call your leader. Now where is Tizu?"

"Protection!" Nathan snorted. "Nobody's bothered you, any of you, have they? We've not given you any cause to be afraid—yet—but don't press your luck, Sadrew, if you take my meaning." Nathan smiled, a dangerous gleam in his eye.

Sadrew flushed and stepped back. Then, feeling the comforting presence of his supporters at his back, he growled, "Is that a threat?"

Nathan opened his eyes wide and shook his head. "Why, no indeed, Citizen Sadrew. It's a promise."

Momentarily speechless, Sadrew flushed an even deeper shade of crimson. But Nathan heard the growing murmur of irate voices in the crowd behind the man. Knowing that the rest of Lann Gheal would back him against these outsiders, his eyes flicked from one angry face to another, waiting, assessing, determined not to be bullied.

Suddenly someone from inside the building pushed him roughly aside. Nathan staggered, and swore. Then Tizu was standing beside him, glaring murderously at the assembled Dymarians.

"Commander," Sadrew said. "I'm glad to see that you're safe—we were worried—"

"Never mind your phony expression of concern for my welfare, Sadrew," Tizu interrupted. "I've heard enough out of you, it's time you and your friends were leaving. It's getting dark, probably past your bedtime."

"We demand protection!" someone in the crowd shouted.

Sadrew folded his arms across his chest and sneered. "Since you've decided to abandon your contract to protect us, we're not going anywhere without some weapons to defend ourselves against these blood-drinking alien monsters."

Tizu snorted. "Oh yeah? Don't bet on it." He surveyed the group, his lip curling in disgust. "A fine lot you are, coming around here demanding protection from aliens. They're Timornans, by the way—people who haven't bothered any of you. In case you haven't figured it out yet, Sadrew, I believe you are the alien here on Timorna, hmm?"

That insight shocked them into silence. Tizu laughed. His voice dripping with contempt, he said, "What happened to that famous Dymarian liberalism of yours? What a bunch of hypocritical assholes, all of you. Listen to yourselves—blood drinking monsters, loathsome aliens—you people joined the Creggan army without telling me, or what?"

There were some embarrassed shuffling and low murmurs among the Dymarians. It had been Creggan intolerance that had started the war on

Dymar, a war that had landed them here on this primitive world. As Tizu scorched them with an accusing glare most dropped their eyes.

Sadrew glanced around at his uncertain supporters, then rallied. "It won't work, Tizu, one of my men saw Kai—saw the blood on his face. When he'd finished feeding on that hapless native, the poor creature was barely alive—it could hardly stand."

Sadrew caught the look of surprise, quickly masked, on Tizu's face and crowed with triumph. "Yes, I thought so. You didn't know about that, did you? Now, either honor your contract to us and get these monsters out of camp, or give us enough weapons to defend ourselves."

Tizu gave Nathan a hard look, then returned his attention to the Dymarians. "Contract? What contract? Lann Gheal never signed any contract with you. We contracted with Bennett to save you from the Creggans, and so we did.

"The contract is over—and we're not releasing any of our weaponry to a bunch of trigger-happy civilians, so get that thought right out of your heads, all of you. You're not in any danger from Kai, so get out of here with this crap."

When no one moved, Sadrew stubbornly holding his ground, Tizu sneered, "You're a real prize, Sadrew, you know that? I don't give a shit what one of your slimy little spies saw. Kai and his Timornans haven't gone anywhere in this camp, except back and forth from their barracks to the sickbay, so I'm not kicking them out. They're helping the sick—doing something useful—which is more than you lot are doing," he added.

"Why are you coming around here trying to start trouble with this crazy tale of yours? If you're feeling lonely, or neglected, and want some attention, I can find you some new accommodations in an empty storeroom, with a nice friendly guard at your door, just to keep you company. Would you like that better?"

He fingered the sidearm at his hip. "Is that what you want, hmm?" When there was no reply, Tizu snarled, "Then get out of here, the lot of you, before I put the whole pack of you bigoted assholes under guard."

Grumbling to one another, the Dymarians drifted away into the growing shadows, sullen under Lann Gheal's united front against them.

Back inside the HQ, Nathan breathed a sigh of relief and closed the door behind them with a satisfied click. "Thanks, Commander. I'd better go and report to the Kashallan—"

As Nathan passed him, Tizu unexpectedly slammed him hard up against the wall. Pinning him, Tizu glared at the big man. "You're not going anywhere, Derek, until I get some answers. Now just what exactly is that shit Sadrew talking about?"

"I don't know," Nathan mumbled, but he looked away, unable to meet the other man's smoldering eyes.

"Don't try to lie to me, Derek. Sadrew may have shit for brains, but he wouldn't have come up with such an outrageous story unless he knows something, or thinks he does. Now tell me the truth. I backed you up out there, damn it, and I won't be made a fool of. Has Kai turned into a vampire, like Sadrew claims?"

"No!" Nathan said, shrugging out of the Commander's hold. He stared angrily back at the other man. "You've seen him walking around in broad daylight, how could he be a vampire and do that?"

"I don't know, Derek, you tell me. This is an alien world; maybe things are different here. Now stop jerking me around, out with it. Is he drinking his followers' blood, or not?"

Nathan sighed. In a low voice, he finally admitted, "Yes."

Jaw clenched and eyes hard, Tizu demanded, "Humans too?"

"No—"

"But not because we haven't asked to," Marti blurted. "The Avairei told me, when I offered, that my blood wasn't right yet—not enough kavay or something."

Tizu turned, gazing at her openmouthed. Putting her hands on her broad hips, she faced all of them defiantly. "Yeah, that's right, I offered, like the others who have been helping him. And I've offered more than once, too. He saved my lover's life, and for that alone, I'd gladly give him half my blood, and then some."

Her dark eyes raked over her former comrades, her lip curling with contempt. "You pack of mangy dogs have no idea how it was for us out there. We haven't told you half of it, but he saved us, not just once, but many times.

"And that morning when that black-hearted overseer would have killed Marnez, he stopped the brute, bargaining for all our lives, in exchange for hosting the symbiont like the Ima wanted. The way I see it, he gave up everything for us. Whatever he needs, I'll give it to him if I can, and so will the rest of the squad."

Into the hushed silence that followed her declaration, Nathan added, "It's the symbiont, Commander, it eats for both of them now. We left Sulas in a hurry, as you've guessed, and Tani's like a little child, in some ways. It wasn't ready to be weaned. It can't eat whatever the grown Khutani do.

"Anyway, the formula we brought for the bondmates to eat is almost gone, and, because of all the added strain put on them by the doctoring, they've had to add blood to make the formula go farther and keep themselves alive." Gray eyes ablaze, his voice quivering with pent-up emotion, Nathan said, "Don't you dare judge him because of some stupid horror vids you watched back home. You don't know what he's been doing for you, or any of the ones that have been sick. Dunnagh hates having to feed like that—but he can't do anything about it. He's starving, damn it, can't you see that, any of you?

"Commander, you made a snide comment before about him needing to go on a diet, but look past the Khutani coiled around his middle. Look at the hollows in his face, or the sharpness of the bones in his back and shoulders—really look at him, damn it! And when you do, also know that you're to blame for part of that weight loss."

"What are you talking about?" Tizu demanded.

"Commander, you're up and moving around, feeling almost back to normal, aren't you? And it's been, what, six or seven days since you collapsed." At Tizu's uncomprehending stare, Nathan let out a bark of mirthless laughter.

"It took us several weeks to recover from the alignment symptoms. Not days, Commander, weeks. The only reason you're this far along in your recovery is because he's been helping you, as well as Bennett and everybody else. And he's damn near killing himself to do it."

A shocked silence followed that revelation. At last Tizu sighed and groped for a chair. He sat down heavily. Now that the adrenaline rush had drained out of him, Nathan saw the exhaustion in his face. Looking up at Nathan, he grumbled, "You've made your point. Go on, get out of here."

At the outer door Tizu stopped them again. "Nathan, watch your back. I wouldn't put anything past Sadrew and his bunch. I'll send some of the men and extra weaponry over to D barracks, just in case you need them."

Without turning, Nathan nodded and stepped out into the night.

Chapter Nine

Sairsa surfaced from troubled dreams, but remained with her eyes closed. Outside the barracks the wind whined, pelting rain clattering against the roof. That wasn't what had awakened her. The storm hit before they'd retired. The staccato drumming of falling rain had been a constant, lulling sound in her sleep. It was something else, but what...?

Then recognizing the moist, rhythmic slap-slapping noise of the couple locked in a passionate embrace beside her, Sairsa inwardly writhed. Oh, Gods—not again! Could she endure this, even with her love for Dunnagh to aid her—could she live like this?

Anger, humiliation and jealousy twisted her insides into painful knots. Taking several deep breaths, she tried to relax her tight muscles and stifle her sobs—praying for them to finish it soon.

No sense making things worse by broadcasting her growing distress; that would be infinitely worse. When this happened before, they had stopped immediately, and turned to offer her comfort. Embarrassing her further, they had forgotten all about their own passion in their concern for her wellbeing.

Pela especially had been very upset, having no idea that she, herself, was the crux of Sairsa's distress. Her solicitude made her feel worse, because she could tell Pela really meant her concern.

Hot tears rolled down Sairsa's cheeks, and she couldn't stop them. Oh, well, from the sounds coming out of the pair right now, they wouldn't be aware of anything but each other for a while. Damn them—this awful place, these strange people, Pela, Tani, and Dunnagh, damn them all.

In a corner of her mind, a little voice said: "You don't have to live like this. No one is forcing you. Dunnagh told you honestly how it must be. He gave you the choice—if you can't accept this crazy menage a trois, then go to Tizu, give him what he wants, and let him marry you."

But is that what I want? And if I can't go to such a marriage with wholehearted love and affection, would that be fair to him? The answer, to her way of thinking, was: No, it would not.

How did she feel about Hukiyo Tizu? Did she, or could she, love him? Being honest with herself, she didn't know. It was Dunnagh that still pulled at her heartstrings, not another. But what she also wanted was the life they had planned on Dymar. That life was gone forever. Gone, all of it gone—her family, her old life, her dreams—all gone.

And what about the child—Dunnagh's child? Men could be so funny about these things. Would Tizu even want her if he had to take the child—another man's child, too? Oh, Gods! This mess was all so complicated, and she felt so frightened and alone.

Oh, Dunnagh, must I lose you too?

WITH A CONTENTED SIGH, Pela flattened herself atop her lover's chest. The Kashallan put his arms around her, pressed her close and kissed her. For a time they clung together, enjoying the last intimate moments of their love. Finally he cradled her to rest in the crook of his arm, and closed his eyes, drifting towards sleep once again.

Then, Dunnagh became aware of his human lover's torment. Glancing at the other occupant of their bed, he sighed.

Inside his middle, Tani stirred, letting him taste its irritation. <<This can't go on, Kasha. This isn't good for the child, or her. Why can't she just make up her mind, and accept us or leave?>>

<<I wish it were that simple for us humans, Tani, but we don't seem to be able to make anything easy for ourselves—especially when it comes to our loves.>>

The symbiont gave a mental expression of disgust. <<You humans certainly do like to complicate things for yourselves, don't you? But what do we do about this? She is obviously not happy staying with us, but she doesn't seem to want to leave you, either.

<<I don't like this,>> Tani complained. <<I know you don't want me to interfere with her precious human free will, Kasha, but I am the healer

here, and I must do something soon. It's not just her I have to be concerned about, it's the child—your child, I might add—that needs looking after, too.>>

"Our Sairsa is sad again," Pela whispered, and started to crawl across him.

Dunnagh stopped her. "No, sweet, not this time. I must do it." Pela hesitated, then touched his now-limp sex. He chuckled softly and hugged her. "No, I wish it was that simple." She gave him a confused look. He hugged her again, then murmured, "Pela, sweet, I'm getting hungry. Would you bring me some of that new formula Dado brought in last night? I know there wasn't much from this batch, but he promised us more, and I am hungry, and—"

She glanced at the sobbing woman curled up like a hurt child. "It is nearly morning; I will bring something for all of us," she announced. Sitting up, she added burning powder to the stone lamp by their bed. There was a hiss and the flickering green flame filled the room. Pela threw a cloak hurriedly around her shoulders and headed for the door.

When she was gone, the Kashallan lay staring at the ceiling, the bondmates trying to come to some inner agreement about what to do next. Still undecided Dunnagh finally said, "Sairsa?"

No answer, but the crying stopped. The woman next to him, lying so still was obviously aware of him, though now pretending to sleep. He sighed, and tried again. "Sairsa, love, talk to me." He put a hand on her shoulder, trying to pull her into an embrace.

AT HIS TOUCH SAIRSA flinched and pulled away. "Don't, please don't, Dunnagh," she begged.

Don't touch me. I don't want the intimacy of the symbiont's probing that will also come with your embrace.

No, she didn't want to be touched by those tentacles. They would lay bare her emotions to both bondmates' scrutiny, and she couldn't stand that. Not right now, when it hurt so bad.

Without turning, she felt him pull away. "If that's what you want."

Silence...

She could hear his rhythmic breathing, but she kept her back to him, hoping he would leave, too. At last, unable to bear it any longer, she rolled on her side to face him. As she'd suspected, he was studying her intently. He looked so hurt and confused, making her want to cry, slap him—or scream.

"Sairsa. I don't know what more I can say or do to help you resolve this for yourself. I want to help—what do you need from me?"

"I don't know either, damn it." Sairsa took a deep breath and tried to control herself. That wasn't his fault, now was it? She pushed away her anger and met his gaze, plunging deep into the blue depths of his eyes, searching for answers.

Who is this creature in bed with me, really?

She had always found Dunnagh to be loving, and gentle. But since he'd acquired the symbiont, she suspected he was also lonely, confused, and so desperately afraid she would leave him.

Unfortunately Dunnagh was only one part of the complex being who lay beside her. The alien was also there, watching her thoughtfully through those deep blue orbs, heavy-lidded now with the afterglow of sexual repletion.

What did she read from that one? Concern for her, yes, but that feeling seemed to be enveloped in layers of frustration, impatience and perhaps even contempt for what it must see as her human foolishness and self-indulgence. Unable to face the truth revealed there any longer, she looked away.

Then, feeling torn apart inside, she felt her stomach cramp, and her muscles spasmed as she curled up in a ball around her own misery again.

This time he ignored her feeble protests and gathered her into his arms, Tani's tentacles sinking deftly under her skin. In spite of the flame of her emotions, she felt her resistance crumbling.

"Damn you, Tani! Stop it I don't want you to make me feel better—let me go!" Against her will, she felt her anger slip away, her taut muscles unwinding, as her body betrayed her. "D-damn-it-t. Stop!"

When she lay quiescent in his arms, he kissed her, and Tani said, "You mustn't do this, Sairsa, it's not good for you, or the child growing inside you, and I think you know that. You must decide whether to stay with us or leave."

Sairsa gasped. How did—of course Tani knew, to a being who could taste a thousand subtleties in her body's biochemistry, something as obvious as a pregnancy would literally scream out its message.

Tani nodded its agreement to her unspoken question. "Yes, I know—I've known since that first day—and so has Dunnagh. But you were so ill, and then there was so much else to concern us, that we haven't found the time to talk to you about it."

Sairsa sobbed in frustration, and pounded her fist weakly on his muscular arm. "D-damn. L-let me g-go!"

"Sairsa, please, love," Dunnagh said. "Tani's right this isn't good for you or the baby."

"Ooo, you sound so self-righteous. Baby. What do you know—either of you, about it? Do you care—does anyone really care about me and the baby?"

Suddenly it all felt so hopeless. How could she fight them? It was too hard; she didn't care about anything—Dunnagh, Hukiyo, the baby. Nothing mattered any more.

He looked confused, and she laughed. "Stupid symbiont—you'll never understand."

"Why do you laugh? Doesn't this breeding please you? Dunnagh is your love, isn't he? Don't you want this child?"

"Tani, frankly I don't know how I feel about it. But I suppose you can tell me, hmm?" She looked into the Kashallan's eyes again. No sign of her lover there now; those had been the Khutani's words, not Dunnagh's. Damn him for running away to hide somewhere in their shared flesh, making her deal with this alien creature alone—damn him!

"I can taste many things, but I don't understand what I taste. Humans are so complicated," it grumbled, "And you and my Kasha aren't giving me much help when I do try."

She giggled. Glassy-eyed from the tranquilizer Tani was giving her through the link, she fought against the drug's effects, and slurred, "Shervess you r-right for even try-ing, sho there."

Those blue eyes widened in exasperation, then Dunnagh's face grimaced. "I think you have had too much. I will neutralize the medicine."

The symbiont laughed, and released her from the link. "By my ancestors, you creatures would try the patience of the Gods themselves."

Sairsa giggled again, but as the symbiont released her, she curled once more protectively about herself with her back to him. Muttering to himself, the Kashallan threw the blanket off and sat up, reaching for his kilt.

Chapter Ten

Pela entered, balancing a tray in both hands. She bumped the door closed with her hip and crossed to put the tray down on the crate acting as a nightstand beside the bed. Her eyes flicked to the tableau on the mattress.

Without comment, she took a flask from the tray, pouring a generous bowlful of formula and handed it to the Kashallan. He took it without comment, and drank. She poured herself a bowl of hot spice-bush tea and sat down beside him.

Silence, thick and heavy filled the room. In the outer room dishes clinked and someone began singing the Morning Prayer to the Mother. Pela finished her bowl and set it down on the tray with a loud clunk.

Lost in his own thoughts, the Kashallan jumped. Pela stood up. Putting her hands on her hips, she faced him. "Hurry up and finish that, so you can get out of here."

Startled, he blinked up at her. "What?"

"You heard me, Dunnagh-Tani. Drink your drink, or take it with you."

He started to protest, but she stamped her foot impatiently and glared in her best imitation of an angry Sagas. "Go do some human thing, or some Khutani thing, I don't care, just go! You had your chance, now this is sister-wife business, not yours—get out!"

Bemused, he stood, grabbed the flask, his cloak, and walked to the door. Giving her one last confused look, he walked out into the main room, shutting the door quietly as he left.

When she heard the door close, Sairsa shifted her position to apprehensively watch the other woman. Pela poured her a bowl of the steaming liquid. "Sit up, Sairsa'meh, and drink this."

Sairsa uncoiled herself and sat up. Throwing part of the blanket over her shoulders for warmth, she took the offered spicy drink and sipped.

Pela sat cross-legged facing her on the mattress, her own cloak across her shoulders. They drank for a while in silence, each unsure how to begin, now that the time had arrived to settle this thing between them.

Pela drained her bowl and set it back on the tray. Taking a deep breath, she asked, "Sairsa'meh, why are you so unhappy? Is it because of me? Do you dislike me so much? Would you like my Ima to find you another sister-wife?"

Startled, Sairsa glanced up from her brooding. "No! Pela, I don't dislike you. You're a beautiful person, and you've been very good to me. Why do you think I dislike you?"

"I don't know; you seem so miserable." She looked down toying with a bluestone ornament on one of her braids. "This isn't how it should be," Pela murmured in a small, scared voice. She swallowed hard, unable to continue. An oily tear dripped from the corner of her eye, rolled off the tip of her nose, and plopped on the bed in front of her.

The depth of Pela's emotion shocked Sairsa—she'd never dreamed. She set her empty bowl on the floor. "Pela?" Sairsa reached out and took one of the woman's furred hands in her own. She stared at it in concentration, as if she'd never seen it before. Only four fingers with tiny retractable claws, but it was soft, her fur was so velvety soft—and alien. "Don't cry, Pela, please."

Pela sniffed and gave Sairsa's hand a little squeeze. When she'd gained control of her voice again she said, "When the Great Mother came to me in my prayers, she told me you were alone—no kin, no clan, no home, all alone. She told me that, even though you were a stranger here, you were well loved by Her." Pela brought her other hand up and traced the curve of a purple spiral on Sairsa's arm. "Well loved."

"When we were fleeing Sulas, the Goddess told me I must find you and take care of you, and that, if I did as She bade me, all would be well, but if not—"

Pela looked into her alien green eyes, and whispered, "I don't know why what my Goddess charged me with doing has gone so wrong. Perhaps I am unworthy. I want to obey, and I want to be your sister-wife and friend, Sairsa'meh. I want everything to be good for all of us, but if you don't want to be with me—"

Sairsa released Pela's hand and looked away, twisting a corner of the blanket in her agitation. How did she feel about this native woman and the group marriage Pela wanted her to share? It was so complicated.

Sairsa admitted to herself that she was honestly fond of the Avairei, but she also didn't like the idea of sharing Dunnagh with her either. All her cultural training rebelled at the idea. She wanted Dunnagh all to herself, wanted things to be as they had planned. But they were never going to be like that, not ever.

Even if she told Pela that, yes, she was the problem, and asked her to leave, it wouldn't matter. The dreams were gone forever. Sairsa wouldn't have Dunnagh to herself—there would always be Tani to come between them. And Pela was right; the Imas might force him to take another mate. And maybe this new 'other' wouldn't be someone she could like or admire, as she did Pela.

No, it still boiled down to one point—whether she was strong enough to set aside the past and accept a Timornan reality. Feeling the other woman's eyes upon her, she met that gaze and took her hand again.

"Pela, I'm growing to like you very much, and I would be proud to call you a friend. But the idea of a 'sister-wife' is so new and foreign to me; well, I'm not sure how I feel about that."

She sighed. "I'm probably saying this badly. It's not you, Pela; it's me. It's not a custom among my people for women to share their men-folk. It feels—unnatural. And, it's hard for me to understand why you don't seem to mind sharing him with me. Do Avairei women share often their mates?"

"No." Another oily tear, falling from her eye, Pela looked down at their clasped hands. "Dunnagh tried to warn me that you might not want this. He said it wasn't the custom among your people, but my Goddess said—I thought—"

Pela choked on a sob. "Among the Avairei when a man is special, and should have many children from more than one woman, then the bond of sister-wives is formed. It is a very sacred thing among us, perhaps because it is so rare.

"You don't seem to understand, Sairsa'meh, I chose you—not Dunnagh or Tani. Among us it is the first wife, or her Ima, who makes the decision to take a sister-wife, not the man. I wanted you to be with us, not just to please Dunnagh, but for me too. Two women who share the same man's semen—who breed together—the bond that is formed between them is closer than the bonds of family and clan. It is very special.

"I know that part of the reason you are so miserable is because you feel all alone now. No family, no clan, no home. But it doesn't have to be that way. There are sacred vows we can take that will bind us to one another. You won't be alone ever again. Will you accept the gift of my love and my bond as sister-wife, Sairsa'meh?"

Sairsa was stunned. She hadn't thought of their relationship like this. Sharing her lover still made her feel uncomfortable, but she could see that it was a great honor in its way, and yet—

"Pela, thank you. It is a precious gift you offer, but it's hard for me too. Dunnagh and I, we had so many dreams, such plans—" Her voice trailed off, as her own throat tightened. She twisted the blanket again, her own tears now falling, spotting the dark fur with glistening sparks of light.

Pela watched her, saying nothing for a while—letting her cry. At last she said, "I know, my Sairsa'meh, I know. You are not the only one to have dreams that will never be."

Sairsa glanced up, startled. Pela nodded. "When my Ima felt it was necessary for the Kashallan to take a mate, so that, if he should die, all wouldn't be lost for my people, my Ima charged me with this mating.

"It was my duty to accept, but it wasn't to my liking. In fact, I was quite frightened of Dunnagh, the big, alien who was to be mine, along with the Khutani.

"And, I mourned for my lover, and what wasn't to be. You see, I had been promised to another since my childhood. We were to be married when our studies were completed—and now..."

She took a shuddering breath. "That's another gift of the red kavay. When I took it to become fertile—it also changed my reluctance to desire."

Sairsa stared, her mouth dropping open. She had had no idea it had been like this for Pela. In fact, judging by what she'd observed, she assumed quite the opposite.

What a fool! I've been acting like a selfish bitch. Oh, Gods, what courage and honor this woman has. She's set aside her own personal desires, yet she is trying to make me happy, when she can never have the one she needs to be happy herself. She's offering me all that she can under the circumstances. If I accept this bond, I can at least have Dunnagh in part. Oh, Pela!

Sairsa had always been a woman who valued her friendships with other women. Self-assured and confident, in the past she had rarely felt jealous or competitive with them. But this unusual situation had changed all that. It had made her behave in ways foreign to her nature. And now, knowing Pela a little better, she felt both admiration and pity for the woman.

She realized, too, that in the religious life in which Pela had been raised and trained, the company of other women must have also been very important, more so, perhaps, than her relations with the opposite sex.

From the few conversations she'd overheard, she'd guessed that Avairei men and women were often friends in maturity, but for the young who were of breeding age, the opposite-sex relationships were often confined to matings only.

It would be natural for Pela—faced with an unwanted marriage to a frightening, alien—to long for another woman, even an alien woman, to share her life, rather than live alone with a stranger.

And there was the added honor of the sister-wife bond in her culture, to show her the way to make the best out of her situation. Yes, Sairsa could understand and sympathize. But now that she and Dunnagh had found each other, couldn't the Avairei woman be set free to marry her own promised lover? When she asked, however, Pela shook her head.

"It isn't that simple, my Sairsa," Pela explained. Taking the human's hand, she placed it on her belly. "I am breeding too. No, there is no going back for either of us, my Sairsa, no going back at all. We are breeding sister-wives, no matter what our lost dreams.

"The question is only: Can we love each other too, and share the bond and the joys of that union, or must we part? You must decide."

You will never be alone again if you agree.

Sairsa sighed. Suddenly her resistance melted away. She took Pela in her arms. She kissed her and stroked her silky, brown fur. She would accept this unusual gift, and the new life that had been offered her. It wasn't going to be easy for any of them, but with Pela's example of quiet courage to guide her, maybe she could set aside old values and dreams.

Later, when their lovemaking was over, she knelt beside Pela in front of the tiny altar in their room. She made her first blood offering, the women swearing the sister-wife vows together. As she did so, Sairsa realized that, for the first time in a long while, she felt happy and at peace.

With her oath she had found not only a sister to share her life and love, but she had also found the blessing of Pela's Goddess. The Mother Timorna's love flooded her heart with ecstasy, wiping away all doubts. In bowing to the Mother's will, and accepting her fate, a new inner strength filled her soul.

Part Four: The Chi'awari'ga

Chapter One

Tobrach crouched to study the faint scratches in the flinty ground. That was surely an Avairei footprint among those larger, blurred markings. His long brown tongue snaked out, its tip touching the surface of the path. The ground was rock hard, and the trail many days old, but Avairei were among the fugitives that left Sulas with the mutants—but this spoor felt wrong somehow.

Why would Blue Eyes bring his followers this way? There was little food or water in this desolate country—not enough for such a large party. There'd been only a few Loti with the outlaws; not enough to transport supplies for so many. Were they eating their dead?

Those who left Sulas with Blue Eyes and the Ima sagas went freely, not as captives. For whatever his reasons, Blue Eyes would want to preserve as many of his new followers as he could. He wouldn't squander their lives in this dried up husk of a land—no matter how many hunting packs of Warlinga were on his back trail.

Something else was happening here. Tobrach rose to his full height; he needed to see the trail from another perspective. He scanned the horizon hoping for inspiration—and maybe a sight of their quarry. Only the mauve sky, and jagged tawny mountains stared back at him. The wind moaned in the rocks up the slope and tossed grit in his face.

Tobrach turned away in disgust. Stupid, even the elements mocked his efforts. Why was he wasting time following this spoor? It was too old and the enemy long gone. Not far down the trail his hunting pack waited in silence, as motionless as statues.

Nostrils flaring, he faced north again. The afternoon sun caused the trail ahead to shimmer with a warm amber glow. It beckoned, its golden beauty seductively urging him onward. His head crest flattened. A tempting lure, but was there deadly magic at work here as well? They were only a small hunting pack; the sign was stale—why should they continue? This was the Ghostlands, enemy territory.

He smelled the acrid stench of the old poisons permeating the rocks. The burning hostility of the land hovered over the pack like a malignant cloud. Were the Umwira wizards using magic to watch him—was there a trap waiting somewhere ahead?

Maybe.

Gormach had magnanimously given him his wish and sent him North. But was he following the fugitives from Sulas, or just another Umwira warband? The longer they followed this uncertain spoor, the more Tobrach doubted it was the right one.

Right one? Was there a right and wrong when hunting the hated enemy? Any trail that led to a kill was the right one; what was he thinking? And yet, his instincts warned him to turn back. There was definitely something amiss. Each step northward burned its wrongness into his gut like a flaming brand.

Blue Eyes never went this way; he was sure of it. And, he was also sure that Gormach had another reason in mind when he'd sent him on this fruitless hunt. Gormach had been too eager to see him gone. Did he know where Blue Eyes and the Ima had gone, and just wanted Tobrach out of the way so he could amuse himself with the captives, without Tobrach interfering? That was certainly a possibility.

Since coming to Tragar Keep two years before, Tobrach had learned to his dismay that his noble cousin was capable of almost any cruelty—if it amused him. If their clan elders in the Yeyen only knew

Tobrach's head crest flattened in disgust at the unbidden memories. He saw once more the helpless mutants vomiting in the moss of his cousin's slave pen. In his mind he heard their piteous wailing as Gormach killed the meaty young male. The flesh had been sweet, but the slaves' grief had spoiled the meal for him. No matter what the others thought, they were more than animals—or stupid Begta. They were an enigma, and he wished he'd been able to talk to them and discover who they were and where they'd really come from.

Gormach had cursed him when he left the hall early that night, and later, he'd beaten him severely when he found out about the bones. Tobrach hadn't understood why Gormach had been so furious when he saw Blue Eyes kinsman's bone around the mutant's neck. What was so wrong with that? All Warlinga wore death strands. He'd just wanted the mutants to have a token to remember the dead one by.

But did Gormach ever need a reason for his brutality?

Someone cleared his throat and spat on the trail behind him, startling Tobrach out of his reverie. He mentally shook himself and returned his attention to the matter at hand. Tobrach walked back to them.

"I see no reason to follow this trail any further into enemy territory. We will go back to where they came out of the underground tunnels and see if we can pick up a better spoor."

They stared at him with unblinking red eyes, unmoving. A gust of wind swirled dust around their scaly feet. Finally his cousin Chi'am said, "But we know the Umwira went this way, cousin, why turn back now?"

"Yes, Chi'am, we know that a warband of Umwira passed this way—sometime in the last twenty-day cycle, but we don't know if it is the same bunch of mutants that our K'San charged us to find." His tail brushed the ground at his back in an uncertain rhythm. Tobrach glanced over his shoulder at the trail that led further north. The sun had shifted; its golden lure was gone.

He turned back to his hunting pack. "It is my decision, as hunt leader, that we should go back. The fugitives from Sulas aren't up in the Ghostlands."

"Maybe not," Chi'am persisted, "but there are plenty of Umwira to hunt. We will find others to kill—what does it matter?"

An old veteran slapped the younger Warlinga with his tail. "Quiet, infant, K'San Tobrach is right. This hunt isn't about hunting for the sport of it. Gormach wants Blue Eyes and the Ima Sagas for the Dingay, if we play around up here chasing our tails till the Sorins come without something to show for our hunt, he will be furious with us. Do you want our K'San to be wrath with you, hmm?"

Chi'am flattened his head crest, and stepped back, muttering a reluctant, "No."

The old hunter grunted and said to Tobrach, "K'San cousin, you are right to turn back. The rains are coming. The wind has shifted and I can smell it. The storm will wipe out what little sign we've been following, maybe catch us in a flash flood too. I doubt if there is any point in stopping at the entrance to the tunnels, though. Rain will have destroyed the spoor before we get there. We might as well go back to the keep."

Tobrach grunted a noncommittal reply. Was it the weather or his soft bed and a barrel of mushroom beer that made the man so eager for a return to Tragar? Tobrach's nostrils widened as another gust of wind blew down the canyon. Now the old hunter brought it to his attention he could smell the rain too. They'd best keep to the high trails on the way back.

Ugly brown storm clouds were looming over the peaks again by the time they neared Tragar Keep. The old fortress's menacing presence was a warning to the hated enemy, and a guardian of the Jeban Pass. It crouched on a ridge overlooking a thorn-choke valley, the rugged peaks of the Rim Wall at its back.

They were about halfway up the ridge when a small party from the fortress marched out to meet them. When he recognized the pack's leader Tobrach dismissed his hunters to go on to the keep ahead of him, falling into step with Gormach's hunt leader, Warega, to hear the news.

Warega was looking particularly grim. That must mean they hadn't found the fugitives yet. A fat droplet of blue rain hit the back of his neck. He shivered and glanced behind him at the oncoming storm, then up at the yawning gates of the keep. Maybe he'd been too eager to return. Was he getting as lazy and debauched as the rest of them? He shivered, blaming it on the cold wind.

"When did you get back, honored elder?"

"Yesterday."

"I hope your hunt was more successful than ours."

Warega gave him a snort of a laugh. "Hardly. The trail south along the Rim Wall is as barren of life as ever. No one, not even a pack of the damned vistri has been along that trail this season. I'd bet my life on it," Warega said. "And, it would appear that the fugitives haven't gone north, judging by your own tail dragging return."

"We found recent sign of a warband on the prowl, but the spoor was stale and petered out just before the first storm washed out all sign of them. I doubt if it were Blue Eyes and the outlaws from Sulas though. They were moving too fast through hard country for a warband with a lot of keep-bred Avairei to care for."

"Mm, you probably were tracking that warband that attacked the guards taking the Ima to Riath—damn their greedy souls. That's why Sagas returned to Sulas in the first place. If it wasn't for them, all the trouble with Blue Eyes never would have happened. The woman would already be in a Dingay cell, and we wouldn't have to be worrying about being caught out in a Sorin and spending the Long Sleep Season jammed down a stinking Begta warren."

Tobrach glanced at him sharply. A shaft of green lightning threw Warega's face into silhouette, making it impossible to see his expression. Was the man joking? Not likely. Years of serving under Gormach had made the man bitter and laconic. When drunk he mourned for the old days when he served under Gormach's famous father.

The son of the great man was a disappointment to them all. Privately Tobrach understood why the Ima Sagas had refused Gormach breeding privileges, but that didn't make his lot as Gormach's heir any easier to bare. As the boom of the thunder receded, he said, "What does our K'San plan to do now?"

"K'San. Warega snorted in disgust. "That drunken lout is a disgrace to our ancient lineage! I wish you would let me— " At a warning growl from Tobrach he subsided. "All right, all right, you've made your position very clear. I don't agree with you. I'll respect your wishes, but look around you, Tobrach. We can't go on like this much longer, and you know that too."

Refusing to be drawn into that argument again, he said, "Just answer the question, Hunt Leader. What is our K'San planning to do?"

"What else is there to do but keep looking," Warega complained. "The Dingay will cut the meat from all our bones if we fail them—Combaron made that crystal clear. The fugitives can't have just disappeared without a trace; I don't believe for one moment their magic is that good. So we keep looking till we find them."

"How? Where does Gormach plan to look for them?"

"Now that you are back and the packs are up to full strength we will probably head west into the Broken Lands tomorrow or the day after."

Tobrach's head crest rose in surprise. "Why there?"

"Think, cousin." Warega grumbled. "You have searched North, I South, and K'San Drucas's packs from the capital will be scouring the eastern slopes of the Jeban pass; where else is there to look, but in the west?"

"But-but there's nothing out there," Tobrach spluttered. "There's nothing but a lot of stinking reeds and some Begta warrens—"

"And the Shallow Sea, don't forget," Warega reminded him.

Tobrach was so startled he stopped in the middle of the trail. Rain pelted his head and ran off his scaly body in bluish rivulets. Warega chuckled. "Close your mouth, cousin or your gut is going to fill with water."

Tobrach shut his mouth with a snap and continued walking. The Shallow Sea. There were bands of the Umwira living across the Shallow Sea, true, but they didn't usually raid this far North. Were their wizards tired of the Ghostlander's monopoly? Had they decided to claim some new hunting territory for themselves? That would explain a lot, if it were true.

The Begta claimed they'd found the mutants in the west, near the Shallow Sea. But they also claimed the mutants had come from out of the sky, and that was as likely as a thorn-bush turning green.

"The Begta."

"Yes, you've figured it out, the Begta." Warega let out a mirthless laugh. "They hold the answer to the puzzle—and our K'San means to get the information out of them—one way, or another."

Chapter Two

Tessa sat beside Singey in the Camp Committee's small meeting room. They were drinking hot spice-bush tea and listening to Bennett arguing with Councilor Arishim and a few of the Dymarian holdouts. Bennett had made his own decision to go with the Kashallan, but he still felt some concern for the Dymarians who were vacillating between the two factions. Most of these people weren't showing symptoms of the alignment yet, so they were reluctant to abandon their hopes of a galactic rescue.

She couldn't really blame them; if she had a choice, she would want to go home, too. Well, no sense thinking about that; she had no choice and that was that. She had to admire Bennett's persistence, though; the man really was trying to make them see the futility of staying here with Sadrew and his cronies.

Bennett had wanted the Kashallan to come to this meeting too, but he had refused. He'd pointed out to Bennett that since the news of his interesting dining habits had spread around the base, his presence might do more harm than good. Reluctantly Bennett had agreed.

Tessa stifled a sigh. This was hopeless; the Dymarians were repeating the same points over and over again. She wished she'd stayed in the barracks with Ima Nansa. The old priestess was teaching her the Avairei written language. Tessa's questing mind was fascinated by the wealth of lore Nansa could impart to her.

Lately Tessa had been feeling more like her old self. With a renewed supply of its formula brought up to the base from the Begta wild pools, Tani's maturing body was finally able to manufacture something to keep her nightmares at bay, and for that she would be eternally grateful.

Through half-closed eyes, she studied her fellow sufferers. Most of the Dymarian holdouts seemed either bored or hostile. Arishim was pretending to be Motherly and sensible, Bennett looked frustrated. Singey's face had assumed the stony mask that concealed his growing rage. Across the table Commander Tizu was watching her; he looked equally bored.

Tizu was an enigma. The Avairei were terrified of him. He hadn't sworn the oath, but he wasn't working against the Kashallan either. At Bennett's insistence, he'd come to the meeting, but he'd kept his opinions to himself. Just as he'd been doing ever since he'd recovered enough to assume his command.

When he caught her look, he rolled his eyes. Tessa covered her mouth quickly in order to stifle a laugh. Giving her a faint smile, he turned as one of his armachda approached. Bending over the armachd whispered something to the Commander in an excited voice.

Around the table conversation petered out, the others noticing the messenger too. "What is it, Commander, trouble?" Bennett asked.

"I don't know. The sentries say there is a large group of Timornans just coming out of the canyons and heading up the cliff trail. Ross wants to know what to do about them." He raised an inquiring eyebrow in Singey's direction.

"I think the Kashallan was expecting the Begta to bring in more of his special formula. That's probably who's coming. I can't think of anyone else who would—"

"These aren't the Begta—" Tizu said.

"Commander," Councilor Arishim interrupted, "Whoever it is, shouldn't we allow them to come in? It's broad daylight. They are showing themselves quite openly—they obviously are here with peaceful intentions. Does it really matter who they are? Surely, with your modern weaponry, you can protect us if they are here to start trouble."

She gave a nervous laugh. "And I'm curious—I want to make as full a report about this planet as I can when we return to civilization."

Tizu studied the faces around the table. "Bored, Councilor?" At her startled expression, he gave her a toothy smile. "All right, why not. You're right, Lann Gheal can handle any trouble the natives might have in mind." He stood. "Okay, Ellis, tell Ross to let them pass, I'll send some of the off duty armachda out to escort them in."

At the mention of strangers coming into camp, a cold chill ran down Tessa's spine, the haunted look coming back into her eyes.

"What's wrong, Tessa?" Singey asked, "Do you want me to take you back to our barracks?" He offered her his arm as he rose.

She shook her head impatiently and stepped back out of reach. "I know you mean well, Philip, but stop treating me like a child. I'm all right. Think, Philip—there's going to be trouble. I just know it—"

"Tessa, Philip." Startled, Tessa swung round. Bennett was standing by the entrance. "Is everything all right?"

Tessa sighed. "I'm fine, Dr. B." Then, noticing that everyone was leaving, she changed the subject by asking, "Where is everybody going?" Tessa and Singey followed the doctor outside.

"The Councilor has decided to head a delegation to greet the newcomers. Evidently, from what Armachd Ross said, these Timornans are very large, so I doubt if they're a party bringing a new supply of formula. They're a type of native we haven't encountered before and she—"

Tessa let out a strangled cry, a hand flying to her mouth. Frozen into immobility, she stared at the men with wide, frightened eyes. Singey put a comforting arm around her shoulder. "Tessa, you're safe here, my dear, the Umwira can't harm you anymore."

Gasping for breath, she clung to him. "Oh, Philip," she cried in Timornan, "I know who it is that's coming. It isn't the Umwira—it's the Butcher! Gormach has found us, and there's going to be trouble."

Singey hugged her trembling body close, but his eyes were hard. "Now, Tessa," he soothed in the same language, "Don't be afraid. He can't hurt you. Look around you—the camp is full of Lann Gheal armachda, with modern weapons. It's not like before. He can't—"

Impatiently she shook herself out of his arms. "Damn it, Philip, you don't understand. I'm not afraid for myself, it's the Kashallan I'm afraid for!" At his blank look, she growled in frustration and took off across the quadrangle.

As she hurried away, Tessa called back over her shoulder, "I don't have time to explain—I've got to find Ima Sagas!" Then she was gone, breaking into a run as she darted around the corner of the mess.

Just ahead of them, the Councilor had paused too. "Is there something wrong, doctor?"

Turning his back to the Councilor, he asked Singey in a low voice, "Philip, what's going on?"

"Tessa thinks she knows who's coming. She's gone to tell the Ima Sagas," he said, not bothering to lower his voice.

"Ah, that's wonderful," Arishim beamed. "In case she doesn't find her right away, you had better come up here with me, Dr. Singey. We'll need someone to translate, and I'd rather you do it than one of Kai's men."

"I'm his man too," Singey muttered, but catching a warning glance from Bennett, he subsided. It wasn't worth arguing with the woman about it—and if it was Gormach—Tessa was right—there would be trouble. Taking a deep, calming breath, he nodded, and joined the Councilor.

Falling into step alongside Bennett, Tizu touched his arm and motioned for him to slow down. When they were far enough behind the rest so as not to be heard, he demanded, "I just saw Tessa racing for D barracks. What's going on, doctor?"

"I'm not sure exactly, Commander. Philip and Tessa were speaking in the Timornan language, and Philip didn't want to translate what they said, but if I were you I'd have my men alerted for trouble."

Tizu snorted. "Ross says they're big, but they're only armed with spears and knives. That's nothing to worry about."

Bennett stopped and faced him. "I wasn't worried about the natives, I was thinking about Kai's squad. Philip said that Tessa thinks she knows who's coming, and she didn't look happy about it.

"She looked scared to death, so I suspect it's someone who they had problems with, and, if so, some of our people might have strong enough feelings about the matter to start something. I'd like to avoid any innocent people getting hurt if possible, wouldn't you?"

"I take your meaning. I'll see to it." He gave Bennett a salute and loped off to alert his men.

Welcoming the diversion, a sizable crowd was gathering around the perimeter of the quadrangle as Nathan strode over to the little group standing prominently in the center. Coming up alongside Singey, he murmured, "I just saw Tessa running for our barracks. What's happening?"

Without turning, Singey said quietly, "We have company coming." He motioned to the far side of the square, where, in the distance, a large band of the tall lizardmen could just be seen approaching.

"Oh shit!"

Singey turned to him then, meeting his eye. "Tessa thinks it's the Tragar bunch. She said something about going to find Sagas, but I'm not sure why. More importantly, though, where's the Kashallan?"

"Pela was after him to let her do his hair again; she claimed he was looking as shaggy as a Loti. Last I saw him, she was dragging him into their room, comb in hand."

"I hope he stays there."

Nathan snorted. "Don't count on it."

"Nathan, can't you—"

The big man shook his head, cutting him off. "I know there's bad blood between them, more than for the rest of us, but I can't interfere; he'd never forgive me for that. No, whatever the Gods intend is just going to have to happen."

Singey made a sour face. "I hope you know what you're doing by not interfering, Nathan."

"Yeah, I do too."

Chapter Three

From the moment they topped the mesa, Tobrach's growing sense of danger had heightened. There had been guards posted there, flat-faced mutants, wearing some kind of dark clothing and carrying those long knives. They had other equipment too that Tobrach was sure were weapons of some alien type, and their unknown nature made him even more worried.

Gormach's Hunt Leader, Warega, was nervous too. Gormach himself, however, seemed unaware, or unconcerned. In his most arrogant manner, he marched his men right by the sentries, pointedly ignoring them.

They'd let them pass without a challenge, but Tobrach noted grimly that not long afterward several more of the dark-clad figures loped up, silently flanking their progress.

It was obvious they were expected, and this new bunch had been sent out to usher them in. These mutants must have some way of communicating with each other over long distances, and that only added to his growing unease.

Gormach was a fool if he thought he could bully his way into getting what he wanted out of this lot. These men weren't sick and demoralized slaves; these were highly disciplined and well-trained warriors, as anyone with sense could see.

A cold stab of fear twisted in his gut. By the Great Hunt Leader, they would be lucky if their own sworn K'San didn't get them all killed this day.

JUST INSIDE THE OPEN square, Gormach halted. Tobrach and Warega moved to flank him, the rest of his kinsman fanning out behind them. He surveyed the camp, taking his time, as if he already owned the place.

At first glance it was not a very impressive sight. “These rectangular buildings look flimsy compared to the solidity of our stone keep,” Warega observed. “They will probably blow down in the first Sorin to hit the plateau.”

“Why would these strange creatures choose to build up here in the first place?” Tobrach wondered.

Warega dipped his head crest and rumbled a laugh. “Whatever the reason, Young Cousin, it certainly was a clever ruse. None of the hunting packs have discovered them until now.”

“Don’t they know the Sorins are almost upon them?” Tobrach asked.

“Perhaps they gain their power from the poisoned winds, like Ghostlanders” Gormach growled. “Unfortunately for them, we’ve found them before the storms; their magics will be weak—just like before.”

Gormach didn’t much care what their reasons for coming to this mesa might be. It was all the same to him, as long as he got what he wanted. But thank the Great Hunt Leader they had found them. Combaron would have flayed him alive if he’d failed to find Sagas and Blue Eyes before the storms forced him to retreat to his keep for the Long-Sleep-Season.

A sizable crowd was gathering on the opposite side of the inner square, their ugly, flat faces staring curiously at himself and his clan. He observed them with amusement, fondly remembering the taste of their exotic flesh. When his business was completed for the Dingay, perhaps he would return with all his hunting packs and—

Beside him Tobrach glanced around nervously, and in a low voice he said, “Cousin, perhaps we should leave; this is not—”

“Shut up, you cowardly, misbegotten son of Begta scum,” he snarled under his breath.

Tobrach flattened his head crest at the insult, but prudently remained silent.

In the middle of the square a small party of what appeared to be officials of some sort waited. “Ah, a welcoming party” he chortled. “How touching.

Among the group, Gormach recognized the dark-skinned mutant and the big gray-eyed male that had been his slaves at Tragar. He silently congratulated himself; it was as he had suspected; the renegades had returned to their own. Scanning the crowd again, Gormach noticed several of the others, watching him. Their hands hovered near the long knives they once again wore.

For just a moment he felt a stab of fear, wondering if Tobrach was right—maybe they should leave. But failing the Dingay would have its own dire consequences.

Banishing any thought of retreat from his mind, he met the gray-eyed male's hostile gaze, gave him an impressive view of his fangs, then drawled, "How nice to come for a visit, and be welcomed by old friends."

The big male reddened but said nothing, only glaring the harder. Gormach was amused. Too bad this one didn't seem to know the mind techniques that made toying with Blue Eyes so diverting. Come to think of it, where was Blue Eyes? Hiding perhaps; no matter, he would find him.

"It was very clever of you to come up here after leaving Sulas," Gormach said. "We might still have been looking for you, except for the fact that we were hungry and happened to catch a few careless Begta." Reaching into a pouch at his waist, Gormach drew out a chain with several metallic disks on it. He tossed it to the big male. "Yours, by chance?

"However did you manage to get loyalty out of a Begta? Most amazing! They endured quite a lot of pain before they told me what I wanted to know. But in the end such faithfulness seemed to make their meat taste that much sweeter."

Nathan caught the dog tags, then put them in his pocket. They had been given to one of Dado's kin. That bunch had been sent to bring back some of the Kashallan's precious formula. Damn, those Begta were just another score to be settled with the sadistic brute. Nathan could imagine the torments the little furballs must have suffered, and how the Butcher would have enjoyed their pain.

Damn. They needed that formula.

To his surprise Nathan realized that he was going to miss Dado and the rest of the trouble-making furballs. Fingering his sidearm, he laughed. "Well, if it takes loyalty and honor to sweeten the stew, I guess we're out of luck. Though your fat carcass would feed us for days, we'd probably all die of food poisoning after the first bite."

Gormach snarled, his crest flattening atop his scaly head, his kinsmen muttering threats behind him. Before the Warlinga could take the insult further, Ima Sagas pushed her way through the group of humans and planted herself in front of him. Folding her arms across her thin chest, she demanded, "What do you want, Gormach?"

"Ah, Ima, how nice to see you," Gormach purred. He bowed over the bulge of his belly.

She snorted. "Don't try your games on me. Why are you here?"

Gormach clicked his tongue in reprimand. "Now, now, there's no need to be rude, good Ima. Surely you remember that High Matri Enaju sent for you? You know why I've come. I've come for you—among other things." He smiled, giving her an impressive view of his fangs.

"Oh, it's all quite official. Ata Combaron has seen to that. He has appointed me and my kinsmen to bring you and your—uh, 'friends' to Riath."

"Combaron!" Sagas gasped, staggering backwards in surprise.

"Yes," Gormach said. The amusement was back in his red eyes. "He's not dead—even though one of you tried very hard to make sure of that. Fortunately—for him—he was found in time.

"But, there are other murders to add to the charges already laid against you." His voice lost its teasing quality and hardened. "And there is the destruction of Sulas itself to answer for. So you see, Ima, you will come with me. Oh, indeed you will!"

"No, she will not!"

Gormach swung round at the sound of that voice. Its owner had come up quietly from between the buildings behind the Warlinga, and stood now, facing them. "Ah, Blue Eyes at last," Gormach chortled. "You've changed—and learned our language—but I'd recognize you anywhere."

The man was dressed in a strange mixture of mutant and Avairei garb. He wore the necklaces and cloak of a high-ranking priest, but his kilt was made of the same black cloth as the rest of the mutants.

Gormach noted with some amusement, the man's long, red mane hung loose on one side of his head, while on the other it had been twisted into several tiny braidlets in the Avairei fashion. Gormach gave him a toothy grin. "Sorry if I interrupted your—uh—beauty treatment, but I was just telling the good Ima here that—"

"I heard what you told her, Gormach, and the answer is no. She isn't going to Riath with you. Nobody here is going to Riath before the Sorins—not even you."

Ignored by the two combatants, Sagas put a hand to her chest and gulped for air. The big male reached out and steadied her. She looked up at him with moist, frightened eyes. Then she took a deep breath and straightened. Teeth bared in a silent snarl she demanded, "Gormach! What do you mean that I destroyed Sulas? That is nothing but a Dingay lie to discredit me and my family!"

Gormach turned his attention back to the priestess his head crest flattened. "It is no lie, Ima; Sulas is dead. You insult my honor," he snarled, his tail lashed the ground angrily. "I would never lie about something like that. But if you will not believe me, perhaps you would consider the word of my young cousin here as more trustworthy."

Tobrach's crest sank, his tail drumming a nervous rhythm behind him. "It is true, Ima, what my cousin says. I have seen it with my own eyes. The pools at Sulas are black and foul smelling now. There is no life there at all. The Holy Ones are either dead—or gone—no one knows."

Sagas reeled. Once more the mutant male steadied her. Gormach had to admit that the priestess seemed genuinely shocked by their news.

But Blue Eyes wasn't surprised at all. Hmm.

Sagas turned to Blue Eyes as if begging him to deny this awful truth. "I'm sorry, Sagas, it is true. When the Dingay tried to kill me—my kin wouldn't stay in a place like that. Someday, perhaps, things will be different. Sulas is no more."

"I see—" Holding herself rigid, she opened her mouth to say something further, but no sound came out. She tried once more, then gave up, and looked down at the ground, a fold of her kilt crumpling in her hand.

"This brings me back to the reason for my visit," Gormach said. "This has been a most diverting little chat, renewing old acquaintances and all that, but it's time to go. You are going to Riath, now!" he growled.

"Some of your accomplices left at Sulas are already in my slave pens at Tragar, and I'm going to bundle the lot of you up to make a gift for High Matri Enaju Dingay. I'm sure she'll be delighted to see you."

Blue Eyes let out a bark of mirthless laughter, shaking his head. "I think there is something wrong with your hearing, Gormach of Tragar. I told you before: Nobody's going to Riath, not me, not Ima Sagas, and definitely not you." He smiled, displaying sharp, triangular teeth in open challenge. "Especially not you—in fact, you will be very lucky to leave this mesa alive today, do you know that? Very lucky indeed!"

Gormach snorted, his head crest rising in mockery. "Really! How very amusing," he drawled. "Am I supposed to be afraid now?"

Behind blue eyes a gray maned female started to scold him about something in their barbaric tongue. Without turning to face her, he made an angry dismissive gesture, cutting her off. She gasped in surprise, but he ignored her.

Speaking in Timornan again, he snarled to his warband, "Keep those ignorant fools out of my affairs."

"Your will, Kashallan," Gray Eyes and the dark-skinned male said.

"Very impressive," Gormach said, "And most amusing. You have them trained well, mutant—your wizard should be pleased."

"Amusing! Is it?" Blue eyes showed him his teeth again. "I wonder if you will think it so amusing when I invoke the power of the Chi'awari'ga upon you."

Every Warlinga in the square froze at the naming of the ancient blood-vengeance ritual challenge. Blue Eyes laughed. He held up the death strand around his neck, fingering the rough beads made from the bones of his dead.

"By the flesh that is now a part of my flesh," he intoned the ancient chant, "and by the soul that is united with mine for this act, I call upon the laws of the Chi'awari'ga and claim the right to seek blood vengeance against my murderer. With the Great Hunt Leader as my witness, I give honor to the Ancient Ones, and swear to be bound by the laws of the challenge. Let my enemy do the same or be forever shamed in the eyes of the Gods and all Timornans. So be it!"

"How dare you mock our traditions, mutant filth!" Warega hissed. He lashed the ground with his tail, others in the pack growling in outrage. Some shouted for Gormach to kill the impudent Umwira without waiting.

"I mean no disrespect," Blue eyes shouted over the growing clamor. "I have only the highest respect for Warlinga traditions. I am no Umwira mutant. They are my enemies, too. If you had paid attention to what the Begta told you, you would know that."

Warega stared at him in disbelief. "Starmen, bah!" Gormach growled a curse and turned a malevolent red eye on his cousin. The slime-sucking, half-bred Begta, this was all his fault! When they got back to Tragar, he was going to—

"Don't blame Tobrach for the challenge, Gormach," Blue Eyes's cool voice said as if divining his intent. "I doubt if he knew the greater significance of his deed. I believe his actions were prompted by nothing more than pity for another's suffering and grief.

"At the time I wondered why you reacted so violently when you found out I had been given the bone of my kinsman to wear. Later, when I was bonded, I found out the answer from my new relatives.

"Congratulations for knowing that tidbit of arcane lore; it would have been so tiresome to have to explain it to you. Still amused, hmm?"

Suddenly feeling trapped Gormach swore a vile oath, but was unable to hold the mutant's blue-eyed stare. He glanced at the grim faces of his kinsmen and inwardly cringed. Did they seriously expect him to fight this puny male? Apparently they did, damn them.

Warega was giving him such a cold stare, that he felt his guts twist into knots. Would his hunting pack kill him if he refused Blue eyes?

As if reading his hunt leader's mind, Blue Eyes pressed, "Do you accept the Chi'awari'ga, or forfeit your stinking blood right here and now."

Snarling, Gormach whirled to face him, sinking into a fighter's crouch. "Yes-s-s, I accept, little mutant," he hissed. "I will feast on your insolent carcass tonight with pleasure."

"NO!" Sagas roared. Drawing herself up to the full height of her priestly authority, she rounded on Blue Eyes. "I forbid it, do you hear! There is too much at stake for you to risk your life in some stupid Warlinga challenge. Kill him if you must; the Gods know the misbegotten filth deserves to die." She pointed a trembling hand at Gray Eyes. "Let your own Hunt Leader do it. He can kill the scum with his star weapons, if you must have it done. Kill all of them, you have the power, but don't risk yourself!"

"Sagas, it is because I do have the power to kill them all, that I cannot. I am sorry, Ima, I won't bow to your will in this matter. Tani and I are agreed. You will just have to accept the outcome of the challenge like everyone else."

"No, Kashallan, please—"

"Enough, Sagas," he snapped, "This discussion is ended." Ignoring her, he turned back to the Warlinga. "According to the tradition we—"

"Wait a minute," Gray Eyes interrupted. "If you two are set on this fight, then before this goes any farther, there's one big problem that needs to be taken care of."

"What are you talking about?" Gormach demanded.

"I'm talking about how this chi—whatever it is—is going to be fought. The way I see it now, the combatants are matched unevenly. What weapons are you going to use?"

Gormach laughed, a malevolent gleam coming into his eyes, then he displayed his teeth and claws. "He made the challenge, let him suffer for his insolence," he crowed. Behind him Gormach heard murmurs of disapproval from his men.

Gray Eyes clicked his tongue in disgust. "Not very sporting of you, Gormach. Too bad he won't let me kill you in the manner which you deserve."

"Nathan," Blue Eyes warned.

"Anyway, this is how I see it. If you two fight with no weapons at all, then Gormach has a definite physical advantage. But if you each fight with the weapons that you are most comfortable with, Dunnagh will have an advantage. Our tools are far superior to yours."

Gray eyes drew out a short rod from a sheath at his waist and a line of fire spurted from the ground just in front of the Warlinga's feet. They leapt backwards, eyes wide. Gray Eyes smiled and replaced his weapon. "I think you take my meaning," he said.

"Before this goes any further, we need to compromise, and decide how this fight is going to take place, so that it's as fair as possible. Then it will be up to the Gods to decide who wins after that."

"I agree," Warega said, returning hesitantly to his former position. "I know something of these ancient rituals. You are right, mutant, they must be carried out honorably, or the Great Hunt Leader will be displeased. I know your people use the long knives, but do they use any weapons like these, perchance?" He held up a long bone-tipped spear for Blue Eyes's inspection.

The Mutant glanced at Blue Eyes and said something to him in their language. Blue Eyes gave him a curt nod. He sighed. "That is a good suggestion, Hunt Leader. There is only one problem. At the moment we don't have any weapons of our own like that for my chieftain to use."

Tobrach stepped forward and generously offered his spear. "In the interests of fairness, I would be honored if you would take my weapon—if it suits you, Blue Eyes."

Blue Eyes hefted the spear, testing its balance and its feel in his hands. He nodded, then bowed to Tobrach. "Thank you, San Tobrach. I am honored."

Gormach directed a scathing look at his cousin, but the fool held his head crest high in defiance. He would pay for that—later.

"Good, that's settled," Gray Eyes said, "The weapons are agreed upon. And the place? Easy enough, part of the quadrangle here can be roped off for the combat. And when?" He scratched his chin thoughtfully, and looked at the sky.

For a change, the rains seemed to be holding off. There were a few clouds beginning to mass on the far horizon, nothing that would bother them for hours yet. "Hmm, let's say we will begin when the sun's shadow reaches that thorn bush over there. That will give us all time to get ready."

Chapter Four

Grim-faced, Dunnagh strode into D barracks. Ignoring the frightened looks of his followers, he went into his room and slammed the door. He wasn't in any mood to listen to their arguments. Alone at last he sighed and sat down on the bed. He must do what he had sworn blood oath to do—and that was that.

<<Kasha, I'm frightened.>>

Dunnagh patted his middle in a futile effort to comfort the symbiont. <<I know, Shalla, so am I, don't you taste it? I'm sorry, Tani, but I must do this. Can you understand?>>

<<Yes, of course I understand, Kasha, it's like the time with the Umwira. You helped me with my enemy. Now it is me who must help you with your enemy. I understand, but I wish it didn't have to be now. Sagas is right—there is so much at stake.>>

<<I know, Shalla, and I wish it could be otherwise, but—>> He looked up as the door opened. Sairsa and Pela stepped into the room. He rose and gathered them into his strong arms. They looked up at him, human woman and Avairei, their faces frightened, eyes sparkling with unshed tears. He kissed each of them tenderly, hugging them tight.

Sairsa choked back a sob. "Oh, Dunnagh, I can't bear this—I just found you again, and now—" Tears began rolling unheeded down her cheeks.

He kissed one of the gleaming drops, tasting its salt on his tongue. He gazed down at her with those fathomless blue eyes of his, and gave her a lopsided grin. "There, there, my love, it will be all right. Don't wish me bad luck by mourning me before I'm gone."

Sairsa blanched. "Oh, Gods, no—I would never!" She buried her face against his chest. "I'm so frightened," she murmured. "I can't stand to lose another that I love. I don't want to be alone."

"Sister," Pela soothed, stroking the human woman's shoulder. "Don't fret so. You aren't alone—you will always have me. Our husband is right; you mustn't take on so. We can help best if we go and pray to the Great Mother to protect him. This crying is no good."

He gave his Avairei mate a grateful look, hugging them close one last time. He kissed each of them fiercely, then released them and stepped back. "I need some time to prepare myself, loves, please."

Pela nodded her understanding. Putting an arm around Sairsa's shoulder, she led her out of the room. He breathed a heavy sigh of relief and flopped back down on the edge of the bed. Tani was right, Dunnagh thought privately. Why did the sadistic monster have to come now. They would have been gone in a few more days—why now?

He was beginning the Caldoni prayers for single combat when the door opened again. He scowled, but this time it was Nathan, and Moraga with a large bundle in her arms. Moraga set the bundle down on the bed, and opened it.

"This be some of Enghus's things," she explained. "You and your wee companion will need some protection from that murdering black-hearted devil, 'cause I don't think he'll fight fair. So it's only right you have these."

Inside the bundle was a leather jerkin, and some of her dead brother's well-padded practice gear. Her twin had been a tall beefy man. Moraga was right; at least some of this stuff would be of use to him. He rose and enfolded her in his arms, holding her tight. "Thank you," he said as he released her. "It's very fitting that I wear his gear; since it is partially to avenge his death that I do this."

She reached for his hand, studied the tentacle casings for a long moment then kissed them. "I be going, and praying for your winning, Ce'awn."

Dunnagh choked. At the door he stopped her. "Moraga, will you stand guard out there? I don't want any of the Avairei coming in here bothering me. Just call me when they're ready for the combat." She nodded, then closed the door.

Grim-faced, Nathan surveyed him, arms folded across his chest. Dunnagh ignored him. Stripping off his Avairei kilt and ornaments, he put on Enghus's practice gear. The shirt and pants fit. He could wear the leather jerkin as well, but much of the rest of the gear was too big, so he reluctantly discarded it. Putting on his combat boots, he sat down once more on the bed and began unbraiding his hair.

For this ritual combat, Dunnagh wanted to wear his hair once more in the tight warrior's braid as he had done while still a Caldoni armachd. Undoing Pela's neatly woven little braidlets, however, was giving his adapted fingers some trouble.

Nathan watched his growing frustration for a while then sat down on the bed beside him and slapped his hands out of the way. "Let me do that," he said. "You're making a proper mess of it."

Dunnagh handed over the brush and comb, turned his back to him, and rested his hands on his knees.

As he brushed, Nathan stole glances at Dunnagh's adapted hands. "You going to be able to manage with that Warlinga spear? It looked heavy and a bit long."

"I'll manage."

Nathan grunted, then let a heavy silence fall between them. He untangled the half-finished braids and began brushing out Dunnagh's long red hair.

Feeling the rhythmic pull of the brush, Dunnagh closed his eyes, and tried to relax and center himself for the combat to come. Time seemed to stand still; no sound from outside penetrated his awareness. It felt good just to sit here and let his beloved friend brush his hair, like in the old days. He smiled to himself, feeling strangely detached.

If I have to die today, let me take this memory with me to the Halls of the Dead.

Nathan finally broke the spell by blurting, "This is one time when I agree with Sagas. We should just kill him. The shit doesn't deserve such an honor as you're giving him."

Dunnagh sighed. Without opening his eyes, he said, "Perhaps you're right, but I swore blood oath on it the night he killed and ate Enghus. I have to do it this way."

Nathan worked a while longer, then he grunted. "I thought so. It would be just like you to do something heroic and stupid like that, without considering the consequences to yourself."

Dunnagh chuckled. "You never change, do you."

"But what about Tani?" Nathan persisted. "It's not just you that's going to face him, you know? If something happens—"

"It's all right, Nathan, I understand why my Kasha must do this. We are of one mind about it," Tani said. Then, in a shy voice, it added, "But thank you for worrying about me, too."

"Mm." Continuing his work, Nathan twined Dunnagh's hair into the tight four-ply warrior's braid that had been passed down as a part of the warrior tradition since the earliest days on Caldon. His eyes stung, but he held himself under rigid control, trying to add, with each twist of the braid, a measure of his own caring and strength, to aid his love in the coming battle.

Suddenly Dunnagh turned, and grabbed hold of his arm. He stared up at Nathan, a pleading, haunted look in his eyes. "Nathan," he begged. "For the sake of all that we've been to each other over the years, and with the power of the Ancient Ones as witness, I, Dunnagh, would lay Gessa upon you."

Face expressionless, Nathan asked, "And they are?"

Still holding him with the feverish intensity of his gaze, Dunnagh said, "The first Geish I lay upon you is to take care of Pela and Sairsa and my children, if I should die."

Nathan nodded. "No surprise you asking. Logical really, though I'm not sure how Tessa is going to take it."

Dunnagh chuckled. "I didn't say you had to marry them—not unless you and they want to. Just take care of them, all right?"

"Oh. Sure, I'd do that even without the Geish." Then, taking a deep breath, his throat tight, Nathan asked, "And the other Geish?"

Turning solemn again, Dunnagh intoned. "Nathan, I would lay the power of this Geish upon you, not for myself, but for my children, who will need you, and for all Timorna. If I don't survive this day, I charge you to go with Sagas to Ticca Keep and give yourself up to a kashallan bonding."

Nathan blanched, bending forward as if he had just been kicked in the gut. Straightening, he stared incredulously at Dunnagh for a long moment, unable to breathe. Then, without a word, he picked up Dunnagh's half-finished braid, and continued to weave.

When he was done, he tied it off, then came around to face him. Looking down at his friend, his heart lurched. All the fear and revulsion he felt for the symbiont and what had been done to Dunnagh was threatening to tear him apart.

He hated this. He was just getting used to Tani, but the thought of one of them eating out some of his insides, then sharing his body with him forever—it made his skin crawl.

If he loves me, how could he ask me to do this? And the answer came from a tiny voice in his head: *Because he has to. The future of this world depends on the kashallan bonds being reformed; there is no one else he could ask. He has no choice.*

"I'm sorry," Dunnagh mumbled. "I know this is a shock." Unable to meet his friend's eye, he looked down at his misshapen hands. He turned them over, studying them as if he'd never seen them before.

"My hands. For you and all the humans here they are the symbol of my new alienness. Even though I've used them only for healing, I know that in spite of your feelings for me, they disgust and frighten even you. I want to understand your revulsion, but I can't. I no longer can perceive the world only through human eyes, no matter how much I try.

"To me, these alien parts of me have become wonderful instruments of sensation and exploration, a way to experience the wonders of life that go far beyond my limited human senses.

"And if I'm brutally honest with myself, I know that my tentacles, gill slits and pointed teeth have torn a hole in the fabric of our love. A hole that may never be mended. More than anything else that grieves me. I wish I could change that rift above all things."

Still looking down at his hands, Dunnagh said, "If I had allowed myself to remember the oath I'd made to the Khutani before we were captured. If I hadn't been so scared and so angry, the night Enghus died—maybe I would have done things differently, I don't know. But I do know how much I'm asking of you, Nathan."

Taking a ragged breath, Nathan nodded his acceptance. He reached down to his waist and drew out his belt knife. Crossing to Pela's little altar, he made the ritual cut on his arm, then allowed his blood to drip into the offering bowl. When he finished, he turned to Dunnagh, still sitting silent on the bed, and held up the bowl.

In a now-calm and deliberate voice, he intoned, "With all the Gods of Timorna and Caldon as witness, I swear by my blood, and by my ancestors' honor, that I accept the Gessa you lay upon me. If you die this day, I will take care of your family to the best of my ability, and," he took a deep breath, "I will accept a Kashallan bonding."

"Thank you, my kinsman," Dunnagh said. "It eases my mind greatly to know that all isn't lost because of my damned heroic stupidity, as you would say."

"I'm not finished," he said fiercely, his voice thick with feeling. "Damn you to the deepest, darkest pit of the underworld, Dunnagh, if you make me keep this oath—you hear me, damn you?"

Tears in his eyes, Dunnagh whispered, "I hear you, Mo Hara."

Chapter Five

Nathan beside him, Dunnagh hefted his borrowed spear and stepped over the barrier into the roped-off enclosure. Gormach, Rhys, and Warega were already there waiting for him. Around the perimeter of the rectangle, the base's inhabitants, who were well enough to be out of bed, were gathered to watch the proceedings.

Dunnagh observed that someone had bullied Gormach into binding his tail around his waist. Good, that would keep the odds a bit more even.

Gormach raised his head crest and let out a mocking laugh, "Do you think that puny skin covering is going to make any difference in the outcome of this combat?"

Ignoring him, Dunnagh bowed to Rhys and Warega. "Thank you, I can see that everything is in order. As the ancient law decrees, this is a fight to the death. Once we begin, no one from outside is to interfere, no matter what happens, is that understood?" The two judges nodded.

Then, he turned to give Nathan a stern glare. The big man hesitated, then reluctantly agreed not to interfere—no matter what happened.

At last he eyed his opponent. "Agreed?"

Gormach gave him a toothy smile. "Agreed."

"We are of like mind, then," Warega said. "In accordance with the ancient custom, you will retire now to opposite sides of this enclosure. I will give you a few moments to pray and to prepare yourselves, then I will lower my spear and give you the signal to begin."

In his corner, Dunnagh took a deep breath, and sank further into the Cumarsaid trance. Through their shared mental link Tani joined him, adding its own sensitivity to their expanded consciousness. Dunnagh glanced at his enemy, studying the muddy vibrations of his aura. He saw fear, anger, and a secretive slyness. That last observation worried him. Was Gormach planning some kind of treachery?

Before he could explore that notion further, Warega shouted for them to begin, and then there was no more time for speculation. Dunnagh sprang into the center of the enclosure.

Holding his spear two-handed like a quarterstaff, Dunnagh circled the big Warlinga cautiously, taking the measure of his adversary. Gormach for the moment seemed content to do the same, allowing Dunnagh to lead him in a wide circular dance of feint and parry.

Then, tiring of this sport, the Warlinga launched his own merciless attack. From within the Cumarsaid Dunnagh allowed his body to flow, without conscious effort, into the graceful movements necessary to counter his opponent's every strike. Back and forth they battled in their deadly dance. Jab, block, thrust, parry.

Tani's gift of extra adrenaline flooded his system. As he had expected, the Warlinga was fast, incredibly fast. Hard-pressed, Dunnagh needed all his skill and Tani's aid to match the big brute's savage attacks.

But it did give Dunnagh a grim satisfaction to be holding his own. Psy shield warding off the war magic illusions sent to trick him, they battled. Thrust and counter-thrust, jab and block, he lost himself in the flow of the combat.

Ignoring the tower of flames seemingly engulfing him, Dunnagh leapt out of reach, preventing his opponent from cornering him. He preferred flight to fighting, when pressed too hard and the odds were against him.

Gormach cursed him for his cowardice. His tactics would never win him the combat, but Dunnagh hoped to wear his opponent down, before standing to fight. In spite of his evasions, he was managing to get in a few good strikes. The Warlinga now had a long gash down his side, made when a wicked last-minute thrust went deeper than he expected.

But as the battle progressed, Dunnagh saw, with growing alarm, that the side wound, along with the other gashes he had inflicted, weren't doing much to slow the fat Warlinga down.

And Dunnagh himself wasn't getting away unscathed. He now sported several long cuts of his own, when his slower human reflexes hadn't proved quick enough to save him from the murderous thrusts of his opponent's blade.

The host feared that if this kept up much longer, he would tire in spite of the symbiont's added help. Grimly he shoved his fear to the back of his mind and hung on.

<<The Warlinga were bred to fight monsters like the Umwira,>> Tani informed him. <<They can compensate for, or ignore, almost any amount of pain and injury when fighting a hated enemy. Even a drunken, lazy Warlinga like Gormach can do that.>>

<<Great.>> Dunnagh dodged a wicked thrust. <<I wish you'd mentioned that sooner.>>

<<I'm sorry, Kasha, I forgot you wouldn't know that.>>

<<Never mind, Shalla, we'll manage.>> Mental shields up, mind and body alert, he kept moving and prayed for a god-sent opportunity to end this deadly game.

DAMN THE CREATURE! The coward kept nipping at his flanks then dodging away, instead of standing to fight, like a proper enemy. Gormach had hoped for a quick victory when he tired of toying with the little mutant and began his murderous offensive.

To his surprise, however, Blue Eyes was matching him, blow for blow. He suddenly realized that the man's skills, both physical and mental, were far better than he had assumed.

Now that blue Eyes had regained his health, he was proving to be a formidable opponent. He would have to work, and work hard, if he wanted to win this deadly duel. The outcome didn't seem quite so certain, and that worried him. In spite of his physical advantages, his easy victory had melted away like snow in the sun. Gormach was not pleased. How had he misjudged the mutant so completely?

Gormach had been unable to penetrate his opponent's mental barriers, so he had no idea what to expect from Blue Eyes, and that uncertainty made him doubly uneasy. The mutant's war magic too had improved since last they sparred.

How had he managed to become this good in the warrior's magical arts in such a short time? Surely he would have noticed if Blue Eyes had tried any tricks like these when he had been his slave. The man had certainly had cause; Gormach had seen to that very carefully. He had taken great pleasure in tormenting Blue Eyes, thinking him too weak to stop him.

What had changed for this one in a few short twenty-day cycles? Had that old witch Sagas bonded him to a Khutani, as the Avairei, who were now captives at Tragar, claimed? Was this hated enemy really part of a bonded kashallan pair? If so, then what he planned to do this day was an unforgivable sacrilege.

Angrily, he pushed such thoughts from his mind. This was nonsense—a fiendish illusion sent into his mind by this mutant devil fighting him. Damn him to the black pit of oblivion. How had the creature managed to get past his shields without him even being aware of the attack? If he continued to think like this, the mutant would have him for sure.

Gormach preferred a sure thing rather than trusting himself to chance—even if that meant fixing the odds in his favor a bit. Under the guise of blocking one of Blue Eyes' thrusts, he loosened the cord that held his tail clamped tight around his waist. He wanted an end to this little farce.

With a roar, Gormach pressed his physical advantage even harder. Coming in close, he feinted, then reversed his thrust, landing a mighty blow from his spear shaft across the back of Blue Eyes' exposed hand. The man let out a startled cry. Gormach gave him a toothy smile.

The blow had caught his adversary off guard, sending the creature's weapon flying in a wide arc out of his reach. Blue Eyes retreated, but, before he could dance out of range and retrieve the spear, Gormach whipped his tail free from around his waist and entangled his opponent's legs. Blue Eyes hit the ground hard, air exploding out of his chest in a painful grunt.

Gormach rumbled a laugh. "At last! I have you now."

Just in time Blue eyes rolled out of range as Gormach flung himself forward in an attempt to pin him. Coming up into a fighter's crouch, Blue Eyes pivoted, then, while Gormach was still bent forward, he snapped a savage kick onto the Warlinga's backside. Gormach sprawled, gasping for air. Pain shot up his backbone and exploded behind his eyes.

Blue Eyes sprang away, grabbing up his spear, as Gormach roared to his feet. "Tail hurt, Cheating Half-bred Begta? Is it broke?"

Damn the foul creature! Fear twisted a little tighter in his gut. His tail hung useless, dragging in the dust. He lunged. Was it broken? Best not think about that now—he would kill him.

Blue Eyes smiled and danced out of range. "Serves you right, you cheating, black-hearted devil. I knew you wouldn't fight fair."

"You'll pay for that, slimeworm!" Gormach snarled, and harried his enemy mercilessly. Once again, he hadn't expected the smaller, less-adept creature to have fended off his attack and escaped. The blow that Blue Eyes had dealt him had been a painful shock, but it wasn't broken as his opponent believed.

His tail was beginning to come back to life now, but he held back, not wishing his adversary to know that fact just yet. He would win this combat, by any means he could. Oh yes, he would win. He would rip this one's arrogant throat out and drink his delicious, mutant blood before too much longer—yes, he would. And he'd enjoy feasting on his insolent flesh too, savoring the sweet taste of his victory, while the dead one's kindred screamed and mourned.

And this time, there would be no offering of the dead one's flesh or bone beads to his kin, so they could make trouble later. He would personally see to that, and take care of Tobrach's meddling while he was at it. This insolent blue-eyed male would be all his, and he would gorge himself to satiation on his deliciously sweet flesh before this day was over.

Gormach could see it now; the man was tiring. His breath was coming harder, his blocks and evasions slower. It wouldn't be long now. He was favoring his injured hand, too. Ah, yes, his hands—there was Blue Eyes' weakness, the part of him most vulnerable to his attacks.

Without being consciously aware of it before, he now saw the ungainly way the enemy held his weapon. Blue Eyes' two middle fingers were placed as if he were unable to bend those fingers around the spear's handle properly. With a sly smile, Gormach began focusing his attention on those vulnerable appendages.

With malicious glee he realized that even light blows from his spear shaft across those fingers made the creature wince with pain. This contest was becoming amusing again; it wouldn't be long now.

Blue Eyes looked into Gormach's eyes as the Warlinga landed another blow on his sensitive hands. Gormach saw the growing fear in those unnatural blue orbs when he realized that the Warlinga had discovered his weakness.

"Hand hurt, Blue Eyes?" Baring his fangs in a smile, Gormach continued his onslaught. He could almost taste the other man's fear now.

Lunging in close, Gormach feinted a downward blow with the tip of his spear at the mutant's hand. When Blue Eyes raised his spear shaft to block the blow, Gormach reversed his strike, and came in low underneath the other man's guard with the butt end of his own weapon. Gormach thrust upward, sending his opponent's weapon spinning harmlessly across the enclosure.

Then before Blue Eyes could retrieve it, Gormach wrapped his now-revived tail around his adversary's waist, pulling the dazed man to him. Blue Eyes cried out as he felt those iron coils tighten about him. He flung himself away, straining at the end of his scaly tether. His panic lent him a frenzied strength, but Gormach only bared his fangs in a satisfied smirk, and pulled him closer.

"Can't dance away now, can you, little mutant?" He would enjoy Blue Eyes's futile struggling for a while before he ended it.

Blue Eyes screamed his defiance, then, abandoning his attempts to escape, he lunged forward and attacked. He pounded the callused sides of his hands against the Warlinga's scaly chest in impotent rage. Gormach laughed, and tightened his grip, forcing his helpless prey into a macabre parody of a lover's embrace.

Gormach threw away his own weapon, raking his claws across his trapped opponent's back, shredding his leather tunic and the flesh beneath. "You're mine now," he hissed. "Your futile attack won't free you. Surrender and be done with it."

Blue Eyes cursed him, but Gormach saw the fear and knew he was exhausted. He rumbled a low laugh and squeezed. Finally, Blue Eyes gave up, and lay limp and panting in his arms.

Except for Blue Eyes labored breathing, a stunned silence fell over the onlookers. No one moved, ensnared by the spell cast by death's imminent presence. The two macabre lovers clung to one another, unaware of anything outside themselves.

Gormach looked down at his prey, savoring the intimate moment. He could feel the man trembling in his embrace. The Warlinga moaned, eagerly pulling the hated one closer. The mutant slumped in his arms, blue eyes closed, head lulling back on his arm, exposing that vulnerable throat

Gormach could see the tiny pulse, just below that tender, pale skin, rhythmically throbbing with its precious store of life's blood. The sight reminded him of the thinness of mutant skin. With no effort at all he could claw open Blue Eyes's neck, and watch the steaming blood pour over his hands in a hot fragrant tide.

It would be so easy to take all that he wanted, so very, very easy. Gormach moaned, the sound welling up from deep in his throat. He convulsively tightened his grip on the man in his pleasure. "Not for long will your life's blood pulse within that tender shell of skin," he promised. "I will taste your sweet blood soon—oh, so s-soon-n."

"Look at me!" Gormach commanded, his voice roughened by his mounting passion. "I want to see death's fear in your eyes. I want to savor your knowledge of your failure."

The blue eyes flew open, focused on his for a moment, then they closed again. Gormach laughed, his clawed hands gently raking Blue Eyes's back. The man let out a stifled moan. "Ah, yes, you know," Gormach crooned. "I saw it in those strange eyes of yours. And it gives me no end of pleasure to know, that you know your life is mine to take. Care to beg me for my mercy?"

Silence.

Gormach laughed again. "No matter, I wouldn't give it anyway—but it would add to my pleasure to hear you grovel."

The mutant trembled but remained silent, eyes closed. "Nothing to say? A pity. But I will feast on your insolent mutant flesh this night, and I will savor every mouthful. Mm, yes, you will be all mine." Gentle as a caress, Gormach took a clawed finger, and traced a line down Blue Eyes's pale cheek to just above the point of the jaw.

When he brought his hand away, a dark line marred the white skin. Droplets of blood welled in the long cut. The intoxicating aroma filled his nostrils. Gormach breathed in deeply, exhaling his fetid breath in a long, pleasurable sigh. He bent and licked the tiny droplets, savoring their exotic taste. Blue eyes shuddered. The Warlinga bent and licked again. "Sweet, so very, very sweet."

Suddenly the man opened his eyes and fixed his enemy with his eerie blue stare. "Gormach, with the Gods as our witness, you have forfeited the Chi'awari'ga and your honor by this treachery. Doesn't the shame of it matter to you at all?"

Gormach chuckled. "Not over much," he admitted. "I got what I wanted—you—that's what matters to me. Nor should you care about such foolish notions either. What good will your honor do you, when I rip out your throat and drink away your life. Your precious honor won't save you from my fangs, so why should you care?"

Blue Eyes shook his head, his expression suddenly pitying. "You are wrong, Warlinga, such things as honor always matter. By your deeds you have forfeited the Chi'awari'ga. Instead of an honorable death, you must suffer my judgment. And for your crimes, you will taste the death that only a kashallan can give."

Still keeping eye contact, Blue Eyes reared back his head, then, thrust it forward like a striking snake. He opened his mouth wide, and for just a moment, a small, gray head popped out, spitting a stream of black, viscous liquid straight into Gormach's startled face.

With a shriek of pain, the Warlinga flung his opponent from him. Staggering blindly around the enclosure, he tore at his face, trying to rid himself of the black goo that was eating away at his flesh.

The onlookers gaped in horrified fascination as Gormach's features blurred, and folded in upon themselves. His cries became more high-pitched as the skin and flesh melted away, exposing the bloody skull beneath. Toppling to the ground, Gormach writhed in agony, his screams fading into a wet, choking gurgle.

At last, the corpse lay motionless. It was over; Dunnagh's promise to the war gods had been fulfilled.

Chapter Six

For a long moment no one moved; then, the spell was broken and several people hurried into the enclosure. Nathan knelt beside the Kashallan, raising him gently into a sitting position. Beside Gormach's lifeless body, Bennett, Singey, and several of the Warlinga hovered. "Don't touch him!" Dunnagh warned, the exhaustion plain to hear in his voice. "Until it dries, that stuff will eat away any flesh it touches."

Just about to examine the corpse, Singey jerked his hand back. "Nathan," Dunnagh said. "Get rid of that, before some fool gets too curious and gets hurt." Dunnagh pointed with his chin at the corpse.

"With pleasure, Ce'awn." Stepping to the fallen Warlinga, he motioned the bystanders to get back. Unholstering his handgun, he set the beam on its maximum setting and fired. The corpse exploded in a blaze of white-hot energy. When it was over, nothing remained of the Butcher but a smoking pile of blowing ash and blackened ground.

Nathan smiled and replaced his weapon. He returned to his friend. "Are you all right?"

His breath still coming in ragged gasps, Dunnagh stared at him incredulous, and tried to laugh. "Nathan, there are times when you have a true genius for asking the stupidest questions." He gave him a feeble grin. "No, I'm not all right, but help me up anyway; I've got to finish this, while I still have some strength left."

Nathan frowned, then, catching Dunnagh's don't-argue-with-me look, he nodded and assisted him to his feet. He swayed, and Nathan steadied him; then he stepped back.

Taking a deep breath, the Kashallan set aside his pain and addressed Tobrach. "What says the new K'San of Tragar? Is the Chi'awari'ga concluded to his satisfaction?"

Tobrach hesitated, glanced at the blackened ground, and said, "It is finished." Then, bowing to the Kashallan he knelt, instinctively holding out his hands, palms downward in the ancient ritual gesture.

The Kashallan blinked, then smiled. "If you would welcome my touch, K'San, you must remove your wrist guards."

Tobrach's head crest rose in a question, but he removed his wrist guards, then held out his hands once more.

Bracing himself against the pain, the Kashallan gingerly extended his tentacles. Slipping them neatly into the tender skin that lay between the hardened scales at just that point, he formed the link.

Tobrach's eyes widened. The Kashallan's lip twitched. "So the form of this ritual has survived, but not the reason for it. Didn't you ever wonder why the skin here lies so tender and exposed? It was bred into your people long ago for just such a touch as mine."

The Kashallan closed his eyes, swayed, but caught himself before Nathan could rush to his assistance. He took a slow breath, and allowed the symbiont part of himself to taste the essence of this trusting man. At last the Kashallan opened his eyes, and smiled down at the awe-struck Warlinga. "I have tasted you and found your flavor sweet. What would you ask of me, Tobrach, of Tragar?"

Tobrach swallowed, then stared up into those alien blue eyes and pronounced in a voice quivering with emotion, "I would ask you to accept my oath of allegiance, Holy One." At the Kashallan's nod, he continued. "As K'San of Tragar, I pledge myself and my kinsmen to the protection of the northern border.

"And I also swear to be bound by your will, Holy One, and that of the Blessed Khutani. I pledge my life to serve and protect you, until my death claims me. By the Great Hunt Leader and by the Great Mother, I so swear."

"So be it," the Kashallan intoned. "And I in turn swear this to you. I pledge to give my own life in service to you and all Timorna. As healer and guardian, I pledge to work for the re-establishment of life on our wounded world. I will be bound to this path until my own death claims me."

He smiled fondly at the Warlinga. "Before I break our link, there is one thing more. Until Sulas can be cleansed and renewed, I charge you, K'San of Tragar, with the protection and care of my Khutani kindred here in the border lands."

Tobrach gasped in surprise. "Willingly I would do this, Kashallan but they are gone—"

"They aren't gone, Faithful One," he said. "I have placed a message to my kindred in your blood. When you return to Tragar, release those Avairei you are holding in your slave pens, take them to the springs beneath the keep.

"Ask the priests to call the Khutani. When the Elders come, make a blood gift to them. They will know my mind and bless you and your house for your loyalty. Do you understand me, K'San?" When Tobrach nodded he released him from the link.

Tobrach's voice trembled with emotion. "Never in living memory has a Warlinga been given such an honor; Holy One. Only the Avairei priests now make the blood gift. Gladly I will do what you command. But, Holy One, won't you come with me to Tragar? I would care for and protect you, too."

"Your offer is tempting, but no. I will go south to Ticca as I've planned. After the Sorins be ready, however, I may need you."

When the Warlinga were gone, the Kashallan turned back to the people still gathered in the quadrangle. They shifted nervously under his gaze. Over the past few days many had experienced his healing touch. Today they witnessed a kashallan's power to destroy.

Their thoughts were as transparent to him as glass; they were frightened. Though cloaked in human form, he wasn't truly human any longer in their minds. He was a stranger, and most definitely dangerous.

At last he spoke, his voice hard. "There is no more time to coddle or argue with you. Soon my people and I leave for Ticca. Either swear to me your allegiance as the Warlinga K'San has just done, and come with me, or stay here and die. It is your choice. And frankly, I don't particularly care anymore which you choose."

Swaying, he waved a hand at the surrounding countryside. "This world was once as lush and as beautiful as Dymar was, before the Creggan invasion. Not like now. My Khutani kindred have kept the knowledge of that beautiful Timorna in their racial memory. We alone remember the time before the great wars.

"I will say this to you one last time. You are welcome here—and needed here. Stop dwelling in the past. Set aside your illusions and accept what fate has decreed for you. Your knowledge and alien skills can help us rebuild this shattered land.

"Can't you forget about your old pampered existence among the stars? Aren't you strong enough to grasp what is offered to you, here and now? If not, then it is better that you die. Timorna is a harsh mother; only the strong, in body and in spirit, have the right to live and breed here. It's up to you now—"

Suddenly drained of strength, he broke off and motioned to Nathan and Singey. Sagging heavily against them, he allowed them to help him back to D barracks.

Chapter Seven

Half supporting, half carrying him, Nathan and Singey managed to get the Kashallan back to the little room he shared with Pela and Sairsa, where he collapsed semiconscious onto the bed. Ensnared in delirium, the Kashallan felt a shroud of darkness closing around him, enfolding him in its inky vastness, promising him peace and rest.

Rest—yes, that's what he wanted. Why couldn't they leave, so he could rest? He desperately tried to tell them that, but for some reason his tongue wasn't working properly, or maybe they just weren't listening to him. Feebly he tried to push them away, all those blurred, unrecognizable faces hovering over him, but they just wouldn't go away or leave him alone.

TEMOG LOOKED UP FROM his examination, and met Sagas's anxious eyes. "Both bondmates are very weak, Sagas," he said. "I will treat the host's wounds in a moment. Though serious, none of his injuries are life threatening.

"It's the symbiont that I am most concerned about. Creating the black kavay, as it did to save their lives, plus all the healing Tani has been doing—I just don't know if they can make it."

"Can't we do something?" Nathan blurted. "We can't let that devil Gormach win! Not now, not after—" He broke off, swallowing.

"San Nathan, we won't let him die. If it is at all possible, we will keep him alive." Turning to Pela, Temog said, "Bring his formula, and I'll try to get him to take some of it."

Nathan held out his strong right arm. "You can add some of my blood to go with it. Tani will be more apt to feed if it can taste fresh blood. The symbiont lately hasn't been very interested in that formula stuff, especially when it isn't fresh."

Temog started to protest, but Nathan cut him off with an angry gesture. "Gods, Temog! Surely we humans have enough kavay in our systems by now to make the gift. It may not be Avairei custom to let anyone else give a blood gift, but most of the native Timornans are already pretty weak from giving, and Dunnagh is our kinsman, and that's got to count for something, doesn't it?"

Temog thought about it for a moment, then nodded. "All right, San Nathan, we will try; perhaps you have a point."

SAGAS LAY RIGID ON her mattress and listened to the restless night sounds around her. It was late. Everyone in the long room was pretending to rest, but like herself they were too frightened to sleep. Behind the closed door to his room she could hear murmuring voices. After this latest episode of their foolishness, the bondmates were so weak. Temog must be in there again, trying to coax the symbiont to drink more of the blood-enriched formula.

"Oh, Holy Mother, don't let the Kashallan die," she prayed.

Stubborn, willful, stupid warrior, how could the host risk so much. And the Khutani, it was so young and susceptible—willing to side with, and follow its bondmate's lead, even when, by doing so, it risked all their dreams and the Makers' plans.

Stupid, stupid child! Sagas gritted her teeth in frustration. Why would he never listen—why would he never let her guide him? She was only trying to do her duty, as she had sworn to the Holy Ones she would. Why?

Unable to contain her fears and frustrations any longer, Sagas sat up. She needed to move—do something; she was too restless to sleep. Perhaps she should go relieve Temog.

But as she rose she noticed over by the altar, two shadowy figures silhouetted against the green flames of a votive lamp. His wives. They'd been sitting there for hours. Sagas scowled; this wasn't good. The women were breeding, and the star woman was still weak from the alignment process. If the Kashallan did die those children would be of inestimable value. His wives needed their rest.

Ever practical, Sagas glanced around the room's dark interior. As she'd expected, her second in rank among the Imas here, Surrel, was awake. Sagas crossed to her bed, and touched Surrel's shoulder.

The priestess sat up immediately, giving her superior a questioning look. Sagas motioned towards the two women by the altar, then, in a low voice, she murmured, "Wake Ata Loran if he's asleep. Tell him to give you a mild sedative for the Kashallan's women.

"They are doing neither themselves nor their unborn children any good by remaining over there any longer. I want them abed, and if they won't go on their own, they will be made to go."

Sagas walked to the altar, putting a firm hand on each woman's shoulder. "You have been here long enough, my children. The Mother, I'm sure, has heard your prayers; all will be well. You must rest now."

Pela nodded obediently and rose, but the other balked, remaining where she was, silently defying her. Sairsa's green eyes were dull from exhaustion. Her naked face was streaked with her tears. Even sitting here, she swayed with weariness, ready to collapse.

Sagas gritted her teeth. Like the rest of her willful kin, Sairsa was being stubborn. *Not this time, my girl; I've had enough human insolence for one day, thank you. Your mate may challenge me and get away with it, but you will not.*

"Daughter, you will do as I say," Sagas said. "You will not be helping the Chosen if you get sick again yourself. And, what of his child? Are you willing to risk losing the babe because of your stubbornness?"

Sairsa's eyes flared wide at that, and she opened her mouth to answer, but Pela intervened. Putting an arm around the larger woman, she hugged her. "Sairsa'meh, please, my Ima is right—you will do our husband no good if you get yourself sick again. He will only worry about you and want to treat you instead of getting well himself."

Pela brushed the hair back off her forehead. "Please, my Sairsa." Reluctantly, the woman nodded and got stiffly to her feet.

Surrel was beside them by then, and, speaking in a low soothing voice, she drew them away to the pallet that had been prepared for them.

Sagas sighed with relief, and knelt by the altar. Surrel would see that they were settled. Good; that was at least one worry off her mind.

"I think you should take your own advice and go to bed yourself, Sagas," Nansa said as she sat down beside her.

Sagas glanced over at the old Ima. "And you, dear Ima? I could say the same about you."

Nansa snorted. "I'll get plenty of rest soon enough, child."

They sat in companionable silence for a time, each staring at the altar's tiny flame, each lost in her own thoughts. At last, while still facing the altar, Sagas let out an exhausted sigh and asked, "Why, Nansa, why? How could he do this—how could either of them risk so much—and for such a stupid reason? Why?

"At every opportunity, he resists or defies me. Ignorant, stubborn, willful—stupid, stupid Warlinga," she raged, rubbing a hand across her face. "Oh, Nansa, if the Kashallan dies—what will become of us? And if he dies, I will have failed them—failed in the sacred duty that the Khutani have given me."

For a long time the old woman was silent, finally she turned to her younger colleague, a spark of compassion in her ancient, knowing eyes. "Sagas, you are like a bright, intense flame burning hot and true. You always were. I am sure that is why the Holy Ones chose you for this difficult task. They knew your will was strong enough and your faith resolute enough, to withstand any test given you.

"But you also have to learn when to surrender and let go. You can't control everything, all the time. Yes, the Chosen and his kin are stubborn and willful. I'd be the first to agree. They have their own ways of doing things. And yes, they will change us and our world. But I have faith that our Makers are aware of all this.

"I trust that they knew that in bringing these wild, barbaric people to Timorna, our lives would be altered. And maybe that was their intent—had you thought of that? Maybe this is all part of what, in their wisdom, they have foreseen."

"But surely this foolish insistence on fighting that degenerate Gormach wasn't part of any plan," she protested. "He could have died, still may—"

"I agree with you there," Nansa said. "That was very stupid. But the unwillingness to forswear an earlier-given oath on the host's part, speaks of courage and a steadfast loyalty. Those are virtues to be highly prized in a host. And though the bondmates chose to keep that vow, they didn't act irresponsibly.

"The Chosen got that big Hunt Leader kinsman of his to pledge himself for a kashallan bonding should this pair be killed. Did you know that, my girl?"

Sagas gaped. Nansa chuckled and patted her hand. "I thought you hadn't known. Nathan told me earlier, when he was so worried. He loves the Chosen deeply, and was willing to do even that for his sake. So you see, dear one, we need only have faith.

"We are all mortal and make mistakes, but the Goddess has a way of looking out for us even when we do stupid, stubborn, willful things that could ruin it all.

"Now go to bed, Sagas—take your own advice. He's not going to die, and soon enough he will be up and challenging your will, so you had best be strong, and rested enough to not let him win." She chuckled softly. "Not without a good fight, anyway, hmm?"

Sagas hesitated, then rose wearily to her feet. "Yes, I'll try to rest. I promised Temog I'd relieve him in a bit. Good night, Ima, and thank you."

WHEN THE WOMAN HAD gone, Nansa sat for a long time staring into the lamp's flickering flame. In the quiet stillness of the night, she felt all fear and worry fall away, leaving her renewed. At peace with herself, and at one with her Goddess, Nansa knew what she must do, and wasn't afraid. The charge had been given, and she would surrender to its will. She would make the gift.

Chapter Eight

Two days later, Temog announced over breakfast that the bondmates were out of danger, and would survive. Nathan had been only the first of Dunnagh's human kin to offer the blood gift. To Temog's surprise, there had been no shortage of volunteers; even some of the aligned humans from the base had wanted to donate.

With a ready supply at hand, the priest decided to put his patient on a force-feeding program, which seemed to be working.

Though still weak, the Kashallan was definitely on the mend. In fact, he felt well enough that evening, to try arguing with Sagas. He had just finished a feeding and was propped up in bed, with a number of his followers clustered around him.

Now that his health was returning, he felt an instinctual urgency to be off this mesa before they could be caught in a Sorin storm. But when he insisted they needed to leave, his followers put up a united front against him, and refused to allow him out of his bed.

"But the Sorins are coming—"

"Yes, they are, and I am the one that has been warning you to leave for quite some time now." Sagas reminded him. "And would you listen?" He opened his mouth, but she hurried on, "and I am also aware of how weak you truly are—"

"I know how weak I am, too, but I can sleep on Barren's back while we are traveling. We need to—"

"No. You will not try to rest and regain your strength while riding on the Loti." She folded her arms across her thin chest and looked down her long sharp nose at him. "In your condition, riding will be almost as exhausting as walking—and you know it."

"But—"

"No buts. If you won't think of yourself, then think of your kindred who are still weak from the alignment. We don't have enough Loti to carry so many, and our supplies. Think for once! You will not leave that bed Until Temog says so. We are all agreed on that."

He glanced at the worried faces of the people gathered around his bed. Nathan, Temog, his wives, Tessa and Singey, they all looked so solemn, and determined. No help coming from that quarter.

"You do look a bit pale, love," Sairsa said. "And I can see your hands trembling—even though you are trying to hide it."

"The rain will be pretty damned cold. Want to ride wet and freezing all day?" Nathan asked.

Not particularly. The Kashallan sighed and threw up his hands in surrender. "All right, you've all made your point. Do what you want then. So, if I'm supposed to rest—get out of here and let me do it," he grumbled.

Secretly, he was relieved, and glad he'd lost this round—but he wasn't going to let them know it. When they left the room, he settled back with a contented sigh against the pillows, and closed his eyes.

"ARE YOU SURE THIS IS what you want to do, Ima?" Temog asked.

"I'm sure," Nansa said. "And as my closest living kin in this place, I expect you and Surrel to respect my wishes in this matter."

Temog and Surrel bowed, then chimed in unison. "Your will, Ima."

"Good." Softening her demeanor, now that she was sure they wouldn't try to stop her, she reached out and took their hands. "I thank you, my dear ones. May the Mother bless you and keep you all safe. It is better this way; you will see, trust me."

Surrel choked back a sob. Temog raised the old woman's hand to his lips and kissed it, his eyes saying what words could not convey. Nansa bowed to them, opened the door to the Kashallan's room, stepped in and closed it firmly behind her.

In the green light from the votive lamp on Pela's little altar, she could see the blanketed figure lying curled on his side upon the bed. How peaceful he looked, like the child that at least a part of him still was. Just a child—both parts of him, a lonely and frightened child, having to grow up too fast, taking on the dangers and responsibilities of a hostile, adult world.

He lay with his head resting on one arm, long red hair snarled around his shoulders like a ruddy shawl. He sighed heavily in his sleep, rolling on to his back. As he did so, the blanket slipped partway off, exposing his torso.

Nansa couldn't help noticing his haggard features and the gaunt body. He had lost a fair bit of body mass since leaving Sulas. So much traveling and fighting, so much healing work, with so little food, these hardships had taken a heavy toll on the host, as well as on the Khutani.

This alien Chosen—what a complicated creature he was. Like the rest of his kin, he was a frustrating, exasperating, yet generous and lovable mixture.

Much of the time Sagas was ready to strangle him. Then he would turn around and do something so incredibly thoughtful and caring, something that no Avairei would ever have dreamed of doing, and then, Sagas would have tears in her eyes. What a diverse and exciting world he and his people must have lived upon, before the Mother called them to her. Nansa smiled.

Chosen, you were picked well. You and your people will change us, whether we like it or not. Truly, this first kashallan-bond child of the pools was blessed; when you were chosen for its companion.

Standing beside him, she could see the young symbiont stirring restlessly within its bondmate's flesh. Tani was growing hungry—it was almost time.

She sat down upon the bed and touched his shoulder. "Wake up, Chosen," she said. "Your bondmate grows hungry; you need to feed."

He grunted. "Feed?" He yawned, rubbed his eyes, then opened those blue orbs and focused them upon her. "Ima?"

"Yes, child, don't you feel your hunger?"

He propped himself up on an elbow, stared at her in bewilderment for a moment, then closed his eyes and considered. When he opened them again, he said, "Yes, I am hungry, but what are you doing here, Ima?"

Nansa brushed the damp red hair from his forehead and looked deep into his eyes. "Child, you know why I'm here."

He looked at her blankly for a moment, then, understanding dawning, he sat up, shaking his head. "No, oh no, Ima—surely there is someone else—I couldn't—"

"This is my choice. Child, you can, and you must. Too much depends on you now. You need to gain back your strength as soon as possible. You must take the gift I am offering, Holy One—for all our sakes."

Nansa saw the symbiont writhe within him. Its hunger was aroused, and she could almost taste Tani's need. The host, however, bulked. Shaking his head stubbornly, he tried to resist. "Ima, I couldn't. I am too weak and hungry, I couldn't hold back—"

Dunnagh gazed at her through his tears, and shook his head again. "No, Ima, I couldn't stop myself, I would—"

Placing her finger upon his lips, she said, "Child, enough, I know that, and I'm neither asking, nor wanting, you to hold back. This is my gift."

Choking on a sob, he buried his face in his hands. She stroked his hair, trying to comfort him. Nansa could feel him trembling, tearing himself apart with his conflicting desires.

"Chosen, listen to me. I am too old. Even riding a Loti, I couldn't make it to Ticca. It is better this way."

Dunnagh resisted, imploring her with his eyes to stop. "No, no, please, Ima, you can make it—"

"Truly, Chosen, I cannot, and you and I both know it. I would die on the journey. Far better this way, when my death can do some good."

When he continued to sob, she took his face between her gnarled old hands, forcing him to look at her once more. "What a wonderful pampered world your home must have been for you to take on so. But you must stop this, Chosen. Your home is Timorna now, and the Mother demands that her children be strong.

"You must set aside this foolishness from your past, and accept this part of your life. For the sake of the Shalla, and for all those who depend on you, you will take my gift and not shame either of us. You will take from me all that you require."

DUNNAGH HAD NEVER THOUGHT of Caldon as a pampered world before. In fact, by galactic standards, it was considered quite primitive, its inhabitants not much better than savages themselves. It was a shock to consider his home, as the priestess must see it, but she had a point. Judged by Timornan conditions, Caldoni were as spoiled as Dymarians.

Since the evacuation, he, like the rest of Lann Gheal, had considered themselves, superior to the soft, self-indulgent Dymarians. He had been contemptuous of their unwillingness to let go of their hopes for rescue and accept reality. Yet here he was, doing the same thing, guilty of the same resistance. It was a humbling realization.

Nansa moved closer. "Hold me," she commanded. He whimpered, giving in to one last wordless protest, then Dunnagh pulled her into his arms, settling her against a shoulder. She smiled at him, her expression softening. Reaching up a grizzled hand, she brushed the tears from his cheek.

"Child, do you know what joy you have given me?" Startled, he stared. Her smile widened. "Yes, joy. Every day since we left Sulas, I have thanked the Great Mother for allowing me to live long enough to witness the forming of a new kashallan bond.

"I feel so blessed. And now, to be given the opportunity, in my dying, to nurture a life once more—it is a blessing as wonderful as when my womb was young and fertile, and I nurtured the life of my children. It is a great honor that you give me, child."

Nestling herself more comfortably against him, Nansa lifted the death strand around his neck and studied the bones. "Though it isn't an Avairei custom, I have asked my kindred to make you and San Nathan and Tessa bone beads to wear. I want you to have one. Will you wear a bead in remembrance of me?"

Dunnagh cleared his throat several times, before the words would come. "Yes, Ima, I will, and it would be my honor."

Letting go the death strand, she stroked his cheek. "Good, I am glad... Now it's time, child. Take all that you need, honor me and my gift. Do what has to be done."

He nodded. Then, adjusting her position, he bent his head to her withered neck and began to feed.

Chapter Nine

The Kashallan brushed his wet hair out of his eyes and pulled the hood of his cloak down lower over his face. Rain. He both wanted it to stop, and feared that it would before they reached their objective. Tall brown reeds thrust their slender stalks towards an olive-green sky. Glancing down at Berren's muddy paws, sloshing through blue-tinged puddles, he shivered.

How long till they camped for the evening? No telling with the clouds blotting out the sun. He shifted his weight to a more comfortable position. Were there enemies following them? Until they were under attack, it would be almost impossible to locate an ambush in this weather. The reeds cut off visibility, the rain dulled sounds and the air stank with the pungent scent of a machete-hacked trail through the undergrowth.

"Are you all right, Kashallan?" Berren's anxious query drifted back to him. When he made no answer, she stopped walking and turned her head, to study the heavily wrapped figure sitting astride her broad back.

"I'm fine, Berren. I was just adjusting my cloak a bit to get the rain out of my face." He patted her soggy shoulder. "Don't fret, I'm feeling much stronger today."

Unconvinced, she studied him a moment longer, then resumed her pace, glancing back over her shoulder from time to time. The Kashallan pointedly ignored her. Berren was a dear, but she could be such a mother hen at times. He was fine—almost.

This was the first day since leaving the base that he'd won his argument with his followers and been allowed to ride, rather than be carried in a litter. Sagas must have put the fear of the black pit of oblivion into the poor Loti, however, because every time he moved, she glanced back at him, her heavy brow wrinkling with concern.

Well, at least he had made his point. He would be tired and sore when they camped tonight, but it would be worth it. He hated being carried in that awful litter like an invalid—even if he did still feel like one.

With the rains as their constant companion, they had been moving steadily down out of the high country for about a nine-day. It had been a difficult journey. Constant downpours made traveling a nightmare. In places they waded through water up to their knees for what seemed like hours. His weakness, combined with the humans still convalescing from the kavay alignment slowed their progress.

They should be farther away from the mesa by now, but it couldn't be helped. The Broken Lands were hard going even for seasoned Warlinga, and his people were far from that.

But it could have been worse. At least he had flasks of his precious formula for the journey. On the day before they left the base. The old Begta shaman Umwa showed up unexpectedly. With a grinning Dado by his side, the shaman marched boldly into camp with his kinsmen, carrying bottles of the bondmates' formula.

In spite of Lann Gheal's surveillance the Begta managed to pass the sentries unnoticed, getting right up to the base itself before they were finally spotted. Ignoring the weapons hastily trained on them by Tizu's startled armachda, the shaman marched his little band into the middle of the quadrangle, as if they owned the place.

When Nathan arrived to translate, the old charlatan pounded his chest and announced in a loud voice, "I, Mighty Umwa, bring guides for journey to Ticca and food for Kashallan. Only Mighty Umwa has magic enough to do this.

"Me, Mighty Umwa with my big, big magics, will see to it, personally, that no more bad Warlingas," the Begta gave Nathan a solemn, yellow-eyed stare, "or other bad enemies, will find Kashallan on the journey to Ticca."

Then, after giving Nathan a few more low-voiced words of advice, he gave Tizu a smug look, turned on his heel and left.

Nathan told Dunnagh all of this later, and admitted that, in spite of himself, he had missed the little furball. He was glad Dado had been off on another errand for the old windbag when Gormach found his cousins, tortured, and then ate them.

He also admitted to feeling much better about their trip south, knowing they would have Begta guides along. Dunnagh had agreed.

Unfortunately, the Kashallan remembered that the old fellow left them with one other piece of advice that they hadn't been able to follow.

The old Begta warned Nathan, "You in bad danger from the Ghostland magics. Take Kashallan and leave soon. Take everybody. If starmans stay here, bad things happen—very bad magics. You go soon!"

Even though his convalescence gave the Dymarians extra time to make up their minds, Sadrew's stories convinced a few to stay on the base with him, no matter what the risk. These people were terrified of the Kashallan, and were determined to wait on the mesa for the rescue ship. No amount of arguing could persuade them to change their minds.

Dunnagh felt bad about leaving them—even that fool Sadrew—but he'd been in no condition to argue with them. And considering the hateful rumors that Sadrew and his cronies spread about him, it was a wonder that he got any of the base's inhabitants to follow him.

Sadrew's hate campaign became so extreme that he ended up losing support, rather than winning it. And his supporters dwindled even further when Councilor Arishim agreed to go with the Timornans.

ARISHIM WAS A PLUMP motherly looking woman dressed in a flowing yellow robe, with a long salt and pepper braid down her back. Bennett brought her to see him soon after Ata Temog announced that he was recovered enough to see a few visitors. As she drew near the bed, he could taste her nervousness even without extending his tentacles to form the link.

With the rumors about Timornan cannibalism and his vampirism flying through the camp, Dunnagh could imagine how hard this must be for her.

Trying not to show his surprise, he wrapped the blanket about himself and swung his legs over the edge of the bed so he could sit facing them. He smiled, and motioned for his guests to come and sit on the cushions beside his bed.

When he saw the color drain from Arishim's golden skin, he inwardly sighed. He'd forgotten about how his smile affected many of the humans on the base. "I'm sorry, Councilor," he said. "I didn't mean to frighten you, please come and sit; you are both welcome guests. I was getting very bored staring at the ceiling."

Taking Arishim's hand Bennett gave him a shaky smile and ushered her forward to sit on the cushions. When they were seated, Bennett cleared his throat and said, "Ce'awn, I know you aren't up to long visits yet, so we won't stay, but Councilor Arishim is planning to come with us. As you have requested, she's here to give you her oath of fealty."

The Kashallan nodded to the doctor, then turned to study Arishim more carefully. "This is welcome news, but forgive me if I seem surprised. You truly wish to come with me?"

Arishim glanced down at his hands resting on his blanketed knees, swallowed hard, then nodded. "Yes, Kashallan, I do." In her lap she clasped her hands together, her knuckles white.

Lips quivering, she gave a nervous laugh, glanced at his hands again, then taking in a deep breath she said, "This decision isn't easy for me—but not for the reason you may think. I understood what you told us after your fight with that horrible creature, Gormach. I've hoped for rescue until now because—" another deep breath, "because I wanted to help my people—all my people.

"I am a duly elected official of the Dymarian government. Ce'awn, you know how bad it was for my people after the Creggan invasion—you were there. I have a responsibility—a duty to my people back there as well as here. We are at war. I couldn't just forget about them and abandon that responsibility—" She broke off, her eyes suddenly brimming with tears. "But I have no choice now."

"Mm, yes I understand now. In spite of all your precautions, you've begun the kavay alignment process. There is no going home for you, even if the ship should come."

"Yes," Arishim whispered. Then her face crumpled, and she placed her hands over her eyes and sobbed.

The two men looked at one another. Reaching into his tunic pocket, Bennett brought out a rumpled handkerchief and placed it in the crying woman's lap. Arishim mumbled her thanks, sniffed and wiped her eyes.

When he saw that she was focusing on him again, the Kashallan said, "I'm very sorry, Councilor. In a way I owe you an apology. I didn't understand why you resisted all attempts to see the truth of your situation. But you are right, if you have begun the alignment, you must come with us. Only a very painful death awaits anyone who remains here."

Arishim shuddered, sniffed again, then nodded and held out her hands palms down, for the link. "I believe you. And if I can't return to my people on Dymar, I still have a responsibility to those of my people who are stranded here with me on Timorna. As Dr. B said, I came to give you my oath, and my help if you will except it."

For answer he reached out and took her hands. Extending his tentacles he gently formed the link. Arishim shuddered, then relaxed, her look one of astonishment.

He laughed, but there was no humor in his eyes. "I am getting quite good at this, actually. It isn't the painful process that you envisioned is it?"

Arishim flushed, her golden skin darkening. "N-no, it isn't."

"It's all right, I know Sadrew's hateful rumors must make it harder for you to trust me. I understand." She gave him a faint smile and nodded. Through the link the Kashallan tasted her anxiety, but he also savored her sincerity and willingness to help him. "I will be very honored to accept your oath, Councilor, and I thank you."

It wasn't possible for him, with his injuries, to take the oath of everyone coming along. Tani just wasn't physically up to the strain of tasting that many people. So as a compromise, he contented himself with taking the oaths of the camp's leaders, like Bennett, Arishim, and Tizu. They in turn, would have to be responsible for the rest.

"Kashallan?"

"Hmm?"

Berren pointed a dripping hand towards a figure dressed in black, all-weather combat gear waiting beside the trail just ahead. "I think your hunt leader wants to speak to you."

As the Loti passed him, Tizu fell into step beside her. He glanced up at Dunnagh, his features blurred under the shadow of his helmet. "You making out all right?"

Dunnagh sighed. A tang of irritation came into his voice as he said, "Don't you start in on me too. Both Nathan and Sagas have been checking on me endlessly. And Berren here," Dunnagh patted the Loti's damp shoulder, "has been clucking like a mother hen every time I shift my weight to a more comfortable position."

"Mm. Is that so."

The man definitely didn't sound impressed.

"You didn't answer my question. I repeat; how are you doing?"

Unable to keep up his pretense under the Commander's penetrating stare, Dunnagh relented and let the weariness show on his face. "I'll make it," he said grimly. "How long before we camp?"

"That depends—on you, maybe. Dado says there's a big kavalpa grove not far after we cross the next wash." Tizu glanced up at the heavy clouds. I'd like to make it past that wash today. If the rain gets any worse it could flood. We'd lose a lot of time if we have to wait till the water falls again. But if you're too—"

Dunnagh made a dismissive gesture with his hand cutting him off. Tizu was right, and they had no time to spare. "Do what you think best, Commander, you're right; we can't afford a delay. I'll manage. Don't worry about me."

Tizu gave him another penetrating look, then grunted. "All right. I'll tell the point man." Using his long machete to hack a parallel trail through the reeds, Tizu trotted off toward the head of the column.

Tizu. Dunnagh watched him disappear among the dripping reeds and thanked the Gods once again for his presence with them.

As commander of Lann Gheal, his fealty would insure the support of the armachda. But the man had prolonged his decision until both Dunnagh and Nathan fretted that he would refuse to accompany them.

Then, one evening as their departure date drew near, a knock on his bedroom door interrupted a particularly tedious discussion with his wives. Sairsa and Pela had been nagging him about getting more rest while he could. The Kashallan looked up with relief as the door opened, and Nathan and Tizu stepped into the room.

Just for a moment, Dunnagh saw the pain in the man's eyes as Tizu took in the intimate tableau upon the bed. He looked away. When he met Dunnagh's gaze once more, a mask of indifference was firmly in place upon his weathered face.

Without a word, he crossed the room and knelt before the Kashallan and held out his hands palm downwards in the ritual gesture. The Kashallan took his hands, extended his tentacles, and formed the connection. "I came to give you my oath, and that for the armachda as well," Tizu announced.

Inwardly relieved Dunnagh nodded and closed his eyes so that Tani could savor the taste of him. Because of the bad feelings over Sairsa that lay between them, the symbiont took extra care in its exam. But the Commander gave his oath honestly, fully aware of the painful death that awaited him if he lied.

When it was finished, Tizu told Dunnagh gruffly, "Still convalescing as you are, you'll need me to help you keep this bunch in line, 'cause Derek here sure can't do it." Nathan scowled, and Dunnagh and Tizu exchanged knowing smiles. Nathan flushed, his scowl deepening.

Dunnagh laughed. "Stop glowering, you know we're teasing you." Nathan grunted looking mollified.

Returning his attention to Tizu Dunnagh sobered and said, "I will be glad of your help, Commander, and thank you. In Timornan fashion, I'm making you one of my new Hunt Leaders. Your experience will be most appreciated. I feel better about the trip knowing that you're coming with us."

"Damned right you should." Giving him a lopsided grin, Tizu brushed his black hair off his forehead, cleared his throat, then without looking at him he said, "Mm, Lann Gheal had a meeting. We took a vote. We all decided, that we were coming."

He shifted his position on the cushion, cleared his throat, then said, "The armachda wanted me to tell you that even if all the human and native Timornans are a bunch of degenerate cannibals, and you yourself are a blood-drinking monster, as Sadrew claims—damn it, you're Lann Gheal's blood-drinking monster.

"The armachda aren't about to abandon their own, to stay here with a bunch of insulting, arrogant assholes that have shit for brains like Sadrew."

That brought tears to Dunnagh's eyes, because, behind the rough joking, he knew how hard this was for the man. While in the link with him, the bondmates also tasted the grief and loneliness that Tizu felt after losing Sairsa to him once and for all.

The Commander couldn't hide his feelings in such an intimate contact. But the Kashallan also could taste Tizu's resolve to do what was required to survive on this world.

Later Nathan confessed how very relieved he was by Tizu's decision. Dunnagh allowed that Nathan was a much better Second than a commander, so it was good that Tizu would be there to take over the corps. For the present, however, because of the language problem, Dunnagh convinced Nathan to continue as a co-commander, until Tizu mastered the Timornan language well enough to be left in charge.

There was another reason for leaving Nathan in charge as well. Most of his Timornan followers disapproved of him making the fiery little Commander his Hunt Leader. They didn't trust Tizu in spite of the oath and the Kashallan's reassurances.

Dunnagh supposed he couldn't blame them. Tizu had given them quite a fright, the night he shot holes in their barracks. It had been the alignment process gone awry, making him crazy, that was at fault, but he couldn't convince them of that. In time they would appreciate Tizu's value, but for the present, it seemed politic to leave Nathan as hunt leader, in spite of his grumbling.

The new relationship between all of them, with its complex blend of rights, and responsibilities, was a strain on everyone. The Avairei and the other Timornans had to learn to trust their new "human Warlinga" in the same way they had always accepted the lizardmen whom the Khutani bred for their protection.

And in turn the humans would be expected to treat the Timornan natives as if they were their relatives. It was all such a tangled mess, and he was still too weak to deal with it.

Time, he prayed that with more time it would all work out.

Epilogue

Sadrew looked up from the computator terminal as another violent gust of wind shook the prefab walls of HQ. Damn! If the winds picked up much more, they might all be buried alive under a pile of rubble. Trust a rich philanthropist like Bennett to be miserly enough to buy cheap, shelters, rather than invest in something that would hold up in a storm.

There was a loud boom and another blinding flash of green lightning lit up the night sky. In HQ the overhead lighting flickered, then steadied once more. Sadrew swore. Damn them, damn them all, and this god-forsaken planet as well!

Time crawled by as they waited for the rescue ship—but rescue was coming, in spite of what those degenerates claimed. Kai had wanted them to abandon the base, to run off and play primitive—with him of course as their lord and master. Most of the fools on the base had believed him, and left, but Sadrew hadn't been fooled by his lies.

And when the ship came back for them, Kai, Bennett, and the rest of that lot would be sorry—oh, yes, he'd see to that. A smile curving his thin lips, he patted the computator pad on the desk. He had it all documented right here. They were going to pay—for everything.

Since Kai and his bunch left, an endless round of boredom, illness, and numerous frustrations had been piling up, one on top of the other. Everyone expected him to fix things. Well he couldn't—and it wasn't his fault, damn them.

Sadrew glanced over at the ever-silent communications unit. Nothing. Day after day they sent out their distress call into the black void of space. All their desperate communications were swallowed up into that hungry maw of emptiness.

Nothing, and still more nothing, and damn Bennett for that too, or that slant-eyed little Commander Tizu—whichever one of them was responsible for leaving him with such inferior equipment.

Thinking of the deserters got him cursing again. It was all here in his report, when the rescue ship came, they'd see. He'd have Tizu up on charges, and as for Bennett—well, it would be interesting to see how long his lily-white reputation lasted when the government assembly learned about how he had abandoned them.

If you live that long, a tiny voice in the back of his mind reminded him. He pushed that thought back down into the pit where it belonged. He'd survive. He'd show them. The ship would come. He was an important person, after all—his family wouldn't let him rot here. Why, just yesterday he thought he'd heard—

Feeling his gut spasm, he bent forward and retched upon the floor. Damn them! Kai and his native rabble had brought the damned virus back into camp again.

Sadrew jumped as a loud peal of thunder crashed overhead, deafening him. He cursed, a moment later, when a blinding flash of green lightning lit up the night, then died away, taking with it all the electrical power on the base.

In the darkness that followed, he waited, hoping the power would kick back on, but when it hadn't after a few minutes, he rose stiffly and started for the door.

Then from outside, he thought he heard the sound of someone screaming, but it was hard to tell over the pounding storm. Stupid fools, he thought irritably. They're like children, afraid of the dark. He hated to go out in this stuff, but he supposed he'd better before someone came over to complain. This wasn't the first time this had happened. Stumbling over a chair in the dark, he stopped and rubbed his bruised shin.

About to open the outer door, he froze. There it was again—that high-pitched screaming. Only this time it was nearer and louder. The cries seemed to be coming from the mess next door. The sound was so primal—so terrifying. There were other sounds too—like people running, tripping over things in the dark. He shivered, suddenly reluctant to venture out into the storm.

Sadrew was backing away from the door when it burst open in front of him. In a flash of lightning, he saw a creature right out of his worst nightmares step into the room.

He screamed.

THE GREAT AVENGER PACED restlessly, gnashing his teeth in frustration. Dragging another whimpering captive in his claws, his Second approached. At his leader's growl of permission to speak, he said, "This is the last of them, Great Avenger. It would appear the blue-eyed one is no longer here."

The Umwira war leader hissed. "Have you checked everywhere? The Master has scryed this place, and he assured me that the insolent mutant and his warband were here."

"He may well have been here—I don't doubt wizard Barak's magics," his Second said. "But Blue Eyes is not here now. This place held many more of these creatures at one time, but the rest are gone. There is nowhere to hide. These ones are sickly and inferior. Perhaps they were left here to die."

"Perhaps," the war leader said. He glanced down in disgust at the mewling bag of filth in the other's grasp. Yes, this one was obviously an inferior specimen of his kind. But if Blue Eyes wasn't here, where had he gone?

Back across the Shallow Sea to some hidden lair, or—May the Fires Preserve Us, had he come back here after their encounter, sent his Avairei slaves west, then taken his warband north into the Ghostlands to launch a counterattack?

As the power of the Sorins increased Blue Eyes's magics, it would be a logical move—one that the Avenger himself would use—if he were Blue Eyes.

That last was a most disturbing thought. From the moment they emerged from the tunnels that connected the Ghostlands with this rugged country, the war leader had felt the power of some unknown magic blocking his attempts to scry out the mesa.

The Master's more powerful sorcery might have been able to break through the barrier, but his own magic could not penetrate it. Crippled by this failure, they'd sneaked in and scouted the terrain, like any lowly slave from the south with no magics. Fortunately for them, these stupid fools hadn't even set up a sentry to give an alarm.

The attack on the camp was swift and deadly, with almost no resistance. But in spite of that, the victory was disappointing. They would have to leave with little more information than they came with.

Ah, well, there were ways—painful ways—to remedy that problem. They would take these captives north—the Master would know how to get answers out of them.

The End

This story is continued in Book Three: *The Outlawed Bond*

Additional information for the Tales of the Kashallans series

Note to the reader: it is my hope that by reading the text of these fantasy books, the alien words peppering the writing are clear on their own. But for those readers who enjoy such things, and those who may get confused from time to time by the many foreign words from the various races and cultures on my imagined world Timorna, I offer the following notes to aid with clarity.

Best wishes and happy reading!

Celu Amberstone

Pronunciations of unfamiliar words:

Consonants

The sound [ch or kh] represents the ck in the word lock [lahkh].

Other consonants are pronounced like in English.

An apostrophe in a word represents a glottal stop.

Vowels

A – like father AI – like in ice AY – like in way

E – like in ate EI – like in island

I – like in see

O - like in low

U – like in too

Y – like in eat

H – when next to a vowel shortens and softens the vowel sound

Timornan words (general)

Timorna [tim-MOR-na] – The name of the uncharted planet where this story takes place.

The Great Destruction – A nuclear holocaust that almost destroyed life on Timorna, thousands of years ago.

The Burning Times – A time when the radioactivity was at its highest, just after the destruction.

Sorins [SOR-inz] – A weather condition in which the wind blows straight out of the north, picking up radioactive dust and other harmful substances as it heads south. During the Sorin seasons all life must seek shelter, or go dormant, to survive.

KHUTANI [KOO-TAH-NEE] – The ancient eel-like symbiotic race living on Timorna in its deep undergrownd waterways, who were responsible for storing the genetic patterns and keeping life alive during the Great Destruction and the Burning Times that followed.

Amla [AHM-la] – The term used by the Khutani and kashallans to refer to a parent.

Amsi [AHM-see] – A Khutani term used to address a peer of its kindred.

K'amsi [k'AHM-see] – A Khutani term of respect for an elder of that race.

Sh'amsi [sh'-AHM-see] – A Khutani term used to address a younger sibling.

kashallan [kah-SHAH-lan] – A host-symbiont bond. A partnership between two intelligent beings sworn to serve as guardians and healers of the planet Timorna.

Kasha [KAH-shuh] – The intimate name a symbiont in a kashallan pair uses for its host.

Shalla [SHAH-luh] – The intimate name a kashallan host uses for his symbiont.

The Kashallan – This term refers to a particular pairing, that of the human, Dunnagh Kai, and Tani, the Khutani symbiont. They are the first bonded pair in over seven hundred years.

Bebech [BEH-bech] – A native race that served as hosts of the Khutani, who were killed off by plague.

kavay [kah-VAY] – A blue substance created by the Khutani that when introduced into a living organism makes its survival possible on Timorna.

kavay alignment – The process by which the body is metabolically changed at such a deep level that, once alignment occurs, a constant supply of kavay must remain in the diet, or death will occur.

Sweh'an [SWAY'-ahn] – Another type of host-symbiont bond, this time between a mortal host and a spirit being from another dimension that will use its powers to aid a host, in exchange for possession of the host body at agreed times, so that it can experience a physical reality.

H'an [h'-AHN] – The host for a Sweh'an spirit.

Swe'a'sa [SWAY'-ah'-sah] – The intimate name the host uses to address her Sweh'an spirit companion.

H'an'si [h'-AHN'-see] – The name the Sweh'an spirit uses to address its host.

Cha'Han [CHA'hahn] – The Avairei priest who is bound to the Sweh'an bonded host as her companion.

Ba'etchat'seh [bah'-AYCHAHT'sah] – The Timornan version of a padded cell, used to discipline the Sweh'an when its behavior while taking its pleasures becomes too troublesome.

Wa'chassey'ul [wa'-CHSAY'-ool] – A Warlinga bound by magic to the will of the Sweh'an as both lover and mortal guardian.

AVAIREI [AH-VYE-RAY] – One of the four intelligent species bred by the Khutani. A furry, bipedal race with cat-like features and a long mane. They are the priests, scholars and healers of their society. Their function is also to care for the Khutani in their underground pools, and to distribute the medicines the Khutani make for the creatures they introduced to their world after the Great Wars nearly destroyed all life on Timorna.

Ata [AH-tuh] – (Father) A term used when addressing a male Avairei.

Ima [EE-muh] – (Mother) A term used when addressing a female Avairei priestess.

Ima Matri [EE-muh MAH-tree] – The priestess who is head of a Avairei keep like Sulas.

High Matri – The head, and ruler over, all of the Avairei family clans.

Ata Leyas [AH-tuh LAY-ahss] – (Healing Father) The male Avairei who is second in command of the religious hierarchy at a keep.

WARLINGA [WOR-LING-ga] – Another of the intelligent species bred by the Khutani. Large two-legged lizardmen naturally endowed with teeth claws and long muscular tails. Their function is to be warriors and hunters. They were bred especially to protect the Khutani-held southern lands from the Umwira, the mutated remnants of the original people who caused the Great Wars.

Chi'awari'ga [CHI'-ah-WAHR-ee'-gah] – An ancient Warlinga ceremony of single combat to settle a feud or other dispute.

Accavett [ah-cah-VET] – The women's quarters in a Warlinga keep.

Sa [sah] – A title of respect for female Warlinga.

San [sahn] – A title of respect for male Warlinga. The terms Sa and San are also used for humans as well because many of them are warriors, too.

LOTI [LOW-TEE] – A third intelligent species. They resemble centaurs with long, shaggy fur. Their function is to farm and care for the land of Timorna. They are also artisans, weavers and craftsmen.

Timornshaya [tim-morn-SHY-uh] – A term of respect offered to the Loti people.

BEGTA [BEKH-TA] – THE last of the four intelligent species created by the Khutani. Small, woolly-furred simian-like people with long arms. They live in the wilder regions of the south. The Begta are an outcast people, hunters and gatherers, who are notorious thieves. They are despised by most other Timornans, and often hunted for food, or sold as slaves.

Domail [dough-MAIL] – A Begta victory dance.

Begtanshay [BEKH-tahn-shay] – A term of respect given to the Begta people by the Khutani and the kashallans in earlier times.

UMWIRA [OOM-WEER-UH] – This is a name given to the mutated descendants of the planet's original intelligent inhabitants by their enemies. Also known as the Ghostlanders, they are the people who were responsible for the Great Destruction. They are the sworn enemies of the Khutani and wish to destroy all that the Khutani have created, so they can reclaim the more favored lands in the South.

Clans of the Western Umwira – The Western Clans are related to the Ghostlanders and descended from the original inhabitants of Timorna; being exposed to the poisons of the north and west where they live, they have mutated and interbred with slaves taken from the Khutani-held lands, so that they don't resemble the peoples before the wars.

The seven clans are: Blue Stone, Sand Mountain, Bitter Water, Red Wind, Rock Salt, Green Clay, Twisted Grass.

Plants and Animals on Timorna

taba worm [TAH-buh] – A long, thin worm that lives among the liru reeds, in both the Swamp and the Broken Lands. Eaten by the Begta. The appearance of a bowl of taba worms is rather like blue spaghetti.

gumati [goo-MAH-tee] – A frog-like creature with four hopping legs, living in the Swamp. Eaten by the Begta.

budasen [BOO-dah-sen] – A stork-like creature with long neck and legs. It has big paddle feet for running across the surface of grassy ponds. Not a bird; it has scales, and can't fly.

pomong [puh-MAHNG] – A lizard-like predator with a long, sharp tail. It preys on the budasen.

snayga [SNAY-guh] – A small predator that swims in large schools. Eating habits like the piranha of old Earth.

vistri [VIST-tree] – A six-legged scaly predator about the size of a large dog, and like dogs hunt in packs. Very dangerous.

winglah [wing-LAH] – Any large creature of the western lands that has through the generations mutated into a dangerous monster because of exposure to the Sorins.

obeylem [oh-BAY-lem] – A large plant-eating creature, living in the Swamp. It has six limbs (four long legs for walking, two short arms for grabbing food), also a long tail and neck. Hunted for their meat.

bolacht [BAh-lach] – A herd beast introduced by the Khutani to meet the needs of the Speir'dina. Provides meat milk wool and can be ridden as well.

madag [MA-dag] – Timorna's answer to a herd dog. Looks something like a small armored dinosaur. Can fight vistri, but gentle with humans and other Khutani-bred races

shri moss [shree] – A short yellow moss, growing everywhere as ground cover.

liru reeds [LEER-roo] – A tall, brown bamboo-like plant growing in the canyons of the Broken Lands and parts of the Swamp.

kavalpa trees [kah-VAHL-puh] – Tall, black trees like weeping willows that usually grow up around a spring or other water source. When their long branches touch the ground, they root themselves, thus forming, over time, large thickets that give shelter to many of Timorna's inhabitants.

masa root [MAHS-suh] – A plant with a large edible root, eaten by most Timornans. Cultivated by the Loti.

lamra [LAM-ruh] – A corn-like grain developed from the liru reeds. A staple food in the diet. Cultivated by the Loti.

dahalli [Da-hal-lee] – A thorny shrub that can grow quite tall with purple broad leaves and bright orange berries that are sweet.

clamisa – A mutated form of masa root growing across the Shallow Sea in the West. A staple of the western Clans

oko – A small armored predator in the western lands it looks something like an armadillo. Thought to be sly by the Western Clans.

dhuura – A sea creature found in the Shallow Sea. It also is a food staple for the Clans of the coast.

leongon – An armored shark-like predator in the Sea.

nagril – A nearly transparent jelly/shrimp-like creature that feeds much of the sea life on Timorna.

cobura – A furred sea animal.

aluutae – A reed/grass-like plant growing in the West used for basket making.

Land features

Ghostlands – This is a wide peninsula of barren land that connects the Favored Southern land with the blackened and radio-active northern continent. Living mostly underground this is the land where a cabal of techno-wizards has control of what is left of the old technology. They also have tremendous Psy powers which they have gained through exposing themselves to mutations sought in the poisoned places in their land.

Broken Lands – A region of canyons and mesas where some of the Begta bands live, and where the humans set up their base.

Yeyen Banai [YAY-yen ban-EYE] – A large valley surrounded by a high rim of mountains. This is where most of Timorna's Khutani-bred population lives.

Rim Wall – The mountains encircling the Yeyen Banai.

Jeban Pass [JAY-bun] – The main route from the Broken Lands through the Rim Wall to the shelter of the Yeyen Banai Valley beyond.

The Great Swamp – A low-lying stretch of land to the south of the Broken Lands. Very dangerous to travel, since it is pockmarked with poisonous pools, and subject to constant earthquakes.

Lake Ticca – A large lake at the edge of the Great Swamp, out of which the Shaden river flows. In its center is the island fortress of Ticca keep.

Shaden Falls [SHAY-den] – The portage around this waterfall is the main southern route from the Swamp through the Rim Wall to the Yeyen Banai Balley.

The Shallow Sea – The straight between the land of the Western Clans of the Umwira and the northwestern edge of the Swamp.

Timornan Keeps and Fortresses

Avairei keeps:
Riath [REE-ahth] – the capital
Sulas [SOO-luss]
Ticca [tee-KAH]
Shaden [SHAY-den]
Ha'limra [ha'-LEEM-rah]
Warlinga fortresses:
Tragar [TRAh-gar]
Meh'gach [MAY'-gakh]

Caldoni words adopted into the Timornan language

Speir'dina [SPEER'-din-uh] – The term chosen by the humans to refer to themselves after they accepted that they had become a part of Timornan society. Literally it means sky people.

Teh'lach [TAY'-lahkh] – A pseudo-family group among the followers of the Kashallan, containing members of several different species.

Speir'van [SPEER'-vahn] – Literally, "sky-woman." Used by the Speir'dina as a term of respect for a high-ranking human woman, such as Sairsa the first kashallan's human wife.

OTHER CALDONI WORDS and phrases

Caldon [KAHL-don] – The world where Dunnagh and many of the Lann Gheal armachda are from.

Cumarsaid [KOO-mar-sayd] – A trance-like state in which the practitioner opens his awareness to communicate psychically with other life. This discipline was practiced as part of the ancient Caldoni warriors' training and is still taught today.

Lann Gheal – A term meaning "Bright Blade," it refers to a mercenary organization formed on Caldon. Their purpose is to keep alive many of the ancient warrior traditions of their race. They are not for sale to the highest bidder in a conflict, and will only fight for what they believe to be right.

armachd (plural: armachda) [ar-MAKHT, ar-MAKHT-uh] – Warrior.

Geish (plural: Gessa) [gaysh, GAY-suh] – A charge or compulsion laid upon someone that binds them to do a certain thing. A Geish is usually of divine origin, but also can be laid by one person on another.

Fir Gall [feer gahl] – A foreigner.

mo – This word means "my," but when used with other words often changes the sound at the beginning of the next word.

Cara [KAH-ruh] – Friend. mo hara [moh HAH-ruh] – My friend—my love. Mo hri [moh hree] – My heart. Mo gra [moh grah] – My love.

Ce'awn [kay'-OUN] – A chieftain. mo he'awn [moh hay'-OUN] – My chieftain.

Ceartachd [Keer-takht] – A word meaning the "rightness" of a thing.

Ca'companachta [kah'-kom-pah-NAKH-tah] – Literally meaning "battle companions," it is a relationship of lovers who also fight together.

Bacach [BAH-kakh] – An unlikable person, an evil man.

Amadan [AH-muh-dahn] – Idiot; can be used affectionately or as an insult.

Dina [DEE-nuh] – People.

kina [KEE-nuh] – Kin or kindred.

le'ayn [lay'-AIN] – Twin. Literally, "half of one."

shenahi [SHEN-ah-hee] – Ancient Caldoni storyteller or bard.

Pibroch [pee-BRAHKH] – A musical instrument like a bagpipe.

Faltia, cuj milla faltia [FAHL-tee-uh, coodge MEE-luh FAHL-tee-uh] – Welcome, a hundred thousand welcomes.

go ra my get [GOR-rah-MY-uh-get] – Thank you.

Ru'a [ROO'-ah] – "The red." It refers to a person with red hair; for example, Dunnagh Ru'a (Red-haired Dunnagh.)

colcannon [kohl-CAN-nun] – A native Caldoni dish made with potatoes, cabbage, and onions.

Also by Celu Amberstone

Renewal
The Prophecy of Manu
Teoni's Giveaway

Rituals
Blessings of the Blood: A Book of Menstrual Lore and Rituals for Women
Deepening the Power: Community Ritual and Sacred Theatre

Tales of the Kashallans
The Dream-Chosen
The Hunted Kashallan
The Outlawed Bond
Uncertain Refuge
Prey of the Umwira
Blood Magic's Snare

Standalone
Refugees and Other Stories

About the Author

Celu is of mixed Cherokee and Scots-Irish ancestry. Celu Amberstone was one of the few young people in her family to take an interest in learning Traditional Native crafts and medicine ways. This interest made several of the older members of her family very happy while annoying others.

Legally blind since birth, she has defied her limitations and spent much of her life avoiding cities. Moving to Canada after falling in love with a Métis-Cree man from Manitoba, she has lived in the rain forests of the west coast, a tepee in the desert and a small village in Canada's arctic. Along the way she also managed to acquire a BA in cultural anthropology and an MA in health education. Celu loves telling stories and reading. She lives in Victoria British Columbia near her grown children and grandchildren.

About the Publisher

Kashallan Press is an independent publisher releasing books by author Celu Amberstone. Among her books are critically-acclaimed works now re-released by Kashallan Press, and new works showcasing her talents in writing both fiction and non-fiction.